D1513254

C016675498

JENNIFER L. ARMENTROUT

Half-Blood
with
Daimon
(A prequel novella)

HODDER

First published in the United States of America in 2011
by Spencer Hill Press

First published in Great Britain in eBook in 2013
by Hodder & Stoughton
An Hachette UK company

First published in paperback in 2014

5

A CIP catalogue record for this title is available from the British Library

Paperback ISBN 978 1 444 79799 2
eBook ISBN 978 1 444 78142 7

Printed and bound by Clays Ltd, St Ives plc

Hodder & Stoughton policy is to use papers that are natural, renewable
and recyclable products and made from wood grown in sustainable
forests. The logging and manufacturing processes are expected to
conform to the environmental regulations of the country of origin.

Hodder & Stoughton Ltd
338 Euston Road
London NW1 3BH

www.hodder.co.uk

For Kathy.
You're missed and loved by many.

Pronunciation Guide for *Half-Blood*
Daimon: DEE-mun
Aether: EE-ther
Hematoi: HEM-a-toy
Apollyon: a-POL-ee-on
Agapi Mou: ah-GAH-pee MOO
Akasha: ah-KAH-sha

HALF-BLOOD

I

My eyes snapped open as the freakish sixth sense kicked my fight or flight response into overdrive. The Georgia humidity and the dust covering the floor made it hard to breathe. Since I'd fled Miami, no place had been safe. This abandoned factory had proved no different.

The daimons were here.

I could hear them on the lower level, searching each room systematically, throwing open doors, slamming them shut. The sound threw me back to a few days ago, when I'd pushed open the door to Mom's bedroom. She'd been in the arms of one of those monsters, beside a broken pot of hibiscus flowers. Purple petals had spilled across the floor, mixing with the blood. The memory twisted my gut into a raw ache, but I couldn't think about her right now.

I jumped to my feet, halting in the narrow hallway, straining to hear how many daimons were here. Three? More? My fingers jerked around the slim handle of the garden spade. I held it up, running my fingers over the sharp edges plated in titanium. The act reminded me of what needed to be done. Daimons loathed titanium. Besides decapitation—which was *way* too gross—titanium was the only thing that would kill them. Named after the Titans, the precious metal was poisonous to those addicted to aether.

Somewhere in the building, a floorboard groaned and gave way. A deep howl broke the silence, starting as a low whine before hitting an intense shrill pitch. The scream sounded inhuman, sick and horrifying. Nothing in this world sounded like a daimon—a hungry daimon.

And it was close.

I darted down the hallway, my tattered sneakers pounding against the worn-out boards. Speed was in my blood, and strands of long, dirty hair streamed behind me. I rounded the corner, knowing I had only seconds—

A whoosh of stale air whirled around me as the daimon grabbed a handful of my shirt, slamming me into the wall. Dust and plaster floated through the air. Black starbursts dotted my vision as I scrambled to my feet. Those soulless, pitch black holes where eyes should have been seemed to stare at me like I was his next meal ticket.

The daimon grasped my shoulder, and I let instinct take over. I twisted around, catching the surprise flickering across his pale face a split second before I kicked. My foot connected with the side of his head. The impact sent him staggering into the opposite wall. I spun around, slamming my hand into him. Surprise turned to horror as the daimon looked down at the garden spade buried deep in his stomach. It didn't matter where we aimed. Titanium always killed a daimon.

A guttural sound escaped his gaping mouth before he exploded into a shimmery blue dust.

With the spade still in hand, I whirled around and took the steps two at a time. I ignored the ache in my hips as I sprinted across the floor. I was going to make it—I had to make it. I'd be super-pissed in the afterlife if I died a virgin in this craphole.

"Little half-blood, where are you running to?"

I stumbled to the side, falling into a large steel press. Twisting around, my heart slammed against my ribs. The daimon appeared a few feet behind me. Like the one upstairs, he looked like a freak. His mouth hung open, exposing sharp, serrated teeth and those all-black holes sent chills over my skin. They reflected no light or life, only signifying death. His cheeks were sunken, skin unearthly pale. Veins popped out, etching over his face like inky snakes. He truly looked like something out of my worst nightmare—something demonic. Only a half-blood could see through the glamour for a few moments. Then the elemental magic took over, revealing what he used to look like. Adonis came to mind—a blond, stunning man.

"What are you doing all alone?" he asked, voice deep and alluring.

I took a step back, my eyes searching the room for an exit. Wannabe Adonis blocked my way out, and I knew I couldn't stand still for long. Daimons could still wield control over the elements. If he hit me with air or fire, I was a goner.

He laughed, the sound lacking humor and life. "Maybe if you beg—and I mean, really beg—I'll let your death be a fast one. Frankly, half-bloods don't really do it for me. Pure-bloods on the other hand," he let out a sound of pleasure, "they're like fine dining. Half-bloods? You're more like fast food."

"Come one step closer, and you'll end up like your buddy upstairs." I hoped I sounded threatening enough. Not likely. "Try me."

His brows rose. "Now you're starting to upset me. That's two of us you've killed."

"You keeping a tally or something?" My heart stopped when the floor behind me creaked. I whirled around, spotting a female daimon. She inched closer, forcing me toward the other daimon.

They were caging me in, giving no opportunity to escape. Another one shrieked somewhere in the pile of crap. Panic and fear choked me. My stomach rolled violently as my fingers trembled around the garden spade. Gods, I wanted to puke.

The ringleader advanced on me. "Do you know what I'm going to do to you?"

I swallowed and fixed a smirk on my face. "Blah. Blah. You're gonna kill me. Blah. I know."

The female's ravenous shriek cut off his response. Obviously, she was very hungry. She circled me like a vulture, ready to rip into me. My eyes narrowed on her. The hungry ones were always the stupidest—the weakest of the bunch. Legend said it was the first taste of aether—the very life force running through our blood—that possessed a pure-blood. A single taste turned one into a daimon and resulted in a lifetime of addiction. There was a good chance I could get past her. The other one . . . well, he was a different story.

I feinted toward the female. Like a druggie going after her fix she came right at me. The male yelled at her to stop, but it was too late. I took off in the opposite direction like an Olympic sprinter, rushing for the door I'd kicked in earlier in the night. Once outside, the odds would be back in my favor. A small window of hope sparked alive and propelled me forward.

The worst possible thing happened. A wall of flames flew up in front of me, burning through benches and shooting at least eight feet into the air. It was real. No illusion. The heat blew back at me and the fire crackled, eating through the walls.

In front of me, *he* walked right through the flames, looking every bit like a daimon hunter should. The fire did not singe his pants nor dirty his shirt. Not a single dark hair was touched by the blaze. Those cool, storm-cloud-colored eyes fixed on me.

It was him—Aiden St. Delphi.

I'd never forget his name or face. The first time I'd caught a glimpse of him standing in front of the training arena, a ridiculous crush had sprung alive. I'd been fourteen and he seventeen. The fact he was a pure-blood hadn't mattered whenever I'd spotted him around campus.

Aiden's presence could mean one thing only: the Sentinels had arrived.

Our eyes met, and then he looked over my shoulder. "Get down."

I didn't need to be told twice. Like a pro, I hit the floor. The pulse of heat shot above me, crashing into the intended target.

The floor shook with the daimon's wild thrashing and her wounded screams filled the air. Only titanium would kill a daimon, but I felt confident that being burnt alive didn't feel too good.

Rising up on my elbows, I peered through my dirty hair as Aiden lowered his hand. A popping sound followed the movement, and the flames vanished as fast as they appeared. Within seconds, only the smells of burnt wood, flesh, and smoke remained.

Two more Sentinels rushed the room. I recognized one of them. Kain Poros: a half-blood a year or so older than me. Once upon a time we had trained together. Kain moved with a grace he'd never had before. He went for the female, and with one quick swoop, he thrust a long, slender dagger into the burnt flesh of her skin. She too became nothing but dust.

The other Sentinel had the air of a pure-blood to him, but I'd never seen him before. He was big—steroids big—and he zeroed in on the daimon I knew was somewhere in this factory but hadn't seen yet. Watching how he moved such a large body around so gracefully made me feel sorely inadequate, especially considering I was still lying sprawled on the floor. I dragged myself to my feet, feeling the terror-fueled adrenaline rush fade.

Without warning, my head exploded in pain as the side of my face hit the floor *hard*. Stunned and confused, it took me a moment to realize the Wannabe Adonis had gotten ahold of my legs. I twisted, but the creep sank his hands deep into my hair and yanked my head back. I dug my fingers into his skin, but it did nothing to alleviate the pressure bearing down on my neck. For a startled moment, I thought he intended to rip my head right off, but he sank razor sharp teeth into my shoulder, tearing through fabric and flesh. I screamed—*really* screamed.

I was on fire—I had to be. The draining burned through my skin; sharp pricks radiated out through every cell in my body. And even though I was only a half-blood, not chock-full of aether like a pure-blood, the daimon continued to drink my essence as though I were. It wasn't my blood he was after; he'd swallow pints of it just to get at the aether. My very spirit shifted as he dragged it into him. Pain became everything.

Suddenly, the daimon lifted his mouth. "What are you?" His whispered voice slurred the words.

There was no time to even think about that question. He was ripped off me and my body slumped forward. I rolled into a messy, bloody ball, sounding more like a wounded animal than anything remotely human. It was the first time I'd ever gotten tagged—drained by a daimon.

Over the small sounds I made, I heard a sickening crunch, and then wild shrieks, but the pain had taken over my senses. It started to pull back from my fingers, sliding its way back to my core where it still blazed. I tried to breathe through it, but *damn* . . .

Gentle hands rolled me onto my back, prying my fingers away from my shoulder. I stared up at Aiden.

"Are you okay? Alexandria? Please say something."

"Alex," I choked out. "Everyone calls me Alex."

He gave a short, relieved laugh. "Okay. Good. Alex, can you stand?"

I think I nodded. Every few seconds a stabbing flash of heat rocked through me, but the hurt had faded into a dull ache. "That really . . . sucked something bad."

Aiden managed to get one arm around me, lifting me to my feet. I swayed as he brushed back my hair and took a look at the damage. "Give it a few minutes. The pain will wear off."

Lifting my head, I looked around. Kain and the other Sentinel were frowning at nearly identical piles of blue dust. The pure-blood faced us. "That should be all of them."

Aiden nodded. "Alex, we need to go. Now. Back to the Covenant."

The Covenant? Not entirely in control of my emotions, I turned to Aiden. He wore all black—the uniform Sentinels wore. For a hot second, that girly crush resurfaced from three years ago. Aiden looked sublime, but fury stomped down that stupid crush.

The Covenant was involved in this—coming to my rescue? Where the hell had they been when one of the daimons had snuck into our house?

He took a step forward, but I didn't see him—I saw my mother's lifeless body again. The last thing she ever saw on this earth was some god-awful daimon's face and the last thing she'd ever felt . . . I shuddered, remembering the body-ripping pain of the daimon's tag.

Aiden took another step toward me. I reacted, a response born out of anger and pain. I launched myself at him, using moves I hadn't practiced in years. Simple things like kicks and punches were one thing, but an offensive attack was something I'd barely learned.

He caught my hand and swung me around so I faced the other direction. In a matter of seconds, he had my arms pinned, but all the pain and the sorrow rose in me, overriding any common sense. I bent forward, intent on getting enough space between us to deliver a vicious back kick.

"Don't," Aiden warned, his voice deceptively soft. "I don't want to hurt you."

My breath came out harsh and ragged. I could feel the warm blood trickling down my neck, mixing with sweat. I kept fighting even though my head swam, and the fact that Aiden held me off so easily only made my world turn red with rage.

"Whoa!" Kain yelled from the sidelines, "Alex, you know us! Don't you remember me? We aren't going to hurt you."

"Shut up!" I broke free of Aiden's grasp, dodging Kain and Mister Steroids. None of them expected me to run from them, but that's what I did.

I made it to the door leading out of the factory, dodged the broken wood and rushed outside. My feet carried me toward the field across the street. My thoughts were a complete mess. Why was I running? Hadn't I been trying to get back to the Covenant since the daimon attack in Miami?

My body didn't want to do this, but I kept running through the tall weeds and prickly bushes. Heavy footsteps sounded behind me, growing closer and closer. My vision blurred a bit, my heart thundered in my chest. I was so confused, so—

A hard body crashed into me, knocking the air right out of my lungs. I went down in a spiraling mess of legs and arms. Somehow, Aiden twisted around and took the brunt of the fall. I landed on top of him, and I stayed there for a moment before he rolled me over, pinning me down into the itchy field grass.

Panic and rage burst through me. "Now? Where were you a week ago? Where was the Covenant when my mother was being killed? Where were you?"

Aiden jerked back, eyes wide. "I'm sorry. We didn't—"

His apology only angered me further. I wanted to hurt him. I wanted to make him let me go. I wanted . . . I wanted . . . I didn't know what the hell I wanted, but I couldn't stop myself from screaming, clawing, and kicking him. Only when Aiden pressed his long, lean body against mine did I stop. His weight, the close proximity, held me immobile.

There wasn't an inch of space between us. I could feel the hard ripple of his abdominal muscles pressing against my stomach, could feel his lips only inches from mine. Suddenly I entertained a wild idea. I wondered if his lips felt as good as they looked . . . because they looked awesome.

That was a wrong thought to have. I had to be crazy—the only plausible excuse for what I was doing and thinking. The way I stared at his lips or the fact I desperately wanted to be kissed—all wrong for a multitude of reasons. Besides the fact I'd just tried to knock his head off, I looked like a mess. Grime dirtied my face beyond recognition; I hadn't showered in a week and I was pretty sure I smelled. I was *that* gross.

But the way he lowered his head, I really thought he was going to kiss me. My entire body tensed in anticipation, like waiting to be kissed for the first time, and this was definitely not the first time I'd been kissed. I'd kissed lots of boys, but not him.

Not a *pure-blood*.

Aiden shifted, pressing down further. I inhaled sharply and my mind raced a million miles a second, spewing out nothing helpful. He moved his right hand to my forehead. Warning bells went off.

He murmured a compulsion, fast and low, too quick for me to make out the words.

Son of a—

A sudden darkness rushed me, void of thought and meaning. There was no fighting something that powerful, and without getting out so much as a word of protest, I sank into its murky depths.

2

Whatever my head rested on felt firm, but oddly comfortable. I snuggled closer, feeling safe and warm—something I hadn't felt since Mom pulled my butt from the Covenant three years ago. Jumping from place to place rarely afforded such a comfort. Something wasn't right.

My eyes flew open.

Son of a bitch.

I jerked back from Aiden's shoulder so fast I cracked my head against the window. "Crap!"

He turned toward me, his dark brows high. "Are you okay?"

I ignored the concern in his voice and glared at him. I had no idea how long I'd been out of it. Judging by the deep blue of the sky outside the tinted windows, I guessed it'd been hours. Pures weren't supposed to use compulsions on halfs who weren't in servitude; it was considered highly unethical since compulsions stripped people of free will, choice, and everything.

Damn Hematoi. Not that they ever cared about ethics.

Before the original demigods had died along with Hercules and Perseus, they'd all shacked up with each other in the way only the Greeks could. Those unions had produced the pure-bloods—the Hematoi—a very, very powerful race. They could wield control over the four elements: air, water, fire, and earth, and manipulate that raw power into spells and compulsions. Pures never were to use their gifts against another pure. Doing so meant imprisonment—or even death in some cases.

Being a half-blood, the product of a pure-blood and ordinary old human—a mongrel by pure standards—I had no control over the elements. My kind was gifted with the same strength and speed the pures had, but we had an extra special gift that set us apart. We could see through the elemental magic the daimons used. The pures couldn't.

There were a lot of us halfs running around, probably more than pure-bloods. Considering pures married to improve their position in our society instead of marrying for love, they tended to fool around—*a lot*. Being that they weren't susceptible to diseases that plagued mortals, I figured they assumed it was okay to forego protection. As it turned out, their half-blood offspring served a very valuable position in the pure-blood society.

"Alex." Aiden frowned as he watched me. "Are you okay?"

"Yeah, I'm fine." I scowled while taking in my surroundings. We were in something big—probably one of the Covenant's super-large Hummers that could plow over an entire village. Pures weren't concerned with things like money and gas mileage. "The bigger the better" was their unofficial motto.

The other pure—the enormous one—was behind the wheel and Kain sat in the passenger seat, silently staring out the window. "Where are we?"

"We're on the coast, just outside of Bald Head Island. We're almost to Deity Island," Aiden answered.

My heart jumped. "What?"

"We're going back to the Covenant, Alex."

The Covenant—the place I'd trained and called home up until three years ago. Sighing, I rubbed the back of my head. "Did the Covenant send you? Or was it . . . my stepfather?"

"The Covenant."

I breathed easier. My pure-blooded stepfather wouldn't be happy to see me. "You work for the Covenant now?"

"No. I'm just a Sentinel. I'm more on loan for the time being. Your uncle sent us to find you." Aiden paused, glancing out the window. "A lot has changed since you've been gone."

I wanted to ask what a Sentinel got accomplished on the well protected Deity Island, but I figured it wasn't any of my business. "What's changed?"

"Well, your uncle is now the Dean of the Covenant."

"Marcus? Wait. What? What happened to Dean Nasso?"

"He died about two years ago."

"Oh." No big surprise there. He'd been old as dirt. I didn't say anything else as I mulled over the fact my uncle was now *Dean* Andros. Ugh. I made a face. I barely knew the man, but the last I remembered, he'd been working his way up through the pure-blood politics. I shouldn't be surprised he'd found his way into such a coveted position.

"Alex, I'm sorry about the compulsion back there." Aiden broke the silence that had stretched between us. "I didn't want you to hurt yourself."

I didn't respond.

"And . . . I'm sorry about your mother. We searched everywhere for you two, but you didn't stay in one place long enough. We were too late."

My heart squeezed in my chest. "Yeah, you were too late."

Another few minutes of silence filled the Hummer. "Why did your mother leave three years ago?"

I peeked through the curtain of my hair. Aiden watched me as he waited for an answer to his loaded question. "I don't know."

Since the age of seven, I had been a half-blood in training—one of the so called "privileged" halfs. We had two options in life—either attend the Covenant or go into the working class. Halfs who had a pure-blood willing to speak for them and foot the cost of an education were enrolled in the Covenant to train as Sentinels or Guards. The other halfs weren't so lucky.

They were rounded up by the Masters, a group of pures who excelled at the art of compulsion. An elixir had been created out of a special blend of poppy flowers and tea. The concoction worked differently in a half's blood. Instead of leaving them lethargic and sleepy, the refined poppy made them compliant and vacant—giving them a high they never came down from. Masters started indentured halfs on the elixir at the age of seven—the age of reason—and continued on in daily doses. No education. No freedom.

The Masters were ultimately responsible for dealing out the elixir and monitoring the behaviors of the halfs in servitude. They were also the ones who marked them on their forehead. A circle with a line through it—the painfully visible sign of slavery.

All halfs feared that future. Even if we did end up training in the Covenant, it took only one wrong move before we were given the drink that keeps on giving. What my mom did by pulling me out of the Covenant without so much as an explanation was a major strike against me.

I was also sure taking half of her husband's—my stepfather's—fortune wouldn't help me out any, either.

Then there were all those times I should've contacted the Covenant and turned my mom in, done what was expected of me. One call—one stupid call—would have saved her life.

The Covenant would hold that against me, too.

The memory of waking up and stumbling into my worst nightmare resurfaced. The day before, she'd asked that I clean up the balcony garden I'd demanded on having, but I'd slept in. By the time I'd gotten up and grabbed the little bag of garden tools, it'd been noon.

Figuring Mom was already working on the garden, I'd gone out on the balcony, but the garden was empty. I'd stood there for a while, staring down at the alley across the street, toying with the garden spade. Then, from the shadows, a man had stepped out—a daimon.

He'd stood there in broad daylight, staring up at me. He'd been so close I could've chucked the spade and hit him. With my heart in my throat, I'd jerked back from the railing. I'd rushed back into the house, screaming for her. There'd been no answer. Rooms had blurred as I'd raced down the tiny hallway toward her bedroom and pushed open the door. What I'd seen would haunt me forever—blood, so much blood, and Mom's eyes, open and vacant, staring at nothing.

"We're here." Kain leaned forward eagerly.

All my thoughts vanished as my stomach did a funny twist. I turned and stared out the window. Deity Island actually consisted of two islands. The pures lived in their fancy homes on the first island. To the outside world, it looked like any normal island community. Small shops and restaurants lined the streets. There were even shops run by mortals and tailored to them. The pristine beaches were to die for.

Daimons didn't like to travel across water. When a pure turned all dark side, their elemental magic twisted and could only be accessed if they were touching earth. Being out of contact weakened them. It made an island the perfect hidey hole for our kind.

It was too early for anyone to be on the streets, and in a matter of minutes we passed over the second bridge. On this part of Deity Island, nestled among marshlands, beaches, and forests virtually untouched by man, stood the Covenant.

Rising up between the endless sea and acres of white beaches, the sprawling sandstone structure we passed was the school where pures and halfs attended classes. With its thick marble columns and strategically placed statues of the gods, it was an intimidating and otherworldly place. Mortals thought the Covenant was an elite private school where none of their children would ever have the privilege of attending. They were right. People had to have something super-special in their blood to make it this far.

Beyond the main building were the dorms and they too boasted more columns and statues. Smaller buildings and bungalows dotted the landscape, and the massive gyms and training facilities sat adjacent to the courtyard. They always reminded me of the ancient coliseums except ours were enclosed; hurricanes could be a real bitch around these parts.

It was all beautiful—a place I loved and hated at the same time. Seeing it now, I realized just how badly I'd missed it . . . and Mom. She'd stayed on the main island while I'd gone to school, but she'd been a fixture around the campus, popping up and taking me to lunch after classes, swaying the old Dean to allow me to stay with her during the weekends. Gods, I just wanted one more chance, one more second to tell her—

I checked myself.

Control—I needed to be in control right now, and caving in to the lingering grief wasn't going to help me. Steeling myself, I climbed out of the Hummer and followed Aiden to the girls' dorm. We were the only ones moving down the silent hallways. With it being the beginning of summer, only a few students would be running around.

"Get cleaned up. I'll return for you in a little bit." He started to turn, but stopped. "I'll find something for you to wear and leave it on the table."

I nodded, at a loss for words. Even though I was trying to push the emotions down, some of them seeped through. Three years ago, my entire future had been perfectly planned. All the Instructors at the Covenant had praised my abilities in the training sessions. They even went as far as to say I could become a Sentinel. Sentinels were the best—and I'd *been* one of the best.

Three years without any training had set me back behind every half. A lifetime of servitude most likely waited for me—a future I couldn't face. Being subject to the pures' wills, having no control or say over anything—the possibility scared the crap out of me.

A possibility made worse by my nearly all-consuming need to hunt daimons.

Fighting them was ingrained in my blood, but after seeing what'd happened to Mom, the desire skyrocketed. Only the Covenant could provide the means for achieving my goals, and my absentee pure-blooded uncle now held my future in his hands.

My footsteps felt heavy as I moved around the familiar rooms. They were fully furnished, seeming larger than I remembered. The room had a separate living area and a decent sized bedroom. And it had its own bathroom. The Covenant offered only the best to its students.

I took a longer than necessary shower, reveling in the feeling of being clean again. People took things like showers for granted. I knew I had. After the daimon attack, I'd hit the road with little cash. Staying alive had turned out to be more important than a shower.

Once I was sure all the grime was washed away, I found the neat stack of clothes left on the small table in front of the couch. Picking them up, I realized at once they were the Covenant-issued training attire. The pants were at least two sizes too big, but I wasn't going to bitch about it. I brought them to my face and inhaled. They smelled so, so clean.

Back in the bathroom, I craned my neck. The daimon had tagged me just where the neck sloped down to the collarbone. The tag would be an angry red color for the next day or so, and then fade to a pale, shiny scar. A daimon's bite never left the skin undamaged. The nearly identical rows of tiny indentations made me queasy and also reminded me of one of my old Instructors. She was a beautiful older woman who'd retired to teach basic defense tactics after a nasty run-in with a daimon. Her arms had been covered with pale, half circle marks a degree or two lighter than her skin tone.

One tag had been bad enough. I couldn't imagine what it must've been like for her. The daimons had tried to turn her by draining her of all her aether. When it came to turning a pure, there was no exchange of blood.

It was a frighteningly simple process.

A daimon placed their lips on the drained pure's, shared some of their aether and—voila!—brand spankin' new daimon. Like infected blood, the tainted aether they passed turned a pure, and nothing could be done to undo the change. The pure was lost forever. As far as we knew, it was the only way a daimon could be made, but then again, it wasn't like we hung around and talked to them. They were killed on sight.

I'd always thought that policy was stupid. No one—not even the Council—knew what the daimons thought to accomplish by killing. If we caught one and actually questioned it, we could learn so much about them. What were their plans—their goals? Did they even have any? Or was it just the need for aether that kept them going? We didn't know. All the Hematoi cared about was stopping them and making sure none of the pures were turned.

Anyway, rumor said our Instructor had waited until the very last moment to strike, therefore foiling the daimon's plans. I remembered staring at those marks and thinking how terrible it was that her otherwise flawless body had been ruined.

My reflection in the fogged mirror stared back at me. This tag would be hard to hide, but it could've been worse. He could've tagged a chunk of my face—daimons could be cruel.

Halfs couldn't be turned, which is why we made such excellent fighters against the daimons. Dying was the worst that could happen to us. Who cared if a half-blood went down in battle? To the pures, we were a dime a dozen.

Sighing, I flipped my hair over my shoulder and pushed away from the mirror just as a soft knock sounded. A second later, Aiden opened the door to my dorm. All six and half feet of him came to an abrupt stop the moment he saw me. Surprise flickered over his face as he stared at the fresh version of me.

What can I say? I cleaned up nicely.

With all the dirt and overall grossness gone, I looked just like my mom. Long dark hair fell down my back; I had those high cheekbones and full lips most pures did. I was a bit curvier than Mom's willowy frame and I didn't have her amazing eyes. Mine were brown, homely old brown.

I tipped my head back, looking him straight in the eyes for the first time. "What?"

He recovered in record time. "Nothing. You ready?"

"I guess so." I snuck another peek at him as he headed out of my room.

Aiden's dark brown waves continually fell over his forehead, brushing against equally dark brows. The lines of his face were nearly perfect, the curve of his jaw strong, and he had the most expressive lips I'd ever seen. But it was those thundercloud eyes I found beautiful. No one had those eyes.

From the brief time he'd held me down in the field, I felt positive the rest of him was just as stunning. Too bad he was a pureblood. Pures equaled hands-off to me and every half out there. Supposedly, the gods had forbidden interactions of the fun kind between halfs and pures eons ago. Something to do with the purity of a pure's blood not being tarnished—a fear a child of such a coupling would be . . . I frowned at Aiden's back.

Would be what—a Cyclops?

I didn't know what might happen, but I did know it was considered very, very bad. Gods got offended, which wasn't a good thing. So since we'd been old enough to understand how babies were made, we half-bloods had been taught to never look at a pure-blood with anything other than respect and admiration. Pures were taught to never taint their bloodline by mixing with a half, but there were times when halfs and pures did hook up. It didn't end pretty, and halfs usually caught the brunt of the punishment.

It wasn't fair, but it was the way this world had existed. The pures were on top of the food chain. They made the rules, controlled the Council, and even ran the Covenant.

Aiden glanced over his shoulder at me. "How many daimons have you killed?"

"Just two." I picked up my pace so I could keep up with his long legged one.

"Just two?" Awe filled his voice. "Do you realize how amazing it is for a half-blood not fully trained to kill one daimon, let alone two?"

"I guess so." I paused, feeling the bubble of anger threatening to boil over. When the daimon had seen me standing in the doorway of Mom's bedroom, he'd launched himself at me . . . and right onto the spade I'd held. *Idiot.* The other daimon hadn't been that dumb. "I would've killed the other one in Miami . . . but I was just—I don't know. I wasn't thinking. I know I should've gone after him, but I panicked."

Aiden stopped and faced me. "Alex, the fact you took down one daimon without training is remarkable. It was brave, but also foolish."

"Well, thanks."

"You're not trained. The daimon could've easily killed you. And the one you brought down in the factory? Another fearless, but foolish act."

I frowned. "I thought you said it was amazing and remarkable."

"It was, but you could've been killed." He walked off ahead.

I struggled to keep up with him. "Why would you even care if I was killed? Why does Marcus care? I don't even know the man, and if he doesn't allow me to resume training, I'm as good as dead, anyways."

"That would be a shame." He looked at me blandly. "You have all the potential in the world."

My eyes narrowed on his back. The sudden urge to push him was almost too great to pass up. We didn't talk after that. Once outside, the breeze played with my hair, and I sucked in the taste of sea salt as the sun warmed my chilled skin.

Aiden led me back to the main school building and up the ridiculous number of stairs that led to the Dean's office. The formidable double doors loomed ahead, and I swallowed hard. I'd spent a lot of time in this office when Dean Nasso had overseen the Covenant.

As the Guards opened the door for us, I remembered the last time I'd been in this office for a lecture. I'd been fourteen, and out of boredom, I'd convinced one of the pures to flood the science wing using the water element. Of course the pure had totally ratted me out.

Nasso had not been pleased.

My first glimpse of the office was exactly how I remembered: perfect and well designed. Several leather chairs sat before a large cherry oak desk. Wildly colored fish zoomed back and forth in the aquarium lining the wall behind the desk.

My uncle stepped into my line of sight and I faltered. It'd been so long since I'd seen him—years really. I'd forgotten how much he looked like Mom. They shared the same eyes—emerald-colored ones that shifted depending on mood. They were eyes only my mother and uncle shared.

Except the last time I'd seen her eyes, they hadn't been vibrant. The icky feeling swelled inside me, pressing on my chest. I stepped forward, pushing it all the way down.

"Alexandria." Marcus's deep and cultured voice snapped me back into the room. "After all these years. To see you again? I am at a loss for words."

Uncle—and I used the term loosely—sounded nothing like a close family member. His tone was cold and plastic. When I met his eyes, I knew right off I was doomed. There was nothing in his stare linking me to him—no happiness or relief at seeing his only niece alive and in one piece. If anything, he looked rather bored.

Someone cleared his throat, drawing my attention to the corner of the office. We weren't alone. Mister Steroids stood in the corner, along with a female pure. She was tall and slender, with cascades of raven-colored hair. I pegged her as an Instructor.

Only pures who had no aspirations for the political games of their world taught for the Covenant or became Sentinels—or pures like Aiden who lived with super-personal reasons for doing so: say, like having his parents murdered by daimons right in front of him when he was a child. That was what'd happened to him. Supposedly, it was why Aiden had chosen to become a Sentinel. He probably wanted some sort of revenge.

Something we had in common.

"Sit down." Marcus motioned to a chair. "We have a lot to discuss."

I pulled my eyes from the pures and treaded forward. Hope flared with their presence. Why else would there be pures here if not to talk about my lack of training and ways to overcome it?

Marcus moved behind his desk and sat. From there, he folded his hands and leveled a look at me. Unease made me sit straighter and my feet dangled above the floor.

"I really don't know where to begin with . . . this mess Rachelle created."

I didn't respond since I wasn't sure I'd heard him correctly.

"First off, she nearly ruined Lucian. Twice." He spoke as if I'd had something to do with it. "The scandal she created when she met your father was bad enough. When she emptied Lucian's bank account and ran off with you? Well, I'm sure even you can understand the lasting implications of such an unwise decision."

Ah, Lucian. Mom's perfect, pure-blooded husband—my stepfather. I could imagine his response. It probably had involved a lot of throwing stuff and bemoaning his poor character judgment. I don't even know if Mom had ever loved him, or if she'd loved my mortal father she'd had an affair with, but I did know Lucian was a total priss.

Marcus continued listing the ways her decisions had hurt Lucian. I pretty much tuned him out. The last I remembered, Lucian was working to secure a spot on the pure-blood Council. Reminiscent of the old Greek Olympian court, the Council had twelve ruling figures, and, out of those twelve, two were Ministers.

Ministers were the most powerful. They ruled the lives of both pures and halfs just as Hera and Zeus ruled Olympia. Needless to say, the Ministers had huge freaking egos.

Each Covenant location held a Council: North Carolina, Tennessee, New York, and the pure-blood university located in South Dakota. The eight Ministers controlled the Council.

"Are you even listening to me, Alexandria?" Marcus frowned at me.

My head jerked up. "Yes . . . you're talking about how bad everything's been for Lucian. I feel sorry for him. Really, I do. I'm sure it pales in comparison to having your life ripped away from you."

A strange look inched across his face. "Are you referring to your mother's fate?"

"You mean your sister's fate?" My eyes narrowed as I met his gaze.

Marcus stared at me, his face going blank. "Rachelle sealed her own fate when she left the safety of our society. What happened to her is truly tragic, but I cannot find it in myself to feel overly upset. When she pulled you away from the Covenant, she proved she gave no thought to Lucian's reputation or for your safety. She was self-centered, irresponsible—"

"She was everything to me!" I jumped to my feet. "She did nothing but think of me! What happened to her was *horrific*— 'tragic' is for people who die in car wrecks!"

His expression didn't change. "She did nothing but think of you? I find that strange. She left the safety of the Covenant and put both of you in danger."

I bit the inside of my cheek.

"Exactly." His gaze turned arctic. "Sit down, Alexandria."

Furious, I forced myself to sit and shut up.

"Did she tell you why you needed to leave the Covenant? Give you any reason to why she would do such a reckless thing?"

I glanced over at the pures. Aiden had retreated to stand beside the other two. The three of them watched this soap opera through poker faces. A lot of help they were proving to be.

"Alexandria, I asked you a question."

The hard wood embedded into my palms as I gripped the chair arms. "I heard you. No. She didn't tell me."

A muscle ticked along Marcus's jaw as he stared at me in silence. "Well, it is a shame."

Since I wasn't sure how to respond, I watched him open up a file on his desk and spread the lined papers out in front of him. Leaning forward, I tried to see what they were.

Clearing his throat, he picked up one of the papers. "As it is, I cannot hold you responsible for what Rachelle did. The gods know she is suffering the consequences."

"I think Alexandria is aware of how her mother suffered," the female pure interrupted. "There is no need to go any further."

Marcus's stare turned glacial. "Yes. I suppose you are correct, Laadan." He turned back to the paper he held between his elegant fingers. "When I was advised you were finally located, I requested your reports to be sent to me."

I winced and sat back in the seat. This wasn't going to be good at all.

"All of your Instructors had nothing but glowing accolades when it came to your training."

A small smile formed on my lips. "I was pretty damn good."

"However," he glanced up, briefly meeting my eyes, "when it comes to your behavior records, I find myself . . . flabbergasted."

My smile shriveled up and died.

"Several write-ups for issues of disrespect toward your

teachers and other students," he continued. "A particular note here, written personally by Instructor Banks, states your level of respect for your superiors is seriously lacking and had been an ongoing issue."

"Instructor Banks had no sense of humor."

Marcus arched a brow. "Then I imagine neither did Instructor Richards nor Instructor Octavian? They also wrote, at times, you were uncontrollable and undisciplined."

Protests died on my lips. I had nothing to say.

"Your problems with respect didn't appear to be your only issues." He picked up another piece of paper and his brows rose. "You were disciplined numerous times for sneaking out of the Covenant, fighting, disruption of class, breaking numerous rules, and oh yes, my personal favorite?" He looked up, smiling tightly. "You had racked up repeated demerits for breaking curfew and for fraternizing in the male dormitory."

I shifted uncomfortably.

"All before the age of fourteen." His lips thinned. "You must be proud."

My eyes widened as I stared at his desk. "I wouldn't say proud."

"Does it matter?"

I looked up. "I . . . guess not?"

The tight smile returned. "Considering your previous behavior, I'm afraid to say there is no way I could allow you to resume training—"

"What?" My voice turned shrill. "Then why am I here?"

Marcus placed the papers back into the file and closed it. "Our communities are always in need of servants. I spoke with Lucian this morning. He has offered you a place in his home. You should be honored."

"No!" I came to my feet once again. Panic and rage seized me. "There is no way you're going to drug me! I won't be a servant in his house or any pure's!"

"Then what?" Marcus folded his hands again and looked at me calmly. "Will you go back to living on the streets? I will not allow that. The decision has already been made. You will not reenter the Covenant."

3

Those words shocked me into silence. All my dreams of vengeance evaporated into nothing. I stared at my uncle, hating him almost as much as I hated daimons.

Mister Steroids cleared his throat. "If I may say something?"

Marcus and I turned toward him. I was surprised he could even speak, but Marcus waved his hand for him to continue.

"She killed two daimons."

"I'm aware of this, Leon." The man who was about to bring down my whole world didn't seem too interested.

"When we found her in Georgia, she was holding her own against two more daimons," Leon continued. "Her potential, if trained properly, is astronomical."

Shocked that this pure would speak for me, I slowly sat down. Marcus still looked unimpressed and those bright green eyes were as hard as ice.

"I understand, but her behavior before the incident with her mother cannot be erased. This is a school, not a daycare center. I do not have the time or the energy to keep an eye on her. I cannot have her running wild through these halls and influencing the other students."

I rolled my eyes. He made me sound like a cunning criminal about to bring down the entire Covenant.

"Then assign someone to her," Leon said. "There are Instructors here during the summer who'll be able to keep an eye on her."

"I don't need a babysitter. It's not like I'm going to burn down a building."

Everyone ignored me.

Marcus sighed. "Even if we assign someone to her, she is behind in her training. There is no way she would be on par with those in her class. Come fall, she will be sorely behind."

This time it was Aiden who spoke. "We would have the entire summer to prepare her. It's possible she could be ready enough to attend classes."

"Who has the time for such an undertaking?" Marcus frowned. "Aiden, you are a Sentinel, not an Instructor. Neither is Leon. And Laadan will be returning to New York shortly. The other Instructors have lives—ones I cannot expect them to drop just for one half-blood."

Aiden's expression was unreadable, and I sure as hell didn't know what provoked the words coming out of his mouth next. "I can work with her. It wouldn't interfere with my duties."

"You're one of the best Sentinels," Marcus shook his head. "It would be a waste of your talent—"

They battled on about what to do to me. I tried interjecting once, but after the warning glare both Leon and Aiden sent my way, I shut up. Marcus continued stating I was a lost cause while Aiden and Leon argued that I could be fixed. My uncle's willingness to turn me over to Lucian stung. Servitude wasn't a pleasant future. Everyone knew that. I'd heard rumors, terrible ones concerning how the pures treated halfs—especially female halfs.

Laadan stepped forward after Aiden and Marcus came to a standstill about what to do with me. Slowly, she flicked her long hair over one shoulder. "How about we make a deal, Dean Andros? If Aiden says he can train her and still do his duties, then you have nothing to lose. If she's not ready by the end of the summer, she doesn't stay."

I twisted back to Marcus, full of hope.

He stared at me for what seemed like forever. "Fine." He leaned back in his chair. "But this is on you, Aiden. Do you understand? Anything—and I mean anything—she does will be a reflection upon you. And trust me, she will do something. She's just like her mother."

Aiden suddenly looked cautious as he glanced back at me. "Yes. I understand."

A wide smile broke out across my face and the cautious look on his face grew, but when I turned back to Marcus, my smile died under his frigid stare.

"I will be less tolerant than your old dean, Alexandria. Do not make me regret this decision."

I nodded, not fully trusting myself to speak. There was a good chance I would mess it all up if I did. Afterwards, Marcus dismissed me with a wave of his hand. I stood and left his office. Laadan and Leon remained, but Aiden followed me.

I turned to him. "Thank you."

Aiden stared at me. "Don't thank me yet."

I smothered a yawn and shrugged. "Well, I just did. I really think Marcus would've shipped me off to Lucian's if it wasn't for you three."

"He would've. Your stepfather is your legal guardian."

I shuddered. "That's reassuring."

He caught my reaction. "Was it something that Lucian did that caused you and your mother to leave?"

"No, but Lucian . . . wasn't particularly fond of me. I'm Mom's love child, you know? He's just Lucian. What's that prick up to, anyways?"

Aiden's brows rose. "That prick is the Minister of Council."

My mouth dropped open. "What? You're kidding, right?"

"Why would I joke about something like that? So you may want to refrain from calling him a prick in public. I doubt it would help your cause."

News that Lucian was now a Minister made my stomach

clench, especially considering he had a "place" for me in his household. I shook my head and pushed that implication far from my thoughts. I had enough immediate concerns other than dealing with him.

"You should get some rest. Come tomorrow, we'll begin training . . . if you feel up to it."

"I do."

Aiden's gaze drifted over my bruised face and then down, as if he could see the many cuts and bruises I'd racked up since I'd fled Miami. "Are you sure?"

I nodded, my gaze falling on the lock of hair he kept pushing off his forehead. "What are we starting with? I didn't start any of the offensive tactics or Silat training."

He shook his head. "I hate to disappoint you, but you won't be starting with Silat training."

That *was* disappointing. I liked daggers and all things that stabbed, and I really would like to know how to use them effectively. I started to head toward my dorm, but Aiden's voice stopped me.

"Alex. Don't . . . let me down. Anything you do will come back on me. Do you understand?"

"Yes. Don't worry. I'm not as bad as Marcus makes me sound."

He looked doubtful. "Fraternizing in the male dorms?"

I flushed. "I was visiting *friends*. Not like I was hooking up with any of them. I was only fourteen. I'm not a ho-bag."

"Well, that's good to know." He walked away.

Sighing, I headed back to my room. I was tired, but all the excitement from getting a second chance had me hyped up. After staring at the bed for an absurd amount of time, I left my room and moved through the empty halls of the girls' dorm. The pures and halfs shared living quarters only at the Covenant. Anyplace else, we were segregated.

I tried to remember what it'd been like to be here. The

rigorous training schedules, ridiculous class work studying things that'd bored me to tears, and all the social games the pures and halfs had played. There's nothing like a bunch of catty teenagers who could either kick your ass halfway across the country or set you on fire with a mere thought. That alone changed who people picked fights with or became friends with. And at the end of the day, it was always good to have a firestarter in your back pocket.

Everyone had a role to play. I'd been considered cool by half-blood standards, but now I had no idea where I would stand come fall.

After roaming the empty common rooms, I left the girls' dorm and headed for one of the smaller buildings near the marshlands. The one story, square building held the cafeteria and rec rooms and surrounded a colorful courtyard.

I slowed as I neared one of the larger rooms. The laughter and crashes radiating from the room proved there were some kids still here over summer vacation. Something flip-flopped inside me. Would they accept me back? Would they even know me? Hell, would they even care?

Taking a deep breath, I pushed open the doors. No one seemed to notice me. Everyone was busy cheering on a pure who floated several pieces of furniture in midair. The young girl was a novice at controlling the air element, which explained all the noise. Mom had used air, too. After all, it was the most common element. Pures could only control one, sometimes two if they were really powerful.

I studied the girl. With her bright red curls and giant blue eyes, she looked about twelve, especially standing next to the towering halfs in her cute jumper. I really didn't have room to talk. I came in at a whopping five and a half feet, which was midget size compared to most of the halfs.

I blamed my mortal father.

Meanwhile, the pure pursed her lips as another chair toppled to the floor and more chuckles erupted from her audience—all except one. Caleb Nicolo. Tall, blond, and all charming smile, Caleb had been my partner in dysfunction when I'd been at the Covenant. I shouldn't have been so surprised to see him here during the summer. His mortal mother had never wanted anything to do with her "weird" child and his pure-blood father was totally on the absentee list.

Caleb stared at me, wide-eyed and stunned. "Holy . . . crap."

Everyone turned at that point, even the pure. With her concentration broken, all the items fell to the floor. Several of the halfs scattered as the couch came down, and then the pool table.

I wiggled my fingers. "Long time no see, huh?"

Caleb snapped out of it and within two seconds, he'd crossed the length of the room and pulled me into a mammoth hug. Then he picked me up and swung me around.

"Where in the hell have you been?" He put me on my feet. "Three years, Alex? What the hell? Do you even know what half of the students said happened to you and your mom? We thought you were dead! I could seriously punch you in the face, like right now."

I could barely hold back my smile. "I've missed you, too."

He kept staring at me like I was some kind of mirage. "I can't believe you're really standing here. You better have a wild story for me."

I laughed. "Like what?"

"You better have had a baby, killed someone, or slept with a pure. Those are your three options. Anything less is totally unacceptable."

"You're so gonna be disappointed, because it wasn't anything exciting."

Caleb dropped his arm around my shoulders and steered me to one of the couches. "Then you gotta tell me what the hell you've been doing and how you got back here. And why you didn't call any of us? There isn't a single place in this world that doesn't have cell service."

"I'd go with she probably killed someone."

I tilted my head back and spotted Jackson Manos in the group of halfs I didn't recognize. He looked exactly as I remembered him. Dark hair parted down the middle, a body made just for girls to drool over, and equally dark, sexy eyes. I gave him my best smile. "Whatever, you douche. I didn't kill anyone."

Jackson shook his head as he approached us. "Do you remember dropping Nick on his neck during take down practice? You nearly killed him. Good thing we heal as quickly as we do or you would've put him out of training for months."

We all laughed at the memory. Poor Nick had spent a week in the infirmary after the incident. Our good time and general curiosity drew the other halfs to the couch. Knowing I had to answer some of the questions regarding my absence eventually, I came up with a pretty bland tale about Mom wanting to live among mortals. Caleb looked at me doubtfully, but he didn't push it.

"What the hell are you wearing, by the way? It looks like the guy's training uniform." Caleb plucked at my sleeve.

"It's all I have." I gave a dramatic, pitiful sigh. "I doubt I'm going to get out anytime soon, and I don't have any money."

He grinned. "I know where they keep all the training clothes here. Tomorrow, I can pick you up some extra stuff in town."

"You don't have to. And besides, I don't think I want you shopping for me. I'd end up looking like a stripper."

Caleb laughed, the skin around his blue eyes crinkling. "Don't worry about it. Dad sent me a near fortune a few weeks ago. Guess he feels bad for being a dick of a father. Anyway, I'll get one of the girls to go with me or something."

The pure—Thea was her name—eventually made her way over to where we sat. She seemed nice and genuinely interested in me, but she asked the one question I feared.

"So has your mother . . . reconciled with Lucian?" she asked in a small, childlike voice.

I forced myself not to show any reaction. "No."

She looked surprised. So did the halfs.

"But . . . they can't divorce," said Caleb. "Are they going to do the separate house, different zip code thing?"

Pures never divorced. They believed their mates were predestined by the gods. I'd always thought it was a load of bull, but the "no-divorce" thing explained why so many of them had affairs.

"Uh . . . no," I said. "Mom . . . didn't make it *out there*."

Caleb's mouth dropped open. "Oh. Man, I'm sorry."

I forced myself to shrug. "It's okay."

"What happened to her?" Jackson asked, as tactless as ever.

Taking a deep breath, I decided to tell them the truth. "A daimon got her."

That led to another round of questions, all of which I answered truthfully. Each of their faces mirrored shock and awe as I got around to the part where I'd fought and killed two of the daimons. Even Jackson seemed impressed. None of them had even seen a daimon in real life.

I didn't go into detail about my meeting with Marcus, but I did tell them my summer wasn't going to be all fun and games. When I mentioned I'd be training with Aiden, a collective groan sounded.

"What?" I looked around the group.

Caleb kicked his legs off my lap and stood. "Aiden is one of the toughest—"

"Roughest," Jackson added solemnly.

"Meanest," threw in a half-blood girl with brown hair cut über-short. I think her name was Elena.

Unease shifted through me. What had I gotten myself into with him? And they weren't done with their descriptions.

"Strongest," another kid added.

Elena glanced around the room, her lips curving. "Sexiest."

There was a round of sighs from the girls, but Caleb frowned. "That's not the point. Man, he's a beast. He's not even an Instructor. He's a Sentinel through and through."

"The last couple of graduating classes got assigned to his area." Jackson shook his head. "He's not even a Guide, but he weeded out over half of them and sent them back as Guards."

"Oh." I shrugged. That didn't sound all that bad. I was about to point that out when a new voice interrupted.

"Well, look who's back? If it isn't our one and only high school drop-out," drawled Lea Samos.

I closed my eyes and counted to ten. I made it to five. "Are you lost, Lea? This isn't where they're handing out the free pregnancy tests."

"Oh, boy." Caleb moved to stand behind the couch, getting out of the way. I didn't blame him. Lea and I had a legendary history. The write-ups Marcus had gone over for fighting had usually involved Lea.

She laughed that husky, throaty laugh I was all too familiar with. I looked up then. She hadn't changed a bit.

Okay. That was a lie.

If anything, Lea had grown more beautiful in the last three years. With her long copper-colored hair, amethyst eyes, and impossibly tanned skin, she looked like some sort of glamorous model. I couldn't help but think of my own boring brown eyes.

While my own stellar reputation had my name whispered on many lips during my time here, Lea had literally prowled the Covenant—No. She'd owned it.

Her eyes dropped the length of me as she stalked across the rec room, taking in the oversized shirt and rumpled jogging pants. One perfectly groomed brow arched. "Don't you look lovely?"

She, of course, was dressed in the tightest and shortest skirt known to man. "Isn't that the same skirt you wore in the third grade? It's getting a little tight. You may want to go up a size or three."

Lea smirked and tossed the mass of hair over her shoulder. She sat in one of the fluorescent moon chairs across from us. "What happened to your face?"

"What happened to yours?" I retorted. "You look like a damn Oompa Loompa. You should lay off the spray tanning, Lea."

There were a couple of snickers from our impromptu audience, but Lea ignored them. She was focused on me—her arch-nemesis. We'd been 'at this since we were seven. Sandbox enemies, I guessed. "You know what I heard this morning?"

I sighed. "What?"

Jackson sauntered to her side, his dark eyes devouring her long legs. He moved behind her and tugged a strand of her hair. "Lea, knock it off. She just got back."

My brows rose as she motioned him down with a flick of her little finger. He lowered his mouth to hers. Slowly, I turned to Caleb. Looking bored with the display, he shrugged. Instructors couldn't prevent the students from hooking up. I mean, come on. With a bunch of teenagers thrown together, it happened, but the Covenant frowned upon it. Usually the students didn't flaunt it.

When they were done tonguing one another, Lea returned to staring at me. "I heard Dean Andros didn't want you back. Your very own uncle wanted to place you into servitude. How sad is that?"

I flipped her off.

"It took three pures to convince her uncle she's worth keeping around."

Caleb snorted. "Alex is one of the best. I doubt it took much convincing."

Lea opened her mouth, but I cut her off. "I *was* one of the best. And it did. Apparently, I have a bad reputation and he felt I had missed too much time."

"What?" Caleb stared at me.

I shrugged. "I have until the end of summer to prove to

Marcus I can get caught up in time to join the rest of the students. It's no big deal, right, Lea?" I faced her, grinning. "I think you remember the last time we sparred? It was a long time ago, but I'm sure you can recall it quite clearly."

A pink flush crawled over her tanned cheeks and her hand crept to her nose in what looked like a subconscious move, drawing an even bigger grin from me. At such a young age, our sparring was supposed to have been an absolutely no-contact training exercise. But one insult had led to another, and I'd broken her nose.

In two places.

It'd also landed me in suspension for three weeks.

Lea's plump lips thinned. "You know what else I know, Alex?"

I folded my arms over my chest. "What?"

"While everyone here may believe whatever lame excuse you gave for your mother leaving, I know the real reason." Her eyes sparkled with malice.

Coldness settled over me. "And how do you know?"

Her lips curved at the corners as she met my stare. I vaguely noticed Jackson moving away from her. "Your mother met with Grandma Piperi."

Grandma Piperi? I rolled my eyes. Piperi was a crazy old woman who was supposed to be an oracle. The pures believed she communed with the gods. I believed she communed with a lot of liquor.

"So?" I said.

"I know what Grandma Piperi said to make your mother go crazy. She was crazy, right?"

I was on my feet without realizing it. "Lea, shut up."

She looked at me, eyes wide and unfazed. "Now Alex, you may want to calm down. One little fight and you'll be cleaning toilets for the rest of your life."

My hands clutched. Had she been in the room, under Marcus's desk or something? How else would she know so much? But Lea was correct, and that sucked. Being the bigger person meant walking away from her. It was harder than I ever imagined, like walking through quicksand. The more I moved, the more the air around me literally demanded that I stay and break her nose again. But I did it, and I made it past her chair without hitting her.

I was a totally different person—a better person.

"Don't you want to know what she said to your mother to make her crazy? To make her leave? You'll be happy to know it had everything to do with you."

I stopped. Just like Lea knew I would.

Caleb appeared at my side and grabbed my arm. "Come on, Alex. If what she's saying is true then you don't need to fall for this crap. You know she doesn't know anything."

Lea twisted around and threw one slender arm over the back of her chair. "But I do. You see, your mother and Piperi weren't alone in the garden. Someone else overheard her conversation."

I shrugged off Caleb's grip and turned around. "Who heard them?"

She shrugged, studying her painted nails. I knew right then and there, I would end up hitting her. "The oracle told your mother you would be the one to kill her. Considering you couldn't stop a daimon from draining her, I guess Piperi meant it in the abstract sense. What good is a half-blood who can't even protect her own mother? Is it any wonder why Marcus didn't want you back?"

There was a moment when no one moved in the room, not even me. Then I smiled at her, right before I grabbed a handful of copper hair and yanked her out of the chair.

Screw being a better person.

4

The way her mouth dropped open as she fell backwards almost made up for her cruel words. Clearly, she hadn't expected me to do anything, thinking the threat of being expelled was far too great. Lea didn't know the power of her own words.

I jerked my arm back, fully intending on undoing whatever the doctors had done to fix that perky little nose of hers, but my fist never landed. In fact, Caleb got to me before I could take another step toward her. He literally carried me out of the rec room, and then put me down and blocked my path back to Lea. There was a wild grin on his face as I tried to dart around him.

"Let me pass, Caleb. I swear to the gods, I'm going to break her face!"

"Back not even a day, Alex. Wow."

"Shut up." I glared at him.

"Alex, knock it off. You get into a fight and you're going to get kicked out. What then? Be a servant for the rest of your life? Anyway, you know she's lying. So let it go."

I glanced down at my hand and noticed several strands of red hair wrapped around my fingers. Sweet.

Caleb saw the vicious gleam in my eye and seemed to realize staying near this room wasn't going to end well. Grabbing my arm, he all but dragged me down the hallway. "She's just a stupid girl. You know she was just talking crap, right?"

"Who knows?" I grumbled. "She's right, you know? I have no idea why Mom left. She could've spoken to Grandma Piperi. I don't know."

"I seriously doubt the oracle said you would kill your mom."

Unconvinced, I punched the front door open.

Caleb followed close behind. "Just forget about it, okay? You've got to focus on training, not Lea and what the oracle may have said."

"Easier said than done."

"Okay. Then you could ask the oracle what she told your mom."

I stared at him.

"What? You could ask the oracle if it bothers you that much."

"There is no way that woman is still alive." I winced at the blinding sun. "It was three years ago when Mom could've talked to her."

Now Caleb gave me the same look.

"What? She can't be. She would have to be . . . like a hundred and fifty years old by now."

Pures had a lot of power and an oracle would have even more, but none of them were immortal.

"Alex, she's the oracle. She'll be alive until the next one comes into power."

I rolled my eyes at Caleb. "She's just a nutty old woman. Communes with the gods? The only things she communes with are the trees and her bridge club."

He made a sound of exasperation. "It never fails to amaze me that being what you are—what we are—you still don't believe in the gods."

"No. I do believe in them. I just think they're absentee land-lords. Right now, they're probably hanging out somewhere in Las Vegas, screwing showgirls and cheating at poker."

Caleb jumped away from me, his feet landing on the white and tan pebbles. "Do not let me be standing next to you when one of them strikes you down."

I laughed. "Yeah, they're really watching and taking care of business. That's why we have daimons running around draining pures and killing mortals for the fun of it."

"That's why the gods have us." Caleb grinned like he'd just explained everything.

"Whatever." We stopped at the end of the stone pathway. From here, we either went to the girls' dorm or the boys'.

The two of us stared across the flooded marsh. Woody plants and low growing bushes dotted the brackish water, making crossing the mess almost impossible. Beyond that was the forest—literally a no man's land. When I was younger I'd thought monsters lived in the dark woods. When I'd gotten older I'd learned that following the marshes led to the main island, giving me a perfect escape route when I'd wanted to sneak around.

"Does the old hag still live in there?" I asked finally. What if I could talk to Piperi?

Caleb nodded. "I guess so, but who knows? She comes down to the campus every once in a while."

"Oh." I squinted in the harsh light. "You know what I was thinking?"

He glanced at me. "What?"

"Mom never told me why we needed to leave, Caleb. Never once during those three years. I think I'd be . . . more okay if I knew why Mom left in the first place. I know it doesn't change anything that happened, but at least I'd know what the hell was so important we had to leave here."

"Only the oracle knows and who knows when she'll be back here? And you can't go to her. She lives way back there. Even I don't venture that far into the marshes. So don't even think about it."

My lips curved at the corners. "All these years, and you still know me so well."

He snickered. "Maybe we can throw her a party and lure her out. I think she was down here for the spring equinox."

"Really?" Maybe if I talked to the oracle she'd give me some answers—or tell my future.

Caleb shrugged. "Can't remember, but speaking of partying, there's going to be one this weekend over on the main island. Zarak's throwing it. You game?"

I stifled a yawn. "Zarak? Wow. I haven't seen him in forever, but I doubt partying is something I'm going to be partaking in anytime soon. I'm permanently grounded."

"What?" Caleb's mouth dropped open. "You can sneak out. You were like the queen of sneaking out."

"Yeah, but that was before my uncle became the dean and I wasn't one step away from being expelled."

Caleb snorted. "Alex, you almost got expelled like three times. Since when has that stopped you? Anyway, I'm sure we can come up with something. Besides, it'll be like a welcome back party for you."

It was a bad idea, but I felt the usual excitement stirring in my belly. "Well . . . I won't be training at night."

"No," agreed Caleb.

A grin tugged at my lips. "And sneaking out never killed anyone."

"Or got them expelled."

We grinned at each other, and just like that, things were the way they'd been before everything had gone to hell.

Caleb and I had a little adventure in the supply room in the main school building after dinner. We swiped every possible article of clothing that would fit me and Caleb promised once again to grab one of the other half girls and go shopping for me the following day. I could only imagine what he'd come back with.

With our arms full, we headed back to my dorm. I was only a little surprised when I spotted Aiden's formidable frame standing by the thick marble columns on the wide porch. Caleb's eyes went wide.

I groaned. "Busted."

My footsteps slowed as we neared him. I couldn't read anything from his stoic expression or by the way he bowed his head toward Caleb in a respectful manner. For once in his entire life, Caleb was struck speechless when Aiden stepped up and took the armful of clothing from him.

"Need I remind you that males are not allowed in the girls' dormitory, Nicolo?"

Caleb shook his head mutely.

He raised his brows as he turned to me. "We need to talk."

I looked at Caleb helplessly, but he backed off with an apologetic half smile. For a hot second, I considered following him. I didn't. "What do we need to talk about?"

Aiden motioned me forward with a curt nod. "You haven't rested at all today, have you?"

I shifted my load to my other arm. "No. I've been catching up with friends."

He seemed to consider that as we made our way down the hall. Thank the gods I'd been given a room on the bottom floor. I hated stairs, and even though the Covenant had more money than I could comprehend, there wasn't a single elevator in the entire campus.

"You should've been resting. Tomorrow won't be easy for you."

"You could always make it easy for me."

Aiden laughed. The sound was a rich, deep noise that would've brought a smile to my face in a different situation. Like one in which he wasn't laughing at me.

I frowned as I pushed the door to my room open. "Why are you allowed in my room if Caleb isn't?"

He arched an eyebrow. "I'm not a student."

"Still a guy." I took my load of clothing to my bedroom, where I dropped them on the floor. "You're not even an Instructor or a Guide. So I think if you're allowed in here, Caleb should be, too."

Aiden studied me for a moment, folding his arms across his chest. "I've been told you were once interested in becoming a Sentinel instead of a Guard."

I plopped down on the bed and grinned up at him. "You've been checking up on me."

"I decided I'd better be prepared."

"I'm sure you were told wonderful things about me."

He rolled his eyes. "Most of what Dean Andros said was correct. You are well known with the Instructors. They did praise your talent and ambition. The other stuff . . . well, that can be expected. You were just a kid—still a kid."

"I'm not a kid."

Aiden's lips twitched as if he wished to smile. "You're still a kid."

My cheeks flushed. It was one thing being told I was a kid by any old person. Who cared? But when it was a super-hot guy telling me that, it didn't leave me all warm and fuzzy inside.

"I'm not a kid," I repeated.

"Really? Then you must be an adult?"

"Sure." I gave him my best smile, the one that usually got me out of trouble.

Aiden was unaffected. "Interesting. An adult would know when to walk away from a fight, Alex. Especially after being warned any questionable behavior could result in their removal from the Covenant."

My smiled faded. "I have no idea what you're talking about, but I would have to agree."

Aiden tipped his head to the side. "You don't?"

"Nope."

A small smile appeared on his lips. It should've served as a warning, but I found myself staring at those lips in place of paying attention to *him*. Suddenly, he crouched in front of me at eye level.

"Then I should be relieved to know what I was told just an

hour ago is false. It wasn't you who yanked a girl—by her hair—out of a chair in the common lounge area."

I opened my mouth to deny it, but my protests died. Dammit. There was *always* someone willing to rat people out.

"Do you understand the precarious position you're in?" His firm gaze held mine. "How foolish it is to allow simple words to lead you to violence?"

Pulling Lea out of the chair had been foolish, but she'd pissed me off. "She was talking about my mother."

"Does it matter? Think about it. It's just words and words mean nothing. Only action does. Are you going to fight every single person who says something about you or your mother? If so, you should go ahead and pack your bags now."

"But—"

"There are going to be rumors—ridiculous rumors about why your mother left. Why you didn't come back. You can't fight every single person who upsets you."

I tipped my head to the side. "I could try."

"Alex, you need to focus on getting back into the Covenant. Right now, you're here as a courtesy. You want revenge against the daimons, right?"

"Yes!" My voice turned fierce as my fists clenched.

"You want to be able to get out there and fight them? Then you need to pay attention to training instead of what people are saying about you."

"But she said I was the reason Mom died!" Hearing my voice crack the way it did, I had to look away. It was weak of me. Embarrassing. Weak and embarrassing were not in a Sentinel's vocabulary.

"Alex, look at me."

I hesitated before I did. For a moment, the hardness in his expression softened. When he looked at me like that, I truly believed he understood my reaction. Maybe he didn't agree with it, but at least he understood why I'd done it.

"You know there was nothing you could do about what happened to your mother." His eyes searched my face. "You do know that, right?"

"I should've done something. I had all that time and I should've called someone. Maybe then..." I ran my hand through my hair and took a deep breath. "Maybe then none of this would've happened."

"Alex, you couldn't have known it would end this way."

"But I did." I closed my eyes, feeling a twisting in my stomach. "We all do. It's what happens when you leave the safety of the community. I knew it would happen, but I was just scared they wouldn't let her back in after leaving. I couldn't... leave her out there by herself."

Aiden was silent for so long, I thought he'd left the room, but then I felt his hand on my shoulder. I opened my eyes, turning my head so I looked down at his hand. His fingers were long and graceful-looking. Deadly, I imagined. But now, they were gentle. Like I had no will of my own, I looked into his silver eyes. I couldn't help but be reminded of what'd passed between us at the factory.

Abruptly, Aiden let go. Running a hand through his hair, he looked unsure of what he was doing. "Look. Get some rest. Eight in the morning will come quick." He turned to leave, but stopped. "And don't leave this room again tonight. I don't want to find out in the morning you burnt down a village while I slept."

There were several retorts I had lined up, all of them clever and snarky, but I squelched them and pulled myself off the bed. Aiden stopped at my door and glanced down the empty hallway.

"Alex, what happened to your mother is not your fault. Placing that kind of guilt on yourself will only hinder you. It will get you nowhere. Do you understand?"

"Yeah," I lied.

Even though I wanted to believe what Aiden said was true, I knew it wasn't. If I'd contacted the Covenant, Mom would still be alive. So yeah, in a way, Lea was right.

I was responsible for my mother's death.

5

The following day was like going back in time for me—up way too early to think straight and wearing clothes made to get my butt kicked in. This time around though, there were a few things different.

Looking at Aiden, for example, it was clear he wasn't going to be like the Instructors I'd had before. They'd been Sentinels or Guards injured on the job, or the ones who'd wanted to settle down. Back then, I'd always ended up with Instructors who were either old as dirt or flat out boring.

Aiden was neither of those things.

He wore the same style of workout pants I'd stolen from the supply closet, but where I wore a modest white shirt, he had on a tank. And boy, did he have arms to show off. His skin didn't sag; he was far from boring, and he was actually out there hunting daimons.

But he did have one thing in common with my old Instructors. The moment I walked into the gym, he was all business. From the way he coached me through several warm-up exercises and ordered me to unroll all the mats, I knew I was going to be hurting by the end of the day.

"How much do you remember from your previous training?"

I looked around, seeing things I hadn't laid eyes on in three years—training mats to ease falls, dummies with skin that felt real, and a first aid kit in every corner. People usually bled at some point in training. But the furthest wall interested me the most. It was covered with wicked-looking knives I'd never gotten to practice with.

"The normal things: textbook stuff, offensive training, kicking and punching techniques." I made a beeline for the weapon wall; it was like compulsion.

"Not much then."

Picking up one of the slender titanium daggers the Sentinels usually carried, I nodded. "The good stuff started just—"

Aiden reached around me, plucking the dagger from my fingers and placing it back on the wall. His fingers lingered over the blade reverently. "You haven't earned the right to touch these weapons, especially *that* one."

At first, I thought he was teasing, but one look at his face told me he wasn't. "Why?"

He didn't answer.

I kind of wanted to touch it again, but I pulled my hand back and walked away from the wall. "I was good at everything I learned. I could hit and kick hard. I could run faster than anyone in my class."

He returned to the center of the room and placed his hands on his narrow hips. "Not much then," he repeated.

My eyes followed him. "You could say that."

"You should get used to this room. We'll be spending eight hours a day in here."

"You're joking, right?"

He didn't look like he was joking. "Down the hall is a gym. You should visit it . . . *often*."

My mouth dropped open.

Aiden gave me a bland look. "You're far too skinny. You need to put some weight on and some muscle." He reached out and tapped my scrawny arm. "Speed and strength, you have naturally. But right now, a ten-year-old could take you on."

I closed my mouth. He had a point. This morning, I'd had to tie the knot twice in my drawstrings to get them to stay up.

"Well, it wasn't like I had three square meals a day. Speaking of which, I'm kinda hungry. Don't I get breakfast?"

The hard look in his eyes softened a little, and for a moment he looked like he had when he'd been in my room the night before. "I brought you a protein shake."

"Ew," I groaned, but when he picked up the plastic container and handed it to me, I took it.

"Drink up. We're going to cover some ground rules first." Aiden stepped back. "Go ahead and sit. I want you to listen."

And there went the softer and kinder look. Rolling my eyes, I sat down and gingerly placed the bottle to my lips. It smelled like stale chocolate and tasted like a watered down milkshake. Gross.

He stood in front of me with those impossibly ripped arms across his chest. "First off: no drinking or smoking."

"Gee. That means I've got to kick the crack habit."

He stared down at me, clearly unimpressed. "You will not be able to leave the Covenant without permission or—don't look at me that way."

"Jeez, how old are you?" I totally knew how old he was, but I wanted to pick.

Aiden cracked his neck. "I turn twenty-one in October."

"Huh." I shook the bottle. "So have you always been so . . . mature?"

His brows furrowed. "Mature?"

"Yeah, you sound like a dad." I deepened my voice and tried to look stern. "'Don't look at me that way' or else."

Aiden blinked slowly. "I don't sound like that and I didn't say 'or else.'"

"But if you had, what would the 'or else' be?" I hid my grin with the bottle.

He glanced to the side, frowning. "Can you just not talk through this?"

"Whatever." I took a drink. "So why can't I leave the island?"

"It's for your safety and my peace of mind." Aiden returned to his original stance, arms over chest, legs spread wide. "You will not leave this island without being accompanied by someone."

"Do my friends count?" I asked, only half serious.

"No."

"Then who's allowed to accompany me?"

Aiden's eyes closed and he sighed. "Either me or one of the other Instructors."

I swished the liquid around in the bottle. "I know the rules, Aiden. You don't have to go over them again."

He looked like he wanted to point out the fact I could probably use a refresher, but he relented. After I was done, he took the shake and walked it back over to where several punching bags were propped against the wall.

I stood and stretched. "So, what am I learning today? I think we should start with anything that doesn't involve you kicking my ass."

His lips twitched as if he was fighting a grin. "The basics."

"The basics." I pouted. "You've got to be kidding me. I know the basics."

"You know enough to not get yourself killed right away." He frowned as I jumped from side to side. "What are you doing?"

I stopped, shrugging. "I'm bored."

Aiden rolled his eyes. "Then let's get started. You won't be bored for very long."

"Yes, master."

He scowled. "Don't call me that. I'm not your master. Only the gods can be called our masters."

"Yes . . ." I paused as his eyes glinted and his jaw tightened, "*sir*."

Aiden stared at me a moment, and then nodded. "Okay. I want to see how you take a fall."

"I almost got one good hit on you in the factory." I felt the need to point that out.

Turning to me, he motioned toward one of the mats. "Almost doesn't count, Alex. It never counts."

I dragged myself over and stopped in front of him as he circled me. "Daimons not only use their strength when they attack, but also elemental magic."

"Yeah. Yeah."

Daimons could be ridiculously strong depending on how many pures or halfs they've drained. Being hit by one of them using the air element was tantamount to getting hit by a freight train. The only time daimons weren't dangerous was when they were draining aether.

"The key is to never let them get you on the ground, but it will happen, even to the best of us. When it does happen, you need to be able to get back up." His gray eyes focused on me.

This was boring. "Aiden, I do remember my training. I know how to take a fall."

"Do you?"

"Taking a fall is the easiest—"

My back slammed into the mat. Pain shot through me. I lay there stunned.

Aiden loomed over me. "That was just a love tap, and you didn't land correctly at all."

"Ow." I wasn't sure I could move.

"You should've landed on your upper back. It's less painful and easier to maneuver out of." He offered his hand. "I thought you knew how to take a fall?"

"Gods," I snapped. "You couldn't have told me first?" I ignored his hand and found I could move. I stood, glaring at him.

A lopsided smile formed on his lips. "Even without a warning, you have a second before you fall. You have more than enough time to position your body correctly."

"Roll the hips and keep your chin down." I scowled, rubbing my back. "Yeah, I remember."

"Then show me." He stopped, eyeing me like I was some kind of weird specimen. "Put your arms up—here. Like this." He positioned my arms so they blocked my chest. "Keep them strong. No spaghetti arms."

"Okay."

He grimaced at my spindly arms. "Well, keep them as strong as you can."

"Hardy har har."

He grinned again. "All right."

Then he hit my arms with the broad side of his. In truth, he didn't hit me hard, but I still fell. And it was the wrong way. I rolled over, wincing.

"Alex, you know what to do."

I rolled over and groaned. "Well . . . apparently it's something I've forgotten."

"Get up." He offered his hand, but I still didn't take it. I stood. "Put your arms up."

I did and braced myself for the inevitable smack. Down I went, over and over again. I spent the next couple of hours on my back, and not in the good way. It got to the point Aiden went through the mechanics of landing as if I were ten.

But finally, out of the useless crap floating around my brain, I pulled out the technique I'd been taught ages ago and I nailed it.

"About time," Aiden muttered.

We broke for lunch, which consisted of me eating alone while Aiden went off to do whatever. About fifteen minutes in, a pure-blood in a white lab coat appeared in front of me. I swallowed the mouthful of food. "Hi?"

"Please follow me," she said.

I glanced down at my half-eaten sub and sighed. I dumped my plate and followed the pure to the med building behind the training facilities. "Am I getting a physical or something?"

She didn't answer.

Any attempt of conversation was ignored and I gave up by the time I hopped up on the table. I watched her go to the cabinet and root around for a few seconds. She turned around, flicking the end of the syringe.

My eyes widened. "Uh ... what is that?"

"Please lift up the sleeve of your shirt."

Wary, I did as instructed. "But what are you giving me— *dammit*!" My skin burned from where she'd jabbed me in the upper arm. "That hurt like hell."

Her lips curved in a faint smile, but her words dripped disgust. "You will be reminded in six months to receive another dose. For the next forty-eight hours, please try to refrain from unprotected sexual activities."

Try to refrain? As if I had uncontrollable animalistic urges and jumped every half in sight? "I'm not a sex-crazed skank, lady."

The pure turned her back, clearly dismissing me. I jumped off the table, tugging my sleeve down. I couldn't believe I'd forgotten about the Covenant's mandatory birth control for female half-bloods. After all, the offspring of two halfs were like mortals and useless to the pures. That had never really bothered me since I doubted I'd ever develop a parental urge. But the pure could have at least given me heads up before she'd stuck me.

When I returned to the training room, Aiden eyed me rubbing my arm, but I didn't explain. From there, he moved on to another favorite of mine: getting knocked down and jumping to my feet.

I sucked at that, too.

By the end of practice, every muscle in my back ached and my thighs felt like someone had sucker-punched them. I was a little slow in rolling the mats. So much so that Aiden eventually took over.

"It'll get easier." He looked up as I limped over to where he was piling the mats. "Your body will get used to it again."

"I hope so."

"You should hold off on the gym for a few days."

I could've hugged him.

"But you should definitely do the warm-up stretches at night. It will help loosen up your muscles. You won't be so sore then."

I followed him to the door. It sounded like good advice. Outside the training room, I waited while Aiden shut the double doors.

"Tomorrow we'll work on the jump some more. Then we'll move on to blocking techniques."

I started to point out I'd learned several blocking techniques, but I remembered how quickly the daimon had tagged me in Georgia. My hand went to my shoulder and over the slightly irregular scar.

"You okay?"

Dropping my hand, I nodded. "Yeah."

As if he could somehow read minds, he stepped forward and brushed my thick ponytail back over my shoulder. The slight touch elicited a shiver. "It's not bad. It'll be gone soon enough."

"It's going to scar—it has already scarred."

"Some would say such scars are badges of honor."

"Really?"

Aiden shook his head. "Yes. It shows how strong and how brave you were. It's nothing to be ashamed of."

"Sure." I forced a quick, bright smile.

I could tell by the look on his face he didn't believe me, but he didn't push it. I limped off, heading back to my room. Caleb waited outside my door with a handful of shopping bags and a nervous look on his face.

"Caleb, you didn't have to do all that. And you're going to get busted over here."

"Then let me in your room before I get caught. And don't worry about the shopping. I got some hot chicks to try clothes on for me. Trust me, mutually beneficial day for me."

I snorted as I limped over to the couch and eased myself down. "Thanks. I owe you."

Caleb launched into all the things I'd missed during my *absence*—that was how I was referring to it now—while I pulled out various jeans, dresses, and shorts I doubted met the Covenant dress code. I shook my head. Where in the hell I was supposed to wear some of this stuff? On a street corner?

Apparently not much had changed. Everyone still snuck off and hooked up with everyone. Lea had successfully pitted two or three boys against one another in hopes of getting between her legs. Jackson looked like the winner if yesterday had been any indication. Two halfs a year older than us, Rosalie and Nathaniel, had graduated and were now Sentinels, and I was beside myself with envy. After today's practice, I doubted Aiden still thought I had any raw potential.

Luke, a half I used to hang out with, had come out of the closet last year—not that being gay or bisexual was even remotely a big deal around here. Being the children of a bunch of horny gods who sure didn't discriminate when choosing their sexual partners left little to be shocked about when it came to sex-related activities.

It appeared I was the only virgin around here. I sighed.

"Was your training that bad?"

"I think I broke my back today," I deadpanned.

He looked like he wanted to laugh. "You didn't break your back. You're just . . . out of practice. In a couple of days, you'll be kicking Aiden's butt."

"Doubtful."

"So what did he want yesterday? Man, I'll be honest. I'm waiting for him to pop in here and beat the crap out of me for being in your room."

"Then you shouldn't be in here if you're scared."

Caleb ignored that. "What did Aiden want yesterday?"

"I think Lea ratted my ass out. Aiden knew about the thing in the rec room. He really didn't bitch me out, but I could've done without the lecture."

"Damn, she is such a bitch sometimes." He sat back in the chair, running a hand through his hair. "Maybe we could burn off her eyebrows or something. I'm sure Zarak would be down with that."

I laughed. "I'm sure that won't help my cause."

"You know, I hooked up—"

"What?" I shrieked, nearly coming off the couch. Wrong move. It hurt. "Please tell me you didn't hook up with Lea?"

He shrugged. "I was bored. She was available. Not bad at all—"

Disgusted, I tossed a pillow at his head and cut him off. "I don't want to know the details. I'm just going to pretend you never admitted to that."

A grin appeared on his lips. "Well, it seems like Lea's determined to get you in trouble if she ratted you out."

I lay back down, thinking about the others in the room. "I don't know. What about the pure who was in the room?"

"Who? Thea?" He shook his head. "There's no way she would've told anyone."

"What's Thea doing here, anyways?"

It was odd to see any pure at the Covenant during the summer. They stayed during the school year, but when summer came, they went off with their parents—probably traveling the world and doing other ridiculously expensive things. Fun, totally cool things. Of course, they had Guards who accompanied them on their adventures, just in case a daimon got any ideas.

"Her parents are on the Council and they don't have any time for her. She's really nice, but super-quiet. I think she's got the hots for Deacon."

"Deacon, as in Aiden's brother?"

"Yup."

I could tell there was something behind the fact Thea liked him. "What's the big deal? They're both pures."

Caleb arched a brow at me, but then seemed to remember I hadn't been here for three years. "Deacon has a reputation."

"Okay." I tried to work out a sudden kink in my back.

"So does Thea. And let's just say Thea wins the purity award."

Good to know I wasn't the only virgin. "And?"

"Deacon's reputation is . . . more of the—hmm, how do I say this nicely?" He paused, looking thoughtful. "Deacon takes after Zeus—that kind of reputation."

"Well . . . opposites attract, I guess."

"Not *that* opposite."

I shrugged, and then winced.

"I almost forgot. You won't believe what I heard today in town. One of the shop owners was busy running her mouth while I was checking out, totally uncaring about who could hear her, but—oh yeah, by the way, that shop owner probably thinks I'm a cross-dresser now."

I giggled.

His eyes narrowed at my apathy. "Anyways, do you remember Kelia Lothos?"

My lips pursed. Kelia Lothos—the name did sound familiar. "Wasn't she a Guard here?"

"Yeah, she's about ten years older than us. She got herself a boyfriend."

"Good for her."

"Wait for it, Alex. You must wait for it. His name is Hector—not sure what his last name is. Anyways, he's a pure from one of the other communities." He stopped for dramatic effect.

I ran a hand over my ponytail, not sure where he was going with any of this.

"He's a freaking pure-blood." He raised his hands. "Remember? Not allowed."

My eyes popped wide. "Oh no, not good."

He shook his head and strands of blond hair fell over his eyes. "I can't believe they were stupid enough to even consider something like that."

The fact that we weren't allowed to have any type of romantic relationship with a pure was a rule ingrained in us since birth. Most half-bloods didn't even question it, but then again, most halfs didn't question much. We were trained into obedience from the get-go.

I tried to find a comfortable position. "What do you think will happen to Kelia?"

Caleb snorted. "She'll probably be stripped of her Guard duties and sent to work in one of the houses."

That filled me with annoyance and resentment. "And Hector will get a smack on the hand. How fair is that?"

He looked at me strangely. "It's not, but that's what happens."

"It's stupid." I felt something tighten in my jaw. "Who cares if a half and a pure get together? Is it really a big enough deal that Kelia has to lose everything?"

Caleb eyes widened. "It's the way it is, Alex. You know that."

I folded my arms, wondering why I felt so strongly about it myself. It was the way things had been for eons, but it seemed so unfair. "It's wrong, Caleb. Kelia's basically going to end up a slave all because she hooked up with a pure."

He was quiet for a moment and then his eyes zeroed in on me. "Does your reaction have anything to do with the fact your new personal trainer happens to be the pure all the chicks drool over?"

I made a face. "Absolutely not—are you insane? He's going to end up killing me." I paused, sinking down in the cushion. "I think he plans on it."

"Whatever."

Stretching out my legs, I pinned him with a glare. "You forget I spent three years out there in the normal world—a world where pures and halfs don't even exist. No one checks someone's godly pedigree before going out with them."

He stared off in the distance a few moments. "What was it like?"

"What was what like?"

Caleb fidgeted on the edge of the chair. "Being out there, away from all of . . . this?"

"Oh." I propped myself onto my elbow. Most halfs had no idea what it was like. Sure, they mingled in the outside world—mingled being the key word—but they were never a part of it, not for any amount of time. Neither were the pures. To our kind, the mortal life seemed like a violent one, where daimons weren't the only evil things people had to worry about.

Yeah, we had our crazies, too. The guys who didn't have the word "no" in their vocabulary, the back-stabbing girls, and people who'd do *anything* to get what they wanted. But it was nothing like the mortal world, and I wasn't sure if that was a good or bad thing.

"Well, it's different. There are so many people who are different. I kinda blended in to a point."

Caleb listened with far too much excitement for his own good as I tried explaining what it was like out there. Whenever we moved around, Mom had used compulsions to get me into the local school system without transcripts. Caleb showed way too much interest in the mortal school system, but it was different than the Covenant. Here, we spent most of our days fighting in class. Out in the mortal world, I'd spent most of my classes staring at the chalkboard.

Being curious about the outside world wasn't necessarily a good thing. It usually led someone to make a run for it. Mom and I had been more successful than most of those who'd ventured out. The Covenant always found the people who tried to live in the outside world.

They'd just found us a little too late.

Caleb tilted his head sideways as he studied me. "How you doing being back here?"

I lay back down, staring up at the ceiling. "Good."

"Seriously?" He stood up. "Because you've been through a lot."

"Yeah, I'm okay."

Caleb made his way over and sat down, practically shoving me on my side.

"Ouch."

"Alex, the crap that's happened has to have, you know, bothered you. It would've messed with me."

I closed my eyes. "Caleb, I appreciate your concern, but you're practically sitting on me."

He shifted, but remained beside me. "Are you gonna talk to me about it?"

"Look. I'm doing okay. It's not like it hasn't bothered me." I pried my eyes open and found him watching me expectedly. "Okay. It's messed with me. Happy?"

"Of course I'm not happy."

One thing I wasn't good at was talking about how I felt. Hell, I wasn't even good at *thinking* about how I felt. But it didn't look like Caleb was moving any time soon. "I . . . try not to think about it. It's better that way."

He frowned. "Really? Do I need to use basic psychology on you and go with, 'it's probably not a good thing you don't think about it?'"

I groaned. "I hate psychobabble, so please don't start."

"Alex?"

I sat up, ignoring the way my back screamed, and pushed him off the couch. He caught himself easily. "What do you want me to say? That I miss my mom? Yes. I miss her. That it totally sucked seeing her get drained by a daimon? Yes, it sucked. Fighting daimons and thinking I was going to die was fun? No. It wasn't fun. That *also* sucked ass."

He nodded, accepting my little rant. "Did you get to have a funeral for her or anything?"

"That's a stupid question, Caleb." I pushed back the hair that had escaped my ponytail. "I didn't get to have a funeral. After I killed the daimon, there was another one. I ran."

His face paled. "Did anyone go back for her body?"

I cringed. "I don't know. I haven't asked."

He seemed to mull it over. "Maybe if you had a ceremony for her, it would help. You know, a little gathering just to remember her."

I leveled a hard look at him. "We're not having a funeral. I mean it. If you even think about something like that, I will risk getting expelled just to kick your ass." Having a funeral meant facing that my mother was dead. The wall—the toughness I'd built around me—would break and I . . . I couldn't deal with that.

"Okay. Okay." He held up his hands. "I just thought it would bring you some closure."

"I have closure. Remember? I saw her die."

This time he was the one to cringe. "Alex . . . I'm so sorry. Gods, I don't even know how you must've felt. I cannot even imagine it."

He then took a step forward, as if he intended to hug me, but I waved him off. Caleb seemed to get I didn't want to talk about it anymore and he switched back to safer topics—more gossip, more tales of Covenant shenanigans.

I remained on the couch after he'd snuck back out of the dorm. I should've been hungry or ready to go socialize, but I wasn't. Our conversation—the part about my mom—lingered like a festering wound. I tried focusing on the gossip I'd learned. I even tried thinking about how nice Jackson looked now—even Caleb, because he'd really filled out in the last three years—but their images were quickly replaced by Aiden and his arms.

And that was *so* wrong.

I shifted back down and went back to staring at the ceiling. I was okay. I was great, actually. Being back at the Covenant was far better than being out there in the normal world or cleaning toilets in some pure's house. I rubbed under my eyes, frowning. I was okay.

I had to be okay.

6

I wanted to curl up in a hole and die.

"There you go." Aiden nodded as I deflected one of his blows. "Use your forearm. Move with purpose."

Move with purpose? How about moving to a spot where I could lie down? That was a purpose I could get behind. Aiden launched himself at me and I blocked his jab. Hell yeah, I was good at that. Next, he swung around, and for someone so freaking tall, he sure could move that body like a ninja.

The heel of his foot slipped past my arms and slammed into my side. The impact barely registered on my pain scale. By now, I'd gotten used to the sharp spike of pain and the throbbing that followed. I inhaled slowly and tried to breathe through the agony. Half-bloods don't show pain in the face of the enemy. At least I remembered that.

Aiden straightened, concern flickering over his face. "You okay?"

I clenched my teeth. "Yes."

He approached me, looking doubtful. "That was a pretty hard hit, Alex. It's okay if it hurts. We'll take a few minutes."

"No." I walked it off while he watched. "I'm fine. Let's try this again."

And we did. Missing a few jabs and kicks was far better than having to run laps like yesterday or spend the entire afternoon in the gym.

That's what'd happened when I'd whined about my back and sides hurting last time. Aiden went through several more blocking techniques a ten-year-old could master while I obsessively watched his movements. Over the past couple of days, I'd realized how far behind I really was, and even I was amazed by the fact I'd managed to kill two daimons.

I couldn't even block most of Aiden's kicks.

"Watch me." He circled me, his body taut. "There is always something that'll give away my next move. It could be a fine tremor of the muscle or a brief glance, but there is always something. When a daimon attacks, it's no different."

I nodded and we squared off again. Aiden moved in with one swipe of the hand. I knocked his arm away, and then the other. It wasn't his jabs or punches I had a problem with. It was his kicks—he spun around so fast. But this time, I saw his eyes drop to my waist.

Twisting into the kick, I brought my arm down in a clean sweeping motion a second too late. His foot connected with my bruised back. I doubled over immediately, grasping my knees as I slowly breathed in and out.

Right away, Aiden was at my side. "Alex?"

"That . . . stung a bit."

"If it makes you feel better, you almost had it this time."

I looked up and gave a short laugh at the sight of his lopsided grin. "Good to hear."

He started to say something, but his grin faded as his voice gave a low warning. "Alex. Stand up."

My back protested such a sudden move, but the moment I saw Marcus at the door, I understood why. I didn't need to look like I'd just gotten the crap knocked out of me in front of him.

Marcus leaned against the door, arms folded. "I wondered how training was going. I see it's moving along expectedly."

Ouch. I took a deep breath. "Would you like to give it a try?"

Marcus's brows rose and he smiled, but Aiden placed a warning hand on my arm. "Don't."

I shook his hand off. I was pretty sure I could take my uncle.

With his perfectly groomed hair and pressed khakis, he looked like a poster child for yacht-club-of-the-month.

"I'm game if you are," I offered again with a bright smile.

"Alex, I'm telling you not to do this. He used to be—"

Marcus pushed away from the wall. "It's all right, Aiden. I wouldn't accept such a ridiculous offer normally, but I find myself feeling charitable."

I snickered. "Charitable?"

"Marcus, this isn't necessary." Aiden moved in front of me. "She's only beginning to learn blocks correctly."

I scowled at Aiden. *Jeez. Way to have my back there, buddy.* My ego roared back to life and I pushed around Aiden. "I think I got him."

Marcus tipped his head back and laughed, but Aiden looked less than amused by the whole situation. "Alex, I'm telling you *not* to do this. Be quiet and listen to me."

I looked at Aiden innocently. "Do what?"

"No. *She has this*, Aiden. Let's see what she's learned. Since she is challenging me, I assume she is ready."

I planted my hands on my hips. "I don't know. I'd feel bad for beating up an old guy."

Marcus's bright emerald gaze settled on me. "Attack me."

"What?"

He looked perplexed, but then he snapped his fingers. "That's right! You haven't learned any real attack moves. Then I shall attack you. You do know defensive blocking techniques?"

Marcus knew about defensive blocking techniques? I shifted my weight and glanced at Aiden. He did not look pleased by any of this. "Yeah."

"Then you should be adeptly trained to defend yourself." Marcus paused and the smile slipped away. "Just picture me as the enemy, Alexandria."

"Oh, that won't be too hard, *Dean Andros*." I raised my hands and motioned him forward. I was a total badass.

Marcus gave no warning other than the fine tremor in his arm right before he moved. I raised my arm, just as Aiden instructed, and blocked the jab. I couldn't fight the wild grin as I deflected another bone-jarring punch. My gaze narrowed on my uncle as he straightened and prepared for another attack.

"Back off." Aiden's voice came from the sidelines, low and harsh. "You're too close."

I pushed forward, blocking another one of Marcus's hits. Cockiness took over. "You've got to be faster—"

Instead of Marcus following through on what I expected would be a pretty damn good roundhouse kick, he grabbed my arm and twisted. As he spun me around he brought his other arm around my neck, placing me in a brutal choke-hold.

My heart slammed against my ribs. Any movement I made only succeeded in twisting my arm to an even more unnatural angle. Within seconds, he'd rendered me helpless. In any other situation, like one where it wasn't *my uncle* holding *me* in a choke-hold, I would've given him props for such quick maneuvering.

He bent his head, speaking directly into my ear. "Now just imagine if I was a daimon," said Marcus. "What do you think would happen next?"

I refused to answer, clenching my teeth.

"Alexandria, I asked you a question. What would happen if I was a daimon?" His grip tightened.

My gaze met Aiden's. He watched the whole thing with helpless anger etched into his face. I could tell there was a part of him that wanted to step in, but he knew he couldn't.

"Do we need to try this again?" asked Marcus.

"No! I'd . . . be dead."

"Yes. You'd be dead." Marcus let go and I stumbled forward. He brushed past me, addressing Aiden. "If you even hope to have her ready by fall, you may want to work on her attitude and make sure she actually takes your instructions next time. If she continues this way, she will fail."

Not taking his eyes off me for one second, he gave Marcus a curt nod.

I silently fumed until the moment Marcus disappeared. "What the hell did I ever do to him?" I rubbed my neck absently. "He could've broken my arm!"

"If he wanted to break your arm, he would have. I told you to be quiet, Alex. What did you expect from Marcus? Did you think he was just some lazy pure-blood who needed protection?" His voice dripped sarcasm.

"Well, he looks like one! How was I supposed to know he was secretly Rambo in Dockers?"

Aiden stalked up to me, reaching out and catching my chin. "You should have known, because I told you not to push him. Yet, you still did. You didn't listen to me. He used to be a Sentinel, Alex."

"What? Marcus was a Sentinel? I didn't know that!"

"I tried to tell you that." Aiden closed his eyes and let go of my chin. Turning away, he ran a hand through his hair. "Marcus is right. You won't be ready in the fall if you don't listen to me." He sighed. "This is why I could never be an Instructor or a Guide. I don't have the patience for this crap."

This was one of those times I knew I needed to shut up, but I couldn't. Angry as hell, I followed him across the mats. "I am listening to you!"

He whirled around. "What part did you listen to, Alex? I explicitly told you not to push him. If you can't listen to me, how can anyone—including Marcus—expect you to listen to your Instructors in the fall?"

He was right, but I was too embarrassed and angry to admit it. "He only did that because he doesn't like me."

He gave an exasperated sound. "It has nothing to do with whether or not he likes you, Alex. It has everything to do with the fact that you don't listen! You've spent too much time out there where you could easily defend yourself against mortals, but you're not in the mortal world anymore."

"I know that. I'm not stupid!"

"Really?" His eyes flashed furious silver. "You are behind every single person here. Even the pure-bloods who'll be attending school in the fall will have the basic knowledge of how to defend themselves. You still want to be a Sentinel? After what you've shown me today, I doubt that is the case. Do you know what makes a Sentinel? Obedience, Alex."

I felt my cheeks flush. The sudden rush of hot tears stung my eyes. I blinked and turned away from him.

Aiden cursed under his breath. "I'm . . . not trying to embarrass you, Alex. But these are the facts. We've only been training for a week and you have a long road ahead of you. You need to listen to me."

Once I was pretty sure I wouldn't start crying, I faced him. "Why did you even stick up for me? When Marcus wanted to hand me over to Lucian?"

Aiden glanced away, frowning. "Because you have potential, and we can't afford to have that potential wasted."

"If I . . . hadn't missed so much time, I know I'd be good."

He turned back to me, eyes shifting back to a softer gray. "I know, but you did miss a lot of time. Now we have to get you back to where you need to be. Battling your uncle is not going to help you."

My shoulders slumped and I looked away. "He hates me. He really does."

"Alex, he doesn't hate you."

"Oh no, I think he does. This was the first time I've seen him since the first morning here, and he was more than eager to prove that I'm a jackass. It's obvious he doesn't want me to be trained."

"That's not the case."

I looked at him. "Really? Then what *is* the case?"

Aiden opened his mouth but closed it.

"Yeah. Exactly."

He was quiet for a few moments. "Were you two ever close?"

I gave a short laugh. "Before? No. I only saw him when he visited Mom. He never paid any attention to me. I always figured he was one of the pures who weren't too fond of . . . my kind."

There were a lot of pures out there who looked down on halfs, seeing us more like second-class citizens than anything else. They knew they needed us, but it didn't change how they viewed us as something other than pure.

"Marcus has never felt that way about . . . halfs."

I shrugged, suddenly tired of talking. "I guess it's just me then." I glanced up and forced a weak smile. "So . . . will you show me what I did wrong?"

"Which part?" His mouth tightened.

"All of it?"

He finally smiled, but the usual banter we shot back and forth at each other during our training sessions disappeared. His direct and formal instructions made his disappointment in me clear. But what could I do? I hadn't known Marcus was Chuck Norris. I'd lost my temper. So what? So why did I feel icky?

After practice, I still couldn't shake the feeling of being an utter failure. Not even when Caleb showed up at my door hours later.

Frowning, I stepped aside and let him in. "You're really good at sneaking into this dorm, Caleb."

He smirked, but it faded as he took in my sweat-stained cloth- ing. "It's Zarak's party. Tonight. Remember?"

"Dammit. No." I kicked the door shut.

"Well, you'd better get ready. Like now. We're already late."

I debated telling him I wasn't feeling up to it, but the idea of sulking around my room didn't seem entertaining. I figured I deserved a night of fun after the day I'd had, and it wasn't like

Aiden or Marcus would know if I decided to go to Zarak's. "I need to take a quick shower first. Make yourself comfortable."

"Sure." He plopped down on the couch and picked up the remote control. "There's going to be a lot of the pures there. Ones who haven't seen you since you've come back. Of course, they know you're back. Everyone is talking about it."

Rolling my eyes, I pushed on the bathroom door and stripped off my clothes. I wasn't worried about Caleb popping in on me. It'd be like walking in on his sister naked; I doubted he wanted to see my goods. As I twisted in front of the mirror, I caught sight of a smorgasbord of bluish splotches covering my back and my sides. Yuck. I turned away.

Caleb continued from the living room. "Lea and Jackson got into a huge fight today, right on the beach for everyone to see. It was fun to watch."

I wasn't so sure about that. After a quick shower, I dried my hair so it fell in somewhat manageable waves. Now what to wear?

"Are you almost done in there? Gods, I'm bored."

"Almost." I pulled out a pair of jeans and a shirt even though I wanted to wear the slutty little black dress Caleb had picked out, but the low back would show all the bruises.

Caleb stood up as I walked into the living room. "You look hot."

I scrunched up my face. "You think this is hot?"

He laughed as he turned toward the door. "No."

By the time we met some other halfs at the edge of campus, Caleb's running monologue about who was going to be at the party had driven out the worst of my foul mood. Caleb kept sneaking looks at one of the girls who'd joined us as we trekked across the bridge to the main island. It was easy to forget about practice and all I'd missed in the last couple of years.

It wasn't hard for us to make it past the Guards. None of them recognized me, or if they did, they didn't care enough to send me back to my room. They were used to kids making their way back and forth between the two islands, especially during the summer.

"Wow." One of the girls let out a low exhale as we skirted along the sand dunes. "The party's definitely in high gear."

She was right. As soon as we rounded the bend, pures and halfs spilled out from the large beach house. It'd been ages since I'd been to Zarak's house. Like Thea, his parents held seats on the Council, had a lot of money, and had little time for their pure-blood offspring.

With its incredible views of the ocean, pale blue siding and whitewashed decks, Zarak's parents' beach house was identical to the house Mom had lived in. I assumed her house still stood on the opposite side of the island. A mixture of grief and happiness flowed through me. I saw myself as a little girl, playing on the porch, running through the sand dunes, laughing, and I saw Mom, smiling down at me. She always had been smiling.

"Hey." Caleb came up behind me. "You doing okay?"

"Yeah."

He slipped his arms around my shoulders and gave them a squeeze. "Come on, you're gonna be like some kind of rock star here. Everyone's going to be happy to see you."

Walking up to the beach house, I did kind of feel like a rock star. Everywhere I looked, someone called my name or rushed over to give me a hug and a warm, "Welcome back." For a while, I lost myself in the sea of familiar faces. Someone shoved a plastic cup in my hand; another topped it off from an open bottle, and before I knew it, I was buzzing happily among old friends.

I headed up the wide steps, hoping to find Zarak somewhere in the house. He was, after all, one of my favorite pure-bloods. Dodging around two halfs making out while still maintaining firm grips on their red plastic cups—*amazing* ability by the way—I slid into the less crowded kitchen. Finally, I spotted the recognizable head of blond curls. He appeared occupied with a pretty blonde.

I was pretty positive I'd be interrupting, but I didn't think Zarak would mind. He had to have missed me. I walked up and tapped my fingers along the curve of his shoulder. It took a moment for him to lift his head and turn around. A pair of startling gray eyes—clearly not Zarak's—met mine.

I took a step back. I'd never seen the boy before, but there was something oddly familiar about those eyes and the planes of his face.

"What do we have here?" He gave me a lazy smile. "A half eager to make my acquaintance?" He looked back at the other girl, then to me.

"Oh, well . . . I thought you were someone else. Sorry."

Amusement sparkled in his eyes. "I guess I was being presumptuous, wasn't I?"

I couldn't help but grin. "Yes, you were."

"But weren't you being presumptuous by assuming I was someone else? Does it matter?" I shook my head. "Well, I should introduce myself." He took a step forward and bowed—literally, bent at the waist and bowed. "I'm Deacon St. Delphi, and you are?"

My jaw almost hit the floor. Honestly, I should've known the minute I saw his eyes. They were nearly identical to Aiden's.

Deacon's lips turned into a smug grin. "I see you've heard of me."

"Yeah, I know your brother."

His brows rose. "My perfect brother knows a half-blood? Interesting. What's your name?"

Clearly annoyed with the lack of attention, the girl behind him huffed and slipped around us. My gaze followed her, but he didn't spare her a glance. "My name's Alexandria Andros, but—"

"But everyone calls you Alex." Deacon sighed. "Yes. I've heard of you, too."

I took a sip of my drink, eyeing him over the cup. "Well then. I'm afraid to ask."

He walked over to the counter and picked up a bottle, taking a healthy gulp. "You're the one my brother spent months chasing after and now is saddled with training."

My smile turned sour. "Saddled with?"

He chuckled, dangling the bottle of liquor from his fingers. "Not that I'd mind being saddled with you. But my brother . . . well, he tends to rarely enjoy what's in front of him. Take me, for example. He spends the bulk of his free time making sure I'm behaving like a good pure instead of enjoying myself. Now . . . he'll spend all his time making sure *you* behave."

That made little sense to me. "I don't think your brother is very fond of me at the moment."

"I doubt that." He offered me the bottle. I shook my head. Pouring himself a drink, he smiled widely. "I'm sure my brother is very fond of you."

"Why would you—"

Sitting the bottle aside, he picked up a glass and placed a finger to the rim. Flames shot around the glass. A second later, he blew the fire out and downed the glass. Another damn firestarter, which was another thing I should've known. Pure's affinities toward certain elements tended to run in families.

"Why would I think that?" Deacon leaned down as if he were about to share a major secret. "Because I know my brother, and I know he wouldn't have volunteered to get any old half-blood up to par. He's not the most patient of people."

I frowned. "He's pretty damn patient with me." Except maybe for today, but I wasn't sharing that.

Deacon gave me a knowing look. "Need I say more?"

"I guess not."

He seemed to find that equally amusing. Wrapping his free

arm around my shoulders, he steered me toward the porch and right into the path of Lea and Elena, the girl I'd met in the lounge my first day back. The only reason I remembered her name was because of her über-short haircut.

I sighed.

Deacon looked sideways at me. "Friends of yours?"

"Not really," I muttered.

"Hey redhead," he murmured. "Looking good."

I had to give it to said redhead. Lea looked exquisite in the slinky red dress that clung to every curve of her body. She was hotness—just too bad she was a complete and total bitch.

Her gaze drifted over me and then Deacon's arm, which still hung over my shoulder. "Oh gods, please tell me you've spilled a drink on your shirt and you're temporarily walking with her to hide the stain. Because Deacon, I'd rather floss my teeth with a daimon's back hair than parade a growth like that around."

Deacon raised his brows at me. "Guess you're right about the 'not really friends' thing."

I gave him a bland look.

He turned a megawatt smile on Lea. He even had dimples, ones I was sure Aiden would have if he ever really smiled. "You have such a pretty mouth for such ugly words."

Lea simpered. "You've never cared about how I've used my mouth before, Deacon."

I gaped at Deacon. "Oh . . . wow."

His lips curved into a half smile, but he didn't respond. I scooted away from him and tugged Caleb back to the sprawling porch. It wasn't too crowded now. Glancing over my shoulder, I noticed that Lea and Deacon had stepped further back into the room.

"Okay. Did I miss something while I was gone?" I asked.

Caleb's face scrunched up. "What are you talking about?"

"Are Lea and Deacon messing around?"

He busted out laughing. "No, but they like to talk a lot of smack."

I hit him on the arm. "Don't laugh at me. What if people thought they were? Lea could get in some major trouble."

"They're not messing around, Alex. Lea's stupid, but not that stupid. Even if they are trying to change the Breed Order laws, no half around here is willingly going to fool around with a pure."

"They're changing the Breed Order?"

"Trying is the key word. Succeeding is a totally different story."

Caleb's eyes shot wide at the unexpected voice. I spun around, nearly dropping my cup. Kain Poros sat on the edge of the railing, dressed in Covenant fatigues. "What are you doing here?"

"Babysitting," Kain grumbled, "and I don't care what you're drinking, so stop looking for a place to dump your cup."

Once I got over my shock at his blasé attitude toward underage drinking, I smiled brightly. "So they're trying to change the Breed Order?"

"Yep, but it's meeting a lot of resistance." He stopped, his gaze narrowing on a half who was getting too close to the bonfire someone had decided to start. "Hey! Yes! You! Get the hell back now."

Caleb reached around me, inconspicuously sitting his cup down. "I hate that they even call it the Breed Order. It sounds so ridiculous."

"I have to agree." Kain nodded. "But that's what they've always called it."

We'd gathered a little audience at this point. "Will someone please fill me in on what the hell they're trying to change?"

"It's a petition to remove the order against the two breeds mixing." A boy with brown hair cropped close to the head smirked.

"A petition to allow halfs and pures to mix?" My eyes went wide. "What brought this on?"

The pure boy snorted. "Don't look too hopeful there. It's not going to happen. Allowing halfs and pures to mix isn't the only thing they're aiming for. The Council isn't going to go against the gods and they sure as hell aren't going to allow halfs on the Council. It's nothing to get excited about."

The strong inclination to launch my cup at his face was hard to ignore, but I doubted Kain would stand for that. "Who are you?"

His eyes sharpened on me, obviously not liking my tone. "Shouldn't I be asking that question, half-blood?"

Caleb cut in before I could respond. "His name is Cody Hale."

I ignored Caleb and scowled at the pure. "Should I know who you are?"

"Knock it off, Alex." Kain climbed off the railing, effectively reminding me of my place in the scheme of things. If Cody said jump, I'd have to say how high. Mouthing off at him wasn't how a half treated a pure—ever. "Anyway, I overheard Council members talking about it. The halfs from the Tennessee Covenant have a strong following. They're petitioning to be on the Council."

"I doubt they'll get anywhere there," Caleb said.

"We don't know," Kain responded. "There's a good chance the Council will hear them in November, and maybe even agree."

My brows rose. "When did this all come about?"

"About a year ago." Kain shrugged. "It's picked up a lot of movement. The South Dakota Covenant is also getting involved. It's about time, too."

"What about here and New York?" I asked.

Caleb snorted. "Alex, the North Carolina branch still exists in the Greek times and with the main Council being located in New York, they're going to hold onto all the old rules and rites. Upstate is a totally different world. It's brutal there."

"If there's such a huge movement then why are Hector and Kelia in so much trouble?" I frowned, remembering Caleb telling me their story.

"Because nothing has passed, and I think our Ministers are looking to make an example out of them." Kain's mouth tightened.

"Yeah, a way of reminding us of where we belong and what happens when we don't follow the rules." Jackson pushed through the little group, smiling in spite of how depressing his words were.

"Oh, for the love of the gods," Kain snapped. Twisting around, he loped off the porch. Two halfs were trying to get a dune buggy started. "You two better not even be within a mile of that thing by the time I get over there. Yes! You two!"

Talk about the petition dwindled off as more plastic cups were passed around. Apparently, political discussion was only socially acceptable before the third cup. I was still mulling over the Breed Order and what it could mean when Jackson sat down on the swing next to me.

I glanced up, smiling. "Hey."

He flashed a charming smile. "Have you seen Lea?"

"Who hasn't?" I giggled.

He didn't find that nearly as funny as I did, but my catty remark served two purposes. Jackson glued himself to my hip the rest of the evening, and when Lea reappeared, her face turned a mottled shade of red when she saw how close Jackson and I were. And we were really super-close on the porch swing. I was practically in his lap.

I tipped my cup at her.

The narrow-eyed look she sent my way said it all. Pleased with myself, I turned back to Jackson with a smug smile. "Your girlfriend doesn't look too happy."

"She hasn't been since you got back." He ran a finger down my arm. "What's going on between you two, anyways?"

Lea and I had always been like this. I imagined it had a lot to do with the fact both of us were aggressive, confrontational, and pretty damn awesome. But there was more; I just couldn't remember it. I shrugged. "Who knows?"

Zarak finally appeared and was most happy to see me. Thanks to him and Cody, everyone was keen on the idea of moving the party elsewhere by taking mommy and daddy's Porsches down to Myrtle.

Since I had my hands full with Jackson, I'd lost track of Caleb at some point, and I hid my half full plastic cup behind the swing. I was okay with the happy buzz, but I was only a few sips away from a dizzy, fall-on-my-face buzz.

"You going with them?"

Frowning, I glanced over at Jackson. "Huh?"

He grinned, leaning in so that his lips almost brushed my ear when he spoke. "Going to Myrtle?"

"Oh," I swung my feet back and forth. "I don't know, but it sounds like fun."

Jackson grabbed my hands, hauling me to my feet. "Zarak's leaving. We can catch a ride with him."

I must've missed the part when he and I had turned into "we," but I didn't protest when he led me down the steps and across the beach. Several of the kids had left already, and I caught a quick glimpse of Lea sliding into the back seat with Deacon. I had no idea where Kain was; I hadn't seen him since the dune buggy incident.

Zarak slid into the driver's seat of the only other car left—at least he seemed okay enough to be behind a wheel. The girl I'd seen earlier with Deacon was taking her sweet time deciding which car was the cooler one.

Growing bored, I leaned against the side of the house while the girl chatted with Lea. Jackson propped himself beside me.

I tipped my head back, loving the way the warm breeze caressed my cheeks. "Shouldn't you be going with her?"

He paused, looking over his shoulder. "She obviously has other plans."

"But she's staring at you," I pointed out. She had her face planted against the window.

"Let her look." He shifted closer, flashing a wicked grin. "She's made her call, hasn't she?"

"Guess so."

"I've made mine." Jackson leaned in to kiss me.

Even though I would've loved to see Lea's face in the aftermath of kissing Jackson, I darted to the side. Jackson was an equal opportunity player and that kind of game I didn't really feel like joining.

He chuckled and made a playful grab for me. He got a good hold on my arm and pulled me back. "You gonna make me chase you?"

My happy buzz had the potential of becoming a very bad one if I kept this crap up. Pulling my arm free, I forced a smile. "You'd better get going. Zarak's going to leave you."

He reached for me again, but I dodged those too-friendly hands. "Aren't you going?"

I shook my head. "Nah. I think I'm going to call it a night."

"I can keep you company if that's what you want. We can take the party back to my dorm or Zarak's room." He started walking backward, toward the car. "I don't think he'd mind. Last chance, Alex."

It took every ounce of my self-control not to laugh. I shook my head and backed off, knowing I looked like a total tease. "Maybe next time." Then I turned around, not giving Jackson another moment to sway me into that car.

Wondering if Caleb had gone to Myrtle, I made my way back across the beach and toward the bridge, passing several silent beach homes. The air around me smelled of sea salt. I loved that smell. It reminded me of Mom and the days we used to spend hanging out on the sand. So caught up in the memories, I only snapped back to reality when a fine shiver coursed down my spine as I neared the bridge.

The scraggly bushes and tall weeds swayed in the cool breeze. Odd since the breeze had been pleasant only minutes before. I took a step forward, scanning the marsh. Gloom covered the bog, but a thicker shadow pulled away from the rest, becoming more solid as the seconds passed.

The wind carried a whisper. *"Lexie . . ."*

I had to be hearing things. Only Mom had called me Lexie, nothing could be out there, but fear still coiled like tight springs in my stomach.

Without warning, strong hands gripped my shoulders and pulled me back. My heart stopped, and for a moment, I didn't know who'd grabbed me from behind. Instinct to lash out kicked into gear, but then I caught the familiar scent of soap and ocean.

Aiden.

"What are you doing?" His voice held a demanding edge.

I twisted around and stared up at him. His eyes were thin slits. Seeing him rendered me speechless for a second. "I . . . there's something out there."

Aiden's hands slipped from my shoulders as he turned to where I pointed. Naturally, there was nothing there but the normal shadows the moon cast across the marshland. He faced me. "There's nothing there. What are you doing out here by yourself? You aren't allowed off the island without supervision, Alex. Never."

Yikes. I took a step back, unsure how to respond.

Then he leaned over, sniffing the air. "You've been drinking."

"Have not."

His brows rose, lips pursed. "What are you doing outside the Covenant?"

I fidgeted with the edge of my shirt. "I was . . . visiting friends, and as I recall, I was told I couldn't leave the island. Technically, I'm still on Deity Island."

He tipped his head to the side, folding his arms. "I'm pretty certain that remaining on the Covenant-controlled island was assumed."

"Well, you know what they say about assuming things."

"Alex." His voice lowered in warning.

"What are you doing out here, creeping around in the dark like some kind of . . . creeper?" Once that last little bit left my mouth, I kind of wanted to slap myself.

Aiden laughed in disbelief. "Not that you need to know, but I was in the process of following a group of idiots to Myrtle Beach."

My jaw dropped. "You were following them?"

"Yes, a handful of us Sentinels were." Aiden's lips curved in an uneven grin. "What? You look surprised. Do you really think we'd let a bunch of teenagers off this island without protection? They may not realize we're always trailing them, but no one gets out of here without us knowing."

"Well . . . that's just fantastic." I stored that little piece of knowledge away. "Why are you still here then?"

He didn't immediately answer the question, since he was busy shuffling me back toward the bridge. "I saw you didn't go with them."

I stumbled. "What . . . exactly did you see?"

He glanced down at me, quirking an eyebrow. "Enough."

Flushing to the roots of my hair, I groaned.

Aiden chuckled low and under his breath, but I heard him. "Why didn't you go with them?"

I debated on pointing out he already knew why, but decided I was already in enough trouble. "I . . . figured I'd engaged in enough stupidity for the evening."

He actually laughed louder then. It was deep and rich. Nice. I glanced up quickly, hoping to see *his* dimples. No such luck. "It's good to hear you say that."

My shoulders slumped. "So how much trouble am I in?"

Aiden seemed to consider that for a few moments. "I'm not going to tell Marcus, if that's what you're hinting at."

Surprised, I grinned up at him. "Thanks."

He looked away, shaking his head. "Don't thank me yet."

I remembered the first time he'd said that to me. I wondered when I was supposed to thank him.

"But I don't want to catch you with a drink in your hand again."

I rolled my eyes. "Jeez, there you go, sounding like a dad again. You need to start sounding like you're twenty."

He ignored that, nodding at the Guards we passed on the opposite end of the bridge. "It's bad enough I have to chase down my brother. Please don't add to my troubles."

I dared a peek at him. He stared straight ahead, a muscle feathering along his jaw. "Yeah . . . he seems like a handful."

"And then some."

I remembered what Deacon said about Aiden making sure I behaved now. "I'm . . . sorry. I don't want you to feel like . . . you have to babysit me."

Aiden gave me a sharp look. "Well . . . thank you."

I twisted my fingers together, feeling tongue-tied for some reason. "It must've been hard having to raise him, practically alone."

He snorted. "You have no idea."

I really didn't. Aiden had been just a kid himself when their parents had been killed. What if I'd had a little brother or sister and I were responsible for them? There was no way. I couldn't even put myself in that situation.

A few moments passed before I asked, "How . . . did you do it?"

"Do what, Alex?"

We passed the bridge and the Covenant loomed ahead of us. I slowed my steps. "How did you take care of Deacon after . . . something so terrible happening?"

A stiff smile formed on his lips. "I had no other choice. I refused to allow Deacon to be handed over to another family. I think . . . my parents would've wanted me to be the one to raise him."

"But that's a lot of responsibility. How did you do it while going to school? Hell, while training?"

Graduating the Covenant didn't mean training ended for a Sentinel. The first year on the job was notoriously fierce. Time was split between shadowing trained Sentinels called Guides and still training in high impact martial art classes and stress tests.

He shoved his hands into the deep pockets of his black, Covenant-issued uniform. "There were times when I considered doing what my family would've wanted for me. Going to college and coming back, engaging in the politics of our world. I know my parents would've wanted me to take care of Deacon, but the last thing they would've ever chosen was for me to become a Sentinel. They never understood . . . this kind of life."

Most pures didn't, and I didn't fully understand it until I'd seen my mother attacked. Not until then did I fully grasp the need for Sentinels. Pushing the troubling thought away, I tried to think of what I remembered about his parents.

They'd been young-looking, like most pures were, and from what I knew, they'd been powerful. "They were on the Council, right?"

He nodded. "But after their death, being a Sentinel was what I wanted."

"Something you *needed*," I corrected softly.

His step slowed and he looked surprised. "You're right. Becoming a Sentinel was something I needed—I still do." He paused, looking away. "You would know. It's what you need."

"Yeah."

"How did you survive?" He turned the question on me.

Growing uncomfortable, I focused on the still water of the

ocean. At night, under the light of the moon, it looked as dark and thick as oil. "I don't know."

"You had no other choice, Alex."

I shrugged. "I guess so."

"You don't like talking about it, do you?"

"Is it obvious?"

We stopped where the pathway split between the dorms. "You don't think it's a good idea for you to talk about it?" His voice held a serious tone that made him sound much older. "You've barely had any time to deal with what happened to your mother . . . what you witnessed and had to do."

I felt something tighten in my jaw. "What I had to do is what all Sentinels have to do. I'm training to kill daimons. And I can't talk to anyone. If Marcus even suspected I had problems dealing with it, he'd hand-deliver me to Lucian."

Aiden stopped and when he looked at me, there was an infinite amount of patience on his face. Once again, I was struck by what Deacon had said. "You're only seventeen. Most Sentinels don't make their first kill until a year or so after graduation."

I sighed; now was a good time to change the subject. "You know what you said about your parents not wanting you to have this kind of life?"

Aiden nodded, a curious look on his face. He probably wondered where the hell I was going with this.

"I think—no, I *know* they would be proud of you, anyways."

He raised one eyebrow. "Do you think that because I offered to train you?"

"No. I think that because I remember you."

My words seemed to catch him off guard. "How? We didn't share any classes or schedules."

"I saw you around a few times. I always knew when you were around," I blurted out.

Aiden's lips tipped at the corners as he stared down at me. "What?"

I took a step back, flushing. "I mean, you had this reputation for being so kickass. Even though you were still in school, everyone knew you were going to be an awesome Sentinel."

"Oh." He laughed again, relaxing a little bit. "I suppose I should be flattered."

I nodded vigorously. "You should be. The halfs look up to you. Well, the ones who want to be Sentinels. Just the other day, they were telling me about how many kills you've made. It's legendary. Especially for a pure—I'm sorry. I don't mean killing a lot of daimons is necessarily a good thing or something to be proud of, but . . . I need to shut up now."

"No. I understand what you're saying. Killing is a necessity of our world. Each one takes its toll, because the daimon used to be a good person. Someone you may have known. It's never easy to take someone's life, but to stare down at someone you once considered a friend is . . . much harder."

I made a face. "I don't know if I could do it . . ." I saw the amusement fade from his face. That must not have been the right response. "I mean, when we see the daimon, we halfs see them for what they truly look like. At least, at first and then we see them for who they used to be. The elemental magic changes them back so they look like they used to. You already know that, of course, even if you don't see through the dark magic like we do. I could do it. I'm sure I could kill someone I once knew."

Aiden's lips pursed and he looked away. "It's hard when it's someone you knew."

"Have you ever fought one you knew before they went all dark side?"

"Yes."

I swallowed. "Did you . . . ?"

"Yes. It wasn't easy." He faced me. "It's getting late, well past your curfew, and you aren't getting off easy for tonight. I expect to see you in the gym tomorrow by eight."

"What?" I'd assumed I had the weekend to myself.

He simply raised his brows. "Do I need to list the rules you've broken?"

I wanted to point out I wasn't the only one who'd broken rules tonight—and that some people who weren't me were still currently breaking rules—but I managed to keep my mouth shut. Even I could acknowledge my punishment could be far worse. Nodding, I started to walk up to my dorm.

"Alex?"

I turned around, figuring he'd changed his mind and was going to order me to see Marcus in the morning and fess up to my bad behavior. "Yeah?"

He brushed a lock of dark hair off his forehead and flashed that lopsided smile. "I remember you."

I scrunched up my face. "What?"

The grin increased to a full smile. And . . . oh, man. He had dimples. The air in my lungs died. "I remember you, too."

8

I was being punished.

It seemed that the part from last night's conversation about not being allowed off the Covenant-controlled island wasn't an assumption. Okay. I totally knew that, but honestly, was it really that big of a deal?

It was a big deal to Aiden.

He carted my butt to the gym first thing in the morning and we spent the better part of the day there. He showed me a few exercises he wanted me to do, a couple of weight reps, and then a whole slew of cardio.

I hated cardio.

While I ran around from one exercise machine to the next, Aiden sat down, stretched out those long legs of his, and cracked open a book that probably weighed as much as I did.

I stared at the leg press machine. "What are you reading?"

He didn't look up. "If you're able to talk while working out then you aren't working out hard enough."

I made a face at his bent head and climbed into the machine. After doing my reps, I realized there was no graceful way of getting out of the thing. Concerned I'd look like an idiot, I stole a quick glance at him before rolling out of the machine.

There were a few more machines he wanted me to work with and I was quiet for the next five minutes or so. "Who reads books that big for fun?"

Aiden lifted his head, pinning me with a bored look. "Who talks to hear themselves speak?"

My eyes widened. "You're in a lovely mood today."

With the obscenely large book balanced on one knee, he turned a page. "You need to work on your upper body strength, Alex. Not your motor speech skills."

I glanced down at the dumbbell and pictured it flying across the room—at his face. But it was such a nice face, and I'd hate to ruin it. Hours went by like this. He'd read his book; I'd annoy him; he'd yell at me, and then I would hop on another machine.

Sad as it was, I was kind of having fun messing with him and I think he was, too. Every so often, a small—and I mean *really* small—smile would grace his lips whenever I'd ask him an irritating question. I wasn't even sure he was paying attention to the book of—

"Alex, stop staring at me and do some cardio." He flipped another page.

I blinked. "I hope that book of yours is on charm and personality skills."

Aha! There was that ghost of a smile. "Cardio—do cardio. You're fast, Alex. Daimons are fast, too, and hungry daimons will be even faster."

My head fell back and I groaned as I dragged myself over to the treadmill he'd pointed to earlier. "How long?"

"Sixty minutes."

Sweet baby in Hades! Was he insane? When I asked that, he didn't find it funny. It took me several tries to get the treadmill working at a speed I could jog to.

Five minutes later, Aiden glanced up and saw how fast I was going. Exasperated with me, he stood and walked over to where I was jogging. Without a word, he increased the speed above four—I'd been at two—and then went back to his wall and his book.

Damn him.

Out of breath and still completely out of shape, I nearly fell off the treadmill when the time hit sixty minutes and slowed to cool-down mode. I glanced over to where Aiden leaned against the wall, engrossed in his mammoth size book.

"What . . . are you reading?"

He glanced up and sighed. "Greek Fables and Legends."

"Oh!" I'd always loved reading what the mortal world wrote about our gods. Some of it was kind of correct while the rest was just bonkers.

"I got it in the library. You know, it's the place you should be hanging out in your spare time instead of drinking."

I shuddered and shook my arms out. "I hate the library. Everyone hates the library here."

Shaking his head, he closed the book. "Why is it that halfs believe there are hellhounds, harpies and furies living in the library? I don't get it."

"Have you not been in the library, seriously? Ugh. It's creepy and you hear stuff all the time. When I was a kid, I heard something growling in there once." I stepped off the treadmill and stopped in front of him. "Caleb heard wings flapping in there, near the bottom level. I'm not kidding."

Aiden laughed deeply. "You guys are ridiculous. There's nothing in the library. And all those creatures have long since been removed from the mortal world. Anyway," he lifted the book and shook it, "It's one of your textbooks."

I dropped down beside him. "Oh. Boring. I can't believe you read textbooks for fun." I paused, considering that. "Never mind. On second thought, I can believe you read textbooks for fun."

He turned his head toward me. "Cool-down stretches."

"Yes, sir!" I saluted him, then stretched out my legs and grabbed my toes. "So what legend are you reading about? How Zeus was the most promiscuous god of them all?" That was a legend the mortals actually got right. He was responsible for most of the original demigods all those years ago.

"No." He handed me the book. "Here. Why don't you take it

and do some reading? I have a feeling after today you're going to spend some long evenings in your room."

I rolled my eyes, but I took the book. After practice, I met with Caleb and bitched for the next hour about how Aiden was being totally uncool. Then I bitched about how he'd disappeared on me last night, leaving me with Jackson.

Friends don't let friends act like ho-bags.

Shortly afterwards, I did go back to my room instead of sneaking off with Caleb. I had a sinking suspicion if I did, I'd get caught, and I really didn't want to spend another day in the gym. It was bad enough I had to spend a good hour or two in it every night.

Bored out of my mind, I picked up the musty smelling book and thumbed through the ancient thing. Half of the book was written in ancient Greek and out of my ability to decipher. It looked like a bunch of squiggly lines to me. After finding the part in English, I discovered it wasn't about legends or fables. It was actually a detailed account of each of the gods, what they represented, and their rise to power. There was even a section on pure-bloods and their lesser halfs—us. Literally, it was how we were listed in this book.

No joke:

The Pure-Blood and their lesser half—the Half-Blood.

I skimmed through those pages, coming to a stop on a small block of text under the name "Ethos Krian." Even I remembered that name. All of us half-bloods did. He was the first of a very select group of half-bloods who could control the elements. But . . . oh, he was more than that. He was the first *Apollyon*—the only half-blood with the ability to control the elements and use the same kind of compulsion the pures could use on mortals.

In other words, the Apollyon was one big, badass of a half-blood.

Ethos Krian, born of a pure-blood and mortal in Naples, year 2848 ED (1256 AD), was the first recorded half-blood to display the abilities of a true Hematoi. As foreseen by the oracle of Rome, at the age of eighteen, the palingenesis awakened Ethos' power.

There are conflicting schools of thought on the origination of the Apollyon and his purpose. Popular belief states the gods who hold court in Olympia bestowed the gift of the four elements and the power of akasha, the fifth and final element, upon Ethos as a measure to ensure no pure-blood's power superseded that of their masters. The Apollyon has a direct linkage to the gods and acts as the Destroyer. The Apollyon is known as "The one who walks among the gods."

Since the birth of Ethos, one Apollyon has been born every generation as dictated by the oracle . . .

The section then proceeded to list the names of the other Apollyons, stopping in the year 3517 in the Hematoi calendar—1925 AD.

We *so* needed updated textbooks.

I skimmed past that part and turned the page. There was another part describing the characteristics of the Apollyon and another passage I was unfamiliar with.

My breath caught as I read it once, then twice. "No way."

Throughout time, only one Apollyon has been born to each generation with exception of what came to be known as "The Tragedy of Solaris." In the year 3203 ED (1611 AD), a second Apollyon was discovered in the New World. The palingenesis awakened Solaris (last name and parentage unknown) into power on her eighteenth birthday, setting in place a chain of startling and dramatic events. To this date, there has never been an explanation of how two Apollyons existed within the same generation or why.

I read the section again. There were *never* two Apollyons. Ever. I'd heard legends when I was a kid about the possibility of two, but I'd chalked them up as . . . well, legends. Continuing on, I quickly ascertained I didn't know jack.

It is believed the First sensed the marking of another Apollyon upon her eighteenth birthday and, unaware of the conse-quences, joined her in the New World. The effects of their union were chronicled as vast and damaging to both pure-bloods and their masters, the gods. Upon meeting, as if they were two halves meant to be one, the powers of Solaris shifted to the First Apollyon, therefore the First became what has always been feared: The God Killer. The power of the First became unstable and destructive.

The reaction from the gods, particularly the Order of Thanatos, was swift and righteous. Both Apollyons were executed without trial.

"Whoa . . ." I slammed the book shut and sat back. The gods, when threatened, didn't mess around. One Apollyon acted as a check and balance system, able to fight anything, but if there were two of them at once?

There was an Apollyon now, but I'd never met him. He was kind of like a celebrity. We knew he was out there somewhere, but we never actually saw him in person. I knew the Apollyon focused on daimons instead carrying out justice against pure-bloods now. Since the creation of the Council, pures no longer thought they could take on the gods—or, at least, they didn't say so openly.

I sat the book aside and turned off the lamp.

Poor Solaris.

Somewhere, the gods had goofed up and created two. It wasn't like it was her fault. She probably hadn't even seen it coming.

* * *

As the excitement of the Summer Solstice bubbled through the Covenant, I settled back into the life of a half-blood in training. The thrill of my presence had worn off, and most of the students who remained at the Covenant during the summer grew used to having me around. Granted, the fact I had killed two daimons secured my awesomeness. Even Lea's bitchy comments became less frequent.

Lea and Jackson broke up, got back together, and as far as I knew, were broken up again.

During the times Jackson was a free man, I developed a routine of avoiding him. Yeah, he was pure sexiness, but he was also super-fast with his hands, and on more than one occasion I'd had to remove them from my butt. Caleb was always quick to point out I had no room to complain since I'd brought it on myself.

Another sort of odd routine developed, but this was between Aiden and me. Being that I was always crabby in the morning, we usually started off practice with stretching and some laps— basically anything that prevented us from talking. By late morning, I was less likely to bite off his head and more receptive to digging into the real stuff. He never mentioned the night he'd busted me at the party and we'd talked about each other's need to become a Sentinel. He also never really explained what he'd meant by, "I remember you."

Of course, I came up with a crap ton of ridiculous explanations. My talent was so amazing that *everyone* knew who I was. Or my antics in and out of the training rooms had made me a legend in my own right. Or I'd been so stunningly beautiful he couldn't help but notice me. That last one was the most absurd. I'd been gawky and a total dweeb then. Not to mention someone like Aiden would never look at a half-blood in that way.

During training, Aiden was stern and rigid in his methods. Only a few times did he seem to slip up and grin when he thought I wasn't looking. But I was always watching.

Who could blame me? Aiden was . . . hotness incarnate. I alternated between staring at those ripped arms and being envious of how he moved with such fluid grace, but it was more than just his ability to make me drool on myself. Never in my life had I met someone so patient and tolerant of me. Gods know I'm annoying as hell, but Aiden treated me as if I were his equal. No pure really did that. The day I'd embarrassed myself by challenging my uncle seemed forgotten, and Aiden did everything to make sure I was coming along as expected.

With his guidance, I was getting used to the demands of training and the toll they took on my body. I even put some weight on. The dweeb part was still up in the air. Aiden *still* wouldn't let me get within ten feet of any of the cool-looking weapons.

On the day of the Summer Solstice, I tried approaching the wall of destruction toward the end of practice.

"Don't even think about it. You'd cut your hand off . . . or mine."

I froze, one hand inches from the wicked dagger. Dammit.

"Alex." Aiden sounded a bit amused. "We only have a little bit of time left. We need to work on your blocking."

Groaning, I pulled myself away from what I really wanted to learn. "Blocking again? That's all we've done for weeks."

Aiden folded his arms across his chest. Today he wore a plain white tee. He made it look good, very good. "That's not all we've done."

"Okay. I'm ready to move onto something else, like practicing with knives or defense against the dark arts. Cool things."

"Did you just quote *Harry Potter*?"

I grinned. "Maybe I did."

He shook his head. "We've been practicing kicks and jabs, Alex. And your blocking still needs work. How many of my kicks have you been able to block today?"

"Well . . ." I grimaced. He already knew the answer. I'd only managed to block a handful. "A couple, but you're fast."

"And daimons are faster than I am."

"I don't know about that." Nothing was as fast as Aiden. Half the time he moved like a blur. But I stepped into position and waited.

Aiden walked me through the maneuvers once more, and I could've sworn he slowed down his kicks just a bit, because I blocked more than I ever had before. We separated, about to start another round of kicks when a whistle sounded from the hallway. The culprit—bronze-haired Luke—stood at the door to the training room. I grinned and waved.

"You're not paying attention," Aiden snapped.

My grin slipped from my face as Luke and a couple of other halfs disappeared from view. "Sorry."

He exhaled slowly and motioned me forward. I complied without argument. "Is he another boy of yours? You're always with that other one."

My hands dropped to my sides. "*What*?"

Aiden brought his leg around fast. I barely had time to block it. "Is he another guy of yours?"

I didn't know if I should laugh, be pissed off, or be ecstatic that he'd noticed I was always with the *other boy*. Flipping my ponytail over my shoulder, I caught his forearm before it connected with my stomach. "Not that it's any of your business, but he wasn't whistling at *me*."

He jerked his hand back, frowning. "What's that supposed to mean?"

I raised my brows at him and waited for him to get it. The moment he did, his eyes widened and his mouth formed a perfect circle. Instead of falling on my ass laughing like I wanted to, I struck out with a vicious kick. Aiming for the vulnerable spot under his ribcage, I almost squealed at how perfect my kick was going to be.

I never made contact.

In one nifty swipe of his arm, he knocked me to the mat. Standing above me, he actually smiled. "Nice try."

I propped myself onto my elbows, scowling. "How come you smile when you knock me down?"

He offered his hand. "It's the little things that make me happy."

I accepted, and he hauled me to my feet. "Good to know." Shrugging, I brushed past him and grabbed my bottle of water. "So . . . um, are you going to the celebrations tonight?"

The Solstice was a big deal for the pures. It kicked off more than a month of social events leading up the Council session in August. Tonight would be the biggest celebration, and if the gods were going to bless them with their presence, tonight would be the night. I doubted any would, but the pures got all dressed in their colorful sheaths just in case.

There would also be a ton of parties held on the main island—none of which us halfs were invited to—and I mean none. And since all the pures' parents would be home, there would be no festivities at Zarak's house. However, rumor had it there would be a beach party hosted by the one and only Jackson. I wasn't sure if I was going to make an appearance or not.

"Probably." Aiden stretched, flashing a strip of taut skin along the band of his pants. "I'm not really big on that stuff, but I need to show up at some of them."

I made myself focus on his face, which was harder than I realized. "Why do you need to?"

He flashed a grin. "It's what we adults have to do, Alex."

I rolled my eyes and took a drink. "You can go and hang out with your friends. It will be fun."

Aiden looked at me strangely.

I lowered the bottle of water. "You do know how to have fun, right?"

"Of course."

Out of nowhere it kind of hit me. I don't think Aiden *could* have fun. Just like I couldn't bear to really, really think about what'd happened to Mom. Survivor's guilt—or at least that's what I thought they called it.

Aiden reached over, tapping my arm. "What are you thinking?"

I glanced up, finding his steady gaze on me. "I was just . . . thinking."

He backed off, slouched against the wall, and eyed me curiously. "Thinking about what?"

"It's hard for you to . . . have fun, isn't it? I mean, I never really see you doing anything. I've only ever seen you with Kain or Leon and never a girl. I did see you once in jeans . . ." I trailed off, flushing. What did seeing him in pants have to do with anything? But that had been an *amazing* sight. "Anyway, I guess it's hard after what happened to your parents."

Aiden pushed off the wall, eyes suddenly a steely gray. "I have friends, Alex, and I know how to have fun."

My cheeks grew even hotter. Obviously, I'd hit a sore spot. Whoops. Feeling very lame, I finished up training and hurried back to my dorm. Sometimes I wondered what I was thinking when I opened my mouth.

Disgusted, I took a quick shower and changed into a pair of shorts. Soon afterwards, I headed back to the hub of the campus to meet up with Caleb in the cafeteria, determined to forget my awkwardness.

Caleb was already there, in deep conversation with another half about who'd gotten better scores in their field exercises at the end of last semester. Since I had yet to take part in any field exercise, I was pretty much left out of the conversation. I felt like a loser.

"You going to the party tonight?" Caleb asked.

I glanced up. "I guess so. Not like I have anything better to do."

"Just don't have a repeat of last time."

I shot him an evil look. "Don't leave me hanging while you run off to Myrtle, you douche."

Caleb chuckled. "You should've come. Lea was bitching up until the moment she saw Jackson without you. She practically ruined everyone's night. Well, Cody actually ruined everyone's night."

I pulled my legs up and leaned back in my seat. This was the first I had heard of that. "What happened?"

He made a face. "Someone brought up the Breed Order crap again, and Cody was really out of it. He started talking smack about it. He was saying stuff about us halfs not belonging on the Council."

"I'm sure that went over well."

He smirked. "Yeah, then he said something about how the two breeds shouldn't mix and all the crap about the purity of their blood." He paused, eyeing someone behind me with great interest.

I twisted around, but I only caught a glimpse of caramel-colored skin and long, curly hair. I turned back to him with a raised brow. "So, what happened?"

"Um . . . a couple of the halfs got pissed. The next thing we know, Cody and Jackson were brawling. Man, they were going at it."

My eyes widened. "What? Did Cody report him?"

"No," said Caleb, grinning. "Zarak talked Cody out of it, but he beat Cody down. It was pretty awesome. Of course, the two idiots made up afterward. They're fine now."

Relieved, I settled back in my seat. Striking a pure—even in self-defense—was a fast way to get kicked out the Covenant. Killing a pure in any situation would get you executed, even if he was trying to cut your head off. As unfair as it was, we had to be careful navigating the politics of the pure-blood world. We could knock the crap out of one another, but when it came to the pures, they were untouchable in more ways than one. And if we happened to break one of the rules . . . well, we were only one step away from a lifetime of servitude—or death.

Shuddering, I thought about my precarious position. If I didn't get accepted in the fall, servitude was what I had to look forward to. There was no way I could allow that. I'd have to leave, but where would I go? What would I do? Live on the streets? Manage to find a job and pretend to be a mortal again?

Pushing those troubling thoughts away, I focused on Jackson's party, which I finally agreed to attend, and a couple of hours later, I found myself there. The little party really wasn't little; it looked like all the halfs who were stuck at the Covenant during the summer had spilled across the beach. Some sprawled across blankets; others reclined in chairs. No one was in the water.

I opted for a comfy-looking blanket beside Luke. Ritter, a younger half with the brightest red hair I'd ever seen, offered me a yellow plastic cup, but I turned it down. Rit hung out with us for a little while, talking about how he was getting ready to travel to California for the rest of the summer. I was only slightly envious.

"You aren't drinking?" asked Luke.

Even I was surprised by my decision, but I shrugged. "I'm not feeling it tonight."

He flicked a long strand of bronze-colored hair out of his eyes. "Did I get you in trouble today during practice?"

"No. I'm usually easily distracted. So it was nothing new."

Luke nudged me, grinning. "I can see why you are distracted. Too bad he's a pure. I'd give my left butt cheek for a piece of that."

"He likes girls."

"So?" Luke laughed at my expression. "What's he like? He seems so quiet. Like you know he'd be good in—"

"Stop right there!" I giggled, throwing up my hand. The movement pulled my sore back muscles.

Luke tipped back his head and laughed. "You can't say you never thought about it."

"He's . . . he's a pure," I said again, like it didn't make him sexy.

Luke shot me a knowing look.

"Okay." I sighed. "He's actually . . . very nice and patient. Most of the time . . . and I just feel weird talking about him. Can we talk about some other hot guy?"

"Oh, yes. Please. Can we talk about another hot guy?" Caleb snorted. "Exactly the thing I want to talk about."

Luke ignored him, his gaze flickering across the beach and settling near a couple of coolers. "How about Jackson?"

I eased onto my back. "Don't say his name."

He chuckled at my pathetic attempt to make myself invisible. "He just showed up *without* Lea. Come to think of it, where in hell is that little ho?"

I refused to look up and draw Jackson's attention. "I have no idea. I haven't seen her."

"Is that a bad thing?" asked Caleb.

"Oh, Alex, here comes your man," Luke announced.

There was nowhere for me to go and I looked helplessly between Caleb and Luke. Neither of them did anything to hide their amusement.

"Alex, where have you've been?" slurred Jackson. "I haven't seen you around."

I squeezed my eyes shut and muttered a dozen curses. "I've been busy with training."

Jackson swayed to the right, toward a distracted Caleb. "Aiden should know you need to get out and have a little fun."

Luke turned and gave me a sly wink before standing. I sat up, but that was as far as I made it. Jackson dropped into the empty space and threw his arm around me, nearly knocking me over.

His breath was too warm and smelled of beer. "You know you're more than welcome to hang out here after the party."

"Oh . . . I don't know about that."

Jackson smiled and moved in closer. Normally I'd find Jackson attractive, but he just grossed me out now. Something was wrong with me. Had to be. "You can't be practicing tomorrow. Not after the celebrations. Even Aiden will be sleeping in."

I doubted that and I found myself wondering if Aiden was having a good time. Did he go to the celebrations and stay? Or did he show up, make an appearance, and bail? I kind of hoped he stayed and had fun. He could use it after spending an entire day holed up with me.

"Alex?"

"Huh?"

Jackson chuckled and slipped his hand over my shoulder. I grabbed it and dropped it in his lap. Undaunted, he reached for me again. "I was asking if you wanted something to drink. Zarak went on a compulsion frenzy and stocked us up for the rest of the summer."

That was good to know. "No. I'm fine. Not thirsty."

Eventually, Jackson grew bored with my lack of interest and roamed off. Grateful, I turned to Caleb. "Smack me next time I even think about talking to a guy. Seriously."

He stared down into his cup, frowning. "What happened with him? Did he come on too strong?" A fierce look came over his face as his eyes narrowed on Jackson's back. "Do I need to hurt him?"

"No!" I laughed. "It's just . . . I don't know." I turned and saw him standing with the female half I'd caught a glimpse of earlier. She was a pretty brunette, ridiculously curvy, and she had a smooth, caramel-colored complexion. "Jackson doesn't do it for me."

"Who does?" His own gaze settled on Jackson's companion.

"Who's that girl?" I asked.

He turned and sighed. "That's Olivia. Her last name is one of those unpronounceable Greek ones. Her father is a mortal; her mom's a pure."

I continued watching the girl. She wore a pair of designer jeans I would've killed for. She also kept avoiding Jackson's wandering hands. "How come this is the first time I'm seeing her?"

"She's been with her dad. I think." He cleared her throat. "She's actually . . . kinda nice."

I looked at him sharply. "You like her, don't you?"

"No! No, of course not." His voice sounded sort of strangled.

My curiosity increased as Caleb's eyes seemed drawn back to Olivia. A red hue colored his cheeks. "Sure. You aren't interested in her at all."

Caleb took a long gulp of his drink. "Shut up, Alex."

I opened my mouth, but whatever I was about to say was cut off when Deacon St. Delphi strolled up out of nowhere. "What the hell?"

Caleb followed my gaze. "Now, that's interesting."

Seeing Deacon on the beach wasn't at all surprising, but seeing him on the night of the solstice when all the pures hovered together was shocking.

It was so very . . . *impure* of him.

Deacon swept the halfs with his cool gaze and a sardonic grin broke across his face when he saw us. Sauntering over, he pulled a shiny silver flask from the pocket of his jeans. "Happy Summer Solstice!"

Caleb choked on his drink. "Same to you."

He took Jackson's empty spot, seemingly unaware of the shocked stares. I cleared my throat. "What . . . are you doing here?"

"What? I got bored over on the main island. All the pomp and circumstance is enough to drive a man sober."

"We can't have that." I took in the red rims around his eyes. "Are you ever sober?"

He seemed to think about that. "Not if I can help it. Things are . . . easier this way."

I knew he was talking about his parents. Unsure of how to respond, I waited for him to continue.

"Aiden hates that I drink so much." He glanced down at his flask. "He's right, you know."

I played with my hair, twisting into a thick rope. "Right about what?"

Deacon tipped his head back, staring at the stars blanketing the night sky. "Everything, but especially the path he chose." He stopped and laughed. "If only he knew that, huh?"

"Aren't they going to know you're gone?" Caleb cut off my words.

"And come over here and ruin all your fun?" Deacon's serious look vanished. "Absolutely. In about an hour, when they start their ritual chanting and crap, someone—most likely my brother—will realize I'm missing and come looking for me."

My mouth dropped open. "Aiden's still there?"

"You came here knowing they would follow you?" Caleb frowned.

Deacon appeared entertained by both statements. "Yes answers all." He brushed a sunny curl off his forehead.

"Crap!" Caleb started to stand while I mulled over the knowledge that Aiden was still partying it up. "Alex, we should go."

"Sit down." Deacon put up a hand. "You have at least an hour. I'll give the party boys enough time to clear out. Trust me."

Caleb didn't seem to hear him. He stared back down the seashore, where Olivia and another half stood close, really close together. Seconds passed while his face hardened. Leaning over, I tugged the hem of his shirt.

He gave me a broad smile. "You know what? I'm pretty tired. I think I'm going to head back to the dorm."

"Boo." Deacon stuck out his lower lip.

I stood. "Sorry."

"Double boo." He shook his head. "And the fun was just starting."

Tossing a quick goodbye to Deacon, I followed Caleb up the beach. We passed Lea coming down the wooden boardwalk.

"Like going after my sloppy seconds?" Lea wrinkled her nose. "How cute."

A second later, I wrapped my hand around her forearm. "Hey."

Lea tried to pull her arm back, but I was stronger than her. "What?"

I smiled my best smile. "Your boyfriend just copped a feel. You obviously aren't doing it for him." I let go then, leaving a very unhappy Lea standing alone.

"Caleb!" I moved to catch up with him.

"I know what you're going to say, so I don't want to hear it."

I brushed my hair behind my ears. "How do you know what I was going to say? All I wanted to point out is if you like the chick back there, you could just—"

With a sideways glance, he raised his brows. "I really don't want to talk about this."

"But . . . I don't understand why you won't admit it. What the hell is the big deal?"

He sighed. "Something happened the night we went to Myrtle."

I tripped over my feet. "What?"

"Not *that*. Well . . . not really, but it came close."

"*What?*" I squealed, punching his arm. "How come you haven't said anything? With the Olivia chick? Jeez, I'm your best friend and you failed to mention this?"

"We both had been drinking, Alex. We were arguing over who called shotgun first . . . and the next thing I know, we're full-on making out."

I bit my lip. "That's kinda hot. So, why won't you talk to her?"

Silence stretched between us before he responded. "Because I like her, really like her, and you would like her, too. She's smart, funny, strong, and her ass is just so—"

"Caleb, okay. I get the point. You really like her. So talk to her."

We headed toward the courtyard nestled between the two dorms. "You don't get it. And you should. Nothing will come out of it. You know how it is for us."

"Huh?" I stared at the intricate designs on the pathway. They were runes and symbols carved into the marble. Some represented various gods while others looked like some child got ahold of a marker and went to town. Actually, it looked like something I'd draw.

"Never mind. I just need to hook up with someone else. Get this stupid whatever out of my system."

I lifted my eyes from the strange markings. "That sounds like a solid plan."

"Maybe I should just hook up with Lea again or someone else. How about you?"

I shot him a dirty look. "Gee, thanks. But seriously, you don't want to hook up with just anyone. You want something . . . meaningful." I stopped, not sure where *that* came from.

Clearly, he didn't either. "Something meaningful? Alex, you've been out in the normal world too long. You know how it is for us. We don't get 'meaningful.'"

I sighed. "Yeah, I know."

"We're either Guards or Sentinels—not husbands, wives, or parents." He stopped, frowning. "Flings and girlfriends. That's what we have. Our duty doesn't allow for much else."

He was right. Being born a half-blood wiped out any chance for a normal, healthy relationship. Like Caleb said, our duty didn't allow for us to form attachments—anything we'd regret giving up or leaving behind. Once we graduated, we could be assigned anywhere and at any given moment we could be yanked and sent somewhere else.

It was a harsh, lonely life, but one with purpose.

I kicked at a small pebble, sending it flying into the thick underbrush. "Just because we won't have the picket fence, doesn't mean . . ." The skin of my forehead creased as a sudden chill brushed over me. It came out of nowhere, and by the sudden confused look on Caleb's face, I knew he felt it, too.

"A boy and a girl, one with a bright and short future, and the other covered in shadows and doubt."

The raspy, ancient-sounding voice brought both of us to a standstill. Caleb and I turned around. The stone bench had been unoccupied a moment ago, but there she was. And she was old, like should've-been-dead-by-now old.

A massive pile of pure white hair sat pinned atop her head, and her skin was dark as coal and heavily lined. Her crooked posture aged her even more, but her eyes were sharp. Intelligent.

I'd never seen her before, but I instinctively knew who she was. "Grandma Piperi?"

She tipped her head back and laughed wildly. I half expected the weight of her hair to topple her over, but she remained upright. "Oh, Alexandria, you seem so surprised. Did you not think I was real?"

Caleb jabbed me with his elbow a few times, but I couldn't stop staring. "You know who I am?"

Her dark eyes flickered to Caleb. "Of course I do." She smoothed her hands over what appeared to be a housecoat. "I also remember your momma."

Disbelief brought me a step closer to the oracle, but shock left me speechless.

"I remember your momma," she went on, nodding her head back and forth. "She came to me three years ago, she did. I spoke the truth to her, you see. The truth was only for her to hear." She paused, her gaze falling back to Caleb. "What are you doing here, child?"

Eyes wide, he shifted uncomfortably. "We were . . . walking back to our dorms."

Grandma Piperi smiled, stretching the papery skin around her mouth. "Do you wish to hear the truth—your truth? What the gods have in store for you?"

Caleb paled. The thing with truths, they usually messed with your head. It didn't matter if it was crazy talk or not.

"Grandma Piperi, what did you tell my mom?" I asked.

"If I told you, what would it change? Fate is fate, you see. Just like love is love." She cackled as if she'd said something funny. "What's written by the gods will come to pass. Most has already. Such a sad affair when children turned against their makers."

I had no clue what she was talking about and I felt pretty sure she was certifiable, but I needed to know what Piperi had said—if she said anything at all. Maybe Caleb was right, and I needed closure. "Please. I need to know what you said to her. What made her leave?"

She tilted her head to the side. "Don't you want to know about your truth, child? That is what's important now. Don't you want to know about love? About what is forbidden and what is fated?"

My arms fell to my sides and I blinked back sudden tears. "I don't want to know about love."

"But you should, my child. You need to know about love. The things people will do for love. All truths come down to love, do they not? One way or another, they do. See, there is a difference between love and need. Sometimes, what you feel is immediate and without rhyme or reason." She sat up a little straighter. "Two people see each across a room or their skin brushes. Their souls recognize the person as their own. It doesn't need time to figure it. The soul always knows . . . whether it's right or wrong."

Caleb grabbed my arm. "Come on. Let's go. She's not telling you anything you want to hear."

"The first . . . the first is always the most powerful." She closed her eyes, sighing. "Then there is need and fate. That is a different type. Need covers itself with love, but need . . . need is never love. Always beware of the one who needs you. There is always a want behind a need, you see."

Caleb let go of my arm and jabbed fiercely at the walkway behind us.

"Sometimes you will mistake need for love. Be careful. The road with need is never a fair one, never a good one. Much like the road you must walk down. Beware of the one who needs."

The lady was a loon, and even though I knew this, her words still sent shivers down my spine. "Why won't the road be easy for me?" I asked, ignoring Caleb.

She stood. Well, as much as she could stand. Since her back hunched forward it stopped her from standing up completely. "Roads are always bumpy, never flat. This one here," she nodded at Caleb with a tiny cackle, "this one has a road full of light."

Caleb stopped pointing behind us. "That's good to know."

"A short road full of light," added Grandma Piperi.

His face fell. "That's . . . good to know."

"What about the road?" I asked again, hoping for an answer that made sense.

"Ah, roads are always shady. Your road is full of shadows, full of deeds which must be done. It comes to those of your kind."

Caleb shot me a meaningful look, but I shook my head. I had no idea what she was talking about, but I was still unwilling to leave. She hobbled past me and I stepped out of the way. My back brushed against something soft and warm, drawing my attention. I turned, finding large purple flowers with bright yellow middles. I shifted closer, inhaling their bittersweet, almost acrid smell.

"Be careful there, child. You be touching nightshade." She stopped, turning back to where we stood. "Very dangerous . . . much like kisses from those who walk among the gods. Intoxicating, sweet, and deadly . . . you need to know how to handle it right. Just a little and you'll be fine. Too much . . . it takes away what makes you who you are." She smiled softly, as if she were remembering something. "The gods move around us, always close by. They are watching and they are waiting to see which one is revealed to be the strongest. They are here now. You see, the end is upon them, upon all of us. Even the gods have little faith."

Caleb passed me another wide-eyed stare. I shrugged, deciding to give it one more chance. "So there's nothing you'll tell me about my mom?"

"Nothing you haven't already been told."

"Wait . . . ?" My skin felt hot and cold all at once. "What . . . Lea said is true? That I was the reason why Mom died?"

"Let's go, Alex. You're right." Caleb took a step back. "She's freaking crazy."

Piperi sighed. "Always ears around these parts, but ears don't always hear correctly."

"Alex, let's go."

I blinked and—I'm not exaggerating—in the time it took me to open my eyes, Grandma Piperi stood in front of me. The old lady moved that fast. Her clawed hand grabbed my shoulder hard enough to make me wince.

She stared up at me with eyes as sharp as blades, and when she spoke, her voice lost its raspy edge. And she didn't sound all that crazy. Oh no, her words were clear and to the point.

"You will kill the ones you love. It is in your blood, in your fate. So the gods have spoken it and so the gods have come to foresee it."

9

"Alex! Watch his hands. You're letting too many blocks get through!"

I nodded at Aiden's harsh words and squared off with Kain again. Aiden was right. Kain was tearing me apart. My movements were too slow, jerky and distracted—mainly due to staying up half the night, replaying the bizarro conversation with Grandma Piperi.

This was a really bad time to be preoccupied. Today was the first practice that included Kain, and I was fighting like a baby. Kain wasn't going easy on me either. Not that I would've wanted that, but I also didn't want to look like a total turd in front of another Sentinel.

Another one of his brutal kicks got through my block and I dodged with only a split second to spare. Dodging was not the point of this exercise. If it were, I'd be excelling at it.

Aiden stalked over to me then, repositioning my arms in a way that would've successfully knocked Kain's leg down. "Watch him. Even the slightest muscle tremor will give away his attack. You have to pay attention, Alex."

"I know." I took a step back and ran my arm over my forehead. "I know. I can do this."

Kain shook his head and walked off to grab his bottle of water while Aiden led me to the other side of the room, his hand wrapped around my upper arm. He bent so we were eye level. "What is your deal today? I know you can do better than this."

I bent to pick up my water, but the bottle was empty. Aiden

handed me his. "I'm just . . . out of it today." I took a drink and handed it back to him.

"I can tell."

I bit my lip, flushing. I was better than this, and gods, I wanted to prove to Aiden I was. If I couldn't get past this then I couldn't move onto anything else—to all those damn cool things I wanted to learn.

"Alex, you've been distracted all day." His eyes met mine and held them. "This better have nothing to do with the party Jackson held on the beach last night."

Good grief, was there nothing this man didn't know? I shook my head. "No."

Aiden gave me a knowing look and took a drink from the bottle before he shoved it back into my hands. "Drink up."

I sighed, turning away from him. "Let's go again, okay?"

Aiden motioned Kain back and then clapped me on the shoulder. "You can do this, Alex."

After collecting myself and taking another gulp of water, I dropped the bottle on the floor. I went back to the center of the mats and nodded at Kain.

Kain watched me wearily. "You ready?"

"Yeah." I clenched my teeth. Kain raised his eyebrows, like he doubted I was going to do anything different this time around.

"All right." He shook his head and we squared off again. "Remember to anticipate my moves."

I blocked his first kick, then his punch. We circled each other for a few rounds while I wondered what the hell Grandma Piperi meant by saying I would kill the ones I loved. That didn't make any sense, because the one person I'd loved was already dead and I sure as hell hadn't killed her. You can't kill someone who's already dead, and it wasn't like I loved—

Kain's boot slammed past my defenses and connected with my stomach. Pain exploded through me, so intense and over- whelming I dropped to my knees. The way I landed put a strain on my battered back. Wincing, I reached around and held my back with one hand and my stomach with another.

I was a total mess.

Kain dropped down in front of me. "Dammit, Alex! What were you doing? You should have never been that close to me!"

"Yeah," I groaned. *Breathe through it. Just breathe through it.* Easier said than done, but I kept telling myself that. I expected Aiden to launch into a major tirade, but he didn't say a word to me. Instead he walked up and jerked Kain up by the scruff of his neck, nearly holding him off the ground.

"Practice is over."

Kain's mouth dropped open and his normally tanned skin paled. "But—"

"Apparently you don't understand." His voice sounded low and dangerous.

I stumbled to my feet. "Aiden, it's my fault. I leaned in." I didn't have to elaborate; it was obvious what I'd done wrong.

Aiden looked over his shoulder at me. A few terse seconds later, he released Kain. "Go."

Kain straightened his shirt while he backed up. When he turned to me, his sea-green eyes were wide. "Alex, I'm sorry."

I waved one hand at him. "No biggie."

Aiden stepped in front of me, dismissing Kain without so much as another word. "Let me take a look at it."

"Oh . . . it's okay." I turned away from him. My eyes burned, but not because of the throbbing pain. I wanted to sit down and cry. I'd walked right into the kick. A child wouldn't have made such a mistake. It was that lame.

He placed a surprisingly gentle hand on my shoulder and turned me back around. The look on his face said he understood my embarrassment. "It's okay, Alex." When I didn't move, he took a step back. "You grabbed your back. I need to make sure you're okay."

Seeing no way out of this, I followed Aiden to one of the

smaller rooms where they kept medical supplies. It was a cold, sterile room like any doctor's office with the exception of the painting of Aphrodite in all her naked glory, which I found odd and a little disturbing.

"Get up on the table."

I wanted nothing more than to run back to my room and sulk in privacy, but I did what he said.

Aiden came back to me, his gaze fixed above my head. "How does your stomach feel?"

"Okay."

"Why did you grab your back?"

"It's sore." I rubbed my hands over my thighs. "I feel like a dork."

"You're not a dork."

"I am. I should've been paying attention. I walked right into the kick. It wasn't Kain's fault."

He seemed to consider that. "I've never seen you so distracted."

For the last month, we'd had eight-hour training days, and I guess during that time he'd seen a lot of things from me. But I'd never been this unfocused.

"You can't afford to be so distracted," he continued gently. "You're coming along remarkably well, but you don't have time to lose. It's almost July and that leaves us about two months to get you caught up. Your uncle has been requesting weekly reports. Don't think he's forgotten about you."

Full of shame and disappointment, my eyes dropped down to my hands. "I know."

Aiden placed his fingers on my chin, guiding my head up. "Why are you so distracted, Alex? You move like you haven't slept and you're acting as if your mind's a million miles from here. If it's not the party last night, is it a guy who has you distracted?"

I cringed. "Look. There are several things I'm not discussing with you. Guys are one of them."

Aiden's eyes widened. "Really? If it's interfering with your training, then it's interfering with me."

"Jeez." I shifted uncomfortably under his intense stare. "There is no guy. I have no guy."

He fell silent, watching me curiously. Those eyes had a calming effect, and even though I knew this was dumb, so stupid, I took a deep breath. "I saw Grandma Piperi last night."

It seemed that Aiden expected me to say anything but that. While his face was impassive as ever, his eyes seemed to deepen. "And?"

"And Lea was right—"

"Alex," he cut me off. "Don't go there. You're not responsible."

"She was right and wrong at the same time." I stopped, sighing at the dubious look on Aiden's face. "Grandma Piperi wouldn't tell me everything. Actually, she told me a bunch of crazy stuff about love and need . . . and gods kissing. Anyway, she told me that I would kill the one I loved, but how is that possible? Mom is already dead."

An odd look flickered over his face, but it was gone before I could figure out what it was. "I thought you said you didn't believe in that kind of stuff."

Of course, he would remember *that* out of the billion random comments I'd made. "I don't, but it's not every day you're told that you're going to kill someone you love."

"So this is what's been bothering you today?"

I squeezed my thighs. "Yes. No. I mean, do you think it was my fault?"

"Oh, Alex." He shook his head. "Do you remember when you asked me why I volunteered to train you?"

"Yeah."

He pushed away from the table I sat on. "Well, I lied to you."

"Yeah." I bit my lip and looked away. "I kinda figured that out already."

"You have?" He sounded surprised.

"You stood up for me because of what happened to your parents." I stole a peek at him. He was quiet as he watched me. "I think I remind you of yourself when it happened."

Aiden stared at me for an eternal second. "You're far more observant than I give you credit for."

"Thanks." I didn't share the fact I'd only figured that out recently.

That lopsided grin appeared. "You're right, if that makes you feel any better. I remember what it was like afterward. You always wonder if there was anything you could've done differently, as pointless as it is, but you get hung up on the 'what if' of it all." The smile disappeared slowly and he turned his face away. "For the longest time, I used to think if I had decided to be a Sentinel earlier, I could've stopped the daimon."

"But you didn't know a daimon was going to attack. You were—are—a pure-blood. So very few of you even . . . choose this life. And you were just a kid. You can't blame yourself for that."

Aiden faced me then, gaze curious. "Then how can you hold yourself responsible for what happened to your mom? You may have realized there was a possibility that a daimon would find you, but you didn't know."

"Yeah." I hated it when he was right.

"You're still holding onto that guilt. So much so that you're reading into what the oracle said. You can't let what she said get to you, Alex. An oracle only talks in possibilities, not facts."

"I thought an oracle talks with gods and the fates," I said dryly.

He looked doubtful. "An oracle sees into the past and the possibility in the future, but it's not set in stone. There is no such thing as a certain fate. Only you are in control of your fate. You aren't responsible for what . . . happened to your mom. You need to let it go."

"Why do you all say it like that? No one says she died.

Everyone is, like, afraid to say that. It's not *what happened*—she was killed."

The shadow appeared on his face again, but he stepped around the table. "Let me look at your back." Before I knew what he was doing, he lifted the back of my shirt and inhaled sharply.

"What?" I asked, but he didn't say anything. He tugged my shirt up further. "Hey—what are you doing?" I smacked his hands away.

He shot around the table, his eyes a gunmetal gray. "What do you think I'm doing? How long has your back been like this?"

I shrank back. "Since we . . . um . . . started blocking training."

"Why didn't you say something about this?"

"It's not a big deal. It doesn't hurt, not really."

Aiden whirled around. "Damn half-bloods. I know you all have a higher than normal tolerance for pain, but *that* is ridiculous. *That* has to hurt."

I stared at his back as he rummaged through the numerous cabinets. "I'm in training." I forced as much maturity into my voice as possible. "We aren't expected to bitch and moan about pain. It's a part of training—a part of being a Sentinel. It happens."

Aiden wheeled around, expression incredulous. "You haven't been training for three years, Alex. Your body—your skin isn't used to it anymore. You cannot let things like that go because you think someone is going to think less of you."

I blinked. "I don't think people are going to think less of me. It's just a . . . couple of damn bruises. Some of them have faded already. See?"

He set a small jar beside me on the table. "Bullshit."

"You've never cussed before." I had the strangest urge to laugh.

"It's not just *a* bruise. Your whole back is black and blue, Alex." Aiden paused, his hands clenching air. "Were you afraid I would think less of you if you brought this up?"

I gave a slight shake of the head. "No."

His lips pressed together. "I didn't expect your body to adapt quickly, and honestly, I should've known."

"Aiden . . . really, it doesn't hurt that bad." The never-ending, dull ache was something I'd gotten used to, so I wasn't really lying.

Picking up the jar, he walked around the table. "This should help, and next time, you will tell me when something is wrong with you."

"All right." I decided not to push my luck. He didn't seem like he'd appreciate any snarky response at this moment. "What is that stuff, anyways?"

He unscrewed the lid. "It's a mixture of Arnica and menthol. Arnica is part of a flower. It acts like an anti-inflammatory and it reduces pain. It should help."

I expected him to hand me the jar, but he dipped his fingers inside it instead. "What are you—?"

"Hold your shirt up. I don't want to get this all over it. It tends to stain clothing."

Dumbfounded, I found myself lifting the edge of my shirt. Once again, there was a sharp intake of breath as he got another look at my back.

"Alex, you can't let something like this go untreated." This time, the anger was gone from his voice. "If you're hurt, you must tell me. I wouldn't have . . ."

Gone so hard on me? Allowed me to practice with Kain and get my ass handed to me? That wasn't what I wanted.

"Don't ever feel like you can't tell me when something's wrong. You've got to trust that I would care if you were hurt."

"It's not your fault. I could've told you—"

He placed his fingers against my skin and I nearly jumped off the table. Not because the salve was cold—don't get me wrong, it was freezing—but they were *his* fingers moving along my back. A pure never touched a half this way. Or maybe they did now. I didn't know, but I couldn't imagine the other pures I knew seeking to ease a half's pain. They usually didn't care enough to.

Aiden silently worked the thick balm across my skin and then up. Eventually his fingers brushed the edge of my sports bra. My skin felt strangely warm, which was odd to me since the stuff was so cold. I focused on the wall in front of me. There was that picture of Aphrodite perched upon a rock. She had this lusty look on her face and her boobs were hanging out for the world to see.

That was *so* not helping.

Aiden continued quietly. Every so often my body jerked on its own accord, and then I felt hot, really hot.

"Did you ever know your biological father?" His quiet voice broke into my thoughts.

I shook my head. "No. He died before I was born."

His deft fingers slid along the side of my stomach. "Do you know anything about him?"

"No. Mom never really talked about him, but I think they used to spend time in Gatlinburg, Tennessee. We would spend Winter Solstice there when she could . . . get away from Lucian. I think . . . being at the cabins made her feel close to him."

"She loved him?"

I nodded. "I think so."

He worked on my lower back now, moving the balm in smooth circles, and every so often the cool scent of menthol reached me. "What were you going to do if the daimons hadn't shown up? You had something to do, right?"

I swallowed. This was an easy question, but I found it hard to concentrate on anything other than his fingers. "Um . . . I wanted to do lots of things."

His fingers stopped and he laughed softly. "Like what?"

"I . . . don't know."

"Did you ever plan on coming back to the Covenant?"

"Yes and no." I swallowed hard. "Before the attack, I never thought I'd see the Covenant again. After it happened, I was trying to get to the one in Nashville, but the daimons . . . kept getting in my way."

"So what were you going to do if the daimons hadn't found you?" He knew not to focus on that horrible week after the attack. He knew I wouldn't talk about it.

"When . . . I was really little, my mom and several Sentinels took a bunch of us kids to the zoo. I loved it—*loved* the animals. I spent the entire summer telling Mom that I belonged in the zoo."

"What?" He sounded incredulous. "You thought you belonged in a zoo?"

I felt a smile tug at my lips. "Yeah, I was a strange child. So . . . it was one of the things I thought I could do. You know, work with animals or something, but . . ." I shrugged, feeling kind of stupid.

"But what, Alex?" I could *feel* his smile.

I stared down at my fingers. "But I always wanted to come back to the Covenant. I needed to. I just didn't fit in with all the normal people. I missed it here, missed having a purpose and knowing what I should be doing."

His fingers left my skin and he was silent for so long I thought something had happened to him. I twisted around to face him. "What?"

He tipped his head to the side. "Nothing."

I crossed my legs and let out a sigh. "You're looking at me like I'm weird."

Aiden sat the jar aside. "You're not weird."

"Then . . . ?" I let my shirt fall back down and grabbed the jar. "You done?" When he nodded I put the lid back on.

Aiden leaned forward, placing his hands on each side of my crossed legs. "The next time you're hurt, I want you to tell me."

When I looked up, he was eye level with me and we were only

inches apart—the closest we'd ever been outside of the training room. "Okay."

"And . . . you're not weird. Well, I've met weirder people than you."

I started to smile, but something in the way Aiden looked at me caught my attention. It was like he was assuming responsibility for me and what I felt. I *knew* he did. Maybe it came from having to care for Deacon . . . and Deacon? I remembered what he'd said last night.

Clearing my throat, I focused on his shoulder. "Does Deacon ever talk about things? You know, about your parents?"

My question caught him off guard. It took him a few seconds to answer. "No. Just like you."

I ignored that. "His drinking? I think he does it so he doesn't have to think about it."

Aiden blinked. "Is that why you do it?"

"No! I don't really do it that much, but that's not the point. What I'm saying . . . ?" Gods, what was I doing? Trying to talk to him about his brother?

"What are you saying?"

Hoping I wasn't over stepping boundaries, I plunged ahead. "I think Deacon drinks so he doesn't feel."

Aiden sighed. "I know. So do all the counselors and teachers. No matter what I do or who I bring him to, he won't open up."

I nodded, understanding how hard it was for Deacon. "He's . . . proud of you. He didn't say it exactly like that, but he's proud of what you're doing."

He blinked. "Why . . . how would you know?"

I shrugged. "I think if you keep at what you're doing, because what you're doing is right, he'll come around."

The serious look remained, and there was more to it than that. He looked worried, and for reasons I didn't even want to acknowledge, it bothered me.

"Hey," I reached out and tapped the hand that rested next to my left leg. "You are—"

The hand that I tapped reached up and clasped mine. I froze as he threaded his fingers through mine. "I'm what?"

Beautiful. Kind. Patient. Perfect. I said none of those things. Instead, I stared at his fingers, wondering if he knew he was holding my hand. "You're always so . . ."

His thumb moved over the top of my hand. The balm made his fingers cool and smooth. "What?"

I looked up, and I was immediately snared. His stare, his soft touch along my hand was doing very strange things. I felt hot and dizzy, like I'd been sitting out in the sun all day. All I could think about was how his hand felt on mine. Then, what his hand would feel like on other parts. I shouldn't be thinking that at all.

Aiden was a *pure*.

The door to our room swung open. I jerked back, my hand falling to my lap.

A big, hulking shadow paused at the door. Mister Steroids—Leon—glanced around the room, his eyes falling to Aiden, who had moved to a much more appropriate distance.

"I've been looking everywhere for you," Leon said.

"What's up?" Aiden asked evenly.

Leon spared at glance at me. He didn't suspect anything. Why would he? Aiden was a well respected pure and I was just a half-blood he was training. "Did she hurt herself?"

"She's fine. What did you need?"

"Marcus needs to see us."

Aiden nodded. He started to follow Leon out, but he stopped at the door. Turning back to me, he was all business again. "We'll talk more about this later."

"Okay," I said, but he was already gone.

My gaze went back to the painting of the goddess of love. I swallowed hard and my grasp on the little jar tightened. There was no way—absolutely no way—I was interested in Aiden in that way. Sure, he was swoon-worthy and really nice, and patient and funny in a dry kind of way. There was a lot about him to like. If he were a half-blood, then there wouldn't be anything wrong. He didn't work for the Covenant, so there wasn't a student hooking up with a teacher kind of problem, and he was only three years older than me. If he were a half-blood, I'd probably have thrown myself at him already.

But Aiden was a freaking pure-blood.

A freaking pure-blood with wonderfully strong fingers and a smile that . . . well, made me feel like there was a nest of butterflies in my stomach. And the way he looked at me—how his eyes shifted from gray to silver in a heartbeat—affected me even now. My stupid little heart leapt in my chest.

10

Sprawled across the mats, going through the motions of the cool-down stretches a couple of days later, Aiden decided to let me in on why Marcus had wanted to see him.

"Lucian is coming."

I stared up at the ceiling, disappointed. "So?"

Instead of looming over me like he usually did, he dropped down beside me on the mat. His leg brushed mine, causing a tightening in my chest. *You're being ridiculous, Alex. Knock it off.* I moved my leg away from his.

"He's going to want to talk to you."

Pushing my weird attraction to him out of my mind, I focused on his words. "Why?"

He bent his knees and dropped his arms over them. "Lucian is your legal guardian. I suppose he's curious to see how your training is coming along."

"Curious?" I kicked my legs into the air. Why? I had no clue. "Lucian has never been interested in anything that had to do with me. Why would he start now?"

His expression tightened for a moment. "Things are different now. With your mom . . ."

"That doesn't matter. It has nothing to do with me."

He still looked strange as he continued to watch me point my toes at the ceiling. "It has everything to do with you." He took a deep breath, seeming to choose his next words wisely. "Lucian is dead set against you returning to the Covenant."

"Good to know Lucian and Marcus share that in common."

His jaw tightened. "Lucian and Marcus share nothing in common."

There he went again, trying to convince me Marcus wasn't the douche I believed him to be. He'd been at it for weeks, talking about how concerned my uncle had appeared when my mom and I had disappeared. Or how relieved Marcus had seemed when he'd notified him I was alive. Nice of Aiden to want to repair the relationship between us, but Aiden didn't realize there was nothing to repair.

Aiden reached over and pushed my legs back down to the mat. "Do you ever sit still for five seconds?"

I grinned, sitting up. "Nope."

He looked like he wanted to smile, but didn't. "Tonight, when you see Lucian, you need to be on your best behavior."

I rolled to my feet, laughing now. "Best behavior? So I shouldn't challenge Lucian to a fight, I guess? I'd win that one. He's a total wimp."

The severe frown that graced his face was a clear indication he wasn't amused. "You do realize your stepfather can over- throw Marcus's decision to allow you to stay here? His authority supersedes your uncle's?"

"Yes." I planted my hands on my hips. "Since Marcus is only allowing me to stay if I prove myself capable of returning to classes in the fall, I don't see what the big deal is."

Aiden came to his feet swiftly. For a moment, I was struck by how quickly he moved. "The big deal is if you mouth off at the Minister like you do with Marcus, you won't get a second chance. No one will be able to help you."

I tore my eyes away from him. "I'm not going to mouth off at him. Honestly, there's nothing Lucian can say to me that will get me riled up. He means nothing to me. Never has."

He looked doubtful. "Try to remember that."

I threw him a grin. "You have such little faith in me."

Surprisingly, Aiden grinned back at me. It made me feel all warm and stupid. "How's your back?"

"Oh. It's doing okay. That . . . stuff really helped."

He stalked across the mats, silver eyes focused on me. "Make sure you put it on every night. The bruises should fade in a couple days."

You could always help put it on again, but I didn't say that. I backed up, keeping a space between us. "Yes, sensei."

Aiden stopped in front of me. "Better get going. The Minister and his Guards will be arriving soon, and all of those at the Covenant will be expected to meet him."

I groaned. Everyone would be wearing a Covenant-issued uniform of some sort and no one had given me one. "I'm going to look like a—"

Aiden placed his hands on my upper arms, obliterating my critical thinking skills. I stared up at him, entertaining a vividly wild scenario in which he pulled me against him and kissed me like the barrel-chested men in those smutty books my mom used to read.

He picked me up and put me on the floor a few feet off the mats. Crouching down, he started to roll up the mats. There went my fantasies. "You'll look like what?" he asked.

I ran my hands over my arms. "What am I supposed to wear? I'm going to stick out and everyone will be looking at me."

He glanced up at me through heavy lashes. "Since when are you bothered by everyone staring at you?"

"Good point." I grinned at him, and then bounced away. "See you later."

By the time I made it to the common lounge, everyone was buzzing about tonight.

It wasn't Lucian that had Caleb pacing the length of the room. Even Lea seemed wound up as she twisted a strand of hair around her fingers. None of us halfs cared much about Lucian personally, but as the Minister of Court he exerted a high level of control over the pures and the halfs. No one could figure out why a Minister would come to the Covenant during the summer, when the vast majority of students were absent.

I was still busy picturing Aiden as a pirate, sweeping me off my feet.

"Do you know anything?" asked Luke.

Before I could answer, Lea chimed in. "How would she know? Lucian barely claims her."

I looked at her blandly. "Was that supposed to hurt my feelings or something?"

She shrugged. "My stepmother visits me every Sunday. Why hasn't Lucian visited you?"

"How would you know?"

Her look was sly. "I know."

"You are so screwing one of the Guards, aren't you?" I frowned at her. "That explains how you always know so much."

Lea's eyes narrowed, much like a cat did when it spotted a mouse.

Snickering, I placed my bet on Clive, a younger Guard who'd been present the first day I'd arrived at the Covenant. He was good-looking, liked to check out the younger girls, and I'd seen him around the dorms a few times.

"Perhaps Lucian is coming to remove you from the Covenant." Lea studied her nails. "I always thought you'd fit in better with the slaves."

Casually, I leaned forward and grabbed one of the thick magazines. I chucked it at Lea's bent head. With half-blood reflexes, she snatched it before it made contact. "Thanks. I needed something to read." She thumbed through it.

As it neared seven, I headed back to my room to get ready. Folded on the coffee table was an olive green, Covenant-issued uniform. My eyes widened as I picked up the uniform and a small note fell out. I opened it with trembling fingers:

Had to guess your size.
See you tonight.

Smiling, I looked inside the pants and discovered they were my size. There was no stopping the wealth of heat spreading over me. What Aiden had done meant the world to me. Tonight I'd look like I actually belonged at the Covenant.

Instead of the black uniforms the trained Sentinels wore, the students donned green outfits of the same cut—reminiscent of army uniforms. And they had all the nifty pockets and hooks meant to carry weapons, which I really liked.

I took a quick shower, and after I put on the uniform I felt a rush. Years had passed since I'd worn this, and there were times when I didn't think I'd ever get to wear it again. Turning in front of the mirror, I had to say I looked good in dress greens.

Excited, I pulled my hair up in a ponytail and left to meet up with Caleb. Together, we headed over to the main campus and a funny surge of nostalgia coursed through me as we entered the largest academy building.

I'd avoided the academy section of the campus since I'd returned, mainly because that was where Marcus had his office. It also seemed unfair to subject myself to all the memories if he decided in a month or two to not let me stay.

Of course, Caleb thought things were going great and Marcus would allow me to stay, but I wasn't so sure. I hadn't even seen him since the day he'd stopped by the gym and I'd made an idiot out of myself. I felt confident that had made a lasting impression. Come to think of it, no wonder Aiden was so worried about what I would say to Lucian.

Shaking my head, I glanced around the crowd of people that filled the grandiose lobby of the school. It seemed like every Guard and Sentinel was in attendance, standing under the statues of the nine muses. The Olympian nine, daughters of Zeus and Mnemosyne, or whoever it was that he hooked up with. Who really knew? The god got around.

The Guards lined every corner and blocked every exit,

looking stony and fierce. The Sentinels stood in the middle, appearing vicious and battle ready.

Not surprising, my eyes found Aiden at once. He stood between Kain and Leon. In my opinion, those three were the most dangerous-looking out of all of them.

Aiden looked up then, his eyes meeting mine. He gave me a little nod, and even though he didn't say anything, his eyes spoke for him. That one glance held a measure of pride and fondness. Maybe he even thought I made the cadet uniform look good. I started to smile, but Caleb led me past them, to the left of the Sentinels where the students belonged. We managed to squeeze in next to Caleb's secret obsession—Olivia. How convenient.

She smiled. "I was wondering if you guys were going to make it."

Caleb said something incoherent, cheeks flushing a ruddy color. I turned away from secondhand embarrassment and I couldn't even look to see Olivia's response. Poor Caleb.

"Looking good, Alex," Jackson whispered.

It never failed. The one guy I didn't want to notice me always did. Glancing up at him, I forced a smile. "Thanks."

He looked as if he thought I truly did appreciate his compliment, but then Lea sauntered in, and I swear, she managed to get the uniform as tight as humanly possible. I looked down at my own and noted that my legs looked nowhere near as good as hers did. Bitch.

I watched as she prowled past the Guards and curved her lips at one of them before squeezing between Luke and Jackson. She murmured something, but my attention had already been caught by something more startling than how good her legs looked.

Half-blood servants stood behind the staff, still and quiet. Row after row of drab gray tunics and washed out white pants made them nearly indistinguishable from each other. Since I'd returned to the Covenant, I'd only caught a glimpse of a servant here and there. It was their job to be invisible, easily overlooked.

Or maybe it was ingrained in us—the free halfs—to ignore their presence. Gods, there were so many of them and they all looked the same: eyes glazed over, expressions vacant, and a crudely tattooed circle with a line through it scarred each of their foreheads. Marking them so visibly ensured that everyone knew their station in the caste system. It hit me all of a sudden.

I could really become one of them.

Swallowing down the sharp spike of panic, I faced the front just in time to see my uncle stalk down the center of the room and stand with his hands folded behind his back. There wasn't a strand of brown hair out of place on Marcus's head, and the dark suit he wore looked so out of place. Even the Instructors who were present were dressed down in comparison to him, wearing Covenant-issued uniforms.

The thick glass and marble front doors swung open as the Council Guards entered. I couldn't help the tiny gasp that escaped my lips. They were an impressive sight to behold, wearing white uniforms and brutal expressions. Then the members of the Council entered. Actually, only two of them floated in behind the Guards. I had no idea who the woman was, but I recognized the man immediately.

Dressed in white robes, Lucian hadn't changed one bit since the last time I'd seen him. His raven-colored hair still hung ridiculously long and his face looked as emotionless as a daimon's. Undeniably, he was a handsome man—like all pures were—but there was something about him that left a bad taste in my mouth.

His air of arrogance fit him like a second skin. As he approached Marcus, his lips twisted into a plastic-looking smile. The two exchanged their greetings. Marcus even bowed slightly. Thank the gods, they didn't expect us to do any of that nonsense. If so, someone would have to force me to my knees with a drop kick.

Lucian was a Minister, but he was no god. He wasn't even royalty. He was just a pure with a lot of power. Oh, and self importance. Couldn't forget that. I'd never understand what Mom had seen in him in the first place.

Money, power, and prestige?

I sighed. No one was perfect—not even her.

Several more Guards followed Lucian and the woman, who I realized was the other Minister. Each of the Guards was identical to the first set, except one. *He* was different, very different from every half-blood here.

The air sucked right out the room the moment *he* stepped into the building.

He was tall—maybe even as tall as Aiden, but I couldn't be sure. His blond hair was pulled back in a small ponytail, showing off his impossibly perfect features and golden complexion. He wore all black, like the Sentinels did. Under a different circumstance—one in which I didn't actually realize what he was—I would've said he was smokin' hot.

"Holy crap," Luke murmured.

A fine undercurrent of electricity permeated the room, coursing over my skin, then through me. I shuddered and took a step back, bumping into Caleb.

"The Apollyon," said someone behind me. Maybe Lea? I had no clue.

Holy crap, indeed.

The Apollyon trailed behind Lucian and Marcus, keeping at a safe enough distance. He wasn't crowding them but could react to any perceived threat. All of us stared, affected by his mere presence.

Unconsciously, I took another step back as the little group neared our side. I don't know what got into me, but suddenly, I wanted to be as far away as possible . . . and I needed to be right here more than anything else in this world. Well . . . maybe not anything, but pretty damn close.

I didn't want to look at him, but I couldn't look away. My stomach lurched when our gazes met. His eyes—they were the strangest color I'd ever seen, and as he got closer, I realized it wasn't my imagination. His eyes were the color of amber, nearly iridescent.

While he continued to stare at me, something happened. It started as a faint line inching down his arms, darkening to an inky black as it reached his fingers. Then, all at once, the thin line spread across the golden hue of his skin and shifted into a multitude of swirly designs. The tattoo shifted and changed, reaching under his shirt and stretching along his neck until the intricate drawings covered the right side of his face. The markings meant something. What, I had no idea. When he passed by us, my breath came out as a harsh gasp.

"You okay?" Caleb frowned down at me.

"Yeah." I smoothed my hair back with shaky hands. "He was . . ."

"Freaking hot." Elena turned to me, her eyes dancing with excitement. "Who knew the Apollyon would be that unbelievably gorgeous?"

Caleb made a face. "He's the Apollyon, Elena. You shouldn't talk about him that way."

My brows knit. "But those markings . . ."

Elena shot Caleb a dirty look. "What markings? And why does it matter if I say he's hot? I doubt he'd be offended."

"What do you mean?" I pushed past Caleb. "You didn't see those . . . tattoos? They appeared out of nowhere. They covered his entire body and his face!"

Elena's lips pursed as she stared at me. "I didn't see anything. Maybe I was just stuck on those lips."

"And that butt," interjected Lea.

"Those arms," added Elena.

"Are you guys being serious?" I glared at each of them. "You didn't see any sort of tattoo?"

They shook their heads.

The guys, with the exception of Luke, looked pretty disgusted with the commotion Elena and Lea were making. So was I. Exasperated, I whirled right into Aiden. "Whoa! Sorry."

He raised his eyebrows. "Don't roam off far." That was all he said.

Caleb pulled me to the side. "What's that all about?"

"Ah, Lucian wants to talk with me or something."

He cringed. "That's gotta be awkward."

"You ain't kidding." I momentarily forgot the Apollyon's tattoos.

Even if I'd wanted to, I didn't get to roam very far. Our little group made it out front and into the setting sun. Everyone appeared to be talking about the Apollyon. No one had expected him to be here or knew how long he'd been one of Lucian's Guards. Since Lucian had taken up residence on the main island, it seemed like someone should've known about the Apollyon's presence earlier. That question switched to a much more interesting one.

"The Apollyon's usually out there hunting daimons." Luke popped up on the railing. "Why would he be reassigned to guard Lucian?"

"Maybe something's going on." Caleb's eyes darted back to the building. "Like something big. Maybe Lucian's been threatened."

"By what?" I frowned, leaning against one of the columns. "He's always surrounded by a crap ton of Guards. Not a single daimon could get close to him."

"Who cares?" Lea sucked in her lower lip and sighed. "The Apollyon is here and he's hot. Do we need to worry with anything else?"

I scrunched up my face. "Wow. You'll make an excellent Sentinel one day."

She sneered at me. "At least *I will* be a Sentinel one day."

My eyes narrowed on Lea, but Olivia's nonstop fidgeting drew my anger. "What is your deal?"

Olivia glanced up, her chocolate-colored eyes huge. "Sorry. It's just . . . I'm so antsy now." She shuddered and wrapped her arms around her waist. "I don't know how you guys can say he's hot. Don't get me wrong, but he's the Apollyon. All that power is frightening."

"All that power is sexy." Lea leaned back, closed her eyes and sighed. "Can you imagine what he's like in—?"

The doors behind us swung open and Aiden motioned me forward. On the steps below, someone made a low noise. I ignored it and left my little group of enemies and friends behind.

"So soon?" I asked once I was inside.

He nodded. "I guess they want to get this over with."

"Oh." I followed Aiden up the stairs. "Hey. Thanks for the uniform." The memory of him getting it for me made me smile.

He glanced over his shoulder. "It wasn't a problem. You look good in it."

My eyebrows shot up as my heart did a cartwheel.

Flushing, Aiden looked away. "I mean . . . it's good to see you in the uniform."

My smile grew to epic proportions. I caught up to him and took the stairs alongside his tall frame. "So . . . the Apollyon ?"

Aiden stiffened. "I had no idea he was going to be with Lucian. His reassignment must've happened not too long ago."

"Why?"

He nudged my arm. "There are some things I cannot disclose, Alex."

Normally I would've balked at that, but the way he said it, in such a teasing manner, made me feel airy and funny. "That's not fair."

Aiden didn't respond to that, and we went up a couple of floors in silence. "Did you . . . feel anything when Seth came in?"

"Seth?"

"The Apollyon is named Seth."

"Oh. That's a boring name. He should be called something more interesting."

He gave a low laugh. "What should he be called then?"

I thought about that for a moment. "I don't know. Something Greek-sounding, or at least, something kickass."

"What would you have named him?"

"I don't know. Something wicked cool, at least. Maybe Apollo. Get it? Apollo. Apollyon."

Aiden laughed. "Anyway, did you feel anything?"

"Yeah . . . it was strange. Almost like an electrical current or something."

He nodded, still smiling. "It's the aether in him. It's very powerful."

We neared the top floor and I wiped a hand over my forehead. Stairs were a bitch. "Why do you ask?"

"You looked a little out of it. It's a bit unsettling the first time you're near him. I would've warned you if I'd realized he was going to be here."

"That wasn't the most disturbing thing."

"Hmm?"

I inhaled deeply. "The . . . tattoos were more unsettling." I watched him closely. His reaction would tell me if I was crazy or something.

Aiden came to a complete stop. "What?"

Oh man, I was crazy.

He came down a step. "What tattoos, Alex?"

I swallowed hard at the sharp look in his eyes. "I thought I saw some markings on him. They weren't there at first, but then they were. I . . . guess I'm seeing things."

Aiden exhaled slowly, his eyes on my face. He reached out, smoothing back a strand of my hair that had come loose. His hand lingered against my cheek, and in that moment, there was nothing more important than him touching me. In a daze, I stared up at him.

All too quickly, his hand dropped to his side and his eyes met mine. I could see there were several things he wanted to say, but for whatever reason, he couldn't. "We have to get going. Marcus is waiting. Alex, try to be as nice as you can be, okay?"

He started back up the stairs, and I hurried to catch up with him. "So, was I seeing things?"

Aiden sent the Guards at the end of the hall a meaningful glance. "I don't know. We'll talk about it later."

Frustrated, I followed him to Marcus's office. Lucian hadn't arrived yet and Marcus sat behind his big, old desk. He looked as he had in the lobby, but minus the suit jacket.

"Come. Have a seat." He motioned me forward.

I trudged across the office, relieved Aiden wasn't leaving me alone. He didn't take the seat next to me but remained along the wall in the same spot he'd stood the first time I'd found myself across from Marcus.

The whole scenario didn't bode well, but I didn't have a lot of time to dwell on it. Even with my back to the door, I knew when Lucian's group approached the office, but he wasn't causing the small hairs on my arms to stand up. The moment the Apollyon entered the room with my stepfather, all the oxygen evaporated.

Fighting my body's almost overpowering need to turn around, I clenched the arms of the chair. I didn't want to acknowledge Lucian, and I didn't want to look at the Apollyon.

Aiden cleared his throat, and my head snapped up. Marcus stared down at me with narrowed eyes. *Oh . . . crap.* My legs felt oddly numb as I forced myself to stand.

Out of the corner of my eye I saw Seth take up position alongside Aiden. He gave the pure-blood a curt nod, which Aiden returned. Because I didn't see those tattoos, I allowed myself to lift my head.

Instantly, our eyes met. His gaze wasn't a flattering one. He was checking me out, but not the way most guys did. Instead he studied me. As close as we were, I realized he was young. I hadn't expected that. With all that power and reputation, I'd expected someone older, but he had to be close to my age.

And he really was . . . beautiful. Well, as beautiful as a guy could be. But his beauty was cold and hard, like he'd been pieced together to look a certain way, but the gods had forgotten to give him a touch of humanity—of life.

I felt the other stares, and when I looked at Aiden, he wore a perplexed expression as he watched me and Seth. Marcus . . . well, he looked expectant, as if he were waiting for something to happen.

"Alexandria." He nodded toward Lucian.

I suppressed the impulse to groan loudly and lifted my hand, wriggling my fingers at the Minister of Council. "Hi."

Someone—either Aiden or Seth—sounded like they swallowed a laugh. But then the unreasonable happened. Lucian stepped forward and wrapped his arms around me. I froze, my arms stuck awkwardly at my sides as the smell of herbs and incense assaulted my senses.

"Oh, Alexandria, it is so good to see you. After all the years, and through all the fear and worry, you're standing here. The gods have answered our prayers." Lucian pulled back, but he kept his hands planted on my shoulders. His dark eyes scanned every inch of my face. "By the gods . . . you look so much like Rachelle."

I had no idea what to do. Of all the reactions I'd expected, this hadn't been a possibility. Whenever I'd been around Lucian in the past, he'd always looked at me with such cool disdain. This bizarre display of affection knocked me speechless.

"The moment Marcus notified me that you were found safe, I rejoiced. I told Marcus I had a place in my home for you." Lucian's eyes settled back on mine, and there was something I didn't trust in that warm gaze. "I would have come sooner, but I was attending to Council business, you see? But your old room . . . from when you stayed with us is still intact. I want you to come home, Alexandria. You do not need to stay here."

My mouth dropped open at that point and I wondered if he had been replaced by a nicer pure-blood in the last three years. "What?"

"I'm sure Alexandria is just overcome by her happiness," Marcus commented blandly.

There was that choked sound again, and I began to suspect that Seth was the culprit. Aiden was too well trained to slip up twice. I stared at Lucian. "I'm . . . just confused."

"Confused? I can imagine. After all that you have been through." Lucian released my shoulders, but then he grabbed my hand. I tried not to let my cringe show. "You're far too young to suffer as you have. The tag . . . it will never go away, will it, dear?"

My free hand went to my neck self-consciously. "No."

He nodded sympathetically, and then led me to the chairs. He let go of my hand, readjusting his robes as he took a seat. I slumped into the other chair.

"You must come home." Lucian's eyes bored into mine. "You don't need to struggle to catch up with the others. This life is no longer necessary for you. I've spoken with Marcus at great length. You can attend the Covenant in the fall as a student, but not one in training."

I couldn't have heard that right. Halfs didn't attend the Covenant as students. They trained or they went into servitude.

Marcus sat down slowly, his bright gaze fastened on me. "Alexandria, Lucian is offering you a chance for a very different life."

I couldn't stop it. The laugh started in my throat and bubbled out. "This . . . this is a joke, right?"

Lucian exchanged a look with Marcus. "No. This is no joke, Alexandria. I know we weren't always close when you were younger, but after all that has happened, I have seen where I have failed you as a father."

I laughed again, earning a disapproving glare from Marcus. "I'm sorry." I gasped as I pulled myself back under control. "This is just so not what I expected."

"You do not need to apologize, my daughter."

I choked. "You're not my father."

"Alexandria!" Marcus warned.

"What?" I looked at my uncle. "He's not."

"It is all right, Marcus," Lucian's voice filled with velvet-covered steel. "When Alexandria was younger, I wasn't much of anything to her. I let my own bitterness rule everything. But now, it all seems so very shallow." He turned to gaze at me. "If I had been a better father figure then maybe you would have called for help when your mother took you away."

I ran a hand over the side of my face, feeling like I'd stepped into a different world—a world where Lucian wasn't a giant douche, and where I still had someone who was technically family and actually cared for me.

"But that is in the past, my dear. I've come to take you back home." Lucian gave me a thin-lipped smile. "I've already spoken with Marcus, and we agree that—considering the circumstances—it would be for the best."

I snapped out of my haze of dumbness. "Wait. I'm catching up, aren't I?" I whirled around in my seat. "Aiden, I'm catching up, right? I'll be ready in the fall."

"Yes." He looked past me at Marcus. "Quicker than I would've thought possible, to be honest."

Thrilled that he hadn't thrown me under the bus, I turned back to my uncle. "I can do this. I have to be a Sentinel. I don't want anything else." My voice rasped with desperation. "I can't do anything else."

For the first time since I'd met Marcus, he actually looked pained, like he was about to say something he didn't want to. "Alexandria, it's not about the training. I'm aware of your progress."

"Then what is it?" I didn't care that I had witnesses to my panic. The walls were closing in, and I didn't even understand why.

"You will be taken care of," Lucian tried to look reassuring. "Alexandria, you can no longer be a Sentinel. Not with such a horrific conflict of interests."

"What?" I looked back and forth between my uncle and step-father. "There's no conflict of interests. More than anyone, I have a reason to be a Sentinel!"

Lucian frowned. "More than anyone, you have a reason *not* to be a Sentinel."

"Minister—" Aiden stepped forward, his eyes narrowing on Lucian.

"I know you've worked hard with her and I appreciate that, St. Delphi. But I cannot allow this." Lucian held up a hand. "What do you think will happen once she graduates? Once she leaves the island?"

"Uh, I'll hunt and kill daimons?"

Lucian turned to me. "Hunt and kill daimons?" His face turned paler than normal—which was saying something—as he turned to Marcus. "She doesn't know, does she?"

Marcus's eyes closed briefly. "No. We thought . . . it would be for the best."

Unease slid down my back. "Know what?"

"Irresponsible," hissed Lucian. He lowered his head, pinching the bridge of his nose.

I shot to my feet. "Know *what*?"

Marcus looked up, his face drawn and colorless. "There's no easy way to say this. Your mother is not dead."

11

Nothing existed but those words.

Marcus stood and edged around his desk. He stopped in front of me. The pained look had returned, but this time it was also mixed with sympathy.

The clicking of the wall clock and the gentle hum of the aquarium motors filled the room. No one spoke; no one pulled their eyes from me. I had no idea how long I stood there staring at him while I tried to piece together what he'd said. Nothing made sense to me at first. Hope and disbelief crashed together, then a horrifying realization as I understood the sympathetic look that had crossed his face. She was still alive, but . . .

"No . . ." I pushed away from the chair, trying to put distance between his words and me. "You're lying. I saw her. The daimon drained her, and I touched her. She was so . . . so cold."

"Alexandria, I'm sorry but—"

"No! It's impossible. She was dead!"

Aiden was at my side, placing a hand on my back. "Alex—"

I twisted out his grasp. His voice—*Oh, gods*—his voice said it all. And when I looked at him, saw the sorrow etched across his striking face, I knew.

"Alex, there was another daimon. You know that." Marcus's voice carried over the sound of rushing blood that filled my ears.

"Yes, but . . ." I remembered how freaked out I'd been. Sobbing and hysterical, I'd shaken her and begged her to wake up, but she hadn't moved.

And then I'd heard someone else outside.

Panicked, I'd barricaded myself into the room and grabbed the money. Things had been blurry then. I'd needed to run. It was what Mom had prepared me to do if something like that ever happened.

My heart stuttered and missed a beat. "She . . . she was still alive? Oh—Oh, my gods. I left her." I wanted to puke all over Marcus's polished shoes. "I left her! I could've helped her! I could've done something!"

"No." Aiden reached for me, but I backed away. "There was nothing you could do."

"The other daimon did it?" I glared at Marcus, demanding an answer.

He nodded. "We assume so."

I started to tremble. "No. Mom wouldn't become . . . it's impossible. You—you're all wrong."

"Alexandria, you know how it could have been done."

Marcus was right. The energy the daimon passed on was tainted. She would've been addicted from the first moment on. It was a cruel way to turn a pure-blood, robbing them of all free will.

I wanted to scream and cry, but I told myself I could handle this. The burning in my eyes told me I was a liar. I turned back to Marcus. "She's . . . a daimon?"

Something akin to pain flickered across his otherwise stoic face. "Yes."

I felt trapped in this room with virtual strangers. My eyes skittered across their faces. Lucian seemed bored with this, surprising considering his earlier outpouring of affection and support. Aiden looked like he was having a hard time keeping his expression blank. And Seth . . . well, he was watching me expectedly. Waiting for me to break down into hysterics, I assumed.

He might get that. I was one step away from a full-blown freak out.

Swallowing against the thick lump in my throat, I tried to slow the wild beating in my chest. "How do you know this?"

"She's my sister. I would know if she were dead."

"You could be wrong." My whisper held a tiny shard of hope. Dead was better than the alternative. There was no coming back once a pure turned into a daimon. No amount of power or begging—not even the gods could fix it.

Marcus shook his head. "She was spotted in Georgia. Right before we found you."

I could tell this hurt him—possibly as much as it hurt me. She'd been his sister after all. Marcus wasn't as emotionless as he made himself out to be.

Then the Apollyon spoke. "You said her mother was seen in Georgia. Was not Alexandria in Georgia when you found her?" His voice was oddly accented, almost musical in quality.

I slowly turned to him.

"Yes." Aiden's dark brows furrowed.

Seth appeared to consider that. "Does it not strike anyone as odd? Could it be her mother remembered her? Was actually following her?"

A strange look crossed Marcus's face. "We're aware of the possibility."

It didn't make sense. When pures were turned, they didn't care about things from their previous lives. Or, at least, that was what we believed. Then again, it wasn't like anyone took the time to question a daimon. They were killed on sight. No questions asked.

"You believe her mother is aware of her. Possibly even looking for her?" Seth asked.

"There's a chance, but we cannot be sure. It could have been a coincidence that she was in Georgia." Marcus's words rang false.

"A coincidence that she was in Georgia in addition to the two other daimons following her?" Aiden asked. Marcus's scowl deepened, but Aiden continued, "You know how I feel about this. We don't know how much of their previous lives daimons retain. There's a chance she's looking for Alex."

The room tilted, and I squeezed my eyes shut. Looking for me? Not as my mother, but as a daimon. For what? The possibilities startled me . . . sickened me.

"It is all the more reason to remove her from the Covenant, St. Delphi. Under my care, Alexandria will be protected by Council Guards and the Apollyon. If Rachelle is hunting her then she will be safest with me."

When I opened my eyes, I realized I was standing in the middle of the room. Each breath I took hurt. The need to give in to the tears was there, but I forced it down, all the way down. I lifted my chin and looked Marcus straight in the eye. "Do you know where she is now?"

Marcus raised his eyebrows as he turned to Lucian, who took a moment before he responded. "I have a dozen of my best Sentinels hunting for her."

I nodded. "And you all—all of you think that knowing that my mother . . . is a daimon will get in the way of me being an effective Sentinel?"

There was a pause. "Not all of us agree, but yes."

"I can't be the first person to face that."

"Of course not," said Marcus, "but you are young, Alexandria, and you . . ."

My breath got caught in my throat again. "I'm what?" Illogical? Distraught? Pissed off? Those were a few things I was feeling right now.

He shook his head. "Things are different for you, Alexandria."

"No. They're not." My voice rasped. "I'm a half-blood. My duty is to kill daimons no matter what. This won't affect me. My mom—she's dead to me."

Marcus stared at me. "Alexandria . . ."

"Will you force her from the Covenant, Minister?" Seth asked.

"*We* will not force her to leave." Marcus interjected, his eyes on me.

Lucian swung toward Marcus. "We agreed on this, Marcus." His strained voice was low. "She needs to be placed under my care."

I knew he was saying a hell of a lot more. I watched Marcus consider whatever that unspoken thing was.

"She can remain at the Covenant." Marcus kept his gaze steady. "Nothing will be jeopardized if she stays here. We can discuss more of this later, don't you agree?"

My eyes widened as I watched the Minister submit to Marcus. "Yes. We will discuss this in great detail."

Marcus nodded before turning to me. "The original deal still holds, Alexandria. You will have to prove to me you are ready to attend in the fall."

I let out the breath I'd been holding. "Is there anything else?"

"No." I turned to leave but Marcus stopped me. "Alexandria . . . I'm sorry for what has happened. Your mother . . . didn't deserve this. Neither do you."

A sincere apology, but it meant nothing to me. I was numb inside, and I wanted nothing more than to be away from all of them. I left the office with my head high, not seeing anyone. I even made it past the Guards, who'd probably heard everything.

"Alex, hold up."

Struggling to control the cyclone of emotions building in me, I whirled around. Aiden had followed me out. I warned him off with a shaky hand. "Don't."

He flinched back. "Alex, let me explain."

Over his shoulder, I saw we weren't alone. The Guards stood by the closed doors to Marcus's office—and so did the Apollyon. He watched us with casual indifference.

I forced my voice low. "You knew this entire time, didn't you? You knew what'd really happened to my mother."

The muscle in his jaw ticked. "Yes. I knew."

Hurt exploded in my chest. Part of me had hoped he hadn't known, that he hadn't kept this from me. I took a step forward. "We've spent every day together and never once did it cross your mind to tell me? Did you think I didn't have a right to know the truth?"

"Of course I thought you had the right, but it wasn't in your best interest. It still isn't. How can you focus on training—focus on preparing to kill daimons—when you know your mother's one of them?"

I opened my mouth, but nothing came out. How could I focus now?

"I'm sorry you had to find out this way, but I don't regret keeping it from you. We could've found her and disposed of the problem without you knowing any different. That was the plan."

"That was the plan? To kill her before I found out she was alive?" My voice grew louder with each word. "You preach to me about trusting you? How in the *hell* can I trust you now?"

Those words struck home. He took a step back, running a hand through his hair. "How does knowing what your mother is make you feel? What does it make you think?"

Hot tears burned in the back of my throat. I was going to break right here in front of him. I started backing up. "Please. Just leave me alone. Leave me alone."

This time, when I turned away, no one stopped me.

In a daze, I climbed into my bed. A sickening feeling settled over me. Part of me wanted to believe everyone was mistaken and Mom wasn't a daimon.

My stomach churned and I curled into myself. Mom was out there, somewhere, and she was killing people. From the moment she'd turned, the need to feed on aether would've consumed her. Nothing else would matter to her. Even if she did remember me it wouldn't be in the same way.

I scrambled from the bed, barely reaching the bathroom in

time. I fell to my knees, clutched the sides of the toilet, and gagged until my body shook. When I was done, I had no strength to stand.

My thoughts whirled into a heady mess. *My mother's a daimon.* Sentinels were out there, hunting her down. But I couldn't replace her warm smile with that of a daimon's. She was my mother.

I pushed away from the toilet and rested my head against my knees. At some point, there was a knock at the door, but I ignored the sound. There was no one I wanted to see, no one I wanted to talk to. I don't know how long I stayed there. It could've been minutes—or hours. I willed myself not to think and to just breathe. The breathing part was easy, but the not thinking part was impossible. Eventually, I crawled to my feet and stared at my reflection.

Mom stared back at me—all except the eyes, the only thing we didn't share. But now . . . now she'd have those gaping sockets and her mouth would be full of jagged teeth.

And if she did see me again, she wouldn't smile or hug me. She wouldn't brush my hair back like she used to. There would be no tears of happiness. She might not even know my name.

She would try to kill me.

And I would try to kill her.

12

By Sunday evening, I couldn't hide in my room anymore. Sick of thinking, sick of being alone, and sick of myself. Somewhere over the past day, my appetite had returned and I was starving.

I managed to make it over to the cafeteria before it closed its doors. Thankfully, it was empty and I was able to eat three slices of cold pizza in peace. The food settled in a dense ball in my stomach, but I managed to get a fourth slice down.

The thick silence of the cafeteria engulfed me. With nothing going on, the endless chatter of my thoughts picked up again. *Mom. Mom. Mom.* Since Friday night, she was all I could think about.

Was there something I could've done differently? Could I have prevented her from turning into a monster? If I hadn't panicked after the attack, maybe I could've fended off the other daimon. I could've saved my mother from such a horrific fate.

Guilt turned the food in my stomach sour. I pushed myself from the table and headed outside just as one of the servants entered to close up for the night. A few kids moved across the quad, but no one I knew very well.

I don't know why I ended up in the main training room. It was past eight, but they never locked these rooms, although the weapons were secured after training sessions. I stopped in front of one of the dummies used for knife practice and the occasional boxing match.

Restlessness itched through me as I stared at the lifelike figure. Tiny nicks and grooves marked the neck, chest, and abdomen. They were the areas where halfs were trained to strike: the solar plexus, heart, neck, and stomach.

I ran my fingers over the indentations. Covenant-issued blades were wickedly sharp, designed to cut through the daimon's skin quickly and do maximum damage.

Eyeing the strike zones marked in red—places to hit or kick if I had to engage a daimon in hand-to-hand combat—I pulled my hair up into a messy twist. Aiden had allowed me to practice with the dummies a few times, probably because he'd gotten tired of me kicking him.

The first punch I threw knocked the dummy back an inch, maybe two. Blah. The second and third blows jarred it back a couple of more inches, but still did nothing for me. The swirling blur of emotions pressed up within me, demanding I cave into it. *Give in. Take Lucian up on his offer. Never risk facing Mom. Let someone else deal.*

I stepped back, resting my hands on my thighs.

My mother was a daimon. As a half-blood I was obligated to kill her. As her daughter I was obligated to . . . what? That answer had eluded me all weekend. What was I supposed to do?

Kill her. Run from her. Save her somehow.

A frustrated shriek escaped me as I swung my leg around and connected with the center of the dummy. It swung back a foot or two, and when it came rushing back at me, I attacked—swinging, punching, and kicking. My anger and disbelief grew with each explosion.

This wasn't fair. None of this was.

Sweat poured off me, dampening my shirt until it clung to my skin and stray hairs stuck to the back of my neck. I couldn't stop. The violence poured out of me, becoming a physical thing. I could taste the anger in the back of my throat—thick like bile and heavy. I tuned into it. I became it.

The rage flowed through me and into my movements until my kicks and jabs became so precise that, if the dummy had been a real person, she'd be dead. Only then was I satisfied. I stumbled back, wiping my hand over my forehead and turned around.

Aiden stood in the doorway.

He came forward, stopping in the center of the room and taking the same position he normally did during our training sessions. He wore jeans, something I rarely saw him in.

Aiden didn't say anything as he watched me. I didn't know what he was thinking or why he was there. I didn't care. Fury still boiled within me. Somehow I imagined it was what being a daimon must feel like, like some kind of unseen force controlled my every move.

Out of control—I was out of control now. Without saying a word, I crossed the distance between us. A wary look flickered across his eyes.

There was no thought behind this, just overwhelming anger and raw hurt. I cocked back my arm and punched him right on the side of his jaw. Fierce pain exploded across my knuckles.

"Dammit!" I bent, bringing my hand back to my chest. I didn't think it would hurt that much. Even worse was the fact I'd barely made an impact on him.

He turned back to me as if I hadn't just punched him in the face and frowned. "Did that make you feel better? Change anything for you?"

I straightened. "No! I'd like to do it again."

"You wanna fight?" He stepped to the side, tipping his head down at me. "Then fight me."

He didn't have to ask me twice. I launched myself at him. He blocked the first jab, but my anger made me quicker than he'd realized. The broad side of my arm slipped past his blocks, cutting him across the chest. It didn't faze him—not one freaking bit. But the pleasure spiked inside me, propelling me forward. Burning with rage and another near feral emotion, I fought harder and better than I ever had in practice.

We circled each other, exchanging blows. Aiden didn't go all out on me, and it only pissed me off. I attacked harder, moving him backwards across the mats. His eyes flared a dangerous silver as he caught my fist inches from connecting with his nose. Bad form to aim above the chest, but screw it.

"That's enough." Aiden pushed me back.

But it wasn't enough. It would never be *enough*. I went to use one of the offensive moves he'd taught me days ago. Aiden moved so he caught me midflight, bringing me down on the mat. Once he had me down he rocked back on his heels.

"I know you're angry." He wasn't even out of breath. I, on the other hand, was gasping for air. "I know you're confused and hurt. What you're feeling is unimaginable."

My chest rose and fell rapidly. I started to sit up, but he pushed me down with one hand. "Yes, I'm angry!"

"You have every right to be."

"You should've told me!" The burning in my eyes increased. "Someone should've told me! If not Marcus, then you should have."

He turned his head away. "You're right."

His softly spoken words didn't ease me. I still heard how he'd said he didn't regret not telling me, that it was for the best. He lowered his hands to his thighs after a few moments.

Wrong move.

I reared off the mat, reaching for his silky hair. Total girl move, but somewhere along the way, I'd lost myself to the anger.

"Stop this!" He captured my wrists easily. Actually, it was embarrassing how quickly he subdued me. This time he pinned me to the mat. "Stop this, Alex," he said again, much lower.

I threw my head back, ready to plant my foot somewhere when our eyes met. I did stop then, with his face inches from mine. The atmosphere changed as one of the wild emotions swirling through me managed to break free and rear its head.

His lean torso and legs pressed against mine in a way that

made me think of other things—stuff that wasn't fighting or killing, but did involve sweating, lots of sweating. Breathing became difficult as we continued to stare at one another. His dark waves had fallen forward into his eyes. He wasn't moving, and I couldn't even if I'd wanted to. I didn't. Oh, gods, I didn't want to move *ever*. I saw the moment he recognized the change in me. Something shifted in those eyes of his and his lips parted.

This was just a harmless, stupid crush. Even as I lifted my head, bringing my lips mere inches from his, I kept telling myself that. I didn't want him. Not this badly—not more than anything I'd ever wanted in life.

I kissed him.

At first, it wasn't much of a kiss. My lips just brushed his, and when he didn't move away, I pushed harder. Aiden seemed too stunned to do much of anything for a few seconds. But then he released my wrists and his hands slid up my arms.

The kiss deepened, full of passion and anger. There was also frustration, so much frustration. Then Aiden pressed down, and I wasn't the one doing the kissing. His lips moved against mine, his fingers pressing into my skin. After only a few seconds he broke off the kiss and sprung away from me.

From several feet away, Aiden crouched on the balls of his feet. His heavy breathing filled the space between us. Eyes wide, they'd dilated until they were almost black.

I sat up and scooted back. What I'd done made it through the thick haze clouding my thoughts. Not only had I punched a pure-blood in the face, I'd also kissed him. Oh . . . *oh, man*. My cheeks flushed; my entire body flushed.

Aiden stood slowly. "It's all right." His voice rasped. "These things happen . . . when you're feeling a lot of stress."

These things happened? I didn't think so. "I . . . can't believe I did that."

"It's just stress." He remained at a safe distance. "It's okay, Alex."

I jumped to my feet. "I think I should go now."

He started forward then, but stopped short, wary of coming any closer. "Alex . . . it's all right."

"Yeah, damn stress thing, huh? Whoa. Okay. Everything is totally okay." I backed up, looking everywhere but at him. "I needed that—not the last thing! Or the thing when I punched you! But the things when I was . . . you know, working out my aggression . . . and stuff. All right . . . see you tomorrow." I fled from the room—from the entire building.

Outside in the thick humid night air, I smacked my forehead and groaned. "Oh, my gods." Somewhere behind me a door opened, so I started down the pathway again.

I really wasn't paying attention to where I was going. Shock and embarrassment didn't adequately describe what I was feeling. Mortification was too lame of a word. Maybe I *could* blame it on stress. I wanted to laugh, except I also wanted to cry.

Would I be able to live this one down? Gods, I couldn't believe I'd actually kissed him. Nor could I believe there'd been a moment where he'd kissed me back, that he'd pressed against me in a way that said he'd wanted it just as badly as I had. That had to have been a figment of my imagination.

I needed a new trainer. I needed a new trainer pronto. There was no way I could ever face him again without keeling over and dying. No way at all and—

Someone stepped in front of me. I moved to the side to avoid whoever it was, but the person blocked me. Pissed I couldn't sulk in privacy, I fired off without looking up. "Gods! Get the hell out of my—" The words died on my lips.

The Apollyon stood in front of me.

"Well, good evening to you." His lips curled in a casual smile.

"Um . . . sorry, I didn't see you." Or *feel* him, which was weird considering both times I'd felt him before actually laying eyes on him.

"Obviously. You were staring at the ground as if it had done something terrible to you."

"Yeah, I'm kinda having a bad weekend . . . that just won't die." I sidestepped him, but he moved in front of me again. "Excuse me." I used possibly my sweetest voice *ever*. He was, after all, the Apollyon.

"Could I just have a few minutes of your time?"

I looked around the empty courtyard, knowing I couldn't refuse him. "Sure, but I need to get back to my dorm soon."

"Then I will walk you there and we can talk."

I nodded, having no freaking clue what he could possibly want to talk to me about. I motioned him forward warily.

"I've been looking for you." He fell into step beside me. "Apparently, you've holed yourself up in your dorm, and your friends have advised me males are not allowed in the dorm. I'm no exception, which I find strange and very irritating. Silly little Covenant rules shouldn't apply to me."

I frowned, not sure what to be skeeved out about more: that he knew who my friends were or that he was looking for me. Both things were equally creepy to me. He could snap my neck like a twig. He was the Apollyon—someone *no one* wanted looking for them.

"So I've been waiting for you to reappear."

Now this *was* creepy. I felt his stare, but I kept my eyes trained ahead. "Why?"

Seth easily fell into step beside me. "I want to know what you are."

I froze and I had to look at him. He was pretty close, not touching. Frankly, he looked like he didn't want to. Caution played across his arresting features as he watched me. "I'm a half-blood."

He arched a blond brow. "Wow. I had no idea you were a half-blood, Alexandria. Color me shocked."

My eyes narrowed on him. "Call me Alex. So why did you ask?"

"Yes, I know. Everyone calls you by some boy's name." His upper lip curled and frustration filled his voice. "Anyway, you know that is not what I'm asking. I want to know what you are."

Pissing off the Apollyon probably wasn't the smartest thing to do, but my mood was somewhere between crappy and really crappy. I folded my arms across my chest. "I'm a girl. You're a boy. Does that clear things up for you?"

One corner of his mouth quirked. "Thank you for the gender lesson. I've always been confused when it comes to boy and girl parts, but once again, not what I'm asking." He stepped forward, tilting his head to the side. "Around May, Lucian requested my presence at Council. They found you around the same time. I find that strange."

My instincts screamed for me to take a step back, but I refused. "Okay?"

"I don't believe in coincidences. Lucian's order has to do with you. So it begs a very important question."

"Which is?

"What is so important about a little girl whose mother is a daimon?" He circled around me. I twisted, following his movement. "Why would Lucian want me here now, but not before? You were right in your dean's office. You would not be the first half or even pure to face down a loved one or a friend in battle. What makes you so special?"

Irritation twitched within me. "I have no clue. Why don't you go and ask him?"

Several short strands escaped the leather thong and fell around his face. "I doubt Lucian is being truthful."

"Lucian doesn't have to be truthful."

"You would know. He is your stepfather."

"Lucian is nothing to me. What you saw in that office was bizarre. He must've been high on power or meth."

"Then you would not be upset if I said he was a pompous ass?"

I bit back my laugh. "Nope."

His lips curved into a half smile. "I intend to figure out why I was pulled away from hunting to guard a girl—"

My brows rose. "You're not guarding me. You're guarding Lucian."

"Is that so? Why would Lucian need me as a Guard? He rarely leaves the Council and is always surrounded by several layers of protection. A fledging Guard could assist him. This is wasting my time."

He had a good point, but I didn't have any answers for him. I shrugged and started walking again, hoping he wouldn't follow, but he did.

"So I'll ask you again. What are you?"

The first two times he'd asked the question, it had just annoyed me, but the third time poked around inside my brain and pushed a memory loose. I thought of the night in the factory. What had the daimon said after he'd tagged me? I stopped, frowning as the words floated to the surface. *"What are you?"* My hand went to my neck, brushing over the ultra-smooth skin of the scar.

Seth's eyes narrowed on me. "What is it?"

I looked up. "You know, you aren't the first person to ask me that. A daimon asked me . . . after he tagged me."

Interest flickered over his face. "Maybe I just need to bite you to find out."

My hand dropped to my side and I cut him a look. He was joking, but it still weirded me out. "Good luck with that."

He smiled this time, flashing a row of perfect white teeth. His smile was nothing like Aiden's, but it was nice. "You don't seem afraid of me."

I took a deep breath. "Why should I be?"

Seth shrugged. "Everyone is afraid of me. Even Lucian— even daimons are afraid of me. You know, they can sense me, and even though they know I am Death to them, they come running right up to me. I'm like fine dining to them. They can't pass me up."

"Yeah . . . and I'm like fast food," I murmured, recalling what the daimon in Georgia had said.

"Maybe . . . or maybe not. Want to hear something strange?"

I glanced around, looking for an escape. My stomach did the icky twisty thing again. "Not really."

He tucked the loose strands of hair behind his ear. "I knew you were here. Not you, so to speak. But I knew someone— someone different. I felt it outside, before I entered the lobby. It was like a magnetic pull. I zeroed in on you immediately."

I felt off the longer I talked to him. "Oh?"

"That has never happened before." He unfolded his arms and reached for me. I jumped back. Annoyance pulled his lips down at the corners.

There were a multitude of reasons why I didn't want him to touch me. Alarmed that he was actually going to, I blurted out the first thing that came to mind. "I saw your tattoos."

Seth froze, one arm outstretched toward me. Surprise shone on his face before his arm fell and he suddenly looked wary. Hell, he no longer looked like he wanted to touch me—or be in the same zip code as me. He backed off this time.

I should've been happy, but it only increased the bundle of nerves forming in my belly. "I . . . have to go. It's late."

The sudden rush of air caused my head to jerk up. Seth moved fast, possibly faster than Aiden, and now he was back in my personal space. "Did you mean what you said in the dean's office? That your mother was dead to you? Do you really believe that?"

Caught off guard by the question, I didn't answer.

He leaned in closer, his voice low but still melodic. "If not, then you better hope you never face her, because she will kill you."

13

Practice was epically awkward the following day. Aiden spent the time pretending I hadn't physically and sexually assaulted him, which created a conflicting set of emotions in me. Part of me was glad he didn't bring it up. And the other part . . . well, that part felt stung. Although it totally made no sense, I wanted him to acknowledge what'd passed between us.

But I did bring the anger to practice. I fought better and blocked more than I ever had. Aiden praised my technique in a truly professional manner, which irked me. When we rolled up the mats at the end of practice, I felt all kinds of confrontational.

"I ran into Seth . . . last night." The words "last night" probably carried a lot more weight than anything else I said. Aiden stiffened, but didn't respond. "He wants to know why Lucian ordered him to Council."

Aiden straightened, brushing his hands across his thighs. "He shouldn't question his orders."

I arched a brow. "He thinks it has something to do with me."

He looked at me then, face impressively blank.

"Does it?"

No answer.

"Does it have something to do with what happened to my mom?" My hands curled into fists at his continued silence. "You said last night I had every right to know what happened to my mother. So I think I have every right to know what the hell is going on. Or are you going to lie to me again?"

That got a response. "I never lied to you before, Alex. I omitted the truth."

I rolled my eyes. "Yeah, that's not lying."

Irritation flared across his features. "Do you think I liked knowing what happened to your mother? Enjoyed seeing how hurt you were when you found out?"

"That's not the point."

"The point is I'm here to train you. To get you ready to attend classes in the fall."

"And nothing else, huh?" The hurt that sprang forth fueled my anger. "Not even the common courtesy of telling me what's going on when you so obviously know what's happening?"

Uncertainty darkened his expression. He shook his head and ran a hand through his hair. The dark waves tumbled back to his forehead like they always did. "I don't know why the Minister ordered Seth to the Council. I'm just a Sentinel, Alex. I'm not privy to the inner workings of the Council, but . . ." He took a deep breath. "I don't entirely trust your stepfather. His display in Marcus's office was . . . abnormal."

Out of all the things I expected him to say, I was shocked he would admit that. It diffused some—not all—of my anger. "What do you think he's up to?"

"It's all I know, Alex. If I was you . . . I'd be careful around Seth. Apollyons can be unstable at times, dangerous. They've been known to lose their tempers, and if he's angry about his relocation . . ."

I nodded, but I wasn't really concerned with that. Aiden left without saying much of anything else. Disappointed, I left the training room and ran into Caleb outside.

The two of us stared at each other.

"So . . . I'm assuming you've heard?" I tried to sound nonchalant.

Caleb nodded, his sky blue eyes sorrowful. "Alex, I'm sorry. It's not right—not fair."

"It's not," I whispered.

Knowing how I was with these kinds of things, he left it alone after that. We didn't bring it up again, and for the rest of the night it was like things were normal. Mom wasn't a daimon, and she wasn't out there draining pures. It was easier to go on, pretending that everything was normal. It worked for a while.

A couple of days later, I got my wish for a new trainer. Well . . . almost. When I opened up the double doors to the main training room Aiden wasn't alone. Kain stood beside him, looking like he clearly remembered our last training session.

My steps slowed as my eyes bounced between the two. "Hey . . . ?"

The look on Aiden's face was unreadable—a common expression since I'd kissed him. "Kain is going to be helping us train three days a week."

"Oh," I felt torn between being excited about learning whatever Kain could show me and disappointed someone else was encroaching on *my* time with Aiden.

I really did have a lot to learn from Kain. He wasn't as fast as Aiden, but I'd come to anticipate the moves Aiden used. With Kain, it was all new. By the end of practice, I felt a little better about the changeup in our training, but there was still a nagging worry Kain's reappearance had something to do with the kiss.

Kain wasn't the only one who kept popping back up. Over the following week, Seth lingered around campus, showing up in the rec room, the cafeteria, and the training room. It made avoiding him—which had been my plan—impossible. Trying to hold my own against Kain with just Aiden watching was bad enough, but having the Apollyon in the mix totally sucked.

Thankfully, today was Kain's off day. He'd accompanied some group of pures on a weekend getaway. I felt bad for him. Yesterday, he'd spent the majority of practice bitching about it. He was a born hunter, not a babysitter. I'd be pissed too if I'd gotten saddled with that assignment.

In practice, we'd finally moved beyond blocking techniques and were working on different types of takedowns. Even though I'd face-planted Aiden several times throughout the day, he was super-patient with me. Besides lying to me about my mom, the guy had to be a saint of some sort.

"You've done really well this week." He gave me a hesitant smile as we headed out.

I shook my head. "Kain kicked my ass in practice yesterday."

Aiden pushed the door open and held it for me. Normally, he left the doors wide open, but lately he'd taken to closing them. "Kain has field experience on you, but you were holding your own against him."

My lips curved upwards. As sad as it was, I lived for those moments when he complimented my improvement. "Thanks."

He nodded. "Do you think it helps to work with Kain?"

We stopped at the doors leading outside. I was kind of stunned he would even ask for my opinion. "Yeah . . . he has different tactics than you. I think it helps that you can see what I'm doing wrong and walk me through it."

"Good. It's what I hoped for."

"Really?" I blurted out. "I thought it was because—never mind."

Aiden's eyes narrowed. "Yes. Why else would I want Kain to help?"

Horrified and embarrassed that I had unwittingly gone *there*, I turned away. "Uh . . . forget I said anything."

"Alex." He said my name in that soft, infinitely patient way. Against my will, I turned back to him. "Bringing Kain in had nothing to do with that night."

I wanted to run and hide. I also wanted to find a muzzle for myself. "It doesn't?"

"No."

"About that night . . ." I took a deep breath. "I'm sorry about hitting you and . . . the other thing."

His eyes deepened, turning more silver than gray. "I accept your apology for hitting me."

I hadn't realized it until then, but we were standing close enough that our shoes touched. I don't know if he had moved, or if I had. "What about the other thing?"

Aiden smiled then, flashing those deep dimples. His arm brushed mine as he reached around and opened the door. "You don't have to apologize for the other thing."

I stumbled into the bright sunlight. "I don't?"

He shook his head, still smiling, and then simply left. Confused and a bit obsessed over what *that* could mean, I joined my friends for dinner and found our newest addition was once again at our table. My smile faded as I saw the open wonder splattered across Caleb's face—the look he got whenever he talked to Seth.

They didn't even look as I sat down at the table with them. Everyone appeared consumed by whatever Seth was telling them. I seemed to be the only one not impressed by him.

"How many kills have you made?" Caleb leaned forward.

Hadn't they already had this conversation? *Oh, yes. Yesterday.* I bit back a sigh of annoyance.

Seth reclined in the plastic chair, one leg propped against the edge of the table. "Over twenty."

"Wow." Elena sighed, a look of pure admiration glossing over her eyes.

I rolled my eyes and took a bite of the dry pot roast.

"You don't know the exact number?" Caleb's brows rose. "I'd keep a list with dates and times."

I found that morbid, but Seth grinned. "Twenty-five. Would have been twenty-six but the last bastard got away from me."

"Got away from the Apollyon?" I took a sip of my water. "Embarrassing."

Caleb's eyes grew to the size of saucers, and honestly, I don't know what'd provoked me to say it—probably that little piece of advice he'd given me the last time we'd talked privately. Seth seemed to take it in stride. He tipped his bottle of water toward me. "How many have you killed?"

"Two." I shoved a forkful of meat into my mouth.

"Not bad for an untrained girl."

I smiled brightly. "Nope."

Caleb shot me a warning look before turning back to Seth. "So . . . how does it feel to use the elements?"

"Amazing." Seth's eyes stayed on me. "I've never been tagged."

I stiffened, hand halfway to my mouth. Ouch.

"What does that feel like, Alex?"

I forced myself to chew the food slowly. "Oh . . . it felt wonderful."

He moved, leaning close enough I could feel his breath on my neck. My entire body locked up. "Nasty little scar you got there."

The fork fell from my fingers, splattering mashed potatoes across the table. I mustered my best "ice princess" look and met his gaze. "You're in my personal space, buddy."

A playful smile graced his lips. "So? What are you going to do about it? Throw your mashed potatoes at me? I'm consumed by terror."

Punch you in the face. That's what I wanted to say and do, but even I wasn't that stupid. Instead, I returned the smile. "Why are you here? Aren't you supposed to be doing important things, like *guarding* Lucian?"

Caleb and the rest of the kids didn't catch my dig, but he did. The smile slipped from his face and he stood. Turning to them, he nodded. "It was nice talking with you all." On his way out he brushed past Olivia. The poor girl looked like she wanted to spaz out.

"Oh, my gods, Alex. He's the Apollyon," hissed Elena.

I cleaned up my mess of mashed potatoes. "Yeah. So?"

She dropped a napkin over the bulk of the potatoes. "Uh . . . you could be a little more respectful towards him."

"I was being respectful. I just wasn't kissing his ass." I raised my brows as I looked at her.

"We weren't kissing his ass." She frowned, scooping up the mess.

I pursed my lips. "Not what it looked like to me."

"Whatever." Caleb exhaled with a whistle. "I mean, wow. He's killed twenty-five daimons. He can wield all four elements plus the fifth—the *fifth*, Alex. Yeah, I'll kiss his ass all day long."

I stifled my groan. "You should start a fan club. Elena can be your vice president."

He smirked. "Maybe I will."

Thankfully, we moved past talking about Seth once Olivia sat down at our table. Caleb was all too happy to see her, and my gaze bounced between the two of them.

"Have you guys heard?" Olivia's coffee-colored eyes widened.

I was half afraid to ask. "What?"

She cast a nervous glance at me. "There was a daimon attack in Lake Lure late last night. The Council just found out. They couldn't get ahold of the group of pures and their Guards."

The information wiped everything else from my thoughts. I wasn't thinking about my rude behavior toward Seth or what Aiden could've meant earlier. I wasn't even thinking about Mom.

Elena gasped. "What? Lake Lure is only four hours from here."

Lake Lure was a small community where several of the pures liked to get away. Just like the place in Gatlinburg where my mom used to take me, it should've been well-guarded. Safe. At least, that was what we'd been told.

"How's it possible?" I hated the way my voice squeaked out.

Olivia shook her head. "I don't know, but several of the Council Guards left with the group this weekend. They had at least two trained Sentinels."

My mouth went dry. No. It couldn't have been the same group—the group Kain had been bitching about babysitting.

"Anyone we know?" Caleb leaned in.

She glanced around, lowering her voice. "Mom couldn't say much more. She was leaving to go investigate . . . the scene, but she did say Kain and Herc were the two Sentinels. I haven't heard anything about what's happened to them, but . . ."

Daimons didn't leave halfs alive.

Silence fell across the table as we processed the news. I swallowed against the sudden tightness in my throat. Kain had been kicking my butt and joking around with me just yesterday. He's good and fast, but if he was missing, it meant he'd been taken for a later snack. Kain was a half, so he couldn't be turned into a daimon.

No. I shook my head. *He got away. They just haven't found him yet.*

Caleb pushed his plate away. Now I wished I hadn't eaten so much. The news was doing gross stuff to the food in my stomach, but all of us pretended we weren't *that* affected. We were in training. In a year or so, we'd be facing this stuff in person.

"What about the pures? Who were they?" Elena's voice trembled.

The look crossing her face filled me with unease. Suddenly, I understood it wasn't just Kain we'd lost.

"There were two families." Olivia swallowed hard. "Liza and Zeke Dikti, and their daughter Letha. The other family was . . . Lea's father and stepmother."

Silence.

None of us moved. I don't even think we breathed. Gods, I hated Lea. Really, I did, but I knew what this felt like. Or, at least, I used to. Finally, Caleb found the ability to speak. "Were Lea or her half sister with them?"

Olivia shook her head. "Dawn stayed at home and Lea is here—*was* here. On the way over, I saw Dawn. She'd come to get her."

"This is so terrible." Elena's face paled. "How old is Dawn?"

"She's around twenty-two." Caleb bit his lip.

"She's old enough to take her parent's seat, but who . . ." Olivia trailed off.

We all knew what she was thinking. Who would want to take a Council seat that way?

Back in my dorm, I found two letters stuck to my door. One was a folded piece of paper and the other was an envelope. The paper contained a scribbled message from Aiden calling off practice tomorrow due to unforeseen events. Obviously, he'd been called to investigate the attack.

I folded up the note and placed it on the table. The envelope was something else entirely; it was from my bipolar stepfather. I didn't read the card. However, there were several hundred dollar bills folded inside it. Those I kept. The card went in the trash bin.

After spending the rest of the evening thinking about what'd happened in Lake Lure, I had trouble sleeping and woke up way too early, filled with an itchy agitation.

By lunch, I'd found out Seth had also taken the four-hour drive with Aiden. More information drifted back to the Covenant as the day progressed. Olivia had been correct. All the pures who'd been in Lake Lure had been massacred. So had the half-blood servants. They'd searched the lake and the grounds, but only four of the Security team had been found. They'd been drained of all their aether. The other two, including Kain, had not been discovered.

Olivia, who'd become our main source of information, filled us in with what she knew. "Some of the dead suffered multiple tags. But the half-bloods they found . . . they were covered in daimon tags."

I read the same, sickening question in the pale faces around the table: *Why?* By birth, half-bloods had less aether in them.

Why would daimons repeatedly drain a half when they had pures who were full of aether?

I swallowed hard. "Do you know how they got past the Guards?"

She shook her head. "Not yet, but there were security cameras around the cabins, so they're hoping the video footage will reveal something."

Some of the halfs tried for some sort of normalcy as the day wore on, and none of us wanted to be alone. But the activity at the pool tables lacked the normal laughs and the game systems sat untouched in front of the televisions.

The sullen atmosphere started to get to me. I retreated to my dorm room after dinner. A few hours later, there was a soft knock on my door. I got up, expecting Caleb or Olivia.

Aiden stood there, and my heart did a weird flip I was beginning to hate.

I asked the stupidest question. "Are you okay?" Of course he wasn't. I mentally kicked myself as he stepped inside and closed the door.

"You've heard?"

No point in lying. "Yeah, I heard last night." I sat down on the edge of the couch.

"I just got back. News travels fast." I'd never seen him so exhausted or grave. His hair looked as if he'd run his hands through it many times, and now it went every which direction. The need to comfort him nearly overpowered me, but there was nothing I could do. He gestured at the couch. "May I?"

I nodded. "It was . . . really bad, wasn't it?"

He sat down, resting his hands on his knees. "It was pretty bad."

"How did they get to them?"

Aiden glanced up. "They caught one of the pures outside. Once the daimons got in—the attack surprised the Guards. There were three daimons . . . and the Sentinels—they fought hard."

I swallowed. Three daimons. The night in Georgia, I'd been surprised by how many were together. Aiden was thinking along the same lines. "The daimons are really starting to work in groups. They're showing a level of restraint in their attacks, an organization they never had before. Two of the half-bloods are missing."

"What do you think it means?"

He shook his head. "We're not sure, but we'll find out."

I had no doubt he would. "I'm . . . sorry you have to deal with this."

A hardness settled across him. He didn't move. "Alex . . . there's something I need to tell you."

"Okay." I wanted to believe the seriousness in his voice was due to all the heavy stuff he had been dealing with all day.

"There were surveillance cameras. They let us get a pretty good idea of what happened outside the house, but not inside." He took a deep breath and lifted his head. Our eyes met. "I came here first."

My chest tightened. "This . . . this is gonna be bad, isn't it?"

Aiden didn't mince words. "Yes."

The air caught in my lungs. "What . . . is it?"

He twisted his long body toward me. "I wanted to make sure you knew before . . . anyone else did. We can't stop people from finding out. There were a lot of people there."

"Okay?"

"Alex, there's no easy way to say this. We saw your mother on the surveillance cameras. She was one of the daimons who attacked them."

I stood, and then I sat right back down. My brain refused to process this. I shook my head as my thoughts went on repeat. *No. No. No. Not her—anyone but her.*

"Alex?"

It felt like I couldn't catch my breath. This was worse than seeing dullness in her eyes as she'd lain on the floor, worse than hearing she'd been turned. This . . . this was worse.

"Alex, I'm so sorry."

I swallowed hard. "Did . . . did she kill any of them?"

"There's no way to know unless we find either of the halfs alive, but I'd assume so. It's what a daimon does."

I blinked back hot tears. *Do not cry. Don't do it.* "Have . . . you seen Lea? Is she okay?"

Astonishment flickered across Aiden's face.

The laugh that came out of me was shaky and broken sounding. "Lea and I aren't friends, but I wouldn't . . ."

"You wouldn't want her to go through this. I know." He reached over and took my hand in his. His fingers felt remarkably warm, strong and grounding. "Alex, there's more to this."

I almost laughed again. "How could there be more?"

His hand tightened around mine. "It can't be a coincidence she is this close to the Covenant. It leaves no doubt she remembers you."

"Oh." I stopped there, unable to go any further. I turned away from Aiden, staring at our hands. Silence stretched out between us, and then he leaned over and wrapped his other arm around my shoulders. Every muscle in my body locked up. Even in a time like this, I could recognize the wrongness of this situation. Aiden shouldn't be offering me any sort of comfort. He probably shouldn't have even come to tell me. Halfs and pures didn't comfort one another.

But with Aiden I never felt like a half-blood and I never thought of him as a pure-blood.

Aiden murmured something I couldn't make out. It sounded like ancient Greek, the language of the gods. I don't know why, but the sound of his voice ripped through the barriers I was trying and failing at stitching together. I sunk forward, resting my head against his shoulder. I squeezed my eyes against the harsh stinging. My breath came out in short, shaky gasps. I don't know how long we stayed like that, his cheek against the top of my head, our fingers wrapped together.

"You show amazing strength," he murmured, stirring the hair around my ear.

I forced my eyes open. "Oh . . . I'm just saving all of this up for years of therapy later."

"You don't give yourself enough credit. What you've had to face? You're very strong." He pulled back, his hand brushing across my cheek so quickly I truly believed I'd imagined the touch. "Alex, I have to go check in with Marcus. He's waiting for me."

I nodded as he let go of my hand and stood. "Could . . . could there be a chance she didn't kill them?"

Aiden stopped by the door. "Alex, I don't know. It would be highly unlikely."

"Will . . . you let me know if they do find either of the halfs alive?" I knew it was pointless.

He nodded. "Yes. Alex . . . if you need anything, let me know." He pulled the door closed with a click behind him.

Alone, I slid to the floor and pressed my head against my knees. There could be a chance Mom hadn't killed anyone. She could be with the other daimons because she didn't know what else to do. Maybe she was confused. Maybe she was coming for me.

I shuddered, pressing further down. My heart hurt. It felt like it was shattering again—all over again. There was the smallest, tiniest chance she hadn't killed anyone. Even I knew how stupid it was to really hold onto that chance, but I did. Because what else did I have? Grandma Piperi's words became clearer to me—not just what she'd said, but what she hadn't.

For whatever reason, Mom had left the safety of the community to pull me away from the Covenant, setting all of this—this huge mess—into motion. During those three years, I'd never once called out for help, never stopped the insanity of living unprotected among mortals.

The countless times I'd done nothing flashed before me. In a way I was responsible for what'd happened to her. Worse yet, if she'd killed those innocent people, I was responsible for their deaths, as well.

My legs didn't shake when I stood. Certainty filled my mind—maybe it'd been made up the night I heard what'd really happened to her. There was a small chance she hadn't committed horrific crimes, but if . . . if the daimon who had been my mother had killed someone, then one way or another, I was going to kill her. She was my responsibility now—my problem.

14

I pretended nothing was wrong the next day in practice. It worked well until we took a break and Aiden asked how I was doing.

I kept my voice even. "I'm fine."

Then I beat the crap out of the dummy.

Toward the end of practice, a surge of energy shimmied down my back right before Seth showed up. He stood by the door, watching quietly. I had the sinking suspicion he was there for me. Groaning, I took my time rolling up the mats.

Aiden nodded in Seth's direction. "Is everything okay?"

"Who knows?" I scowled.

Aiden straightened, coming to his full height. "Has he been bothering you?"

A huge part of me wanted to say yes, but in reality, Seth hadn't really bothered me. And if he had, what could Aiden do about it? Aiden was a badass Sentinel warrior, but Seth was the Apollyon. Where Aiden controlled fire—*pretty awesome*—and he could fight, Seth controlled all four elements—*pretty scary*—and could wipe the floor with Aiden's face.

Aiden stared at Seth in a way that said he had no problem confronting Seth on my behalf. As stupid as it seemed, I felt a smile tug my lips.

So wrong.

Forcing the smile off my face, I skirted around Aiden. "I'll see you later, okay?"

He nodded, eyes still trained on Seth. *Okay then.* Grabbing my bottle of water off the floor, I trudged across the floor. I nodded at Seth as I passed him, half-hoping he was there to partake in the epic stare down with Aiden and nothing else, but he turned and immediately fell into step with me.

Seth's smile looked self-satisfied. "Your trainer does not like me."

"He's not *my* trainer. He's a Sentinel." I kept walking. "And I doubt he's even concerned with you."

Seth chuckled. "Your trainer, who is also a Sentinel, barely spoke to me while we were in Lake Lure. And when he did, I would say it was quite coldly. It hurt my feelings."

I doubted that. "He probably wasn't up to making friends considering what was going on."

"Considering your mother was a part of the attack party?" He raised a casual eyebrow. "He seemed abnormally affected when we reviewed the recordings and saw her."

His words were a well-placed smack in the face. Stopping, I faced him. "Seth, what do you want?"

He tipped his head back. A dark cloud rolled in overhead, casting a gray gloom over the quad. It was going to storm. "I wanted to see how you were doing. Is that so wrong?"

I thought about that. "Yes. You don't know me. Why would you care?"

He looked down, meeting my eyes. "Okay. I don't really care. But you're the reason I'm stuck in this hillbilly rathole, babysitting a self-righteous prick."

My eyes widened. The lilt of his voice made those words sound classy. It was almost funny. "You know, I really don't care about that right now." I stopped as several halfs passed us. They looked at us—looked at *me*. I did my best to ignore their stares.

"Of course you don't. Your mother murdered a classmate's family. My mind would be elsewhere, too."

"Gods!" I gaped. "Really, that was great." I walked off ahead.

Seth followed. "That wasn't . . . very nice of me. I've been told I'm painfully blunt. Perhaps I should work on that."

"Yeah, perhaps you should go do it right now." I tossed the words over my shoulder.

Undaunted, he caught up with me. "I asked Lucian, you know. I asked why I was here."

I gritted my teeth and kept walking. The ominous looking clouds continued to roll in. The sky looked like it was going to split open any moment.

"Do you know how he responded? He asked what I thought about you."

I was only half curious to hear his response.

"He was eager to hear what I had to say." Lightning shot across the sky, striking off the coast. A fraction of a second later, thunder silenced the conversation. I picked up my pace as the girls' dorm came into view. "Don't you want to know?"

"No."

Another flash of lightning lit the sky. This time it struck inland, somewhere beyond the marshes. It was close, too close. "You lie."

I spun around. My smartass response died before it fully took form. Inky marks broke the golden tone of his skin on every piece of exposed flesh. They twisted into designs, held for a few seconds, and then moved into another form. *What were they?*

I tore my eyes from his arms, but the tattoos stretched across his otherwise flawless cheek, etching toward the corners of his eyes. An urge to touch them slammed into me.

"You see them again, don't you?"

There was no point in lying. "Yeah."

Anger and confusion flared deep in his eyes. Lightning shrieked across the sky. "That's impossible."

Thunder sounded so loud I flinched. It clicked into place. "The storm . . . you're doing it."

"It happens when I get moody. I'm pretty irritable right now."

Seth took a step forward, towering over me. "I wouldn't be so temperamental if I knew what was going on. I need to know how you can see the marks of the Apollyon."

I forced myself to meet his eyes. That was a mistake—a huge, stupid mistake.

Power surged, raw and intense. I felt it crawl over my skin and slither down my spine.

And at once, my head emptied of everything except the need to find the source of the crazy power. *I need to get away as fast as possible.* Instead, in sort of a daze, I stepped forward. It had to be what he was. The energy coursing through him had this kind of pulling effect, one that gripped pures, halfs . . . even daimons.

I was feeling those effects now. The wildness that lingered in me reared its head and urged me forward. It urged me to touch him, because I was pretty sure whatever was happening would somehow be exposed the moment our skin touched.

Seth didn't move as I gazed up at him. He looked as if he was working to put together a puzzle and I was one of the pieces. The lazy smile faded and his lips parted. He inhaled sharply and reached out with one hand.

It took a lot, but I ducked away. Seth didn't follow. As soon as I stepped inside the dorm, the sky ripped open, and another flash of blinding light cut across the dark sky. Somewhere, not too far away, it struck once again.

Later that night, I confided in Caleb as we stood together in the back of the packed rec room. The rain had driven everyone inside and our privacy wasn't guaranteed for long.

"Do you remember what Grandma Piperi said?"

His brows rose. "Not really. She said a lot of crazy stuff. Why?"

I played with my hair, twirling it around my finger. "Sometimes I think she isn't so crazy."

"Wait. What? You're the person who said she was crazy."

"Well, that was before my mom turned all dark side and started killing people."

Caleb glanced around the room. "Alex."

No one was listening, although people looked over every once in a while and whispered. "It's true. What did Piperi say? 'You'll kill the ones you love?' I thought it sounded crazy, but that was before I knew Mom was a daimon. We're training to kill daimons. Seems pretty obvious, doesn't it?"

"Look. Alex, there is no way you'd ever be put in that situation."

"She's about four hours from here. Why do you think she ended up in North Carolina?"

"I don't know, but the Sentinels will get her before you . . ." He trailed off at the look on my face. "You won't have to deal with it. You're in the Covenant for the next year, Alex."

In other words, a Sentinel would kill her before I graduated, eliminating the chance of our paths ever crossing. I really didn't know what to think about that.

"Alex, are you doing okay?" He tipped his head, watching me closely. "I mean . . . really doing okay?"

I shrugged off his concern. "Aiden said they couldn't be sure Mom was actually a part of the attack. She was on the camera, but . . ."

"Alex." Understanding and sadness grew on his face. "She's a daimon, Alex. I know you want to think she's not. I understand that, but don't forget what she's become."

"I haven't!" Several kids by the pool table looked up. I lowered my voice. "Look. All I'm saying is there could be a chance, a small chance she is—"

"That she's what? Not a daimon?" He grabbed my arm, pulling me around one of the arcade games. "Alex, she was with the group of daimons who killed Lea's family."

I pulled my arm free. "Caleb, she came to North Carolina.

Why else would she come here if she didn't remember me, want to see me?"

"She could want to kill you, Alex. That's for starters. She's already killed."

"You don't know! No one does."

His chin came up. "What if she did?"

My anger faded into determination. "Then I'll find her and kill her myself. But I know Mom. She would fight what she has become."

Caleb ran a hand through his hair and clasped the back of his neck. "Alex, I think you . . . *oh*."

I frowned. "You think what?"

His expression took on the awed look he got whenever he saw Seth.

Twisting around confirmed my suspicions. Seth stalked through the doors, immediately surrounded by his groupies. "You know, you keep getting that look on your face whenever he comes around, people are gonna start to talk."

"Whatever."

I changed the subject. "By the way, what's up between you and Olivia? Did you talk to her about Myrtle?"

"No, I didn't. Nothing's up between me and her." Caleb faced me, his expression curious now. "What's up with you and Seth? Wait, let me rephrase that: What's up with you when it comes to Seth?"

I rolled my eyes. "I just don't . . . like him. And don't change the subject."

He made a face. "How can you not like him? He's the Apollyon. As half-bloods, we're obligated to like him. He's the only one who can control the elements."

"Whatever."

"Alex. Look at him." He tried to turn me around, but I held my ground. "Oh, wait. He's looking over here."

I pushed him back further. "He's not coming over here, is he?"

He grinned. "Yes—*No*. Wait. Elena cut him off."

"Oh, thank the gods."

Caleb's brows furrowed. "What's your deal?"

"He's weird and . . ."

He leaned closer. "And what? Come on. Tell me. You have to tell me. I'm your best friend. Tell me why you hate him." His eyes narrowed. "Is it because you're undeniably attracted to him?"

I giggled. "Gods. No. You'll think the real reason is even crazier."

"Try me."

So I told him about Seth's suspicions considering why he'd been ordered here and about the tattoos being real, but I left out that part about me wanting to touch him. That was too embarrassing for me to even speak out loud. He looked utterly mystified . . . and excited.

He practically bounced. "The tattoos are real? Only you can see them?"

"Apparently." I sighed, glancing over my shoulder. Elena stood awful close to Seth. "I have no idea what it all means, but Seth isn't too happy about it. The storm earlier? The rain? That was him."

"What? I've heard of some of the pures being able to control the weather, but I've never seen it." He sneaked a glimpse at him. "Wow. That's amazing."

"Would you get the awestruck look off your face for two seconds? It's creeping me out."

He chucked me in the arm. "Okay. I need to focus." It took visible effort for him not to look at Seth. It wasn't because Caleb was attracted to him. Honestly, Seth was just chock-full of aether. None of us could help it. "Why would Lucian's order have something to do with you?"

"Good question." Then it hit me. "Maybe Lucian fears I'm a risk. You know, because of Mom? Maybe he brought Seth here just in case I'd do something."

"Do what? Let her in here? Hold a welcoming party for your mom?" Disbelief filled his voice. "You wouldn't do that, and I don't even think Lucian would consider that."

I nodded, but my new idea carried a lot of weight. It would explain why Lucian didn't want me returning to the Covenant. At his house, I'd be under constant surveillance, but here I pretty much roamed around freely. The only flaw in that idea: did Lucian really think I'd do something that terrible?

"It's probably nothing." Caleb chewed on his lower lip. "I mean, what could it be? It can't mean anything."

"It has to mean something. I have to figure it out."

Caleb stared at me. "Do you think . . . you're focusing on this because of . . . everything that's happened?"

Well, of course I was, but that wasn't the point. "No."

"Maybe stress is making you read more into it."

"I'm not reading into anything," I snapped. He didn't look like he agreed. Exasperated with him and the conversation, I looked over the rec room. Elena still had Seth cornered, but that wasn't what drew my attention. Jackson was in the room.

He leaned against one of the pool tables beside Cody and another male half. His swarthy complexion seemed unusually pale and he looked like he hadn't slept recently. I couldn't blame him. While I didn't know the current status of his relationship with Lea, he had to be worried about her, upset over what'd happened to her parents.

My gaze shifted to Cody. For a second, our eyes met from across the room. I didn't expect a smile or anything, but his icy stare and disgusted look still cut through me. Confused, I watched as he bent down and said something to Jackson.

I took a shuddering breath. "I think they're talking about me."

"Who?" Caleb turned. "Oh. Jackson and Cody? You're just being paranoid."

"Do you think they . . . know?"

"About your mom?" He shook his head. "They know she's a daimon, but I don't think they know she was at Lake Lure."

"Aiden said people would find out." My voice tightened.

Caleb seemed to grow taller as he picked up on my fear. "No one will blame you. No one will hold it against you. They can't, because it has nothing to do with you."

I nodded, wanting to believe him. "Sure. I guess you're right."

Over the next week, the whispers increased. People stared. People talked. At first, no one had the guts to say anything to me directly, but the pures . . . well, they knew I couldn't touch them.

On the way back to the training rooms after lunch, I passed Cody in the courtyard. I kept my head down and barreled past him, but I heard his words anyway. "You shouldn't be here."

My head jerked up, but he was already halfway down the walkway. I headed back to training, his words replaying over and over again. I couldn't have misheard them.

Aiden gave me a puzzled look when I entered the training room. As training neared the end, I finally said something. "Do you think there's a chance . . . my mom didn't attack those people?"

He dropped the mat and faced me. "If she didn't then it would change what we know about daimons, wouldn't it?"

I nodded solemnly. Daimons needed to drain aether to survive. Mom would be no exception. "But they could . . . drain without killing, right?"

"They could, but daimons rarely see the point in not killing. Even turning a pure requires an amount of restraint most daimons don't have."

None of the pures had been turned in Lake Lure. The attacking daimons had shown no restraint.

"Alex?"

I looked up, not surprised to see that he was standing in front of me. Concern lined his face. I forced a smile. "Part of me hopes that she's still in there somehow. That she isn't all evil, and she's still Mom."

"I know." His voice was soft.

"That part in me, it's so lame, because I know—I *really* know she's bad and she needs to be stopped."

Aiden stepped forward, his eyes were so bright and so warm. I wanted to forget about everything and fall into those eyes. Carefully, he reached out and with those fingers, he tucked back the strand of hair that always ended up in my face. I shivered, unable to help it.

"There is nothing wrong with hope, Alex."

"But?"

"But you have to know when to let hope go." He brought the tips of his fingers across my cheek. His hand dropped and he stepped back, the connection broken. "Do you remember why you said you needed to be in the Covenant?"

The question knocked me off guard. "Yeah . . . I needed to fight daimons. I have to."

Aiden nodded. "And do you still need that? Even after knowing that your mother is one of them?"

I thought about that for a moment. "Yes. They're still out there, killing. They . . . have to be stopped. I still need that even though Mom's one of them."

A small smile played over his lips. "Then there is hope."

"Hope for what?"

He brushed past me, stopping only long enough to give me a knowing look. "Hope for you."

I watched him leave, confused by his words. Hope for me? Hope that the kids would forget my mother was a daimon who quite possibly had slaughtered a classmate's family?

Later that night, I felt the stares in the common lounge. Eventually, word did reach me. Some of them—pures and halfs—didn't think I could be trusted. Not with Mom so close and so deadly. It was stupid.

But it got worse. Now people questioned why we'd left three years ago, and why I'd never returned to the Covenant during that time. Rumors circulated. My favorite? Mom had become a daimon long before that terrible night in Miami. And some people believed it.

Days passed, and only a few halfs spoke to me. None of the pures did. Seth wasn't helping matters either, and damn, he made it impossible to steer clear of him. He was everywhere: in the courtyard after practice, eating dinner with Caleb and Luke. He even showed up randomly during practice, always watching quietly. It was annoying and creepy.

A certain *look* would cross Aiden's face whenever Seth stopped by. I liked to tell myself it was a mixture of dislike and protectiveness. Though today we made it through practice without Seth showing up, so I didn't get to further examine the look. What a shame. I watched as Aiden grabbed one of the dummies we'd been practicing with and dragged it toward the wall. The thing weighed a ton, but he moved it around like it weighed nothing.

"Need any help?" I offered anyway.

He shook his head and placed it against the wall. "Come over here."

"What's up?"

"You see this?" He pointed at the dummy's chest. There were several indentations in the flesh-like material. When I nodded, he ran his fingertips over them. "These are from your jabs today." His voice filled with pride, and it was better than any look he could give Seth. "That is how strong your hits have become. Remarkable."

I beamed. "Wow. I have the fingers of death."

He chuckled softly. "And this is from your kicks." He brushed his hands over the dummy's hip. Part of the material had been knocked in. And part of me was envious of the dummy. I wanted his fingers to touch me like that. "There are students your age who've gone through years of training and can't inflict that kind of damage."

"I'm the kung fu master. So what do you say? Am I ready to play with the grownup toys?"

Aiden glanced over at the wall, the one I badly wanted to touch. "Possibly."

The idea of training with the knives made me want to do a happy dance, but it also reminded me of what the knives were used for. "Can I ask you a personal question?"

He only looked a bit weary. "Yes."

"If... your parents had been turned, what would you have done?"

Aiden paused before he answered. "I would've hunted them down. Alex, they wouldn't have wanted that kind of life, to lose all their morals and ideals—to kill. They wouldn't have wanted that."

I swallowed, my eyes still trained on the wall. "But they... were your parents."

"They *were* my parents, but they wouldn't have been once they'd turned." Aiden stepped beside me, and I felt his eyes on me. "At some point we have to let go of the attachment. If it's not your... mother, it could be any other person you know or love. If that day comes, you'd have to face that they're not the same person they used to be."

I nodded absently. Aiden was technically right, but in the end, his parents hadn't been turned. They'd been killed, so he'd never really faced something like this.

He steered me away from the wall at that point. "You're stronger than you realize, Alex. Being a Sentinel is a way of life for you, not just a better option like it is for some of the others."

Once again, his words brought a wealth of warmth. "How do you know I'm so strong? I could be rocking back and forth in my room for all you know."

He gave me a weird look, but shook his head. "No. You're

always . . . so alive, even when you're going through something that would darken the souls of most." He stopped there, becoming aware of what he'd said. The hollows of his cheeks flushed. "Anyway, you're incredibly determined—to the point of stubbornness. You wouldn't stop until you succeeded. Alex, you know what's right and what's not. I'm not worried about you not being strong. I'm worried about you being *too* strong."

My heart sort of swelled. He . . . *cared* for me, and he'd hesitated before answering the question about his parents. Somehow, it made me feel better about my own conflicted emotions, and he did bring up a valid point. No matter who I faced out there, if they were daimons, it was my duty to kill them. It was why I was training now. In a way, I was actually training to kill her.

I took a deep breath. "You know . . . I hate when you're right."

He laughed as I made a face at him. "But you've been right when you don't even realize it."

"Huh?"

"When you said I didn't know how to have fun—the day of the solstice? You were right. After my parents were killed, I had to grow up real fast. Leon says my personality got left behind somewhere." He paused, chuckling softly. "I guess he was right, too."

"How would Leon know? He's like talking to a statue of Apollo. Anyway, you're funny—when you want to be. And nice, and smart, really smart. You have the best personality I've—"

"Okay." Laughing, he held up his hands. "I get it, and I do have fun. Training you is fun and definitely not boring."

I murmured something incoherent, because my chest, well, it was doing that fluttery thing again. Practice was over, and even though I wanted to stay with him, there were no other reasons for me to hang out. I headed for the doors.

"Alex?"

My stomach tightened. "Yeah?"

He stood a few feet away. "I think it would be a good idea . . . if you don't wear *that* to practice again."

Oh. I'd forgotten what I was wearing. It was a pair of questionable shorts Caleb had picked up for me. I hadn't even thought he'd noticed. Looking at Aiden now, I realized he *had* noticed. I fixed an overly innocent look on my face. "Do you find these shorts distracting?"

Aiden gave me one of his rare smiles. Every cell in my body warmed. I even forgot about the terrible thing I was training for. His smile had that kind of impact.

"It's not the shorts I find distracting." He brushed past me, stopping at the door. "In our next practice I may let you train with the daggers if we have time."

My distracting shorts and everything else were forgotten for the time being. "No way. You're being serious?"

He tried to look serious, but his grin looked a bit mischievous. "I think it wouldn't hurt, but only for a little bit. I think it will help . . . you get a feel on how to handle them."

I glanced back at the wall of weapons. I wasn't even allowed to touch them, and now he was going to let me actually practice with them. It was like graduating kindergarten. Hell, it was like Christmas Eve.

Without thinking, I closed the distance between us and hugged him. Aiden immediately stiffened, obviously caught off guard. It was just a simple hug, but the tension racked up several degrees. I suddenly wondered what it would feel like if I rested my head against his chest like I had when he'd come back from Lake Lure. Or if his arms came around me and he held me, but not out of comfort. Or if I kissed him again like I had that night . . . would he kiss me back?

"You're far too pretty to be dressed like that." His breath stirred my hair. "And you're entirely too excited to be working with knives."

I flushed, stepping back. *What?* Aiden thought I was pretty?

It took me several moments to work past that. "I'm bloodthirsty. What can I say?"

Aiden's eyes dropped, and I decided I needed to go to the store and find as many pairs of minuscule shorts as I could get my hands on.

15

Just before dawn, the funeral for those murdered at Lake Lure began and . . . well, it sucked in the way all funerals did. Following ancient Greek tradition, the funeral consisted of three parts. All of the bodies—the ones recovered—were laid out before the funeral began. I stayed in the back of the funeral home, refusing to go anywhere near the dead. I paid my respects from a healthy distance.

The three bodies of the Dikti family, Lea's father and step-mother, and the Guards were wrapped in linen and draped in gold. From there, the funeral procession began, and it was long. The bodies were lifted onto pyres and carried through the main street. All tourist activity had been cut off to Deity Island, and the streets were filled with pure-blood and half-blood mourners.

The students who remained at the Covenant stood out from the crowd. We were the ones dressed in black sundresses or party dresses. None of us really had anything appropriate to wear to a funeral. I had on a black tube dress and flip flops. They were the best I had.

I stayed close to Caleb and Olivia, and I only caught a quick glimpse of Lea and Dawn at the cemetery. The sisters shared the same coppery red hair and impossibly thin bodies, and even with puffy eyes, Dawn was absolutely stunning.

Hematoi didn't bury the dead. After burning the remains they erected massive marble effigy statues. The artist's render-ing of the one that would honor the Samos family depicted their images set on a pedestal carved with a Greek verse about immortality among the gods. The round pedestal already occupied the site.

The jewels and gold were removed from the bodies and placed on the pedestal. I really wanted to leave at that point, but it would've been the height of disrespect. I turned away as they lit the pyres, but I still heard the crackling as the fire ate away at their shrouded corpses. I shuddered, hating the finality of it, hating that these were quite possibly my mother's victims.

Slowly, the mourners broke apart. Some headed back home; others went to small receptions held in the homes of the families. I trailed behind Caleb and Olivia, going back to the Covenant, away from all the death and despair.

As we passed the pyres, my eyes found Aiden. He stood with Leon, a few feet away from Dawn and Lea. He looked up—almost as if he'd sensed me—and our eyes met. He made no other acknowledgement, but I could tell he approved of my presence. Yesterday, before the talk about hunting loved ones and the shorts incident when he'd said I was pretty, I'd mentioned I was unsure if I should come or not, considering Mom had been one of the daimons.

Aiden had looked at me with that serious frown. "You'd feel more guilty for not going and paying your respects. You deserve to do that. Just as much as anyone else, Alex."

He was right, of course. I hated funerals, but I would've felt bad if I hadn't come.

Now, he nodded slightly before turning to Dawn. He reached out and touched her arm. A lock of dark hair fell over his forehead as he bent his head, offering his condolences. I turned my attention to the large iron gates separating the town from the plot of meaningless statues. Seth stood there, dressed in his black uniform. There was no doubt he was watching us. I ignored him as we left the cemetery.

For the rest of the day, I tried to forget that we'd lost so many innocent people.

And that Mom had been responsible.

I didn't get to do anything with the daggers in the next practice. When I pitched a fit about this, Aiden watched on with amused patience.

"Come on." I pushed the mats off the floor. "How am I supposed to get caught up when I can't even touch a dagger?"

Aiden nudged me out of the way and took over mat duty. "I need to make sure you know how to defend yourself—"

"She hasn't practiced with Covenant blades at all?"

Seth leaned against the door frame, arms folded across his chest. He watched us with a lazy expression, but his eyes were extraordinarily bright.

Aiden straightened, barely bothering to look at him. "I would swear I shut and locked that door."

Seth smirked. "I unlocked and opened the door."

"How'd you do that?" I asked. "The door locks from the inside."

"Apollyon secrets. Can't give them away." He winked at me before turning those amber eyes on Aiden. "How can she be prepared to fight if she doesn't know how to wield the only weapon she will have against a daimon?"

Seth gained cool points in my book with that question. I looked at Aiden expectedly. The cold, distasteful expression *he* wore earned way more cool points.

"I was unaware that you had any say in her training." Aiden arched a coal black eyebrow.

"I don't." Seth pushed off the wall and sauntered across the training room. He plucked one of the daggers off the wall and faced us. "I'm sure I could convince Marcus or Lucian to let Alex have a few rounds with me. Would you like that, Alex?"

I felt Aiden stiffen beside me and I shook my head. "No. Not really."

A slow smile crept across Seth's face as he flipped the dagger in his hand. "Really, I'd let you play . . . with the grown-up toys." He stopped in front of me, offering the blade handle first. "Here. Take it."

My gaze fell to the shiny metal in his hand. The end had been sharpened to a brutal point. Like I was under a powerful compulsion, I reached for it.

Aiden's hand clamped down on Seth's, pulling the dagger and Seth's hand out of my reach. Startled, I looked up at Aiden. His furious silver eyes met and held Seth's. "She will train with the daggers when I decide so. Not you. Your presence here is not welcome."

Seth's eyes flicked to Aiden's hand. His smile didn't falter once. "Awfully controlling, aren't you? Since when do pures care so much about what a half-blood touches or doesn't touch?"

"Since when would an Apollyon concern himself with a half-blood girl? One would think he had better things to do."

"One would think a pure-blood would know better than to fall for—"

"Okay." I stepped between the two, cutting off only the gods knew what Seth was about to say. "Time to play nice, boys." Neither of them seemed to hear *or* see me. Sighing, I grabbed Aiden's arm. He looked at me then. "Practice is over, right?"

Reluctantly, he let go of Seth's wrist and backed off. Even he looked surprised by his response, but he watched Seth intently. "For now—yes."

Seth shrugged and flipped the blade over again, his gaze centered on me once more. "I actually don't have anything better to do than concern myself with a *half-blood girl.*"

There was something about the way he spoke that gave me the chills. Or it could have been the skill which he handled the blade with. "I think I'll pass."

After that, Aiden and I left the training room, neither of us speaking. I wasn't sure why Aiden had reacted as strongly as he did or why Seth felt the need to push Aiden like that. But by the time I met up with Caleb, I pushed it to the furthest corners of my brain to dwell on later.

Caleb decided we needed fun, and fun existed on the main island at Zarak's weekly movie night. He always got his hands on movies just released in the theater, and since none of us got to go to places like that very often, it was a big deal to watch whatever the mortal world currently obsessed over. I was surprised he was still holding it after the funerals yesterday, but I assumed everyone needed to let loose a bit, remind themselves they were still alive.

But as soon as we arrived at his house, I knew things weren't going to be fun. Everyone stopped talking when we walked down into the basement that'd been converted into a mini-theater. Pures and halfs alike stared at me, and the moment Caleb followed Olivia upstairs, people started whispering.

Pretending like I wasn't at all bothered, I sat down on one of the unoccupied love seats and focused on a spot on the wall. Pride kept me from fleeing the room. After a few minutes, Deacon broke free of the cluster of kids and joined me.

"How're you doing?"

I slid him a glance. "Great."

He offered me a drink out of his flask. I took it and swallowed a mouthful, watching him out of the corner of my eye. "Careful," he chuckled as he pried the flask out of my fingers.

The liquid scorched my throat and made my eyes burn. "Jeez, what is that stuff?"

Deacon shrugged. "It's my own special mix."

"Well . . . it's certainly special."

Someone from the other side of the room whispered something I couldn't make out, but Cody busted into laughter. Feeling paranoid, I tried to ignore him.

"They're talking about you."

Slowly, I looked at Deacon. "Thanks, buddy."

"Everyone is." He shrugged as he flipped the flask over in his hands. "Frankly, I don't care. Your mom's a daimon. So what? It's not like you can help it."

"It really doesn't bother you?" Of all people, I thought it should bother him.

"No. You're not responsible for what your mother did."

"Or didn't do." I bit my lip, staring at the floor. "No one knows if she did anything."

Deacon raised his eyebrows as he took a long drink. "You're right."

The group across from us erupted in snickers and sly looks. Zarak shook his head, turning his attention to the remote in his hand.

"I think I hate them," I muttered, wishing I hadn't decided to come here.

"They're just scared." He gave a pointed look at the knot of people across the room. "They all fear being turned. The daimons have never been this close, Alex. Four hours isn't that far away, and it could've been any of them. It could've been their deaths."

I shivered and yearned for another drink from Deacon's flask. It was really warming. "Why aren't you afraid?"

"We all got to die sometime, right?"

"That's dark."

"But my brother would never allow something like that to happen to me," he added. "He'd die first . . . and he'd never let that happen either. Speaking of my brother, how's he been treating my favorite half-blood?"

"Uh . . . good, really good."

Cody's loud voice rang out. "The only reason she's still here is because her stepfather is the Minister and her uncle is the dean."

All week I'd been ignoring the snide whispers and awful

stares, but this—this I couldn't ignore. There'd be no saving face if I did.

I leaned forward in my chair, resting my arms on my knees. "What's that supposed to mean?"

No one dared to speak as Cody lifted his head toward me. "The only reason you're still here is because of who you're related to. Any other half would've been thrown into servitude."

Taking a deep breath, I searched my memories for something calming. I came up empty. "Why would that happen, Cody?"

Deacon shifted away from me, flask in hand.

"You brought your mother back here. That's why. Those pures died because your mother's out there looking for you! If you weren't here, they'd still be alive."

"Crap." Zarak stood, clearing his chair from my path. Just in time, too. I flew across the room, stopping in front of Cody.

"You're going to regret saying that."

Cody's lip twisted into a smirk. He wasn't afraid of me. "Wow. Threatening a pure will get you kicked out the Covenant. Maybe that's what you want? Then you can be reunited with your mother."

My jaw hit the floor and my fist was about to hit his. Deacon intervened, wrapping one arm around my waist. He picked me up and set me in the opposite direction.

"Out." He didn't give me much of an option with his hand on my back, pushing me toward the glass doors.

Being outside didn't calm the rage in me. "I'm going to kill him!"

"No, you're not." Deacon shoved the flask in my hand. "Take a drink. It will help."

I unscrewed the lid and took a healthy swallow. The liquid scorched my insides and it only fueled my anger. I tried inching past Deacon, but for someone so slender and untrained, he proved a viable roadblock.

Damn him.

"I'm not letting you go in there. Your uncle may be the Minister, but if you beat up Cody, your ass is a goner."

He was right, but I smiled. "It'd be worth it."

"Would it be worth it?" He stepped to the side, blond curls falling into his eyes as he blocked me again. "How do you think Aiden would feel?"

The question hit me in the chest. "Huh?"

"If you get kicked out, what would my brother think?"

I unclenched my hands. "I . . . don't know."

Deacon tipped his flask at me. "He'd blame himself. Think he didn't train or counsel you well enough. Do you want that?"

My eyes narrowed. I didn't like his logical reasoning. "Just like he counsels you not to be drunk all the time? And yet you are. How do you think that makes him feel?"

He slowly lowered the flask. "Touché."

A few seconds later, backup arrived. "What the hell happened?" Caleb demanded.

"Some of your friends aren't playing nice." Deacon tipped his head back toward the door.

Caleb frowned as he walked to me. "Did one of them do something to you?" Anger flashed across his face when I told him what Cody had said. "Are you kidding me?"

I crossed my arms. "Do I look like I'm kidding?"

"No. Let's just head back to the other island. Those assholes in there don't understand."

"No one understands," I shot back, anger still flooding my system. "You can stay here with *your* friends, but I'm heading back. This was a terrible idea."

"Hey!" Caleb's eyebrows shot up. "They're not my friends. You are! And I do understand, Alex. I know you're going through a lot."

I whirled on Caleb. I knew I was being unreasonable, but I couldn't stop. "You *understand?* How in the hell could you possibly understand? Your mother doesn't want to be around you!

Your father is still alive! He isn't a daimon, Caleb. How in the hell can you understand?"

He held out his hands as if he could somehow physically stop my words. Pain flickered across his face. "Alex? Gods."

Deacon shoved the flask in his pocket, sighing. "Alex, try to calm down. You have an audience."

He was so right. People had come outside at some point, loitering on the sprawling deck, watching with anticipation. They'd wanted a fight earlier and had been denied it. I took a deep breath and tried to rein in my anger. I failed. "Every stupid person here thinks I'm the reason why those people died!"

Disbelief shone on Caleb's face. "That can't be true. Look. You're just stressed out. Let's go back—"

My restraint broke. Closing the distance between us, I wondered if I would hit my best friend. Quite possibly, but I never got to find out. Out of nowhere, Seth appeared at my side, dressed in black like he always was. Did he never take that uniform off?

His presence not only stunned me into immobility, it also had a quieting effect on everyone around us. He took one long, hard look at me and then spoke in that lyrical, accented voice of his. "That is enough."

I would've told anyone else to screw off, but this wasn't a normal situation, and Seth wasn't a normal person. We stared each other down. Clearly, he expected me to heed his warning or else.

With visible effort, I backed off. Caleb took a step toward me, but Deacon grabbed his arm. "Let her go."

And I went. I made it past several houses before Seth caught up to me. "You let a bunch of pures get you that upset?"

"You're such a stalker, Seth. How long were you standing there?"

"I am *not* a stalker, and I was standing there long enough to realize you have no self-control and you're unstable. I kind of like that about you—mainly because I find it entertaining. But you have to know that you are not responsible for what your mother did. Who cares what a bunch of spoiled pures think?"

"You don't know if my mom did anything!"

"Are you serious?" His eyes searched my face. He found what he was looking for. "You are! Now I can add stupid to my list of adjectives for describing you."

I wondered what the other adjectives were. "Whatever. Just leave me alone."

Seth cut me off. "She's a daimon. She kills—*kills* innocent people, Alex. That's what daimons do. There is no reason behind it. That's what she is doing, but it is not your fault."

I really wanted to kick or punch him, but neither of those things would be smart. See, I did have self-control and intelligence. I sidestepped him, but Seth wasn't having it. He reached out, his hand closing around my forearm. Flesh against flesh.

The world exploded.

A surge of electricity shot through my body. It was like the feeling I got whenever he was near, but a hundred times stronger. I couldn't speak, and the longer Seth held on, the more powerful the rush grew. What I was feeling was insane. What I was *seeing* was insane. Intense, bright blue light wrapped around his hand. It twisted like a cord, crackling and twining itself around my arm, his hand. Instinctively, I knew it was connecting us—binding us together.

Forever.

"No. No, this isn't possible!" Seth's body had gone rigid.

I really wished he'd let go of my arm, because his fingers dug into my skin and something . . . something else was happening. I felt *it* move inside me, twisting and wrapping itself through my core, and with each coil I knew it was linking us together.

Emotions and thoughts that weren't my own raced at me. They came in a blinding light, followed by vibrant colors spinning and shifting until I was able to comprehend and make sense of some of it.

This isn't possible.

This is going to get us both killed.

I gasped for air. Seth's thoughts slithered around mine and his emotions rolled and tumbled through the both of us. Abruptly, it all stopped as a door slammed shut in my mind. The colors receded, and finally, the blue cord shimmered into a faint glow before disappearing.

"Uh . . . your tattoos are back."

Seth blinked as he stared down at where his hand was still around my arm. "This . . . can't be happening."

"What . . . did happen? Cuz if you know, I'd really like to be filled in on this."

He looked up, his eyes glowed in the darkness. The bewildered look faded, replaced by anger. "We're going to die."

That wasn't what I wanted to hear. "I—*what*?"

Whatever he knew finally clicked into place for him. His lips thinned, and then he started walking, dragging me along behind him.

"Wait! Where are we going?"

"They knew! They knew this entire time. Now I understand why Lucian ordered me to Council when they found you."

My feet slipped in the sand as I stumbled to keep up with him. I lost a sandal in the process, then lost the other one a couple of steps later. Dammit, I liked those sandals. "Seth! You're going to have to slow down and tell me what's going on."

He shot me a dangerous look over his shoulder. "Your pretentious stepfather is going to tell us what is going on."

I didn't like to admit it, but I was scared, really freaking scared. *Apollyons can be unstable—dangerous even.* No joke. Seth picked up the pace, dragging me behind him. I slipped. My knee caught the hem of my cotton dress, ripping it. With an impatient groan, he hauled me to my feet and continued.

Lightning zipped through the sky as he continued to drag me across the island. It struck a docked boat only a few yards away. The light stunned me, but Seth ignored the mess his anger had created.

"Stop!" I dug my feet into the sand. "The boat's on fire! We have to do something!"

Seth whirled around, his eyes luminous. He yanked me against him. "It's of no concern to us."

Heavy breaths heaved within my chest. "Seth . . . you're scaring me."

His expression remained hard and fierce, but his grip around my arm loosened a bit. "It's not me you should be scared of. Come on."

He pulled me past the burning boat and up the silent coastline.

Seth turned when he spotted Lucian's house, taking the wide porch steps two at a time. Clearly, he didn't care if I could keep up with him or not. He let go then and started banging on the door like the police did on television.

Two fearsome-looking Guards opened the door. The first one spared me only a quick glance before fastening narrowed eyes on Seth.

Seth's chin came up. "We need to see Lucian now."

The Guard straightened. "The Minister has retired for the evening. You will have—"

A brutal burst of wind rushed from behind us. For a second, I couldn't see past the mess of hair blowing in my face, but when I did, my heart stopped. The near hurricane force gust hit the Guard in the chest, slamming him back and pinning him halfway up the wall of my stepfather's opulent foyer. The wind quieted, but the Guard remained up against the wall.

Seth stepped in through the door and looked at the other Guard. "Go get Lucian. Now."

The Guard peeled his eyes off his coworker and hurried off

to do Seth's bidding. I followed Seth in, my hands shaking so badly I held them together. "Seth? Seth, what are you doing? You need to stop. Like right now. You can't do this! Busting into Lucian's house—"

"Be quiet."

Retreating to the furthest corner of the foyer, I stared at the Guard. The air crackled with tension and power—the Apollyon kind of power. I pressed against the wall as it crawled over my skin and inched its way deep inside me.

A decent amount of commotion and movement at the top of the stairs drew my attention. Lucian came down the winding staircase, clad in pajama bottoms and a loose shirt. Seeing him like that made me giggle, but it came out kind of short and hysterical.

Lucian noted my semi-petrified position in the corner, and then glanced at the Guard suspended up against the wall. Finally, he gave Seth a strangely calm look. "What is this about?"

"I want to know how long you were going to continue this madness before the both of us were slaughtered in our sleep!"

My mouth dropped open.

Lucian's voice remained level and cool. "Let the Guard down and I will tell you everything."

Seth didn't look like he wanted to, but he dropped the Guard, and not very gently. The poor man crashed to the floor. "I want to know the truth."

Lucian nodded. "Why don't we move into the sitting room? Alexandria looks like she could really sit down."

Seth glanced over his shoulder with a frown, as if he'd forgotten about me. I must've looked pretty pitiful, because he nodded. I half debated making a run for it, but I doubted I'd get very far. Besides, beyond the fear, I was also curious as hell as to what was going on.

We went into a small room with glass walls. I practically collapsed in the white wicker chair. The Guards followed us, but

Lucian waved them off. "Please notify Dean Andros that Seth and Alexandria are here. He will understand." The Guards hesitated but Lucian assured them with a dismissive nod. When they left, he faced Seth. "Sit?"

"I prefer to stand."

"Um . . . there's a boat on fire outside." My voice sounded tight and too high. "Someone might want to check it out."

"It will be taken care of." Lucian sat in one of the chairs beside me. "Alexandria, I have not been entirely forthcoming with you."

A tiny scoff huffed out of me. "Really."

He leaned forward, resting his hands against his checkered pajama bottoms. "Three years ago, the oracle told your mother that, on your eighteenth birthday, you would become the Apollyon."

I laughed out loud. "That. Is. Ridiculous."

"Is it?" Seth turned to face me. He looked like he wanted to shake me.

"Um . . . yes!" My eyes widened. "There's only one of you guys . . ." My voice trailed off as I remembered what I'd read in the book Aiden had loaned me. All at once, I felt hot and cold.

"Before Rachelle left, she confided in Marcus. He didn't agree with her decisions, but she felt she needed to protect you."

"Protect me from what?" As soon as those words left my mouth, I already knew the answer. *Protect me from what'd happened to Solaris.* I shook my head. "No. This is just too crazy. The oracle didn't tell Mom that!"

"You are referencing the other part, the one where she said you will kill the ones you love? That is not the important part. What is important is you will become another Apollyon." He turned to Seth, smiling. "Having Seth here was the best way to discover if what the oracle had said was correct."

Seth paced the length of the sitting room. "It makes perfect sense. Why I . . . sensed you the first day. No wonder your mother left here. She probably thought she could somehow hide you among the mortals." He turned and eyed Lucian. "Why would you want to bring us together? You know what will happen."

"We do not know what will happen." Lucian returned his gaze. "There have not been two of you in over four hundred years. Things have changed since then. So have the gods."

My eyes bounced between them. "Guys ... I know what you're saying, but you're wrong. There's no way I'm *what* he is. There's no way."

"Then how do you explain what happened outside?" Seth glared at me.

Taking a deep breath, I ignored him. "It's not possible."

"What did happen?" Lucian sounded curious.

Lucian's eyes danced between us as Seth explained about the blue cord and how, for a few seconds, we'd heard each other's thoughts.

It was clear he wasn't surprised.

"It is really nothing to be concerned about. What you experienced was just a way of recognizing one another. This is the reason I assigned you here, Seth. We had to see if she was the other half. The possibility—it was too great an opportunity to pass up. I just didn't expect it to take this long for you two to come together."

"Is it worth the risk?" Seth frowned. "If the gods didn't know about her before, they will soon. You could have just let this be. Is her life nothing to you?"

My stepfather leaned forward, his eyes meeting Seth's. "Do you understand what this means? Not just for you, but our kind? Two of you will change everything, Seth. Yes. You're powerful now, but when she turns eighteen your power will become limitless."

That seemed to perk Seth's interest. "But the gods—they won't allow that to happen."

Lucian leaned back. "The gods ... have not spoken to us in ages, Seth."

"*What?*" Seth and I both shouted. That was some serious stuff right there.

Lucian flicked his wrist in a dismissive manner. "They have removed themselves, and the Council does not believe they will intervene on anything. Besides, if the gods are curious or concerned, they already know about Alexandria. If the oracle has seen it then the gods already know. They *have* to be aware of her."

I didn't believe Lucian. Not for one second. "They weren't aware of Solaris!"

Both of them looked at me. A line formed between Lucian's brows. "How do you know of Solaris?"

"I . . . I read about her. They killed both of the Apollyons."

Lucian shook his head. "You do not know the whole truth behind that. The other Apollyon attacked the Council and Solaris was obligated to stop him. She did not. That is why they were executed."

I frowned. The book hadn't said anything like that.

Seth finally sat. "What do you have to gain from this?"

Lucian's eyes went wide. "With you two, we can eliminate the daimons without risking so many lives. We could change the rules—the laws surrounding half-bloods, the marriage decrees, the Council. Why, anything could be possible."

I wanted to punch him in the gut. Lucian didn't care about halfs.

"What rules of the Council do you wish to see changed?" Seth watched Lucian's face.

"These are things best discussed later, Seth." He waved his hand at me, smiling that weird, icky smile again. "She's fated to be your other half."

Seth turned and gave me a long look. "Could be worse, I suppose."

Okay, that creeped me out. "What do you mean by *that*?"

"You two are like puzzle pieces. You fit together. Your power will feed his . . . and vice versa." Lucian smiled. "Really, it is amazing. You are his other half, Alexandria. You are fated to be with him. You belong to him."

It felt like something heavy sat on my chest. "Oh. *Oh*. No."

Seth frowned at me. "You don't have to sound so disgusted."

The other day I'd felt compelled to touch him, I'd thought it was just because of what he was, but could it be because of what *we* were? I shuddered. "Disgusted? It's . . . revolting! Do you hear yourselves?"

Seth sighed. "Now you're just being insulting."

I ignored that, ignored *him*. "I . . . don't belong to anyone."

Lucian met my stare, and I was struck by the intensity. "But you do."

"This is insane!"

"When she turns eighteen," Seth pursed his lips, "the power—her power shifts to me."

"Yes." Lucian nodded eagerly. "Once she goes through the palingenesis—the Awakening—at eighteen, all you have to do is touch her."

"Then . . ." He didn't need to say it. We all knew.

Seth would become a God Killer.

He turned to Lucian. "Who knows about this?"

"Marcus knows, as does Alexandria's mother."

My heart dropped.

Seth glanced at me, his expression unreadable. "It explains why she has come so close to the Covenant when most daimons wouldn't dare, but why? A half can't be turned."

"Why else would a daimon want to get their hands on an Apollyon? Even now, the aether in Alexandria could feed them for months." Lucian gestured at me. "What do you think will happen if her mother has her after she goes through the palingenesis?"

I couldn't believe what I was hearing. "You think she's here so I can be like some sort of meal plan for her?"

He glanced up. "Why else would she be here, Alexandria? It is why I was against you being in the Covenant, as was Marcus. It had nothing to do with the time you've lost or your previous behavior. There was a chance we could not stop Rachelle by the time you would graduate. The risk was too great that you would come face to face with her and falter in your duty. I cannot allow a daimon to get their hands on an Apollyon."

"But now it's different?" I asked.

"Yes." Lucian stood, placing his hands on my shoulders. "With her so close, we will be able to find her. You will never have to face her. This is a good thing, Alexandria."

"A good thing?" I gave a harsh laugh and shrugged off his hands. "This is all twisted and . . . sick."

Seth whipped his head in my direction. "Alex, you can't just ignore this. Ignore what you are. What *we* are—"

I threw my hand up between us. "Oh, don't even go there, buddy. We aren't anything! We will never be anything! Okay?"

He rolled his eyes, clearly bored with my protests.

I started backing out of the room. "I seriously don't want to hear about any of this again. I'm just going to pretend this conversation didn't take place."

"Alex. Stop." Seth stepped toward me.

I glared at him. "Don't follow me! I mean it, Seth. I don't care if you can throw me through the air. If you follow me, I'll jump off a freaking bridge and take you with me!"

"Let her go." Lucian gave an elegant wave of his hand. "She needs time to . . . come to grips with this."

Surprisingly, Seth listened. I left then, slamming the front door behind me. My thoughts bounced around my head in a chaotic mess on the way back to the island. I barely noticed the air was no longer thick with smoke. Someone had taken care of the boat fire. The Guards at the bridge looked bored when they waved me through.

Minutes later, I crossed the campus and the section of sandy beach separating the faculty and guest lodging from the rest of campus. Under no circumstance was I—or any student for that matter—allowed to wander around their housing, but I needed to talk to someone—I needed Aiden.

Aiden could make sense out of this. He would know what to do.

Since most of the little houses were empty for the summer, it was easy to figure out which one was his. Only one of the nearly identical cottages had a light on inside. I stopped in front of the door and hesitated. Coming here—not only would I get in trouble, but so would Aiden. I couldn't even begin to wonder what they'd do if I were discovered in a pure-blood's cabin at this time of night. But I needed him, and that was more important than consequences.

Aiden answered after a few seconds, taking seeing me standing at his door remarkably well. "What's wrong?"

It wasn't late, but he stood there dressed as if he'd been in bed. The low-slung pajama bottoms looked better on him than Lucian. So did the tank top. "I need to talk to you."

His gaze dropped the length of me. "Where are your shoes? Why are you covered in sand? Alex, talk to me now. What happened?"

I looked down dumbly—my sandals? They were lost somewhere on the main island, never to be seen again. Sighing, I pushed the tangled strands of hair back. "I know I shouldn't be here, but I didn't know who else to go to."

Aiden reached out and took hold of my arms in a gentle grasp. Without saying a word, he led me into his cottage.

16

As Aiden guided me to his couch and sat me down, he had this look about him. It was sort of dangerous and comforting at the same time. "Let me . . . get you a glass of water."

My gaze crawled over his living room. It wasn't much bigger than my room back in the dorm, and much like mine, it was devoid of anything decorative. There were no pictures, favorite paintings, or artwork cluttering the walls. Instead, books and comics lay scattered across the coffee table, lined the numerous bookshelves, and sat stacked on his small computer desk. No television. He was a reader—probably even read the comics in ancient Greek. For some reason, that made me smile.

Then I noticed the corner of the room, between the bookshelf and the desk. A guitar leaned against the wall, and several colorful guitar picks formed a line on one of the shelves—every color except black. I knew it—those hands were used for something graceful and artsy. I wondered if I could ever get him to play for me. I'd always had a thing for guys who played guitars.

"You play?" I tipped my chin toward the guitar.

"Occasionally." He handed me a glass of water, and I downed it before he sat beside me. "Thirsty?"

"Mmm." I wiped away a few drops off my lips. "Thanks. What's up with the picks?"

He glanced at the guitar. "I collect them. A weird habit of mine, I guess."

"You need a black one."

"I guess I do." Aiden took the glass and set it on the coffee table, frowning when he noticed the tremble in my hands. "Alex, what happened?"

My laugh hitched in my throat. "It's going to sound crazy." I stole a quick peek at him, and seeing the concern for me on his face was nearly my undoing.

"Alex . . . you can tell me. I won't judge you."

I kind of wondered what he'd thought happened.

His hand came out and wrapped around mine. "You trust me, right?"

I stared at our hands, those fingers. *You are fated to be with him.* Those words had a shattering effect on me. I pulled my hands free and stood. "Yes. I did. I do. This is just so crazy."

Aiden remained seated, but his eyes followed my erratic pacing. "Try starting at the beginning."

I nodded, smoothing my hands over my dress. I started with the party. The look on Aiden's face hardened when I told him what Cody had said and turned even more dangerous when I explained how Seth had killed someone's boat. I told him everything, even the skeevy part with Seth, and how we were "two halves" or whatever. Aiden was a remarkable listener. He didn't ask any questions, but I knew he caught everything I threw down.

"So, it can't be true, right? I mean, none of this is real." I returned to prowling the length of his living room. "Lucian said it was why Mom left. The oracle told her that I was the second Apollyon and that she was afraid that the gods would . . . kill me, I guess." My laugh sounded a little shrill.

Aiden ran a hand through his hair. "I suspected something strange when Lucian wanted to bring you back to his house. And when you said you'd seen Seth's markings . . . I can't believe I've been around someone so rare this entire time. When do you turn eighteen, Alex?"

I slid my hands down my sides nervously. "March fourth." Less than a year from now.

Aiden rubbed his chin. "When you spoke to the oracle, did she say anything like this?"

"No, she only said I would kill the ones I love. Nothing about this, but she said so much crazy stuff." I swallowed, hearing the blood rushing in my veins. "I mean, looking back, some of the things she said made sense, but I just didn't understand."

"How could you understand?" He came around the small wooden table. "Now we know why your mother would take such a risk in leaving the safety of the island. She wanted to protect you. The story of Solaris is truly tragic, but she stood against the Council and the gods. That's what sealed their fate. Not what was written about them in the books."

"Why would Solaris do that? Didn't she know what would happen?"

"Some say she fell in love with the First. When he stood against the Council, she defended him."

"That's so stupid." I rolled my eyes. "She basically committed suicide. That isn't love."

Aiden gave the briefest of smiles. "People do the damndest things when they're in love, Alex. Look at what your mother did. It's a different kind of love, but she left everything because she loved you."

"I never understood why she left." My voice sounded young and fragile. "Now I know. She really did leave to protect me." The knowledge sat like curdled milk in my stomach. "You know, I kinda hated her for pulling me away from here. I never understood why she would do something so risky and stupid, but she did it to protect me."

"It must bring you some sort of peace to know why, doesn't it?"

"Peace? I don't know. All I can think is if I wasn't some kind of giant freak, she'd still be alive."

My words caused a flicker of pain to cross his face. "You

can't blame yourself for this. I will *not* allow it, Alex. You've come too far for this."

I nodded, looking away. Aiden could believe whatever he wanted, but if I hadn't been the second coming of the Apollyon then none of this would've happened. "I hate this. I hate not having control."

"But you do have control, Alex. What you are gives you more control than anyone else."

"How so? According to Lucian, I'm Seth's own personal electrical outlet or something. Who knows? No one does."

"You're right. No one knows. When you turn eighteen—"

"I'll be a giant freak."

"That's not what I was going to say."

I raised my eyebrows and looked at him. "Okay. When I turn eighteen the gods are going to kill me in my sleep? That's what Seth said."

Anger turned his eyes dark gray. "The gods have to be aware of you. I know this doesn't make you feel better, but if they wanted to . . . get rid of you, they would have already. So when you turn eighteen, anything will be possible."

"You're acting like this is a good thing."

"It could be, Alex. With two of you—"

"You sound like Lucian!" I moved away from him. "Next you're going to be telling me I'm Seth's super-special other half and I belong to him, as if I'm some sort of object instead of a person!"

"I'm not saying that." He closed the distance, putting his hands on my shoulders. I shivered under the weight of his hands. "Do you remember what I said about fate?" I shook my head. I remembered how he'd found my shorts distracting. I had that wonderful subjective memory feature. "Only you have control over your future, Alex. Only you have control over what you want."

"You really think so?"

He nodded. "Yes."

I shook my head, doubtful that I could believe in anything at this point, and started to slip away, but Aiden's hands tightened around my shoulders. An instant later, he gathered me close to him. I hesitated, because being this close to him was possibly the sweetest kind of torture.

I needed to break away . . . move as far away as possible, but his arms circled my shoulders. Slowly, carefully, I rested my head against his chest. My hands fell to the curve of his back and I inhaled deeply. His scent, a mixture of the sea and soap, filled me. The steady beat of his heart under my cheek warmed and comforted me. It was just a hug, but gods, it meant so much. It meant *everything*.

"I don't want to be to this Apollyon thing." I closed my eyes. "I don't even like to be in the same country as Seth. I don't want any of this."

Aiden smoothed his hand down my back. "I know. It's overwhelming and scary, but you're not alone. We'll figure this out. Everything is going to be okay."

I pressed closer. Time seemed to slow down, allowing me a few moments of the simple pleasure of being in his arms, but then his fingers sifted through my hair, finding their way to my scalp, and from there, he guided my head back.

"You don't have anything to worry about, Alex. I'm not going to let anything happen to you."

Those forbidden words wrapped around my heart, forever etching into my soul. Our eyes met. Silence stretched between us as we stared at each other. His eyes shifted to fierce silver and his other arm slid to my waist, tightening. His fingers drifted from my hair and slowly traced the curve of my cheekbone. My pulse thrummed through me as his intense stare followed his fingertips. He moved them down my face and then over my parted lips.

We shouldn't be doing this. He was a pure-blood. Everything

could come to a crashing end for us if we were caught, but it didn't matter. Right now, being with him seemed worth whatever consequence could come from it. This was right, like it was meant to be. There was no logical explanation for it.

Then he leaned forward and rested his cheek against mine. Hot tingles spread through me as his lips moved against my ear. "You should tell me to stop."

I didn't say a word.

Aiden made a deep sound in his throat. His hand slid up my back, leaving a trail of fire in its wake, and his lips moved across my cheek, stopping to hover above mine. I forgot how to breathe, and most importantly, how to think.

He moved, ever so slightly, and his lips brushed across mine once, and then twice. It was such a soft, beautiful kiss, but when the kiss deepened, it wasn't a shy one. This was one of dangerously pent-up need, a desire that'd been denied far too long. The kiss felt fierce, demanding, and soul burning.

Aiden pulled me to him, pressing me right up against his body. And when he kissed me again, it left both of us breathless. Our hands tangled with each other's bodies as we made it back to his bedroom. My hands found their way under his shirt and over the taut skin of his sides. We separated long enough for me to get the shirt off, and gods, each hard ripple was as breathtaking as I'd imagined.

Easing me down on his bed, his hands glided from my face to my arms. Next his hand traveled over my stomach, then my hip, and under the hem of my dress. Somehow, the top of my dress ended up at my waist, and his mouth moved over my body. I melted into him, his kisses, and his touch. My fingers dug into the tight skin of his arms, and my insides were in tight coils. Every place our bodies touched, sparks flew.

Aiden pulled his lips away from mine, and I made a sound of protest, but then his mouth trailed across my throat and to the base of my neck. My skin burned and my thoughts were on fire.

His name was barely a whisper, but I felt his lips curve against my skin.

His gaze and fingers followed some unseen path as he rolled me on top. "You're so beautiful. So brave, so full of life." He guided my head down and dropped a sweet kiss against the scar on my neck. "You have no idea, do you? You have so much life in you, so much."

I tipped my head and he kissed the tip of my nose. "Really?"

"Yes." He brushed my hair back from my face. "Since the night I saw you in Georgia, you've been under my skin. You got *inside* me, became a part of me. I can't shake it. It's wrong." He shifted us, rolling me across the bed until he leaned above me. "*Agapi mou*, I can't . . ." He brought his lips down to mine once more.

There were no more words. Our kisses hardened, his lips and hands took on a purpose that could only mean one thing. I'd never gone this far with a guy before, but I knew I wanted to be with him. There was no doubt, only certainty. Everything in my world hinged on this moment.

Aiden lifted his head, staring down at me with *that* question in his eyes. "Do you trust me?"

I ran my fingers over his cheek, then his parted lips. "Yes."

He made a deep sound in his throat and caught my hand. Bringing it to his lips, he pressed a kiss against each fingertip, then my palm and then my lips.

And that was when someone knocked on the door.

We both froze against one another. His eyes, still cloudy with hunger, met mine. A second passed, and another. I thought he was going to ignore it. Gods, I wanted him to ignore it. Badly. Deeply. My life depended on it. But the knock came again, and this time a voice accompanied it.

"Aiden, open this door. Now."

Leon.

Crap. That was all I could think. We were so busted. I didn't know what to do. I just lay there, wide-eyed and naked. Totally freaking naked.

Never taking his eyes off me, Aiden slowly lifted himself and stood. Only when he bent to retrieve the shirt I'd tossed aside did he break eye contact. He left the bedroom without a sound and closed the door behind him.

I stayed there for a few moments, caught in disbelief. The mood was completely ruined—obviously, and I was still naked. Anyone could bust in here, and here I was, sprawled across the bed. *His* bed . . .

Freaked out more than I ever could've imagined, I jumped up and grabbed my dress. Throwing it on, I looked for a place to hide, but Leon's words froze me.

"I didn't mean to wake you, but I figured you'd want to know this immediately. They've found Kain. He's alive."

I listened, my stomach in my throat, as Aiden managed to convince Leon that he would meet him in the infirmary, while I absolutely refused to look at his bed. My head came up as Aiden opened the door. "I heard."

Aiden nodded, his gray eyes filled with inner conflict. "I'll let you know what he says."

I stepped forward. "I want to come. I have to hear what he says."

"Alex, it's past your curfew, and how would you know to be in the infirmary?"

Dammit. I hated it when he was right. "But I can sneak in there. The rooms are just separated with partition walls. I could stay behind them—"

"Alex." Loverboy was gone. Shoot. "You need to go back to your dorm. Now. I promise I'll tell you everything he says, okay?"

Seeing no way to win this argument, I nodded. We waited a couple of more minutes before we left his house. At the door, Aiden paused, his fingers curling at his side.

My brow furrowed. "What?"

Aiden's gaze settled on me, and the air left my lungs. Passion slammed into me, hard and hot. The look on his face—in his eyes—sent shivers through me. Without saying a word, he cupped my face and brought his lips to mine. The kiss took whatever air I had left in me. It was heady and deep, heart-stopping. I never wanted it to end, but it did. Aiden pulled back, his fingers slowly trailing away from my cheeks.

"Don't do anything stupid." His voice sounded thick. Then he disappeared into the darkness outside of his cottage.

I stumbled back to my dorm on rubbery knees, replaying what'd happened between us. Those kisses, his touch, and the way he'd looked at me were forever branded in my mind. Two seconds from losing my virginity.

Two freaking seconds.

But that last kiss—there was something in it, something that filled me with nervousness and heartache. Once inside my room, I paced back and forth. With learning that I'd become a second Apollyon on my birthday, what'd happened between Aiden and me, and Kain's unexpected reappearance, I was wired. I took a shower. I even straightened my room, but nothing could wear me out. Right now, Aiden and the other Sentinels were questioning Kain—getting the answers I needed. Was Mom a killer?

Hours went by as I waited for Aiden to come by with news, but he never did. I fell into a restless sleep and woke way too early. I had about an hour before training would begin, and there was no way I could wait any longer. The plan formed in my mind. I threw on my gym clothes and hurried outside.

The sun had just crested the horizon, but the humidity made the air murky. I avoided the Guards on patrol, skirting the sides of the buildings as I made my way to the infirmary. Cool air greeted me inside the narrow building. I moved through corridors lined with smaller offices and a couple of larger rooms equipped to handle medical emergencies. The pure-blood doctors lived on the main island and only staffed the infirmary during the school year. This early on a summer morning, only a few nurses would be in the building.

I already had excuses ready if I ran into one of those nurses. I had killer cramps. I'd broken my toe. I'd even say I needed a pregnancy test if it meant I could get to where they had Kain, but I didn't need any of my excuses. The medical compound was tomb-silent as I prowled down the dimly lit hallway. After checking several of the smaller rooms, I stumbled into a ward used to accommodate several patients at once. Instinct led me past the empty gurneys and beyond the pea green curtain.

I froze, the papery thin fabric fluttering behind me.

Kain sat in the middle of the bed, dressed in loose jogging pants and nothing more. Dull locks of hair hid most of his downturned face, but his chest . . . Swallowing down the sudden rise of bile, I could only stare.

His chest, incredibly pale, was covered with crescent-shaped tags and thin slices that looked like they'd been made by one of our Covenant-issued daggers. There wasn't much space on him that wasn't marked.

He lifted his head. His blue eyes stood out against a corpse-like pallor. I inched closer, feeling something in my chest tighten. He looked so bad, and when he smiled at me, he looked worse. His skin was so washed-out that his lips looked blood red. A tiny bit of guilt flashed inside me. Maybe I could've waited to question him, but in typical Alex fashion, I jumped in.

"Kain? Are you okay?"

"I . . . think so."

"I wanted . . . to ask you some questions if . . . it's okay with you?"

"You want to ask about your mother?" He looked down at his hands.

Relief crashed through me. I wouldn't have to explain myself. I stepped closer. "Yes."

He was quiet as he continued staring down at his hands. He was holding something, but I couldn't see what it was. "I told the others I didn't remember anything."

I wanted to sit down and cry. Kain had been my only hope. "You don't?"

"That's what I told them."

An odd sound came from behind the green curtain on the other side of Kain's bed, like cloth dragging across a smooth floor. My brows knitted as I looked past him.

"Is . . . is someone back there?"

The only answer was a low gurgling. Dread came out of nowhere, inching down my spine, demanding that I flee this room now. I pushed past the bed and threw back the curtain. My lips parted in silent scream.

Three pure-blood nurses lay sprawled on the bloody floor. One still clung to life. An angry red line ripped across her throat as she pulled herself across the small distance. I reached for her, but with one last bubble of a noise, she was gone. Rooted to the spot, I couldn't think or breathe.

Throats slashed. All dead.

"Lexie."

No one but Mom called me that—no one. I turned around, my hand fluttering to my mouth. Kain remained on the opposite side of the bed, staring down into his hands.

"I think the nickname Lexie is far better than Alex, but what do I know?" He laughed, and it sounded cold, humorless. Dead. "I didn't know anything until now."

I bolted.

Kain moved surprisingly fast for someone who'd been tortured for weeks. He was in front of me before I made it to the door, Covenant dagger in hand.

My eyes froze on the dagger. "Why?"

"Why?" His voice mimicked mine. "Don't you get it? No. Of course you don't. I didn't get it either. They tried it on the Guards first, but they drained them too fast. They died."

Something was so, so wrong with him. The torture could have done it; all those tags could've driven him crazy. But it didn't really matter why he'd gone insane, because he was most definitely a lunatic—and I was cornered.

"By the time they got to be me, they'd learned from their mistakes. Gotta drain our kind slowly." He glanced down at the dagger. "But we aren't like them. We don't change like them."

I backed up, swallowing down the fear. My training vanished. I knew how to deal with a daimon, but a friend driven crazy was a different story.

"I was hungry, so hungry. There's nothing like it. I had to."

Horrifying realization set in. I took another step back just as he launched himself at me. He was so fast, faster than he'd ever been. Before I could even fully register the swing, his fist connected with my face. I flew back, crashing into one of those little tables. It happened so quickly I couldn't break my fall. I landed in a messy heap, dazed and tasting blood in my mouth.

Kain was on me immediately, yanking me to my feet and flinging me across the room. I hit the edge of the bed hard, and then the floor. Scrambling to my feet, I ignored the pain and faced the one thing that could not be.

Beyond reason or explanation, I had no doubt that Kain was no longer a half-blood. Only one thing moved as quickly as he did. Impossible as it was, he was a daimon.

17

Besides being abnormally pale, Kain looked like . . . Kain. It explained how none of the other half-bloods had sensed it in him. Nothing about him gave off a warning that something was horribly wrong. Well . . . except the pile of dead bodies behind the curtain.

I reached for what looked like a heart monitor machine, hurling it at his head. Not surprisingly, he knocked it aside.

He laughed that sick laugh again. "Can't you do better than that? Remember our training sessions? How easily I got the best of you?"

I ignored that painful reminder, figuring it was best to keep him talking until I had a better option. "How is this possible? You're a half-blood."

He nodded, switching the blade to his other hand. "Weren't you paying attention? I already told you. They drain our kind slowly, and gods, did it hurt like hell. I wanted to die a thousand times, but I didn't. And now? I'm better than I ever was. Faster. Stronger. You can't fight me. None of you can." He lifted the dagger and wiggled it back and forth. "The feeding part is messy, but it works."

I glanced over his shoulder. There was a small chance I could make it to the doorway. I was still fast and not badly hurt. "That . . . has to suck."

He shrugged, seeming like the old Kain—so much so it stole my breath. "You get used to it when you're hungry."

That was reassuring. I inched to my left.

"I saw your mother."

Every instinct in me screamed not to listen to him. "Did you . . . talk to her?"

"She was frenzied, killing and taking great pleasure in it, too. She was the one who turned me." He licked his lips. "She's coming for you, did you know that?"

"Where is she?" I didn't expect him to answer, but he did.

"You leave the safety of the Covenant and you'll find her . . . or she'll find you. But that's not going to happen."

"Oh?" I whispered, but I already knew. I wasn't stupid. Mom wasn't going to get a chance at my aether, because Kain was going to cut me and drain me.

"You know the one thing that sucks about being a daimon? I'm always so damn hungry. But you? I'm certain you'll feel like nothing else. It's a good thing you came to me. Trusted me." His blue eyes dropped to my neck—to where my frantic pulse beat. "She'll keep killing 'til she finds you or 'til you're dead. And you are going to die."

That was my cue to make my move. I pushed with all my strength, but it was no use. Kain blocked my only route of escape. With no other option but to fight him, I squared off, weaponless and out-skilled.

His too-red lips quirked. "Do you really want to try that?"

I forced as much boldness in my voice as possible. "Do you?"

This time, when he grabbed for me, I kicked out and caught the hand holding the dagger. It flew from his grasp, clattering against the floor. Before I could celebrate the small victory, his meaty fist lashed out, and it appeared he remembered how poor my blocking skills were. The punch got me in the stomach, doubling me over.

A rush of air stirred my hair, giving me only a second to straighten myself. I was a goner—no doubt about it. But as I lifted my head, it wasn't Kain standing in front of me.

It was Aiden.

He didn't say anything to Kain. Somehow, he just *knew* as he forced me backwards, away from the daimon half-blood. Kain turned his attention on Aiden. He let out a howl, eerily similar to the one the daimon had made in Georgia. They circled one another, and with Kain weaponless, Aiden had the upper hand. They exchanged vicious blows—no longer partners, but enemies to the core. Then Aiden made his move. He thrust the titanium dagger deep into Kain's stomach.

The impossible happened—Kain didn't fall.

Aiden stepped back, revealing Kain's startled face. He looked down at the gaping wound and started to laugh. It should've been a kill shot, but as cold understanding set in, I realized we had more to learn about daimon half-bloods.

They were immune to titanium.

Aiden kicked out at Kain, who blocked and whirled to deliver a kick of his own. A medical machine crashed against the wall. I gaped at them, frozen in place. I couldn't just stand here. I went for the dagger on the floor.

"Get back!" Aiden yelled as my fingers wrapped around the cool titanium.

I looked up, seeing the reinforcements—and the Apollyon.

"Move back!" Seth's voice thundered through the chaos.

Aiden jumped forward, pushing me against the wall and shielding me with his body. My hands fell to his chest. I turned my head as Seth stepped in front of the Sentinels, one arm stretched out in front of him.

Seconds later, something I could only describe as a lightning bolt erupted from his hand. The flash of blue light—so intense and brilliant—obscured everything in the room. *Akasha*—the fifth and final element: only the gods and the Apollyon could harness it.

"Don't look," Aiden whispered.

I pressed my face into his chest as the air filled with the crackling sound of the most powerful element known to the Hematoi.

Kain's horrific screams rose above it as *akasha* crashed into him. I shuddered, pushing further into Aiden. The screams—I would never forget those screams.

Aiden's hold tightened around me until the agonized screeching stopped and Kain's body thumped to the floor. Aiden pulled back then, the tips of his fingers brushed over my split and swollen lip. For the briefest second, his eyes latched onto mine. In one look, there was so much. Pain. Relief. Fury.

Everyone rushed into the room at once. In the chaos, Aiden quickly checked me over before handing me off to Seth. "Get her out of here."

Seth pulled me past the Sentinels as Aiden turned his attention to the crumpled body. In the hallway, we passed Marcus and several more Guards. He spared us a brief glance. Seth led me down the hallway, silent until he shoved me into another room at the end.

He closed the door behind him and then slowly approached me. "Are you all right?"

I backed up until I pressed against the wall furthest from him, breathing heavily.

"Alex?" His eyes narrowed.

In a matter of hours, everything had changed. Our world— *my world*—was no longer the same. It was too much. Mom, the crazy stuff with Seth, last night with Aiden, and now this? I cracked wide open. Sliding down the wall, I sat with my knees pressed against my chest. I laughed.

"Alex, get up." His voice carried that musical lilt, but it sounded strained. "This is a lot, I know this. But you have to pull yourself together. They are going to come in here—soon. They will want answers. Last night, Kain was normal—as normal as Kain could be. Now he was a daimon. They're going to want to know what happened."

Kain had been a daimon then, but no one knew that. No one

could have known last night. I stared at Seth blankly. What did he want me to say? That I was fine?

He tried again, crouching down in front of me. "Alex, you can't let them see you like this. Do you understand me? You cannot let the other Sentinels or your uncle see you like this."

Did it matter? The rules had changed. Seth couldn't be everywhere. We would go out there and die. Worse yet, we could be turned. I could be turned. Just like Mom. That thought brought forth a flicker of sanity. If I lost it, what good would I be? What about Mom? Who would fix this—fix what she'd become?

Seth glanced back over his shoulder at the door. "Alex, you're starting to worry me. Insult me . . . or something."

A weak smile stretched my lips. "You're a bigger freak than I could've ever possibly imagined."

He laughed, and my ears must've been fooling me, because he sounded relieved. "You're just as big as a freak as I am. What do you have to say about that?"

I cringed, my fingers tightening around my knees. "I hate you."

"You can't hate me, Alex. You don't even know me."

"It doesn't matter. I hate what you mean to me. I hate not having control. I hate that everyone has lied to me." On a roll now, I straightened my legs. "And I hate what *this* means. The Sentinels will die out there, one after another. I hate that I still think of my mother . . . as my *mother*."

Seth leaned forward and grasped my chin. The shock of his touch wasn't as shattering as before, but the bizarre transfer of energy still shimmied through me. "Then take the hate and do something about it, Alex. Use the hate. Don't sit here like there is no hope for them—for us."

For us? Did he mean for our kind or for him and me?

"You saw what I can do. You will be able to do that. Together, we can stop them. Without you, we cannot. And damn it, I need you to be strong. What good are you if you end up a damn servant because you cannot deal?"

Well . . . I guess that answered my question. I smacked his hand away. "Get out of my face."

He leaned in closer. "What exactly are you going to do about it?"

I shot him a warning look. "I don't care if you can shoot lightning from your hand. I will kick you in the face."

"Why doesn't that surprise me? Could it do with the fact you know I will not hurt you—that I cannot?"

"Probably." I really wasn't sure about that. Twenty-four hours ago he'd dragged me clear across an island.

"That doesn't sound particularly fair, does it?"

"This whole stuff with you isn't fair." I poked his chest with my finger. "You have the control in this."

Seth made an exasperated sound. He reached out and clasped the sides of my head. "*You* have all the control. Don't you get it?"

Annoyed, I grabbed his wrists. "Let go."

He twisted his hands and grasped mine. Those amber eyes flared, like he was up for the challenge. After a few terse moments, he broke away and stood. "There's the attitude I have come to know and loathe."

I flipped him off, but the bad thing was, his general annoyingness had somehow reached me. Not that I'd admit it. Ever.

He grabbed a towel off the shelf. After dampening it, he tossed it to me. "Clean yourself up." He sent a devilish grin my way. "I can't have my little Apollyon-in-training looking like a mess."

My fingers clenched around the towel. "If you ever say something that stupid again, I will smother you in your sleep."

His golden brows rose. "Little Alex, are you suggesting that we sleep together?"

Stunned by how he came to *that* conclusion, I lowered the towel. "What? No!"

"Then how could you smother me in my sleep unless you were in bed with me?" He gave a sly grin. "Think about it."

"Oh, shut up."

He shrugged and glanced at the door. "They're coming."

I was only half-curious to know how he knew that, but as I dabbed the cloth under my swollen lip, the door swung open. Marcus entered first, and Aiden appeared behind him. His gaze swept to me, checking me over once more. The look on his face said he wanted to come to me, but with Marcus and half a dozen Sentinels present, it was impossible. I fought down the need to be in his arms and turned my attention to my uncle.

Marcus met my eyes. "I need to know exactly what happened."

So I told them everything I remembered. Marcus remained impassive through all of it. He asked the appropriate questions and when it was over, I wanted to stumble back to my room. Reliving what'd happened to Kain had drained my soul.

Marcus gave me permission to leave, and I climbed to my feet while he gave orders to Leon and Aiden. "Notify the other Covenants. I'll take care of the Council."

Aiden had followed me out into the hall. "Didn't I ask you to not do something stupid?"

I winced. "Yes, but I didn't know—didn't think Kain would be like that."

Aiden shook his head, running a hand through his hair. Then he asked the one question no one else had thought to ask. "Did he say anything about your mother?"

"He said she killed them." I inhaled sharply. "That she took great pleasure in it."

Sympathy shone in those cool eyes. "Alex, I'm sorry. I know you hoped that wasn't the case. Are you okay?"

Not really, but I wanted to be strong for him. "Yes."

He pressed his lips together. "We'll . . . talk later, okay? I'll let you know when we'll have practice again. Things will be chaotic the next couple of days."

"Aiden . . . Kain said she was looking for me. That she was coming for me."

There must've been something in my voice, because he was in front of me so quickly. He reached out and cupped my cheek, his voice so unyielding I didn't doubt a word he said. "I won't allow that to happen. Ever. You will never face her."

I swallowed. His closeness, his touch, evoked so many memories; it took me a moment to respond. "But if I did, I could do it."

"Did Kain say anything else to you about your mother?"

She'll keep killing 'til she finds you—

"No." I shook my head as the guilt ate a hole in my soul.

His hand dropped to his chest, where he rubbed a spot above his heart. "You're going to do something stupid again."

I smiled weakly. "Well, usually I do about once a day."

Aiden raised a brow, his bright eyes amused for a moment. "No, that's not what I meant."

"Then what did you mean?"

He shook his head. "It's nothing. We'll talk soon." He passed Seth on the way back to the room. For a moment, both of their expressions hardened to stone. There may've been mutual respect in their faces, but there was definitely mutual dislike, as well.

I left before Seth could stop me. By the time I made it back to the girls' dorm, several of the students were on the porch. News traveled fast even though it was still early, but the most shocking part was Lea stood among them.

Seeing her caused my heart to clench. She looked terrible by Lea standards—meaning she looked like the rest of us on a good day. I wasn't sure what to say to her. We weren't friends, but what she was going through was unimaginable.

What could I say? No amount of apologies or words of condolence would make anything better for her, but as I got closer to her, I saw the red look to her eyes, the tight line of her normally plump lips, and the overall air of desolation surrounding her. It provoked a memory of how I'd felt when I'd thought my mom had died. Now, take that and multiply it by two; that was how Lea felt.

Our gazes locked and my lame apology rolled out of my mouth. "I'm sorry . . . for everything."

Surprisingly, Lea nodded as she passed me on the way in. I trailed behind her, wishing she'd called me a bitch or made fun of my face. That was better than this. Weary and sore, I pushed down the hallway and passed a group of girls. There were whispers, and they were right. My mother was a murderous daimon.

In my room, I crashed. Still dressed in my clothes, I slept the kind of sleep people only got after facing something so vast and life-changing. Somewhere, in that half-lucid state before I was completely out of it, I realized that when Seth and I had touched in the medical room, there'd been no blue cord.

Aiden sent a note the following day saying practice was still cancelled. He didn't mention when he'd contact me again. Over the hours, a nagging worry developed. Did Aiden regret what'd happened between us? Did he still want me? Were we ever going to talk again?

My priorities were pretty messed up, but I couldn't help it. Since I'd woken up, all I could think about was what'd almost happened between the two of us. And when I did, I felt hot *and* embarrassed.

I stared at the mammoth book he'd loaned me. I'd left it on the floor next to the couch. An idea popped in my head. I could return the book to him—innocent enough reason to seek him out. My mind was made up before I knew it. Grabbing the book, I yanked open the door.

Caleb stood there, one hand raised as if he was about to knock and the other holding a pizza box. "Oh!" He stepped back, startled.

"Hey." I couldn't meet his eyes.

He lowered his hand. Our almost-fight lingered between us like bad blood. "So you're reading Greek fables now?"

"Um . . ." I glanced down at the damn thing. "Yeah . . . I guess."

Caleb sucked his lower lip in, a nervous habit carried over from childhood. "I know what happened. I mean . . . your face kinda says it all."

Absently, my fingers went to my cut lip.

"I wanted to make sure you were okay."

I nodded. "I am."

"Look. I brought food." He held up the box with a grin. "And I'm gonna get caught if you don't let me in or go outside."

"All right." I dropped the book on the floor and followed him out.

On the way to the courtyard, I opted for a safe topic. "I saw Lea yesterday morning."

He nodded. "She came back late the night before. She's been pretty low-key. Even though she's a complete bitch, I feel sorry for her."

"Have you talked to her?"

Caleb nodded. "She's hanging in there. I'm not sure if it's really hit her, you know?"

I understood more than he probably could. We found a shady spot under some large olive trees and sat. I picked at the pizza, arranging my pepperoni slices into a gross-looking smiley face.

"Alex, what really happened to Kain?" His voice dropped to a whisper. "Everyone's saying he was a daimon, but that can't be possible, right?"

I looked up from my food. "He was a daimon."

The sun peeked through the branches, catching the strands of Caleb's hair and turning them a bright gold color. "How did the Sentinels not know that?"

"He looked just like he always did. His eyes were fine, his

teeth normal." I leaned back against the tree and crossed my legs at the ankles. "There was no way to tell. I didn't know until . . . I saw the pures." An image I could never erase.

He swallowed, staring down at his pizza. "More funerals," he murmured. Then louder, "I can't believe this. All this time and there's never been a daimon half. How is it even possible?"

I told him what Kain had said, figuring there was no reason to keep it a secret. His reaction was typical: heavy and deep. Falling in battle meant death for us, and we'd never had to consider anything else.

Caleb frowned. "What if Kain wasn't the first? What if other daimons figured it out and we just didn't know?"

We looked at one another. Swallowing, I dropped my pizza back onto the plate. "Then we picked a hell of a time to be graduating in the spring, huh?"

The two of us laughed . . . nervously. Then I returned to rearranging my pizza, thinking about everything else that had happened. Images of shirtless Aiden flashed before me. The way he'd looked at me and kissed me. The touch of Aiden's fingertips was slowly replaced by the touch of Seth's and the blue cord.

"What are you thinking?" Caleb inched closer and continued when I didn't answer. "What do you know? You have that look on your face! The one you got when we were thirteen and you walked in on Instructor Lethos and Michaels totally making out in the storage room!"

"Ew!" My face scrunched up at the memory. Damn him for remembering the grossest things. "It's nothing. I'm just think-ing . . . about everything. It's been a long couple of days."

"Everything's changed."

I glanced over at Caleb, feeling for him. "Yes."

"They're going to have to change the way we're trained, you know?" He continued in possibly the softest voice I'd ever heard him use. "Daimons always had the strength and speed, but now we'll be fighting half-bloods trained just like us. They'll know our techniques, moves—everything."

"A lot of us are going to die out there. More than ever before."

"But we have the Apollyon." He reached over and squeezed my hand. "Now you've got to like him. He's going to save our butts out there."

The need to tell him everything almost overwhelmed me, but I looked away, training my eyes on the bushy, bitter-smelling flowers. I couldn't remember what they were called. Nightsoot or something? What had Grandma Piperi said about them? Like the kisses from those who walk among the gods . . .

I turned back to Caleb and realized we weren't alone anymore. Olivia stood beside him, arms wrapped tightly around her waist. He told her what happened, and he didn't act like a love-struck idiot, which was good. Finally, she sat down and sent me a sympathetic look. I guessed my face was pretty messed up, but I hadn't really looked at it.

Caleb said something funny and Olivia laughed. I laughed, too, but Caleb glanced at me, catching the false tone of it. I tried to pull myself into their conversation, but I couldn't. Each of us spent the rest of the day trying to forget one thing or another. Caleb and Olivia focused on anything besides the cold reality of halfs being turned into daimons. And me? Well, I tried to forget everything.

When dusk settled around us, we headed back to our dorms, making plans to meet up for lunch tomorrow. Alone, Caleb stopped me before I headed up the porch steps. "Alex, I know you've been going through a lot. On top of everything else, school is going to be starting in two weeks. You've got a lot of stress on you. And I'm sorry about what happened the night at Zarak's."

School was starting in two weeks? Holy crap, I didn't even realize. "I should be the one apologizing." I meant it. "I'm sorry for being such a bitch."

He laughed and gave me a quick hug. Pulling back, his smile faded. "You sure you're okay?"

"Yeah." I watched him start to turn around. "Caleb?"

He stopped, waiting.

"Mom . . . did kill those people at Lake Lure. She was the one who turned Kain."

"I . . . I'm sorry." He took a step forward, his hands coming up and then falling to his sides. "She's not your mother anymore. It's not her doing this."

"I know." The mother I'd known wouldn't take pleasure in killing bugs. She never would've harmed another living, breathing person. "Kain said she'd keep killing until she finds me."

He looked like he didn't know what to say. "Alex, she'd keep killing no matter what. I know this is going to sound terrible, but the Sentinels will find her. They'll stop her."

I nodded, toying with the edge of my shirt. "It should be me who stops her. She's my mother."

Caleb frowned. "It should be *anyone* but you since she *was* your mother. I—" The frown faded from his face as he stared at me. "Alex, you wouldn't go after her, would you?"

"No!" I forced a laugh. "I'm not crazy."

He continued to stare at me.

"Look. I wouldn't even know where to find her," I told him, but Kain's words came right back at me. *You leave the safety of the Covenant and you'll find her or she'll find you.*

"Why don't you sneak back with me? We can download a crap ton of illegal movies and watch them. We can even break into the cafeteria and steal a bunch of food. How about that? Sounds like fun, right?"

It kind of did, but . . . "No. I'm really tired, Caleb. The last couple of days have . . ."

"Sucked?"

"Yeah, you can say that." I backed off then. "I'll see you for breakfast? I doubt I'll have practice."

"Okay." He still looked worried. "If you change your mind, you know where to find me."

I nodded and headed inside the dorm. There was another white envelope shoved in the little crack. When I saw Lucian's sprawling handwriting, there was a weird sinking feeling in my chest. Nothing from Aiden.

"Gods." I opened it up and quickly discarded it without reading it. Although, I was collecting a rather large sum of money. This one contained three hundred, and I stashed it with the rest of the cash. Once things calmed down, I was going to do some serious shopping.

After changing into a pair of cotton pajama bottoms and a tank, I picked up the book of Greek legends and brought it back to the bed, thumbing to the section about the Apollyon. I read the passage over and over again, looking for something that could tell me what was going to happen when I turned eighteen, but the book told me nothing I didn't already know.

Which wasn't much of anything.

I must've fallen asleep, because the next thing I knew I was staring at the ceiling in my dark bedroom. I sat up and pushed back the tangled mess of hair. Disoriented and still half asleep, I tried to remember what I'd dreamed.

Mom.

We'd been at the zoo in my dream. It was just like when I was a kid, but I was older and Mom ... Mom had been killing all the animals, ripping their throats out and laughing. The whole time, I'd just stood by and watched her. Never once did I try to stop her.

I swung my legs over the edge of the bed and sat there as my stomach twisted. *She'll keep killing 'til she finds you.* I stood, my legs feeling strangely weak. Was that why Kain had come back here? Had Mom somehow known I would seek him out and he would relay this message?

No. It wasn't possible. Kain came back to the Covenant, because he was . . .

Why had he come back to a place full of people ready to kill him?

Another memory stood out, brighter than the rest. It was of Aiden and me standing in front of the dummies in the training room. I'd asked him what he would do if his parents had been turned.

"I would've hunted them down. They wouldn't have wanted that kind of life."

I squeezed my eyes shut.

Mom would have rather been killed than become a monster preying on every living creature. And right now, she was out there, killing and hunting—waiting. Somehow, I ended up in front of my closet, my fingers drifting over the Covenant uniform.

Then I'd find her and kill her myself. My own words burned in my mind. There was no doubt what needed to be done. It was crazy and reckless—stupid even—but the plan took form. Cold, steely determination settled over me, and I stopped thinking.

I started acting.

It was early—way too early for anyone to be roaming the grounds of the Covenant. Only the shadows of the patrolling Guards moved under the moonlight. Getting to the secure warehouse behind the training arenas wasn't as hard as I thought it might be. The Guards were more concerned with possible weaknesses in the perimeter. Once inside, I found my way to where they kept the uniforms. My hands snatched one that fit and my heart raced as I quickly changed into it. I didn't need a mirror to tell me how I looked—I'd always known I'd look damn good in a Sentinel uniform. Black was a very flattering color for me.

The Hematoi used the earth element to glamour the uniforms so the mortal world wouldn't suspect we were some paramilitary organization. To a mortal, the uniform looked like plain old jeans and a shirt, but to a half-blood, it was a sign of the highest position a half-blood could obtain. Only the best wore this uniform.

There was a good chance this was the first and the last time I'd ever wear it. If I made it back . . . I'd probably be expelled. If I didn't make it back, well, that was something I couldn't think about.

You're going to do something stupid. My feet tripped up when I remembered what Aiden had said. Yeah. This was pretty stupid. How had he known? My heart turned over. Aiden always knew what I was thinking. He didn't need a blue cord or a crazy oracle's word to know me. He just did.

I couldn't think about him right now or what he'd do if he found out what I was up to. I grabbed a cap off the top shelf, twisted my hair up under it, and pulled it down so it shadowed most of my face.

Then I turned my attention to the weapons room—one-stop shopping for just about any deadly knife, gun, and almost anything that stabbed and decapitated. As sick as it was, I was kind of excited to be in here. I wasn't sure what that said about me as a person, but then again, killing was part of being a half-blood, just like it was to a daimon. Neither of our kinds could escape that—only the pures could.

I opted for two daggers. One hooked onto the side of my right thigh, and the other collapsed from six inches to two with a mere touch of a button on the handle. I put that one in my pocket along the seam of my pants. I grabbed a gun and made sure it was loaded.

Titanium encased bullets. Deadly stuff in here.

With one last look at the room of death and dismemberment, I gave a little sigh and did what both Caleb and Aiden probably had feared. I left the safety of the Covenant.

18

Holy crap. My disguise worked.

I stayed in the shadows for the most part, refusing to let myself think about my actions. As I crossed the first bridge, the Guards simply nodded. One even catcalled, obviously mistaking me for someone legal.

While I navigated the empty streets of the main island, I thought about the times I'd killed. I had two daimon kills under my belt. I could do this. Mom would be no different.

She couldn't be any different.

Being a young daimon, she would have speed and strength, but she'd never had any serious training. Not like the kind I'd had. I'd be faster and stronger than her. Aiden had practically beaten into me the fact young, newly turned daimons would be concerned about one thing only: draining. At three months, she'd be considered a newbie—a baby daimon.

I would just have to strike while she still looked like a daimon, before the elemental magic settled over her and she looked like . . . Mom.

The main bridge proved to be a little more difficult to cross, but thankfully, those Guards didn't have a lot of contact with the students. None of them recognized me, but they wanted to chat. It slowed me down enough to make my confidence waver.

Until one said, "Be safe and come back, Sentinel," and stepped aside.

Sentinel. It was what I'd always wanted to be upon

graduation, taking the more proactive route of dealing with daimons instead of guarding pures or their communities.

Once again, I stuck to the shadows as I made my way around the fishing and cruising boats. The townsfolk on Bald Head Island were used to the "intensely private" people from Deity Island, but there was something about us they sensed. They didn't know what it was that made them back off at the same time they wanted to be close to us.

Living among mortals for three years had been a truly craptastic experience for me. The teenagers had wanted to be close to me while their parents had said I was "one of *those* kids" they needed to stay away from. Whatever that meant.

I wondered what those parents would think if they knew exactly what I was—an almost-trained killing machine. I guess they'd been right to order their offspring to steer clear.

When I left the docks, I stuck to the sides of the buildings. I wasn't sure where to go, but I had a feeling I wouldn't have to go far. And I was right. About ten minutes into what I lovingly referred to as the normal world, I heard quick footsteps behind me. I spun around to face my would-be attacker, gun drawn and leveled.

"Caleb?" I felt something halfway between disbelief and relief.

He stood a few feet behind me, blue eyes wide and arms raised. He wore pajamas, a white shirt, and flip-flops. "Put your gun down!" he hissed. "Gods. You're gonna accidentally shoot me or something."

I lowered the gun and grabbed his arm, dragging him into an alley. "Caleb, what are you doing here? Are you crazy?"

"I could ask you the same question." He glared at me. "I was following you, obviously."

I shook my head and shoved my gun back into the waist of my pants. I'd forgotten a holster—go figure. "You need to go back to the Covenant. Now. Dammit, Caleb! What were you thinking?"

"What are *you* thinking?" He glowered as he threw the question back at me. "I knew you were going to do something incredibly stupid. That's why I couldn't sleep at all. I sat by my damn window and waited. Low and behold, I see your crazy ass sneaking across the quad!"

"How in the hell did you even get past the Guards in your *Mario Brothers* pajamas?"

He glanced down at them, shrugging. "I have my ways."

"Your ways?" I didn't have time for this. Stepping away from him, I pointed in the direction of the bridge. "You need to get back there, where it's safe."

He folded his arms across his chest stubbornly. "Not without you."

"Oh, for the love of the gods!" My temper snapped. "I don't need this right now. You don't understand."

"Don't start with the 'I don't understand' crap. This isn't about understanding anything! This is about you getting yourself killed! This is suicide, Alex. This isn't brave. It isn't smart. This isn't about duty or some misguided guilt you—"

His eyes widened again as *something* landed a couple of feet behind me. I whirled around, and at the same time, Caleb grabbed the dagger from my pants as I pulled the gun.

It was her.

She stood there, in the center of the alley. It was her . . . except it wasn't. It had her long, dark hair that fell in soft waves, framing her pale, ghastly white face—those high cheekbones and familiar lips. But darkness existed where her eyes should have been. Inky veins covered her cheeks, and if she smiled, there'd be a row of nasty, sharp teeth in her mouth.

It was my mother . . . as a daimon.

The shock of seeing her—seeing her beautiful, loving face twisted into such a grotesque mask—caused my arm to waver, my finger to twitch over the trigger. It was her . . . but it wasn't.

I knew from where she stood, there was no way she could

defend herself against a gunshot to the chest. I had the upper hand with my gun filled with titanium bullets—a full clip of them, actually. I could light her up right here and all of this would be over.

She hadn't moved, not an inch.

And now she looked like Mom. The elemental magic cloaked the daimon in her, and she stared at me with those bright, emerald-colored eyes. Her face was still pale, but no longer riddled with thick veins. She looked like she had the night before she'd turned—smiling at me, holding my gaze with hers.

"Lexie," she murmured, but I heard her loud and clear. It was her voice. Just hearing it did wonderful and awful things to me.

She was beautiful, stunning, and very much alive—daimon or not.

"Alex! Do it! Do—!" Caleb cried out.

A quick glance behind me confirmed Mom wasn't alone. Another dark-haired daimon now had a hand around Caleb's throat. He didn't move to kill him or to tag him. He simply held him.

"Lexie, look at me."

Unable to deny the sound of her voice, I turned back to her. She stood closer—close enough a bullet would leave one hell of a hole in her chest. And close enough I caught the scent of vanilla—her favorite perfume.

My gaze flickered over her face, each line of it familiar and beautiful to me. As I stared into her eyes, I remembered the strangest things. Memories of our summers together, the day she'd taken me to the zoo and told me my father's name, the look on her face when she'd told me we needed to leave the Covenant, and the way she'd looked sprawled across the floor in her tiny bedroom.

I faltered. I couldn't catch my breath as I stared into those eyes. This was my mother—*my mother!* She had raised me, treated me like I was the most precious thing in the world. And

I had been her everything—her reason for living. I couldn't move.

Do it! She's not your mother anymore! My arm trembled. *Do it! Do it!*

A scream of frustration tore through me and my arm dropped to my side. Seconds, only seconds had passed and yet, it felt like an eternity. I couldn't do it.

Her lips curved into a smug smile. Caleb gave a yelp from behind me, and then pain exploded alongside my temple. I slipped into the sweet darkness of oblivion.

I woke up to a splitting headache and a dry, bitter taste in the back of my mouth. It took me a few minutes to remember what'd happened. A mixture of horror and disappointment jerked me upright, on alert despite the throbbing ache radiating down the side of my face. I touched my head gingerly, feeling a knot the size of an egg.

Woozy, I looked around the lavishly furnished room. The cedar log walls, the large bed covered in satin sheets, the plasma television, the handcrafted furniture, all of it appeared familiar to me. It was one of the bedrooms in the cabin we used to visit, the one I'd slept in a half a dozen times. A pot of purple hibiscus flowers sat beside the bed—Mom's favorite. She had a thing for purple flowers.

Shock and dismay set in. I remembered this room. Oh, gods. This wasn't good. Nope.

I was in freaking Gatlinburg, Tennessee—more than five hours away from the Covenant. Five hours. Worse yet, I didn't see Caleb. Creeping over to the door, I paused and listened. Not a sound. I glanced at the glass doors leading out to the deck, but there was no way I could leave. I had to find Caleb . . . if he was still alive.

I clamped down on that thought. He had to be alive. There could be no other way.

Of course, my gun was gone and Caleb had taken my dagger. There was nothing in this room I could use as a weapon. If I started breaking stuff apart, it would draw attention, and it wasn't like any of this stuff could be converted into a weapon. Anything that might've been made of titanium had been stripped away.

I tried the doorknob and found it unlocked. I inched the door open and looked around. The sun rose outside, pushing the shadows out of the living area and kitchen. A large round table sat in the middle of the room, surrounded by six matching chairs. Two of the chairs had been pulled back, as if they'd been occupied. Several empty beer bottles rested on the carved oak surface. Daimons drank beer? I had no clue. There were two large couches, nice ones covered in luxurious brown fabric.

Across the room, the television was on, but muted—one of those big thin-screen ones, mounted on the wall. I went to the table and picked up a beer bottle. It wouldn't kill a daimon, but at least it was a weapon.

A muffled scream drew my attention to one of the back rooms. If I remembered right, there were two more bedrooms, another living area, and a game room. All of the doors were closed. I crept closer, freezing as the sound came again from the master bedroom.

I clenched the bottle in my hand and murmured a soft prayer. I wasn't sure what god I was praying to, but I really hoped one of them answered. Then I kicked the door. The hinges creaked and gave way as the wood around the knob splintered. The door swung open.

My breath caught in my throat at the nightmare unfolding before me. Caleb was pinned to the bed. A blond daimon was on him, his rough hands covering his mouth and holding him down while he tagged his arm. The sounds the daimon made as he drained Caleb's blood to get at the aether horrified me.

At the sound of my rage-fueled screams, the daimon lifted his head. His empty stare bored straight through me. I launched myself away from the door, bottle raised high in the air. It wouldn't kill him, but I was going to make it hurt.

Except it never happened.

So caught up on what the daimon was doing to Caleb, I didn't check the room. Stupid. But dammit, these were the kind of things I'd missed out on when I'd left the Covenant. I just knew to act and fight. Not to think.

Someone snatched me from behind. My arm twisted back until I dropped the bottle to the floor. The two chairs pushed back from the table flashed before me. Should've seen this one coming. Struggling proved useless from this position, but I still kicked out and tried to wrench my body away. It only succeeded in causing the daimon to tighten his grip until it became painful.

"Now. Now. Daniel isn't going to kill your friend." The voice came from behind my ear. "Not yet."

Daniel smiled, flashing a row of bloodstained teeth. In a blink he stood in front of me, tilting his head to the side. The glamour took over, revealing the pure-blood characteristics. He would've been beautiful if it weren't for the rivulets of blood dripping down his chin.

Caleb's body jerked every few seconds. Aftershocks of the tag—I would know. His bare arms revealed not one but two daimon tags. Furious, I screamed at the daimon in front of me. "I'm going to kill you!"

Daniel laughed and wiped the back of his hand over his chin. "And I'm going to love tasting you." He sniffed me—*literally* sniffed me. "I can almost taste you now."

I kicked out, catching him in the chest. He staggered a couple of feet back, hitting the bed. Caleb groaned and tried to sit up. Daniel coldcocked Caleb. I cried out, struggling like a rabid animal, but the daimon knocked me to the floor.

And then I was flying up, but no one was touching me. I hit

the wall so hard the plaster cracked, along with what felt like every bone in my body. There I stayed, pinned with my feet dangling several feet off the floor. The daimon controlled the air element—something else I hadn't learned how to defend myself against.

"You need to learn to play nice. Both of you." The other daimon held his hand up. He had a Southern accent—smooth and deep. He stepped up to where I hung, leaned in and patted the top of my foot. It was the daimon from the alley, the dark-haired one who'd been with Mom. "We do get hungry, you know? And with you here . . . well, it gnaws out our insides. It's like a fire inside of us."

I tried to pull away from the wall, but I didn't move. "Stay away from him!"

He ignored me, walking over to Caleb's motionless frame. "We aren't new daimons by any means, but you . . . make it hard to resist the lure of the aether. Just a hit. That's all we want." He ran his fingertips down Caleb's face. "But we can't. Not 'til Rachelle returns."

"Don't touch him." I barely recognized my own, low voice.

He glanced back at me and waved his hand as if it were an after-thought. I hit the floor feet first, and then fell to my knees. I ignored the way my stomach muscles pulled and pushed to my feet. Without thinking about anything other than getting him away from Caleb, I rushed him. The dark-haired daimon shook his head and simply threw his arm up. My body slammed into the wall, knocking several framed paintings to the floor. This—*this* was nothing like training.

And this time I didn't get up.

Clearly annoyed, he pushed away from Caleb. He advanced on me, and I screamed, swinging on him. He caught my arm and then my other, hauling me to my feet.

With both arms rendered useless, I had only my legs. Aiden had always praised my kicks, and with that thought in mind, I pushed my upper back against the wall. Using the daimon's arms and the wall for support, I pulled my legs up to my chest and kicked out.

I caught him right in the chest, and by the startled look on his face he hadn't expected it. He fell back several feet, and I hit the floor once again.

Daniel shot away from the bed and dug his hands into my hair, wrenching my neck back. For a moment, a sick sense of déjà hit me, but there was no Aiden to save me now—no cavalry would be arriving.

As I struggled with Daniel, the dark-haired daimon dropped down in front of me. With his hands resting on his knees and the lazy smile splayed across his face, he looked like he was about to talk about the weather with me. He was that casual.

"What's going on here?"

Daniel released me at the sound of my mother's sharp and angry voice. I struggled to my feet, twisting toward her. I couldn't help the mixture of terror and love coursing through me. She stood in the doorway, surveying the damage with a critical eye. I only saw the glamour. I couldn't see her true form.

I was so screwed.

"Eric?" She directed her scowl at the dark-haired one.

"Your daughter . . . she's not happy with the current state of things."

I couldn't pull my eyes off of her as she stepped over a piece of broken wood. "My daughter better not have one hair on her head missing."

Eric glanced over at Daniel. "Her hair is perfectly fine. She's fine. So is the other half-blood."

"Oh. Yes." She turned to Caleb. "I remember him. Is he your boyfriend, Lexie? Sweet of him to tag along either way. Stupid, but sweet."

"Mom." My voice cracked.

She turned to me with a smile—a big, beautiful smile. "Lexie?"

"Please . . ." I swallowed. "Please let Caleb go."

She tsked and shook her head. "I cannot allow that."

My insides twisted. "Please. He . . . just, please."

"Baby, I can't. I need him." She reached out and brushed back my hair, the way she used to. I flinched, and she frowned. "I knew you would come. I know you. The guilt and the fear would eat at you. What I didn't plan on was him, but I'm not mad. See? He's going to stay."

"You could let him go." My chin trembled.

Her hand drifted down my cheek. "I can't. He's going to ensure that you cooperate with me. If you do everything I tell you to do, he'll live through this. I won't let them kill him or turn him."

I wasn't stupid enough to be hopeful. There was a catch, probably a big and terrible one.

She stepped away, turning her attention to the two male daimons. "What have you told her?"

Eric's chin came up. "Nothing."

My mother nodded. Her voice was the same, but I realized as she talked, it lacked what actually had made it hers. There was no softness in it, no emotion. It was hard, flat—not hers. "Good." She faced me once more. "I want you to understand one thing, Lexie. I love you very, very much."

I blinked, backing against the wall. Her words hurt more than any physical blow could. "How can you love me? You're a daimon."

"I'm still your mother," she replied in the same flat tone, "and you still love me. That's why you didn't kill me when you had the chance."

An act and truth I was already regretting, but looking at her now, I could only see her—Mom. I closed my eyes, willing myself to see the daimon, the monster inside of her. When I opened my eyes, she was still the same.

Her lips twisted into a smile. "You can't go back to the

Covenant. I cannot allow that. I have to keep you away from there. Permanently."

My gaze fell to Caleb. Daniel inched his way closer to him. "Why?" I could keep my cool as long as the bastard didn't touch him again.

"I need to keep you away from the Apollyon."

I blinked, not expecting that. "What?"

"He will take everything from you. Your power, your gifts—everything. He is the First, Lexie. Whether he knows it or not, he will drain everything from you so he can become the God Killer. There will be nothing left of you when he is done. The Council—they know this. They don't care. All they want is the God Killer, but Thanatos will never allow that to happen."

I backed up, shaking my head. Mom was utterly crazy.

"They don't care what it will do to you. I can't allow that. Do you understand?" She stalked forward, coming to a stop in front of me. "That's why I must do this. I must turn you into a daimon."

The room spun and for a moment, I thought I would pass out.

"I have no other choice." She caught my hand, pulling it to where her heart beat. She held it there. "As a daimon, you will be faster and stronger than you are now. You will be immune to titanium. You will have great power . . . when you turn eighteen you will be unstoppable."

"No." I pulled my hand back. "No!"

"You have no idea what you are saying 'no' to. I thought I lived before, but now I am truly living." She held her free hand in front of my face, wriggling her fingers once, then twice. A tiny spark flew from her fingertips, and then her entire hand was on fire.

I jerked back, but her grip increased on my hand.

"Fire, Lexie. I could barely control the air element as a pure-blood, but as a daimon, I can control *fire*."

"But you're killing people! How does that make it okay?"

"You get used to it." She shrugged dismissively. "You'll get used to it."

My blood froze in my veins. "You sound . . . freaking insane."

She looked at me blandly. "You say that now, but you'll see. The Council wants everyone to believe the daimons are soulless, evil creatures. Why? Fear. They know we are far more powerful, and in the end, we will win this war. We are like gods. No. We *are* gods."

Daniel practically licked his lips in anticipation as he eyed me. Sickness and fear clawed through me, and I shook my head. "No. Don't do this. Please."

"It's the only way." She turned away, glancing back at me over her shoulder. "Don't make me force you into this."

I looked at her, wondering how I could've hesitated in the alley. There was nothing about this thing in front of me was my mother. Nothing. "You're freaking insane."

She whipped around, expression hardening. "I told you not to make me force you into this. Daniel!"

I pushed off the wall as Daniel grabbed for Caleb, who groaned as he started to come around. Mom caught me before I could reach them. The daimon bent his head to his arm.

Horror twisted through me. "No! Stop!"

Daniel laughed a moment before his teeth cut into flesh. Caleb jackknifed across the bed, eyes going wild as his terrified screams filled the cabin. I pushed at my mom, but I couldn't get past her. She was strong, so unbelievably strong.

"Eric, come here."

Eric seemed to be more than happy to oblige. His dark eyes flared with hunger. Revulsion and fear filled me, and my struggles renewed.

Mom's hold tightened around my waist. "Remember what I told you, Eric. Small bites, every hour and no more. If she fights you, kill the boy. If she complies, leave the boy alone."

I turned cold. "No! No!"

"I'm sorry, baby. This is going to hurt, but if you don't fight them, it will be over soon. It's the only option, Lexie. I'd never be able to control you any other way. You'll see. It will be for the best in the end. I promise you."

Then she shoved me at Eric.

19

Just like that.

What a bitch.

I screamed and twisted back to her as Eric pulled me into his arms. "Don't let them do this!"

She raised her hand. "Eric."

The daimon flipped me around. I kicked and I threatened every possible method of death and dismemberment, but it didn't stop him. The daimon smiled at me through my rant. Then his fingers squeezed, and in a millisecond, his teeth sank through the soft flesh of my arm.

Red-hot fire shot through me. I reared back, trying to escape the burning, but it followed my movements. Over my screams, I could hear Caleb yelling and begging for them to stop. Neither Mom nor the daimon paid any attention to him. The pain slithered through every part of my body as Eric continued to drain. The room tilted, and there was a pretty good chance I was going to pass out.

"Enough," she murmured.

The daimon lifted its face. "She tastes divine."

"It's the aether. She has more in her than a pure does."

Eric let go of me then, and I fell to my knees, shaking. There was nothing—absolutely nothing that felt like that. Even the aftershocks of the tagging stole my breath. Gasping for air, I stayed there until the fire dulled to nothing more than an ache.

Only then did I realize Caleb was silent. I lifted my head and saw him staring at me. There was a dazed look to his eyes, as if somehow he'd managed to remove himself from this place, left his body or something. I wanted to be wherever he was.

"Now, that wasn't too bad?" Mom grasped my shoulders and forced me back against the wall.

"Don't touch me." My words came out weak and slurred.

She gave me a cold smile. "I know you're upset, but you'll see. We'll change the world together."

Daniel returned to Caleb's side, but he didn't move. The way Daniel looked at him made me think he wanted to do bad things to Caleb. Abruptly, the oracle's words came back to me.

One with a bright and short future.

Caleb would die. Horror forced me toward the bed. This couldn't be happening! In an instant, Eric had me pinned back against the wall. Blood—*my* blood—still stained his lips. Once he was sure I wouldn't move again, he let go and leaned back with a smug half-smile.

Sickened, I pushed down my own pain and fear. "Mom . . . please let Caleb go. Please. I'll do anything." And I meant it. There was no way I was going to let Caleb die in this godforsaken place. "Please, just let him go."

She studied me silently. "What would you do?"

My voice broke. "Anything. Just let him go."

"Would you promise not to fight me or run?"

The oracle's words kept replaying over and over, like some sick chant. There was no telling how much more of this he could take. Caleb's color was chalky, sickly. What was about to happen was fated, wasn't it? Had the gods already seen this? And if I chose not to fight, I would be turned into a daimon.

I swallowed down the taste of bile. "Yes. I promise."

Her gaze flickered over Caleb and the daimon. She sighed. "He stays, but since you made a promise, I'll make you one. They will not touch him again, but his presence will make sure you keep your promise."

Snapping out of his daze, Caleb frantically shook his head at me, but I agreed again. I wanted him out of here, but for now, this was the best I could do. I sat opposite the bed with my back pressed against the wall, eyes trained on Caleb and Daniel. Eric took up position beside me. All I could do was hope someone had checked on us by now. Maybe Aiden finally had come to talk to me or start practice again. Maybe someone had checked on Caleb, and someone at the Covenant put two and two together. If not, in a horrible twist of fate, the next time I saw Aiden, he would try to kill me.

And I doubted he would falter like I had.

Daniel turned from Caleb and stared at the fresh tag on my arm. I squeezed my eyes shut and turned my head. Next was Daniel's turn, and I had a feeling he was going to make it as painful as possible. My eyes burned as I pushed against the wall, wishing I could somehow disappear into it.

An hour came and went, and my body tensed as Daniel knelt down and pried my other arm from my chest. This was wrong, so wrong. There was no way to prepare for this, and when Eric placed his hand over my mouth, Daniel bit into my wrist.

I sagged against the wall, reeling after it was over. Like clockwork, Daniel and Eric took turns tagging me. Mom blabbed on and on about how we would eradicate the Council members, starting first with Lucian. We would then sit on the thrones, and even the gods would bow before us. The tables would turn, she said, and the daimons would rule over not just the pure-bloods, but the mortal world, too.

"We'll have to take down the First, but when you're a daimon Apollyon you'll be stronger than him—better than him."

Mom was really, absolutely nuts.

I learned about their draining. Maybe she was trying to prepare me for my new life? Pures kept them wired for days, halfs only for a few hours, and mortals, well, they killed them for the fun of it. Too bad there wasn't a pure I could hand over to the daimons now. That may sound terrible, but my arms were covered in crescent-shaped bites, much like my old instructor had been scarred. And I'd pitied her—ironic.

The draining continued. Pieces of who I was disappeared with each tag. I no longer pressed away when Daniel dipped down or Eric leaned over. I didn't even scream. And the whole time, *she* stood by and watched it all. I was losing myself to this sick madness, and my soul turned dark and desperate.

Eventually, she left to go check the roads. Not once did she feed off me. I supposed she'd bagged herself a pure earlier, but when she left, I immediately wanted her back. With her gone, Daniel got bold, and though it made me want to vomit, I let him get close. Every so often, he would run the tips of his fingers over my arms, around the bite marks. At least it kept his attention off of Caleb.

"I can already feel it," murmured Eric.

I'd forgotten he was still there. Even though he was tagging the hell out of me, I preferred him to Daniel. "Feel what?" My voice sounded sleepy.

"The aether, I'm buzzing from it. Almost like I could do anything." He reached over and poked one of the bites, causing me to wince. "Do you feel it leaving you? Going into me?"

Refusing to answer him, I lowered my head to my bent knees. He sounded high . . . and I felt sick—my soul felt sick. By the time Daniel tipped my neck back, I was exhausted and near delirious from the pain. Caleb hadn't moved in a while, and Eric didn't need to cover my mouth anymore. I only whimpered as the teeth pierced the skin at the base of my neck.

Eric made soothing noises as Daniel drained me, his thumb tracing the wild pounding of my pulse. "It'll be over soon. You'll see. Just a couple more tags, and it will be over. A whole new world is waiting for you."

After Daniel was done, I slumped to the side. The room spun, tilted. I had a hard time focusing on what Eric was talking about.

"We're going to change the half-bloods first. They can't be

spotted like us. They don't need elemental magic. All over the world, we will launch our attack. It will be beautiful." Eric smiled at the thought. "The Covenants will be infiltrated . . . and then the Council."

It was a good enough plan, one that could easily become a scary reality. Eric didn't seem bothered by the lack of conversational input. He continued on, and I found it hard to keep my eyes open. Fear and anxiety had ridden me hard. I dozed off. For how long, I didn't know, but something jarred me awake.

Weary and confused, I lifted my head in time to see Daniel standing in front of me. Had it already been another hour? Was this it? I couldn't help but wonder if they were preparing for the last bite, the last drop of aether and the last of my soul.

"Daniel, it's not time."

"I don't care. You're getting more than I am. You're practically glowing. Look at me!" Daniel scowled. "I don't look like you."

Eric wasn't glowing, but his skin had taken on a healthy infusion. He looked . . . like a normal pure-blood. Daniel, on the other hand, was still sheet-white.

Eric shook his head. "She'll kill you."

Daniel dropped down in front of me and shoved a hand through my hair, wrenching my head back. "Not if she doesn't know. How would she? I just want one more."

"Don't . . . let him." My weak voice held a pleading edge, but if Eric was concerned with Daniel's fate, he sure didn't show it or try to stop him.

There was a spare spot on my neck still bite-free. I silently begged that he wouldn't go for that. I don't know why I cared at this point, but dammit, I still had some smidge of vanity left.

"She probably likes it," Daniel said. A stuttered heartbeat later, he sank his teeth into that one little spot and his lips moved against my skin. The pain shot through me, causing me to go rigid. His one hand tightened in my hair and his other got friendly, slipping over my shoulder and down further.

Out of everything that was happening, this—*this* was too much. With every ounce of strength I had in me, I lifted my hands and dug my nails into the sides of his face.

Daniel reared back, howling. My shirt ripped in the process, but the sound—the look on his face filled me with a sick sense of satisfaction. Deep and angry-looking welts formed on his face, beading with fresh blood. Blindly, he lashed out and caught me in the eye, toppling me into Eric.

"Hell!" Eric leapt to his feet and I ate the floor.

I curled onto my side and into a fetal position. Above me, I felt Eric push Daniel back, yelling in his face, but I wasn't listening. Something long and thin dug into my thigh. I slowly rolled over, inching my fingers down until they closed over the object hidden in the seam of my pants.

The knife—the retractable one.

Suddenly, Eric lifted me up and straightened me so that I looked at him. Something wet and warm ran down the side of my face, dripping into my right eye. Blood. Not like I had much more I could afford to lose.

Over his shoulder, I saw that Caleb was awake. He stared at me, and I tried to send him a message, but as it was, Eric was doing a good job of blocking him. From the front of the house, we heard the door open, and the click of my mother's heels resonated through the cabin. Eric let go of me and backed clear across the room. My lips curved into a sad little smirk. He knew. I knew.

Mom was going to be pissed when she got a look at my face.

She stepped into the room, and her eyes narrowed on me. In a second, she was kneeling in front of me, tipping my head back. "What has happened here?"

Blood loss and exhaustion addled my thoughts. Moments went by as I stared at her. I couldn't remember where I was or how I got there. All I wanted to do was press my face against her, for her to hold me and to tell me everything would be okay.

She was my mother, and she would stop them. She had to, especially something this vile, this horrendous. "Mom? Look . . . look at what they've done to me."

"Shh." She smoothed my hair back from my face.

"Please . . . please make him stop." I gripped her in a weak hug, wanting to climb into her arms, wanting her to hold me. She didn't. As she turned away from me, I cried out and reached for her.

No. This—this *thing* in front of me wasn't my mother. My mother would never have turned her back on me. She would've held me, comforted me. I snapped out of it, blinking slowly.

"Who did this to her face?" Her voice was so cold, so deadly and so unlike Mom, but at the same time I heard the edge in her words. Recognizing her tone from the many times she'd yelled at me for getting in trouble—it was the tone that happened right before she launched into a major bitch-fest. Eric and Daniel didn't know. They didn't know my mother like I did.

"Who do you think?" Eric sneered.

She pressed cool lips against my forehead, and I squeezed my eyes shut. She wasn't my Mom. "I gave you both explicit orders." She straightened, her eyes falling to Daniel.

Reality settled around me once more, and I came to my knees. I couldn't think about her anymore, couldn't see her as my mom. I made my decision. *Screw fate*. My eyes met Caleb's, and I nodded at Mom's back and mouthed the words, "Get ready." I could only hope he understood.

"That is simply unacceptable." That was the only warning she gave. She launched herself at Daniel, knocking him over Caleb. The two daimons crashed to the floor, swinging and tearing at one another.

I seized the opportunity. Scrambling to my feet, I grabbed for Caleb.

Thankfully, he got the message. He slid off the bed as Eric went after Daniel, too. I staggered to my feet just as Mom pulled

Daniel to *his* feet. He was a good foot taller than her, but she threw him around the room like he was nothing. There was a moment when I couldn't move. Her strength was shocking, unnatural.

Dizzy and nauseous, I stumbled away from the room with Caleb in tow. We raced through the cabin and out the front door. Rain pounded on the roof of the deck, almost but not quite silencing the wet, sloppy crunch from inside the house. The sound propelled both of us over the railing. Forgetting how high the decks were, I hit the ground hard, falling to my knees.

"Lexie!"

My mother's voice pushed me to my feet. Glancing beside me, I saw Caleb do the same. We ran, half sliding and half falling down the muddy hill. Branches slapped me in the face, pulled on my clothing and hair, but I kept running. All that gym time paid off. My muscles pushed past the pain and the lack of blood.

"Alexandria!"

We weren't fast enough. Caleb's startled yelp spun me around. My mom plucked him up from behind, tossing him sideways. Shock flickered over his face right before he slammed into a thick maple tree. I screamed, backtracking to where he'd fallen.

A barrier of flames went up, pushing me back. The fire destroyed everything in its path as it spread. Caleb rolled to his side, barely escaping it. I stumbled backward as the world burned in red and violet colored flames. The rain did nothing to beat down the unnatural fire.

And there she stood—tall and straight, like a terrible goddess of death. Twice now, I'd failed to see that. In the alley in Bald Head and moments earlier in the cabin, right after I'd realized I had a Covenant dagger in my pocket.

"Lexie, you promised me you wouldn't run." She sounded surprisingly calm.

Did I? My hand slipped into the side pocket. "I lied."

"I took care of Daniel. You won't have to worry about him." She edged closer. "Everything is going to be okay now. Lexie, you should sit down. You're bleeding all over the place."

I glanced down at myself. Running had gotten my blood pulsing. I could feel it trickling down my arms and neck. I was kind of surprised I had any left in me. Out of the corner of my eye, a shot of dark blue darted between the flames.

"Just do it, Rachelle. She's weak." Fury and impatience colored Eric's words. "Take care of it and let's get the hell out of here!"

That was so true. Light-headed and off-balance, a bunny rabbit could get the best of me right now. "Don't come any closer."

My mother laughed. "Lexie, this will be over soon. I know you're scared, but you have nothing to worry about. I'm going to take care of everything. Don't you trust me? I'm your mother."

I backed up, stopping when I felt the heat from the flames. "You're not my mother."

She moved forward. Somewhere in the distance, I thought I heard my name being called. His voice—*Aiden's*. It had to be a hallucination, because neither Eric nor my mom reacted to the sound, but even if it was just a sad manifestation of my subconscious, it gave me strength to keep standing. My fingers slid over the slender dagger. How had they missed this? "You're not my mother," I said again, my voice sounding hoarse.

"Baby, you're confused. I'm your mother."

My thumb brushed over the release button. "You died in Miami."

Her eyes held a dangerous glint. "Alexandria . . . there is no other option."

Wait, a voice whispered in my head, *wait until her defenses are down*. If she saw the blade, it would be over. I needed her to believe she'd won. I needed her vulnerable. Though, the strange thing was, I was almost a hundred percent certain the voice didn't belong to me. But that really didn't matter right now.

"There's another option. You could just kill me."

"No. You will join me." Her voice sounded like it had in the room, right before she'd killed Daniel for touching me. How messed up was that? "And since you broke your promise, I will have to kill your little boyfriend over there. That is, if he hasn't been burned alive yet."

Everything came down to this moment. Die or kill her. Be turned into a monster or kill her. The breath I drew in wasn't enough. "You're already dead," I whispered, "and I'd rather be dead than become what you are."

"You will thank me later." Moving inhumanly fast, she wrapped her hand through my hair and jerked my head back.

The handle of the dagger felt awkward, wrong even. Sucking in air, I pushed the little button. There wasn't a lot of space between us, but I still got my arm in between us. It wouldn't be a precise hit, not at this angle, but it would kill.

You will kill the ones you love.

Fate had been right about that.

My mother jerked back, her mouth gaping open in surprise. She looked down. So did I. My hand was flush with her chest, and the blade had sunk through her skin like titanium did when it met the flesh of a daimon.

She stumbled backward as I withdrew the dagger. Her face contorted and blurred. Bright, beautiful eyes met mine, and then they disappeared. Like a switch had been thrown, the fire circling us ceased to exist.

Her scream filled the forest, and my screams overcame hers. She slumped just as my legs refused to cooperate. We both folded into ourselves at the same time, except I collapsed into a messy heap and she buckled into herself. There was a moment—it was quick—but I saw the glimmer of relief cross her face. In that instant, she was Mom. She really was. And then she started to flake apart, fading until there was nothing left but a fine layer of blue dust.

I sagged forward, resting my head against the damp ground, vaguely aware of Eric running and the rain hammering me. Months of grief and loss swirled inside me, invading every cell, every pore. Nothing existed but the raw pain of a different kind of hurting. The tags and the bruises faded in comparison to it. Anguish consumed me. I wanted to die—to just cave in like Mom had. I'd killed her—my mother. Daimon or not, I'd killed her.

Time stopped. It could've been minutes or hours, but eventually there were voices. People called my name, called Caleb's, but I couldn't answer. Everything sounded far away and unreal.

Then strong hands surrounded me, lifting me up. My head fell back and cool rain splattered off my cheeks. "Alex, look at me. Please."

Recognizing the voice, I opened my eyes. Aiden stared down at me, face pale and drawn. He looked stricken as his gaze roamed over the many bite marks. "Hey," I murmured.

"It's going to be okay." His voice held a panicked, desperate edge. He ran wet fingers over my cheeks, catching my chin. "I need you to keep your eyes open and talk to me. Everything's going to be okay."

I felt funny, so I doubted that. There were so many voices, some I recognized and some I didn't. Somewhere I heard Seth. "Where's . . . Caleb?"

"He's okay. We have him—Alex, stay with me. Talk to me."

"You were . . . right." I swallowed, needing to tell someone—to tell him. "She was relieved. I saw it . . ."

"Alex?" Aiden stood, cradling me to his chest. I felt his heart thundering under my cheek and then I felt nothing at all.

20

I woke up staring at the soft glow of fluorescent ceiling lights. I wasn't sure what'd woken me or where I was.

"Alex."

I turned my head and met his pale gray eyes. Aiden sat on the edge of the bed. Dark waves of hair fell over his forehead. He looked different to me. Shadows bloomed under his eyes.

"Hey," I croaked.

Aiden smiled that wonderful full smile that was so rare, so beautiful. He reached over and with just the tips of his fingers, he brushed a few strands of hair off my forehead. "How are you feeling?"

"Okay. I'm . . . thirsty." I tried clearing my throat again.

He leaned over, the bed dipping slightly as he grabbed a glass off the bedside table. Helping me sit up, he waited while I gulped the cool water. "More?"

I shook my head. Sitting up, I got a better view of the unfamiliar room. I was hooked up to half a dozen tubes, but I wasn't in the Covenant. "Where are we?"

"We're at the Nashville Covenant. We couldn't risk the time it would've taken us to get you back to North Carolina." He paused, seeming to choose his next words. "Alex, why did you do this?"

I leaned back and closed my eyes. "I'm in a lot of trouble, aren't I?"

"You stole a Sentinel uniform. You also stole weapons and left the grounds without permission. Untrained and unprepared, you left to hunt down your mother. What you did was so reckless, so dangerous. You could've been killed, Alex. So yes, you're in trouble."

"I kinda of figured that." I sighed, opening my eyes. "Marcus is going to expel me now, isn't he?"

Sympathy shone on his face. "I don't know. Marcus is very upset. He would've come here, but he's been with the Council. Everyone's in an uproar over what happened to Kain and the implications."

"Everything's changed," I murmured to myself.

"Hmm?"

I took a deep breath. "Caleb shouldn't be in trouble. He tried to stop me, but . . . where is he?"

"He's here, in a different room. And he's been awake for the last day, asking for you. He has a couple bruised ribs, but he'll be okay. He's going to head back later today, but you'll need to stay for a little while longer."

Relief washed through me. I relaxed back against the fluffy pillows. "How long have I been asleep?"

He fiddled with the blankets, adjusting them around me. "Two days."

"Whoa."

"You were pretty bad off, Alex. I thought . . ."

I looked at him, my eyes finding his and remaining there. "Thought what?"

Aiden exhaled softly. "I thought I—*we* thought we'd lost you. I've never seen so many tags on a person still . . . living." His eyes fell shut briefly. They were a startling color when they reopened—a beautiful silver. "You scared me. You really did."

There was an odd pain in my chest, sort of a dull aching. "I didn't mean to. I thought—"

"What did you think, Alex? Did you think at all?" Aiden lowered his chin. A muscle feathered along his jaw. "It doesn't matter now. Caleb told us everything."

I was sure what he meant by "everything" was her crazed ranting, the daimons, and those horrible, terrible hours in the bedroom. "Caleb shouldn't be punished. He really did try to stop me, but we got caught in an alley . . . and I saw her. I should've . . . killed her then, but I couldn't. I failed, and I could've gotten Caleb killed."

Aiden faced me again. "I know."

I swallowed. "I had to do it. She was going to keep killing, Aiden. I couldn't stand around and wait for the Sentinels to find her. Yeah, it was stupid. Look at me." I lifted my bandaged arms. "I know it was stupid, but she was my mother. I had to do it."

Aiden was quiet as he stared at me. "Why didn't you come to me instead of running off and doing this?"

"Because you were busy with what happened with Kain and you would've stopped me."

Anger flared behind his eyes. "Damn straight I would've stopped you—prevented *this* from happening to you!"

I flinched. "That's why I couldn't come to you."

"You never should've faced what you did. None of us wanted you to go through this. What you must be feeling . . ."

"I'm dealing." I clamped down on the sudden pressure in the back of my throat.

He ran a hand through his hair. It looked like he'd done that several times in the last two days. "You're so foolishly brave."

His words brought back the memory of the night in his . . . bed. "You've said that before."

"Yes. And I meant it then. If I'd only known how foolishly brave you truly were, I would've locked you in your room."

"I also kinda figured that, too."

He didn't say anything to that and we sat in silence for a long time. Then he started to stand. "You need to get some rest. I'll check in on you in a little while."

"Don't leave. Not yet."

Aiden stared at me as if he could read what was going on

inside me. "I know what you want to talk about, but now is not that time. You need to get better. Then we can talk."

My fingers tightened around the blanket. "I want to talk about it now."

"Alex." His voice was soft.

"Aiden?"

His lips twitched at my response, but then his eyes met mine and held them in their depths. "The night—what happened between us was . . . well, it shouldn't have ever happened."

Ouch. It was a struggle to keep my face blank and not show how much those words hurt.

"Do you . . . do you regret it? What happened between us?" If he said yes, I think I'd die.

"As wrong as this is, I don't regret it. I can't." He looked away then, drawing in a deep breath. "I lost control, lost sight of what's important to you—to me."

"I wasn't complaining."

He looked at me warily. "Alex, you're not making this easy."

I sat up further, ignoring the way the tubes pulled on my arms. "Why should I? I like you. I like being around you. I do trust you. I'm not naïve and dumb. I wanted you. I still do."

His hands clenched against the blanket tucked around my legs. "I'm not saying you're naïve or dumb, Alex. But dammit, I nearly destroyed both of our futures in a matter of minutes. What do you think would've happened if we'd been caught?"

I shrugged, but I knew what could've happened. It wouldn't have been pretty. "But we weren't caught." Then something occurred to me. Maybe it had nothing to do with the actual rules. "Is it because I'm Seth's freakier half? Is that why?"

"No. It has absolutely nothing to do with that."

"Then why?"

Aiden stared at me like he could somehow get me to understand by his stare alone. "It has nothing to do with you being the

Apollyon. Alex, you know that I don't see you as anything different than me, but . . . the Council will."

"Pures do this—they do it all the time and don't get caught."

"I know that there are some pure-bloods who break the rule, but they do it because they don't care about what happens to the other person, and *I* care about what happens to you." His eyes searched mine intently. "I care about you more than I should and that's why I'm not going to put you in that situation and jeopardize your future."

Desperate, I searched for a way we could make this work. We had to, but the look on Aiden's face stole my breath, my protests.

He closed his eyes and took another deep breath. "Both of us need to be Sentinels, right? You know why I have to do this. I know why you have to do this. I lost control, forgetting to see what could come of this. I could've ended whatever chances you had of becoming a Sentinel, but worse than that, I could have stolen your future. It doesn't matter what you are or what you'll become when you turn eighteen. The Council would ensure that you were removed from the Covenant, and I . . . would never forgive myself for that."

"But the Breed Order—"

"The Breed Order hasn't been changed, and with the knowledge that halfs can turn, I doubt it ever will. Whatever ground the halfs have gained was lost the moment the daimons discovered that your kind can be changed."

Well . . . that was depressing, but not as crushing as this. Everything about the moments we'd shared had been magical, perfect, and so right. There was no way I could've mistaken the look in his eyes or the way he'd touched me. Looking at him now, I knew I still wasn't mistaking that look of near desperation, of lust and something far stronger.

I tried to joke. "But I'm the Apollyon. What can they really say? At eighteen, I could just zap anyone who gives us a hard time."

His lips twitched. "That doesn't matter. These rules have been in place since the time the gods walked among mortals. Not even Lucian or Marcus would be able to stop what would happen. You'd be given the elixir and placed into servitude, Alex. And I couldn't live with myself knowing what that would do to you. To see you lose everything that makes you who you are? I couldn't bear that. I couldn't live seeing you like the rest of the servants. You have too much life for that, too much life to lose for me."

I shifted closer, my legs brushing his hands and my face only inches from his. I knew I looked a mess, but I also knew Aiden saw past that. "Don't you want me?"

Groaning low in his throat, he pressed his forehead against mine. "You know the answer to that. I still . . . want you, but we can't be together, Alex. Pures and halfs can't be together in that way. We can't forget that."

"I hate rules." I sighed, feeling the burning in my throat again. I'd wanted him to hold me ever since the moment I'd woken up. And our blood wouldn't even allow that.

He sounded like he wanted to laugh but knew it would only provoke me further. He sighed. "But we have to follow them, Alex. I can't be the reason you lose everything."

Rules could suck it. There were only a few inches between us, and if I moved just a little bit more, our lips would touch. I wondered what he would think about our future then. If I just kissed him, would he care about the rules? About what people would think?

Almost like he sensed what I was thinking, he murmured, "You are so reckless."

The last time I'd been awake, I thought I'd never smile again, but I did smile. "I know."

Aiden shifted and pressed his lips against my forehead. He lingered a few seconds, and before I could do anything, which sucked, because I *was* feeling pretty damn reckless, he pushed himself away. "I . . . I will always care for you, but we won't do this. We can't. Do you understand?"

I stared at him, knowing that he was right, but he was also wrong. He wanted this as much as I did, but he was too concerned by what could happen to *me*. Part of me liked him even more for that, but my heart . . . well, it was cracking. The only thing that kept it from shattering completely was the fleeting look of desire and fondness that flickered over his face as he backed toward the door.

"Get some rest," he said when I didn't answer. "I'll check on you later."

I scooted back down, but then something else occurred to me. "Aiden?"

He stopped, turning around. "Yes?"

"How did you all find us?"

His face hardened. "Seth."

Confused, I sat up again. "What? How?"

Aiden shook his head slightly. "I don't know. He showed up real early in the morning—the morning you left—and said something was wrong and you were in danger. I checked your room and saw that you were gone. Once we got on the road, he knew where to find you. Somehow, he could sense where you were. I don't know how, but he did. Seth was the reason we were able to find you."

Two days later, I returned to the Covenant, pumped full of blood and fluids. As soon as I arrived, I was taken to the infirmary to be checked over again. Aiden sat beside me as the doctor removed the white gauze that covered every piece of exposed skin.

Needless to say, I looked torn up. Several crescent-shape bites marked each arm. They were still pretty red-looking and while the doctor made some herb mixture that "should" help minimize the scarring, I rummaged through the cabinets.

"What are you looking for?" Aiden asked.

"A mirror."

He knew why. Sometimes, as annoying as it could be, it was like we shared the same brain. "It's not that bad, Alex."

I shot him a look over my shoulder. "I wanna see."

Aiden tried again to get me to sit back down, but I refused to listen until he got up and found a small plastic mirror. Without saying a word, he handed it to me.

"Thank you." I lifted the mirror and nearly dropped it.

The deep purple that covered my right eye and spread toward my hairline wasn't bad. It would fade in a couple of days. A black eye wasn't a big deal. I liked to think I looked sort of badass with it. However, the tags on each side of my neck were horrendous. Some of them looked deep, almost as if patches of skin had been ripped out and fused back together, the flesh uneven and crimson in color. The redness would fade, but the scars left behind would be deep and obvious.

My fingers tightened around the plastic handle. "It—I look horrible."

He was immediately by my side. "No. They'll fade, and before you know it, no one will even notice."

I shook my head. I couldn't hide this—not all of these.

"Besides," he said in the same gentle voice, "these are scars to be proud of. Look at what you've survived. These scars will make you stronger, more beautiful in the end."

"You said that before—about the first one."

"The same still stands, Alex. I promise you."

Slowly, I placed the mirror down on the little counter and . . . I broke.

It wasn't the scars or what Aiden had said. It was what those scars would forever be a reminder of—losing Mom in Miami. All the terrible things she'd done and allowed to happen. And what I had done—killing her. They were big, powerful sobs. The kind I couldn't really breathe or think around. I tried to pull myself back together, but I failed.

I sat down in the middle of the doctor's office and cried. I wanted my mom, but she would never answer, never comfort me. She was gone, really gone this time. The yawning hole opened up in me and the grief, it just poured out, and it kept coming and coming.

Aiden knelt beside me, placing his arms around my bent shoulders. He didn't say a single word. He just let me cry it out, and after months of forcing myself to just push through it, all the pain and hurt had built up into the massive knot that finally unraveled.

Once I'd cried myself out, I wasn't sure how much time had passed. My head hurt, my throat felt raw, and my eyes were puffy. But in a weird way, I felt better, like I could finally breathe again, really breathe. All these months, I'd been slowly suffocating and I hadn't realized it until that moment.

I sniffled and winced at the dull pain in the back of my head. "Remember what you said about how your parents wouldn't have wanted a life like that?"

His fingers moved soothingly over my taut shoulders. "Yes. I remember."

"She didn't. I saw it just before she . . . was gone. She looked relieved. She really did."

"You released her from a horrible existence. That's what your mother would've wanted."

A few minutes passed. I still couldn't look up. "Do you think she's in a better place now?" I asked, my voice sounding small.

"Of course she is." Man, he really sounded like he believed it, too. "Where she is . . . she is no longer suffering. It's paradise—a place so beautiful that we can't even begin to imagine what it must be like."

I assumed he was talking about Elysia—a place very much like heaven. I took a deep breath and wiped under my eyes. "If anyone deserved it, she really does. I know it looks bad since she became a daimon, but she would never have chosen that."

"I know, Alex. The gods know that, too."

Slowly, I pieced myself back together and climbed to my feet. "Sorry to . . . unload all of that on you." I stole a quick peek at him.

Aiden frowned. "Don't ever feel sorry for this, Alex. I've told you before, if you ever need anything you can come to me."

"Thanks for . . . everything."

He nodded, stepping aside as I shuffled past him. "Alex?" He picked up a jar from the counter. The doctor must have come in at some point. "Don't forget this."

I took the jar and murmured my thanks. Bleary-eyed, I followed him out and into the vivid sun. It hurt my head and my eyes, but in a way, the sun still felt good on my skin. I was alive.

We stood for a moment on the marbled pathway, both of us staring out across the courtyard and the ocean beyond. I wondered what he was thinking.

"You going back to your dorm?" he asked.

"Yeah."

We didn't talk about our conversation in Nashville or about that night at his place, but it lingered on my mind as we made our way to the dorms. Walking as close as we were, it was hard not to think about it, but when I thought about Caleb, all thoughts of romance—or lack thereof—fled. I really needed to see him.

"See you . . . around?"

Aiden nodded as he stared across the quad. A few halfs lounged on the benches between the dorms. A pure was with them. She was making it rain over one spot. Kind of cool.

I sighed, stalling. "All right . . ."

"Alex?"

"Yes?"

He stared down at me, a soft smile tugging at his lips. "You're going to be okay."

"Yeah . . . I am. I guess it takes more than a couple of hungry daimons to bring me down, huh?"

He laughed, and the sound nearly knocked the air out of my chest. I loved the way he laughed. I looked up at him, a small smile tugging at my own lips. Like always, our eyes met and something deep flared between us. Even out here, out in the open as we were, *it* was still there.

Aiden stepped back. There was nothing left to say. I gave him a tiny wave and watched until he disappeared from view, then I cut across the courtyard and headed to Caleb's room. I wasn't worried about getting caught going into the boys' dorm. We hadn't gotten a chance to talk since everything had gone down. He opened the door after the first knock, wearing sweats and a loose shirt.

"Hey," I said.

He smiled and pushed the door open further. The grin immediately turned into a grimace and he clutched his sides. "Crap. I keep forgetting not to move a certain way."

"You doing okay?"

"Yeah, my ribs are just a little sore. You?"

I followed him back to the bedroom and sat cross-legged on the bed. "Good. Just got checked out by the doctor here."

He eased himself down on the bed beside me. A frown crossed his face as he studied me. "Those tags? Why haven't they healed like mine?"

I glanced down at his arms. Four days later and the only reminder were the bruised ribs and a couple of pale scars dotting his arms. "I don't know. The doc said they would fade in a few days. He gave me a jar of stuff to rub on them." I patted my pocket. "It's pretty bad looking, isn't it?"

"No. You kinda look like . . . like I should be afraid of you kicking my ass or something."

I laughed. "That's because I *can* kick your ass."

He raised his eyebrows. "Alex, I was kind of out of it in the woods, but I heard you . . ."

"Killed her?" I leaned over and grabbed an extra pillow. "Yeah, I did."

My bluntness caused him to flinch. "I'm . . . really sorry. I wish I knew what to say to make it easier for you."

"You don't need to say anything about it." Stretching out beside him, I stared up at the little green stars all over the ceiling. At night, they glowed. "Caleb, I'm sorry I dragged you into that mess."

"No. You didn't drag me into anything."

"You shouldn't have been there. What Daniel was doing—"

His hand clenched beside me. I don't think he saw me notice, but I did. "You didn't—"

"You shouldn't have been there."

He waved his hand, cutting me off. "Stop it. I made the decision to follow you. I could've gone to one of the Guards or the Sentinels. Instead, I followed you. It was my choice."

I stared at him and saw he was actually serious. He looked like he hadn't been sleeping well. I looked away. "I'm sorry . . . you had to go through this."

"It's okay, all right? Look. What are friends for if they can't share a few hours with psychotic daimons? We can look at it as a bonding experience."

I snorted. "Bonding experience?"

He nodded and started telling me about all the halfs who'd visited him since he came back to the Covenant. When he mentioned Olivia, he got that dopey look on his face. Suddenly I wondered if I got the dopey smile on my face when I thought of Aiden. Gods, I hoped not.

"So a skunk humped my leg earlier," Caleb went on.

"*What?*"

He laughed, and then winced. "You haven't been listening to me."

"Sorry." I blinked. "I kind of dazed out there."

"I could tell."

I then had an evil case of word vomit. "I almost hooked up with Aiden."

Caleb's mouth dropped open. It took him a couple of tries to say something coherent. "You do mean you almost hooked him like, say, with a fishing pole or something?"

My brows furrowed at that imagery. "No."

"A right hook to the jaw then?"

I shook my head.

He stared at me, his face draining of all color. "Alex, what in the hell are you thinking? Are you out of your mind? Do you want to end up in servitude? Wow. Oh, my gods, you're insane."

I cringed. "I said we *almost* hooked up, Caleb. Chill out."

"Almost?" He threw up his arms, then winced. "The Council—the *Masters* don't care about almost. Man, here I thought Aiden was cool. Freaking pure-bloods, they don't give two shits about what happens to us. Risk your entire future to just get between—"

"Hey. Aiden isn't like that."

Caleb looked at me blandly. "He isn't?"

"No." I rubbed my eyes. "Aiden's not going to risk my future. Trust me. He's nothing like the rest of them. I'd trust him with my life, Caleb."

He considered that silently. "How did it happen?"

"I'm not going to go into details, you perv. It was something that . . . just happened, but it's over. I just had to tell someone, but you have to promise me you won't say anything."

"Of course, I wouldn't. I can't believe you'd even have to worry about that."

"I know, but I feel better saying it. Okay?"

"Alex . . . you really care about him, don't you?"

I squeezed my eyes shut. "Yeah, I do."

"You do realize how wrong that is?"

"Yes, but . . . he's so different from any pure we know. He doesn't think like them. He's kind and he's really funny once you get to know him. He doesn't put up with any of my crap, and I kind of like him for that. I don't know. Aiden just gets me."

"And you do realize that all of that means nothing?" Caleb said. "That it can't go anywhere?"

That knowledge hurt more than it should. I sighed. "I know. Can we . . . talk about something else?"

Caleb lapsed into silence, thinking only gods know what. "Have you seen Seth?"

I propped myself up on one elbow. "No. He didn't stop by when I was in Nashville and I haven't really been anywhere today. Why?"

He did his best to shrug. With his bruised ribs, it came off a bit lopsided. "I figured you'd see him since . . ."

"Since what?"

"I know I was in and out of it back in the cabin, Alex, but your mom said you were another Apollyon." He watched me closely.

My stomach turned over and I flopped back on the bed, silent. Caleb still watched me. Waiting. I took a deep breath and told him everything in one big rush, stopping for a breath right before I told him Seth would become the God Killer. When it was over, Caleb stared at me as if I had three heads. "What?"

He blinked and shook his head. "It's just . . . you shouldn't *be*, Alex. I remember my *History and Civilization* class last year. We talked about the Apollyons and what happened to Solaris. This is . . . wow."

"Wow isn't the word I'm aiming for." I pushed myself up and crossed my legs. "I mean, it's pretty cool. Right? At eighteen, I'll either be obliterated or sucked dry by Seth instead of legally buying cigarettes."

"But—"

"Not that I *would* smoke. I guess I could pick up the habit. Maybe, just maybe, I'll be all energized long enough to use *akasha*, because I saw Seth use it and it was damn cool. I'd like to hit a daimon or two with that."

Caleb scowled. "You're not taking this serious at all."

"Oh, I am. This is what I like to call coping with the impossible."

He wasn't impressed by my strategy. "You said Solaris was killed because the First Apollyon attacked the Council, right? Not because of what she was?"

I shrugged. "So as long as Seth doesn't go crazy, then I guess I'm okay."

"Why didn't Solaris stand against him?"

"Because she fell in love with him or something lame like that."

"Then don't fall in love with Seth."

"I really don't think that'll be a problem."

He didn't look entirely convinced. "Thought you guys belonged together or something?"

"Not in that way!" I forced my voice calmer. "It's like our energy responds to one another. It's nothing more than that. I'm just made to . . . I don't know, complete him. How freaking lame is that?"

He gave me a concerned look. "Alex, what are you going to do about this?"

"What can I do? I'm not going to stop living . . . or give up on my life, because of what *might* happen. Something really bad may come out of this or something really good or . . . nothing at all. I don't know, but I do know I'm going to focus on being one . . ." I stopped, surprised by my own words. Whoa. It was one of those really mature, really rare moments in my life.

Dammit. Where was Aiden to witness this?

"Focus on what?"

A wide smile crept across my face. "Focus on being one kick-ass Sentinel."

Caleb still didn't buy it, but I brought up Olivia and he was successfully distracted. Eventually I got up to leave. On the way out, I had an idea. It kind of came out of nowhere, but the moment it popped in my head, I knew I had to do it. "Can you meet me tomorrow night around eight?"

His gaze met mine. Somehow, I think he knew what I was going to ask, because he was already nodding. "I want to have . . . something for my mom." I squeezed my arms around my waist. "Like a memorial service or something. I mean, you don't have to."

"Of course I'll be there."

Flushing, I nodded. "Thanks."

Upon returning to my room, I found two letters stuck in the door—one from Lucian and one from Marcus. I was tempted to trash both of them but I opened up the one from my uncle.

It was a good thing I did. The message was simple, loud, and clear.

Alexandria,
Please come see me immediately.
Marcus.

Crap.

I tossed both of the letters on the small table in front of my couch and closed the door behind me. My thoughts swirled with what Marcus could want to talk to me about. Gee, the possibilities were endless. The stunt I'd just pulled, my future at the Covenant, or the whole Apollyon thing. Good gods, I could really be expelled and sent to live with Lucian.

How could I've forgotten about that?

When I finally did make it over to his office, the sun had started its slow descent over the waters, and the hazy light sent a rainbow of colors shimmering over the ocean. I tried to prepare myself for our meeting, but I didn't know what Marcus was going to do. Would he expel me? My stomach twisted uncomfortably. What would I do? Live with Lucian? Go into servitude? Neither of those were options I could live with.

The Guards gave me a curt nod before they opened the door to Marcus's office and stepped aside. My smile was more of a grimace, but elation swelled inside me when I recognized who stood beside the massive bulk that was Leon.

Aiden gave me a small, reassuring smile as the Guards closed the door behind me, but the moment I turned to Marcus, my skin turned cold.

He looked furious.

21

It was possibly the first time I'd ever seen him show any extreme emotion. I settled in for what I assumed would be a giant bitch-fest.

"First and foremost, I'm glad to see that you're alive and in one piece." Then his gaze dropped to my neck and finally, my arms. "Barely in one piece."

I bristled, but I managed to keep my mouth shut.

"What you did showed you have absolutely no regard for your life or the lives of others—"

"I have a regard for other people's lives!"

Aiden shot me a warning glare that said *shut up.*

"Going after a daimon—any daimon—untrained and unprepared is the height of reckless and idiotic behavior. Of all people, you should know the consequences. With what you are, what you will become, I cannot stress how irresponsible your actions were . . ." Marcus continued, but I tuned out at that point.

Instead, I wondered how long Leon had known what I was. Lucian had said only he and Marcus had been aware of what Piperi had told my mom, but a thought struck me. Leon had been the first to come to my defense when they'd brought me back to the Covenant. Had he always known? I looked up at my uncle, not really paying attention to what he was saying. There was always the chance they hadn't been honest with me about who knew. Hell, Lucian and Marcus hadn't been honest about a lot of things.

"If it hadn't been for Seth, you'd be dead or worse. And your friend Mr. Nicolo would have met the same fate."

My attention perked a bit. Where in the hell was Seth at, anyway? I'd half expected him to've weaseled his way into this meeting.

"Do you have anything to say for yourself?"

"Um . . ." I stole a quick glance at Aiden before answering. "It was really stupid of me."

Marcus arched a perfectly groomed brow at me. "Is that all?"

"No." I shook my head. "I shouldn't have done it, but I don't regret it." I could feel Aiden's eyes boring through me. Swallowing, I leaned forward and placed my hands on Marcus's desk. "I regret that Caleb got hurt and the other daimon got away, but she was my mother—my responsibility. You don't understand, but I had to do it."

He leaned back in his chair as he studied me. "Believe it or not, I do understand. It doesn't make your actions justified or intelligent, but I do understand your motivation."

Surprised, I fell back in the chair in silence.

"Alexandria, a lot of things have changed. With the daimons able to turn half-bloods, it's altered the way we must face every situation." He paused, the tips of his fingers resting under his chin. "The Council is calling a special meeting during the November sessions in New York to discuss the ramifications. Since you were an eyewitness to their plans, you will be attending. Your testimony will help decide how the Council will act against this new threat."

"My testimony?"

Marcus nodded. "You were privy to the daimons' plans. The Council needs to hear exactly what you were told."

"But that was just Mom . . ." I trailed off, unsure of how much Leon knew.

My uncle seemed to understand. "It is highly doubtful Rachelle discovered that half-bloods could be turned. It's more likely that she witnessed another daimon doing it. She wanted you . . . for her own reasons."

He had a good point. Based on what she'd said, it did seem like there was some big master plan—more than just her merry band of psychos. And then there was Eric; he was still out there, hyped up on Apollyon aether. The gods only knew what he was getting himself into.

"There is something else we need to discuss." He had my attention again. "I've met with Aiden and have reviewed your progress."

He really had my attention. I tried to sound brave and confident. "Lay it on me."

Marcus looked amused, if only for a second. "Aiden has advised me that you have progressed enough to continue at the Covenant." He picked up the dreaded file and opened it. I sank in my seat, remembering the last time he'd taken a gander at it. "You have a strong handle on the techniques of defense and offensive combat, but I see here you haven't started Silat training or defense against the elements, and you're extremely behind on your studies. You haven't even taken a class on recon or basic guarding technique—"

"I don't want to be a Guard," I pointed out. "And I can catch up on the class stuff. I know I can."

"Whether or not you want to be a Guard or a Sentinel is not even a concern at this point, Alexandria."

"But—"

"Aiden has agreed to continue your training," Marcus closed the file, "throughout the school year. He believes with his help and with the time you spend with the Instructors, you will be able to fully catch up."

I tried my hardest not to look at Aiden, but I almost came out of my seat. Once school began, Aiden didn't have to continue training me. He was a Sentinel full-time. Giving up his free time for me *had* to mean something.

"I have to be honest, Alexandria. I'm not sure it will be enough, but I do have to take into consideration all you have recently accomplished. Even without all the training and classroom experience, you have proven that your ability is . . . beyond some of our seasoned Sentinels."

"But—*wait*. What?"

Marcus smiled, and it wasn't fake or cold. In that one moment, he reminded me so much of Mom I couldn't fight the way the proverbial wall between us cracked. However, his next words blew that barrier to pieces. "If you can graduate in the spring, I am confident you will make an outstanding Sentinel."

Stunned, I stared at him. I'd expected him to try to send me back to Lucian so I'd be under the Council's thumb well before I turned eighteen, but it was the fact Marcus had actually complimented me that knocked me over.

Finally, I found my voice. "So . . . I can stay?"

"Yes. Once classes start up, you will need to spend extra time getting caught up."

A tiny part of me wanted to jump up and hug the man, but that reaction would be so uncool. So I managed a totally calm, "Thank you."

Marcus nodded. "I've worked out an agreement with Aiden to split training with Seth. We both agreed that would be for the best. There are things that Seth will be . . . better suited for as time progresses."

I was too happy about being allowed to stay to care about spending mandatory time with Seth. After three years of being in limbo when it came to my future, I could barely contain the relief and excitement rushing through me. I nodded eagerly as Marcus outlined a plan for me to get caught up on my studies and how I would alternate days between Aiden and Seth.

When my meeting with Marcus was over, I still wanted to hug him. "Is that all?"

His emerald gaze settled on me. "Yes . . . for now."

A wide grin broke out across my face. "Thank you, Marcus."

Marcus nodded, and still grinning, I shot to my feet. On the way out, Aiden and I exchanged relieved looks before I shut the door behind me. I bounced out of the main building and all the way to my dorm. I couldn't wipe the smile off my face. Such terrible things had happened, but out of all the misery, things were starting to look up.

Once inside my dorm room, I kicked off my shoes and stripped off my shirt. My tank got stuck in the shirt during the process. Turning and tugging on my shirt, I—

"Please don't stop with just the shirt."

"Holy crap!" I clutched my chest in surprise.

Seth sat on my bed, hands folded in his lap. His hair hung loose around his face. There was a devious smirk on his face that said he'd totally gotten a glimpse of my lacy bra.

"What are you doing in here?" Almost as an afterthought I added, "And on my bed?"

"Waiting for you."

I stared at him. Part of me wanted Seth to leave, but I was also curious. I sat down beside him, running my hands over the tops of my thighs. I wasn't exactly nervous, but I kind of felt like I wanted to crawl out of my skin. Seth was the first to break the strange silence that spread between us.

"You look terrible."

"Thanks." I groaned and held up my arms. The purplish-red splotches covered every portion of my arms, but I knew my neck . . . well, it was bad. For a few minutes I'd forgotten about it. "I really appreciate you pointing it out."

Seth tipped his head at me and shrugged. "I've seen worse. There was a Sentinel who got cornered once in New York City. Really was a pretty girl—a little older than you—and just had to be a Sentinel instead of a Guard. A daimon took a bite out of her face just to prove a—"

"Ugh. Okay. I get what you're saying: it could be worse. Try telling me when I don't look like I went to third base with a vampire. So why are you here?"

"I wanted to talk to you."

"About?" I stared at my feet and wiggled my toes.

"Us."

Wearily, I lifted my head and looked at him. "There's no—"

He reached out and placed one finger over my lips. "I have something really important to say about that matter, and after you give me a chance to say it, I'm not going to push or ever bring it up again. Okay?"

I should've knocked his hand down, demanded he leave, or at least, leaned back. Instead, I gently brushed his fingers away. "Before you go any further, I want to say something."

Seth's brows rose curiously. "Okay."

I took a deep breath and stared down at my toes again. "Thank you for doing whatever . . . it was you did to find us. If it wasn't for you then I'd probably be dead—or slicing and dicing someone right now. So . . . thank you."

He was silent for so long I checked out what he was doing. Seth just stared at me with this dumb look on his face. To keep from smiling, I looked away. "What?"

"I think that's possibly the nicest thing you have said to me. Ever."

I laughed. "No it's not. I've said nice things to you before."

"Like what?"

There had to be another situation when I'd said something nice. "Like . . . when . . ." I couldn't think of anything. Jeez, I was a bitch. "Okay. That *is* the first nice thing I've said to you."

"I think I need a moment to recognize and cherish this."

I rolled my eyes. "Moving on, what did you want to talk about?"

Seth turned serious. "I wanted to be up front on a few things with you."

"Like what?" I scooted back against the pillows lining the top of the bed, moving my legs so they weren't touching him.

His brows furrowed. "Like what the future has in store for us."

I sighed. "Seth, nothing is going to happen between—"

"Aren't you even a little bit curious as to how I found you? Don't you want to know how I did that?"

"Yeah, come to think of it, I would like to know."

Seth leaned back on one arm, twisting onto his side. The movement sent locks of golden hair forward, sliding over his jaw. His hip was far too close to my curled toes. Not that he seemed to care. "I was having a really good dream about this chick I met in Houston and we were—"

I groaned. "Seth."

"All of a sudden, I was hurled out of the dream. I woke up, and my heart was racing, sweat pouring. I had no idea why. I felt sick—sick to my soul."

I pulled my knees to my chest. "Why?"

"Getting there, Alex. It took me a while to realize nothing was wrong with me, but the feeling wouldn't go away. Then I felt it—the first tag. It was like I was on fire and the pain—it was something real. For a second, I actually thought I had been tagged. It struck me then. It was *you* I was feeling. I went to Aiden—"

"Why did you go to him?"

"Because I figured if anyone knew where you were, it would be him. Lot of help he proved to be, though. He had no clue."

How did he come to that conclusion? That was something better left untouched for now. "So you felt what I was feeling?"

Seth nodded. "Every. Single. Tag. Like it was my skin being ripped into and my aether being drained. I never felt anything like it." He looked away. A few moments passed before he spoke again. "I don't know how you . . . dealt with it. It felt like my soul was being torn apart, but it was *your* soul."

Sort of struck dumb by what he was explaining, I listened quietly.

"Once we realized you weren't in your room, Aiden figured out what you had done. We left immediately, and I can barely explain how I knew where to go. It was like something was leading me. Instinct maybe?" He shrugged, staring down at his hand. "I don't know. I just knew to head west, and when we got close to the Tennessee line, Aiden said you once mentioned Gatlinburg. As soon as he said that, I knew where you were."

"But how? Did any of this happen before? When I was fighting Kain?"

He looked up and shook his head. "I don't think so. Whatever changed did so after then. The only thing I can come up with is that the longer I'm around you, the more . . . connected we are, and since I've already gone through the change, I can tune into those kind of things better."

I frowned. "It makes no sense."

"It will." He sighed. "When Lucian said we were two halfs made to be a whole, he wasn't kidding. If you had hung around that night at his house, you would've learned some interesting things. It would make things . . . so much easier."

Ah, damn. That night only made me think of one thing: Aiden. It was a struggle, but I managed to push him into the furthest corner of my mind. "What kind of things?"

Seth sat up and faced me in one fluid motion. "The gods know you are going to hate this, but oh, what the hell. The longer we are around each other, the more connected we will become— to the point neither of us will really know where one begins and the other ends."

I sat up a bit straighter. "I don't like the sound of that."

"Yeah . . . well, me neither. But this is what's going to go down. I know how you are with control. You're kind of like me in that sense. I don't like not being able to control what I'm feeling. Just like you, but it's not going to matter. Even now, it's already affecting me."

"What's affecting you?"

He seemed to struggle for the right words. "Being around you is already affecting me. I can tap into *akasha* easily, sensing you when you're hurt, and even now, I can feel it." He paused, taking a deep breath. "It's the power in you—the aether. It calls to me, and you haven't even changed yet. What do you think it's going to be like when you do? When you turn eighteen?"

I didn't know and I really didn't like where any of this was heading. "You know what will happen, don't you?"

Seth nodded again and looked away. "Once it happens, it will be a thousand times—no, a million times stronger. What I want, you will want. We will share the same thoughts, needs, and desires. Supposedly, it works both ways, but I'll be stronger than you. Whatever you want may end up being skewed by what I want. I am the First, Alex. All it takes is one touch and that power shifts to me."

Panic reared and I failed at pushing it down. I started to rise, but Seth placed his hands on my knees. Thank the gods I was wearing jeans because if his skin touched mine and that goofy swirly crap started happening right now, I'd probably lose it.

"Alex, hear me out."

"Hear you out? You're saying I'll have no control over anything." I shook my head frantically. The wild movement stretched the tender skin on my throat, but I ignored the sting. "That can't happen. I can't deal with that. I don't believe in being fated to someone—or even fate."

"Alex, calm down. Look. I know this is probably up there with the worst things that can happen to you, but you have time."

"What do you mean I have time?"

"None of this affects you now. You won't want anything I want right now." He let go of my knees and leaned back—away from *me*. "But it doesn't work that way for me. Being near you means the connection is choking the crap out of me. Like right now, your heart is racing. So is mine. Being this close to you is like . . . being inside your head, but you still have time."

Processing all of this wasn't easy. I mean, I got what he was saying. Since he'd gone through the whole palingenesis thing, whatever it was between us was already wrapping its super-special cord around him, but not me. Not until I turned eighteen. Then? "Why didn't Lucian tell me any of this?"

"You didn't stick around, Alex."

I made a face at him. "I don't like any of this, Seth. We're talking seven months here. In seven months, I'll be eighteen."

"I know. Seven months of me helping you train, so try to imagine what the hell I'll be feeling this whole entire time."

I tried, but couldn't. "This isn't going to work."

He leaned forward and tucked a strand of blond hair behind his ear. "That's what I'm thinking. I came up with an idea. Now, hear me out on this. I can deal with this for right now, because even though it's strong, it's not that strong. It's doable—for me, but after you Awaken, things will change. If we can't handle it—if *you* can't handle it, then we'll separate. I'll leave. You won't be able to because of school, but I can. I'll go to the other end of the earth."

"But the Council—Lucian—he wants you here, with me." I rolled my eyes. "For whatever reason. He's ordered you here."

Seth shrugged, and then he flopped down onto his back. "Whatever. Screw the Council. I'm the Apollyon. What the hell can Lucian do to me?"

Those were dangerous, rebellious words. I kind of liked them. "You'd actually do that for me?"

He turned his gaze to me, smiling slightly. "Yes. I would actually do that. You seem surprised."

One of my legs dropped off the side of the bed as I leaned over him. "Yes. Why would you? It sounds like everything comes up rosy for you."

"Do you think I'm a bad person or something?" He continued to smile up at me.

I blinked, a bit taken aback. "No . . . I don't think that."

"Then why would you think I'd force this upon you? Being apart won't stop the connection from growing stronger, but it will stop the shifting of power. Things . . . will be intense once the transfer happens. If I leave, we will each still be our own person."

Out of nowhere, it struck me. "This is for you. You don't think you'll be able to handle it."

He only acknowledged my words with a sardonic twist to his lips.

This connection thing must actually bother him if he really thought he wouldn't be able to handle it down the road. Wrong as it may be, it kind of made me feel better about the situation. In the end, if things became too much, there was a way out. I still had control. So did Seth.

"What are you thinking?"

Snapping out of my thoughts, I looked down at him. "The next seven months are really going to suck for you."

Seth tipped his head back and laughed. "Ah, I don't know about that. This—*this thing*—has its benefits."

I sat back, folding my arms. "How so?"

He smiled.

"What are *you* thinking?"

"That we've actually held an entire conversation without insulting one another. Next thing you know, you'll actually consider me a friend."

"Baby steps, Seth. Baby steps."

He turned back to staring at my ceiling. There were no stars that glowed, just ordinary old, dull white paint. Without thinking, I moved again, reaching out and touching the hand resting near my thigh. Call it an experiment, but I wanted to see what would happen.

Seth's head whipped in my direction. "What are you doing?"

"Nothing." And nothing was what happened. Confused, I wrapped my fingers around his.

"Doesn't look like nothing," His eyes narrowed on me.

"I guess so." Giving up on my impromptu test, I lifted my hand. "Shouldn't you be—" Whatever I was about to say died on my lips. Incredibly fast, Seth grabbed my hand and threaded his fingers through mine.

"Is this what you wanted?" he asked, ever so casually.

It happened. Being so close to him this time, I could see where the markings came from. The thick veins in his hand were the first to darken, branching out before spreading up his arm. Mesmerized, I watched the inky tats cover every piece of exposed skin. Before my eyes, they shifted away from his veins, swirling around his skin. Breaking off into different designs as he—we—continued to hold hands.

"What do they mean?" I looked up. His eyes were closed. "The markings?"

"They are . . . the marks of the Apollyon." He answered slowly, as if he were having trouble forming words and sentences. "They are runes and spells . . . meant to offer protection . . . or in our case, alert each other to our presence . . . or something. They mean other stuff, too."

"Oh." The runes glided down his skin, toward the tips of his fingers. Call me crazy, but I was confident that those markings were reacting to where our skin touched, and for a split second, I really believed those glyphs would jump his skin and spread across my flesh.

"Will . . . I look like this one day?"

"Hmm?"

I pulled my gaze from our hands and looked up. Seth's eyes were still closed, his expression relaxed. Actually, it was more than that. He looked . . . content. Pleased. I'd never seen him so calm. "Is this one of the benefits?" I meant it as a joke, but the realization smacked me upside the head before he could respond. It *was* because he was close to me. Something as simple as that did affect him. *I* affected him that way.

I recalled what he'd said after my run-in with Kain. "I really do have all the power in this."

His eyes opened and they shone like two giant, tawny jewels. "What?"

My fingers tightened around his, and his lips parted, allowing a sharp sigh to leak out. Then, slowly, carefully, I loosened my hold on his fingers. Interesting. "Nothing."

"I never should have told you the truth about that." His voice held a certain rough edge to it. "You do, at least for now."

I ignored the last part and pulled my hand free before the marks could touch my skin. We didn't say anything for a couple of minutes. I leaned back against the pillows and Seth closed his eyes once more. During that stretch of silence, I watched the steady rise and fall of his chest. He almost looked like he was sleeping. Relaxed as he was, the beauty of his face didn't look so cold or methodical. This time, I was the first to break the silence.

"So . . . what are you doing?"

"Now?" He sounded sleepy. "I'm making up plans. Things I'm going to show you—in training, of course."

My brows rose. "I don't see how there is anything you can show me that Aiden can't."

Seth laughed then, and when he spoke, his voice was smug and knowing. "Oh, Alex, I have a lot to show you. Things that Aiden will never be able to teach you."

Staring down at him, I admitted to myself that there was a teeny tiny part of me that actually looked forward to whatever it was that he planned on showing me. I felt confident that it would be entertaining if not fruitful.

We really didn't talk after that, and all too soon, the excitement of everything faded, leaving me exhausted. My eyelids started to get too heavy to keep open, and I wanted nothing more than to kick Seth over, so I could lie down. As it was, he took up quite a bit of space sprawled across the middle of *my* bed.

Not all that surprising, Seth opened his eyes then and looked at me. When he gave a little half smile and pushed himself to his feet, I wondered if he'd sensed he was about to get a roundhouse kick in his side.

There went the element of surprise.

"You leaving?" I asked, because really, I had no idea what else to say.

Seth didn't answer. He lifted his arms above his head and stretched, showing off a row of taut muscles as the black shirt rode up his stomach. The image of a cat flashed before me. That was how he moved, feline and predatory. It was a subtle grace neither human nor half.

"Do you know what your name means? Your real name—Alexandria?"

I shook my head.

He smiled slowly. "It means 'Defender of Man' in Greek."

"Oh. That sounds cool. What does your name—?"

Suddenly, he bent at the waist and swooped in. He was so damn fast I didn't even have a chance to jerk back, which by the way, is totally a natural reaction when the Apollyon comes at someone *that* quickly.

He brushed his lips over my forehead, lingering only long enough I could be positive he'd placed a gentle kiss against my skin before straightening.

"Good night, Alexandria, Defender of Man."

Stunned, I mumbled something along the lines of goodbye, but he was gone before I could fully get the words out. I reached up and brushed my fingers over the spot his lips had touched. His gesture was weird, unexpected, wrong, and . . . sweet.

I eased down and stretched out my legs. Staring up at the ceiling, I wondered what the next couple of months held in store for me. For the most part, I came up empty. Everything had changed—I had changed, but the one thing I could be sure about was between Aiden and Seth, I'd be learning lots of things.

★ ★ ★

The following afternoon, I remembered the card from Lucian I'd dropped on the table. I slipped my finger under the crease and tore it open. I slid the money out, and for the first time, I actually read the note.

It wasn't bad or too fake, but still, nothing stirred in my chest as I stared down at his elegant handwriting. No matter how much money he sent me or how many letters he personally wrote, he couldn't buy my love or erase the suspicion surrounding him like a thick cloud.

But his money was going to buy me some pretty sweet shoes soon.

With that thought in mind, I showered and found something to wear that covered the worst of the tags. Keeping my hair down helped with the neck situation, but it didn't cover all the splotches.

To my surprise, the Guards didn't stop me when I crossed the bridge to the main island, but as I prowled the main street, I had a feeling of being watched. A quick glance over my shoulder confirmed my suspicions. One of the Guards had broken away from his partner on the bridge and kept a discreet distance behind me. Perhaps Lucian or Marcus worried I'd make another run for it . . . or do something else incredibly irresponsible.

I tossed the Guard a saucy grin before darting into one of the boardwalk's tourist shops owned by the pures but run by mortals. The one I dove into featured an assortment of home-made candles, mosaic tiles made out of crushed shells, and sea salt baths. Smiling to myself, I sensed I'd be spending some of Lucian's money here.

Excited by all the girl stuff I planned on indulging in, I considered the simple pleasures of life often overlooked when preparing to kill daimons. Bubble baths were usually a low priority. I grabbed a few white votive candles in little pine-wood spirit boats and a handful of big, chunky ones—the kind that smelled like they'd overdosed in a *Bath and Body Works* sweatshop.

At the checkout counter, I ignored the way the obviously mortal clerk kept staring at my neck. Pures used compulsions on the mortals who lived near the Covenant, convincing them that all the weird things they saw were actually normal. This chick looked like she could use another dose.

"Is that all?" She stuttered over the last word, forcing her gaze away from my scars.

I shifted uncomfortably. Was this going to be how people acted until the damn tags faded? My eyes dropped from her to a set of ocean-themed stationery next to the register. "Can I add that?"

The girl nodded, sending highlighted hair across her face. Unable to look at me directly, she rang me up pretty quick.

Once outside the store, I sat on one of the white benches lining the street and scribbled a couple of lines. After sealing the envelope, I headed across the street and cut between a bookstore and a novelty shop.

I didn't need to look behind to know the Guard still trailed me. Ten minutes later, I climbed the wide steps to Lucian's beach house and slid the note through the crack under his door.

There was a good chance he wouldn't even get it, but at least I'd attempted to thank him. I'd feel less guilty about spending my mini-fortune on my back-to-school wardrobe. After all, I couldn't wear dress greens and workout clothes all year long.

I rushed off his porch just in case he was actually home and caught me there. With my bag of smelly goodness, I started back to the Covenant-controlled island.

"Miss Andros?"

Letting out a huge sigh, I turned and faced the Guard turned stalker. He stood by his partner now, a bland look on his face. "Yeah?"

"The next time you wish to leave the Covenant, please gain permission."

I rolled my eyes, but nodded. I'd come full circle since I'd returned to the Covenant. I still needed a babysitter.

Back on the campus, I made one more stop before I met up with Caleb: the courtyard. Hibiscuses had been Mom's favorite flower, and I found several in bloom. I liked to think they smelled like the tropics but I could never really catch any scent from them. Mom had just liked how beautiful they were. I snatched about a half of dozen and left the garden.

As I neared the girls' dorm, I spotted Lea sitting on the front porch with a few other half girls. She looked a lot better than the last time I'd seen her.

She tipped her chin when I passed her, using one über-tanned hand to flick her gloriously shiny hair over her shoulder. Silence stretched between us, and then she opened her mouth.

"Don't you look lovelier than normal?" She pushed away from the thick columns and bit her plump lower lip. "Well . . . at least the tags draw the attention away from your face. Guess that's a good thing, huh?"

I didn't know whether to laugh or punch her in the face. Either way, as ridiculous as it sounded, it felt good to see Lea back to her bitchy self.

"What?" She narrowed her eyes in challenge. "You have nothing to say?"

I thought it over. "I'm sorry . . . you're so tan I thought you were a leather chair."

She smirked as she strutted by me. "Whatever. Freak."

Normally those words would have started a never-ending battle of insults, but this time, I let it slide. I had better things to do. Inside my room, I separated the candles and the little boats used to guide spirits into the afterlife. The meaning was totally symbolic, but since I didn't have a body or a gravesite, it was the best I could come up with.

I took my time getting ready. I wanted to look nice—well, as nice as I could look with half my body covered in tags. When I felt satisfied my hair didn't look like a frizz ball and the dress I'd worn to the earlier funerals wasn't covered in lint, I picked up a light cardigan. Slipping it over my arms, I gathered up my stuff and headed off to meet up with Caleb.

He was already down by the water, near the edge of the marshlands and where the staff cottages sat. It was the best, most private place to do such a thing, and I felt glad for that. Seeing Caleb in his nice clothes felt like a punch to my chest.

He must've dug a pair of black trousers out of the bottom of his closet, as they were a couple of inches too short for him. Even though Mom had tried to kill Caleb, he'd dressed up out of respect for her memory and for me. Something stuck in my throat. I swallowed, but the sensation didn't go away.

Sympathy radiated from Caleb as he stepped forward and took the flowers out of my hand. Quietly, he set about setting up the little boats, and I plucked off the soft petals and sprinkled them in the boats. I thought she . . . would've liked the extra touch.

Staring down at the three boats, I swallowed again. One for Mom, one for Kain, and one for all the others who had died. "I really appreciate this," I said. "Thank you."

"I'm just glad you're doing this."

The burning in my eyes increased and my throat tightened.

"And you wanted to include me," he added.

Oh, gods. He was going to make it happen. I was going to cry.

Caleb edged closer to me and wrapped his arm around my shoulders. "It's okay."

A single tear snuck out. I caught it with the tip of my finger before it made its way down my cheek, but then came another fat tear . . . and another. I wiped at my face with the back of my hand. "I'm sorry," I sniffled.

"No," Caleb shook his head, "don't be sorry."

I nodded and took a deep breath. After a few moments, I reined the tears back in and forced a wan smile.

We were kind of lost in each other's arms for a while. Both of us had something to mourn—something we'd lost. Perhaps Caleb needed this, too. Time seemed to slow down until we were ready.

I looked at the candles. "Shoot." I'd forgotten a lighter.

"Need a light?"

We turned toward the deep, rich voice. I recognized the sound all the way down to my soul.

Aiden stood a short distance from us, his hands shoved deep into the pockets of his jeans. The setting sun created a halo affect around him, and for a tiny moment, I almost believed he was actually a god and not a pure.

I blinked, but he didn't disappear. He was really here. "Yes."

He stepped forward and touched each vanilla candle with the tip of his finger. Abnormally bright flames sparked and grew, unfazed by the breeze coming off the ocean. When he was done, he stood and looked at me. Pride and reassurance filled his gaze, and I knew he approved of what I was doing.

I swallowed back more tears as Aiden retreated back to where he'd been standing. With effort, I tore my gaze from him and picked up my little boat. Caleb followed suit, and we walked to where the water turned to white, wispy foam, licking at our knees—far enough out that the surf wouldn't carry the boats back in.

Caleb sat the two boats down first. His lips moved, but I couldn't hear what he said. Possibly a prayer? I couldn't be sure, but after a few moments, he let go of his boats and the waves carried them off.

So much stuff ran through my head as I stared down at my boat. I closed my eyes, seeing her beautiful smile. I pictured her nodding and telling me it was okay, okay to let it all go now. And I guess, in a way, it was okay. She was in a better place. I really believed that. There'd always be some sort of guilt. Everything she'd done from the moment the oracle had spoken to her had led to this, but it was over—finally over. Bending down, I set the spirit boat on the water.

"Thank you for everything, for all you gave up for me." I paused, feeling the slick wetness running down my face. "I miss you so much. I'll always love you."

My fingers lingered around the boat for a second more, and then the foamy waves carried the boat from me. Further and further out, the three boats went, their candles still glowing. The sky had darkened by the time I lost sight of the boats and their soft light. Caleb waited for me on the sand, and beyond him stood Aiden. If Caleb thought anything about Aiden's presence, it didn't show on his face.

Carefully, I made my way back to the beach. The distance between Aiden and me seemed to evaporate, and it was only the two of us. A small smile crept over his lips as I approached him.

"Thank you," I whispered.

Aiden seemed to understand I was thanking him for more than just a light. He spoke in a low voice so only I could hear him. "When my parents died, I never thought I'd find peace again. I know you have, and for that, I'm happy. You deserve it, Alex."

"Did . . . you ever find peace?"

He reached out and brushed his fingers over the curve of my cheek. It was such a quick gesture I knew Caleb never saw it. "Yes. I have now."

I inhaled sharply, wanting to say so much to him, but I couldn't. I like to think he knew, and he probably did. Aiden stepped back, and with one last look, he turned and headed home.

I watched until Aiden became nothing more than a faint shadow. Returning to where Caleb sat, I dropped down beside him and placed my head on his shoulder. Every so often, the salt water would tickle our toes, and I'd catch the scent of vanilla from the breeze rolling off the ocean. The air felt warm and pleasant, but the edge of the gentle wind held a soft chill, signifying autumn was on its way. But for right now, the sand felt warm on the island off the Carolina coast and the air still smelled of summer.

And now, the bonus prequel novella DAIMON . . .

DAIMON

A *Covenant* novella

Before

I

She smelled like mothballs and death.

The elderly Hematoi Minister facing me looked like she had just crawled out of the tomb she'd been stored in for a couple hundred years. Her skin was wrinkled and thin, like old parchment, and each breath she took I swore would be her last. I hadn't ever seen anyone that old, but of course I'd only been seven and even the pizza guy had seemed ancient to me.

The crowd murmured its disapproval behind me; I'd forgotten that simple half-bloods like me weren't supposed to look a Minister in the eye. Being the pure-blood spawn of demigods, the Hematoi had huge egos.

I looked at my mother, who stood beside me on the raised dais. She was one of the Hematoi, but she wasn't anything like them. Her green eyes flashed a pleading look to cooperate, to not be the incorrigible and disobedient little girl she knew I could be.

I didn't know why she was so frightened; I was the one facing the crypt keeper. And if I survived this poor excuse for tradition without ending up carrying this hag's bedpan for the rest of my life, it would be a miracle worthy of the gods that supposedly were watching over all of us.

"Alexandria Andros?" The Minister's voice sounded like sandpaper over rough wood. She clucked her tongue. "She is far too small. Her arms are as thin as the shoots of new olive branches." She bent over to study me more closely, and I half expected her to fall in my face. "And her eyes, they are the color of dirt, hardly remarkable. She barely has any blood of the Hematoi in her. She is more mortal than any we have seen this day."

The Minister's eyes were the color of the sky before a violent storm. They were a mixture of purple and blue, a sign of her heritage. All the Hematoi had startling eye colors. Most of the half-bloods did too, but for some reason I'd missed the whole cool eye color boat when I'd been born.

The statements had continued on for what seemed like forever to me and all I could think about was ice cream and maybe taking a nap. Other Ministers had come down to check me over, whispering to each other as they circled me. I kept glancing at my mother and she'd smile reassuringly, letting me know that all of this was normal and that I was doing okay— great, even.

That was, until the old lady started pinching every piece of my exposed skin and then some. I'd always had this thing about being touched. If I didn't touch someone then I believed they shouldn't touch me. Grandma had apparently missed that memo.

She'd reached out and pinched my belly through my dress with her bony fingers. "She has no meat on her. How can we expect her to fight and defend us? She is not worthy to train at the Covenant and serve beside the children of the gods."

I'd never seen a god, but my mom told me they were always among us, always watching. I'd also never seen a pegasus or a chimera, but she'd sworn they also existed. Even at seven I'd had a hard time believing the stories; it had strained my fledgling faith to accept that the gods still cared about the world they had so diligently populated with their children in a way only the gods could.

"She's nothing more than a pathetic, little half-blood," the ancient woman had continued. "I say send her to the Masters. I'm in need of a little girl to clean my toilets."

Then she had twisted her fingers cruelly.

And I had kicked her shin.

I'd never forget the look on my mother's face, like she'd been caught between terror and full-blown panic, ready to run between them and snatch me away. There were a few gasps of outrage, but there were also a few deep chuckles.

"She has fire," one of the male Ministers had said. Another stepped forward, "She will do fine as a Guard, maybe even a Sentinel."

To this day I had no idea how I'd proved my worthiness after kicking the Minister in the leg. But I had. Not that it meant a damn thing now that I was seventeen and had been nowhere near the Hematoi world for the last three years. Even in the normal world I hadn't stopped doing stupid things.

Actually, I was prone to random acts of stupidity. I considered it to be one of my talents.

"You're doing it again, Alex." Matt's hand tightened around mine.

I blinked slowly, bringing his face into focus. "Doing what?"

"You got this look on your face." He tugged me against his chest, snaking an arm around my waist. "It's like you're thinking about something universally deep. Like your head is a thousand miles away, somewhere up in the clouds, on a different planet or something."

Matt Richardson wanted to join Greenpeace and save some whales. He was the pretty boy next door who'd sworn off eating red meat. Whatever. He was my current attempt to blend with the mortals, and he'd convinced me to sneak out and go to a bonfire on the beach with a bunch of people I barely knew.

I had bad taste in boys.

Previously, I'd crushed on a brooding academic who'd written poems on the back of his school books and styled his dyed, jet black hair so it'd covered his hazel eyes. He'd written a song about me. I'd laughed, and that relationship had been over before it got started. The year before that was probably my most embarrassing—the bleached blond, JV football captain with sky blue eyes. Months had gone by with us barely exchanging a "hey" and "do you have a pencil?" before we'd finally met up at a party. We'd talked. He'd kissed me and mauled my boobs, all the while smelling like cheap beer. I'd punched him and broken his jaw. Mom had moved me to a different town after that and lectured me about not hitting as hard as I could, reminding me that a normal girl couldn't throw punches like that.

Normal girls didn't want their boobs mauled either, and I wholly believed if they could've landed a fist like I could, they would have.

I smiled up at Matt. "I'm not thinking about anything."

"You're not thinking at all?" Matt lowered his head. The edges of his blond hair tickled my cheeks. Thank the gods he'd gotten over the "trying to grow dreads" stage in his life. "Nothing going on in that pretty head of yours?"

Something was going on in my head, but it wasn't what Matt hoped for. As I stared into his green eyes, I thought about my very first crush—the forbidden, older guy with thundercloud eyes—the one so far out of my league he might as well have been a different species.

Technically, I guess he was.

Even now, I wanted to spin-kick myself in my face for that one. I was like a walking romance novel character, thinking love conquers everything and all that crap. Sure. Love in my world usually ended up with someone hearing "I smite thee!" as she was cursed to be some lame flower for the rest of her life.

The gods and their children could be petty like that.

I sometimes wondered if my mom had sensed my budding obsession with the pure-blood guy and that was why she'd yanked my happy butt out of the only world I'd known—the only world I really belonged to. Pures were so off limits to halfs like me.

"Alex?" Matt brushed his lips over my cheek, moving ever so slowly toward my lips.

"Well, maybe something." I lifted up onto the tips of my toes and circled my arms around his neck. "Can you guess what I'm thinking about right now?"

"That you wish you hadn't left your shoes back at the fire, because I do. The sand is really cold. Global warming is a bitch."

"Not what I had in mind."

He frowned. "You're not thinking about history class, are you? That would be kind of lame, Alex."

I wiggled out of his grasp, sighing. "Never mind, Matt."

Chuckling, he reached out and wrapped his arms back around me. "I'm just kidding."

Doubtful, but I let him lower his lips to mine. His mouth was warm and dry, the most a girl could ask from a seventeen-year-old boy. But to be fair, Matt was a pretty damn good kisser. His lips moved against mine slowly and when he parted them, I didn't sock him in the stomach or anything like that. I returned the kiss.

Matt's hands dropped to my hips and he eased me down in the sand, supporting himself with one arm as he hovered over me and trailed kisses over my chin, down my throat. I stared up at the dark sky riddled with bright stars and very few clouds. A beautiful night—a normal night, I realized. There was something romantic about all of it, in the way he cradled my cheek when his mouth returned to mine and whispered my name like I was some kind of mystery he'd never be able to figure out. I felt warm and pleasant, not rip-my-clothes-off-and-do-me excited, but this wasn't bad. I could get used to this. Especially when I closed my eyes and pictured Matt's eyes turning gray and his hair much, much darker.

Then he slipped his hand under the hem of my sundress.

My eyes snapped open and I quickly reached down, pulling his hand out from between my legs. "Matt!"

"What?" He lifted his head, his eyes a murky green. "Why'd you stop me?"

Why had I stopped him? I suddenly felt like Miss Purity Princess guarding her virginity from wayward boys. Why? The answer actually came to me pretty quickly. I didn't want to give up my V-card on a beach with sand finding its way into unseemly places. My legs already felt like they'd been well exfoliated.

But it was more than that. I really wasn't in the here and now with Matt, not when I was picturing him with gray eyes and dark hair, wanting him to be someone else.

Someone I would never see again . . . and could never have.

2

"Alex?" Matt nuzzled a spot on my neck. "What's wrong?"

Using a bit of my natural strength, I rolled him off me and sat up. I readjusted the top of my dress, thankful for the darkness. "Sorry. I'm just not into it right now."

Matt remained sprawled beside me, staring up at the sky like I had moments before. "Did . . . did I do something wrong?"

My stomach twisted and felt funny. Matt was such a nice guy. I turned to him, grabbing his hand. I threaded my fingers through his, the way he liked it. "No. Not at all."

He pulled his hand free and rubbed it across his brow. "You always do this."

I frowned. Did I?

"It's not just that." Matt sat up, dropping his long arms over his bent knees. "I don't feel like I know you, Alex. You know, like really know who you are. And we've been dating how long?"

"A couple of months." I hoped that was correct. Then I felt like a douche for taking a guess. Gods, I was turning into a terrible person.

A small smile pulled at his lips. "You know everything about me. How old I was when I got into a club for the first time. What college I want to go to. The foods I hate and how I can't stand carbonated drinks. The first time I broke a bone—"

"Falling off your skateboard." I felt good about remembering that.

Matt laughed softly. "Yeah, you're right. But I don't know anything about you."

I nudged him with my shoulder. "That's not true."

"It is." He glanced at me, the smile on his face fading. "You don't ever talk about yourself."

Okay. He had a point, but it wasn't like I could tell him anything. I could see me now. Guess what? You ever watch *Clash of the Titans* or read any Greek fables? Well, those gods are real and yeah, I'm sort of a descendant of them. Kind of like the stepchild no one wants to claim. Oh, and I hadn't even been around mortals until three years ago. Can we still be friends?

Not going to happen.

So I shrugged and said, "There's really isn't anything to tell. I'm pretty boring."

Matt sighed. "I don't even know where you're from."

"I moved here from Texas. I've told you that." Strands of hair kept escaping my hand, blowing across my face and over his shoulder. I needed a haircut. "It's not a big secret."

"But were you born there?"

I looked away, watching the ocean. The sea was so dark it looked purple and unfriendly. I pulled my gaze away and stared down the shore. Two figures walked along, clearly male. "No," I said finally.

"Then where were you born?"

I fought the soft touch of annoyance as I focused on the guys near the shore, hunkered down as the wind picked up, pelting them with a fine sheen of cold water. A storm was coming.

"Alex?" Matt climbed to his feet, shaking his head. "See? You can't even tell me where you were born. What's up with that?"

My mom thought that the less people knew about us the better. She was incredibly paranoid, believing if anybody knew too much then the Covenant would find us. Was that such a bad thing? I kind of wanted them to find us, to put an end to this craziness.

Growing frustrated, Matt dragged his fingers through his hair. "I think I'm just going to head back to the group."

I watched him turn around before I scrambled to my feet. "Wait."

He turned around, brows raised.

I took a shallow breath, then another. "I was born on this stupid island no one has ever heard of. It's off the coast of North Carolina."

Surprise flickered across his features and he took a step toward me. "What island?"

"Seriously, you wouldn't have heard of it." I folded my arms over my chest as goosebumps crawled over my skin. "It's near Bald Head Island."

A wide smile spread across his face, and I knew the skin around his eyes was crinkling like it did whenever he was exceptionally happy about something. "Was that so hard?"

"Yes." I pouted and then smiled, because Matt had the kind of smile that was infectious, a smile that reminded me of the best friend I hadn't seen in years. Maybe that's why I was drawn to Matt. My own grin started to fade as I wondered what my former partner in mayhem was doing right now.

Matt dropped his hands on my arms, slowly uncrossing them. "Wanna head back?" He nodded down the beach, at the group of kids clustered around the bonfire. "Or stay here . . . ?"

He'd left the offer open, but I knew what he meant. Stay here and kiss some more, forget some more. It didn't sound like a bad idea. I swayed toward him. Over his shoulder, I spotted the two guys again. They were almost on us and I sighed, now recognizing them.

"We have company." I stepped back.

Matt glanced over his shoulder at the two guys. "Great. It's Ren and Stimpy."

I giggled at the accurate description. During the few times I'd actually met the gruesome twosome, I refused to learn their real names. Ren was tall and lanky, his dark brown hair so full of hair gel it could be labeled a dangerous weapon in most states.

Stimpy was the shorter and wider of the two, shaved bald and built like a locomotive. The two were known for causing trouble wherever they went, especially Stimpy and his questionable weightlifting program. They were two years older than us, having graduated from Matt's high school before I even stepped foot in Florida. But they still hung out with the younger crowd, no doubt scoping out impressionable girls. There'd been some bad rumors about those two.

Even in the pale moonlight I could tell their skin was a healthy shade of orange. Their overly broad smiles were obscenely white. The shorter one whispered something and they fist bumped each other.

Not unexpectedly, I didn't like them.

"Hey!" Ren called out as the pair's swagger slowed down. "What's up, Matt, my man?"

Matt shoved his hands in the pockets of his cargo shorts. "Nothing much—you?"

Ren glanced at Stimpy, then back to Matt. Ren's neon pink polo shirt looked painted on his scrawny frame, at least three sizes too small. "We're just chillin'. Gonna head out to the clubs later." Ren looked at me for the first time, his eyes drifting over my dress and down my legs.

I puked a little in my mouth.

"I've seen you around a few times," Ren said, bobbing his head to and fro. I wondered if it was some kind of weird mating dance. "What's your name, sweetness?"

"Her name's Alex," answered Stimpy in all his shifty eyed glory. "It's a guy's name."

I stifled my groan. "My mom wanted a boy."

Ren looked confused.

"Actually it's short for Alexandria," Matt explained. "She just likes to be called Alex."

I grinned at Matt, but he was watching the two guys closely. A muscle feathered along his jaw.

"Thanks for the clarification, bud." Stimpy crossed his massive arms, eyeballing Matt.

Catching Stimpy's look, I shifted closer to Matt.

Ren, still staring at my legs, made a sound that was a cross between a grunt and a moan. "Damn girl. Is your daddy a thief?"

"What?" I'd never actually met my dad. Maybe he was. All I knew was that he'd been mortal. Hopefully, he'd been nothing like these two ass-hats.

Ren flexed his nonexistent muscles, smiling. "Well, then who stole those diamonds and put them in your eyes?"

"Wow." I blinked and turned to Matt. "Why don't you ever say such romantic stuff like that to me, Matt? I'm hurt."

Matt didn't grin like I expected. His gaze kept bouncing between the two, and I could see his hands balling into fists inside his pockets. There was a certain edge to his eyes, to the way his lips were drawn into a tight line. My amusement vanished in an instant. He was . . . scared?

I reached for Matt's arm. "Come on, let's head back."

"Wait." Stimpy clapped Matt on the shoulder with enough force to cause Matt to stumble backward a few inches. "Kind of rude of you guys to just run off."

A rush of warm air crawled up my spine and spread over my skin. My muscles tensed with anticipation. "Don't touch him," I warned softly.

Out of surprise, Stimpy dropped his hand and stared at me. Then he smiled. "She's a bossy one."

"Alex," Matt hissed, staring at me with wide eyes. "It's okay. Don't make a big deal out of it."

He hadn't seen me make a big deal yet.

"The 'tude must come with the name." Ren laughed. "Why don't we go party? I know a bouncer down at Zero who can get us in. We all can have a good time." Then he grabbed for me.

Ren may have meant to do it playfully, but it was seriously

the wrong move. I still had a serious issue with being touched when I didn't want to be. I caught his arm. "Was your mom a gardener?" I asked innocently.

"What?" Ren's mouth hung open slightly.

"Because a face like yours belongs planted on the ground." I twisted his arm back. Shock flickered over his features. There was a second when our gazes locked, and I could tell he wasn't sure how I'd gained the upper hand so quickly.

It had been three years since I'd seriously fought anyone, but unused muscles woke up and my brain sort of clicked off. I dipped under the arm I held, bringing it along with me as I clipped his knee with my foot.

The next second Ren ate sand.

3

Staring down at the guy sprawled spread-eagle in the sand, I realized I kind of missed fighting, especially the rush of adrenaline and the "Damn, I rock" feeling that came along with taking someone down. But then again, fighting mortals was nothing like fighting my own kind or the things I'd once trained to kill. This had been effortless. If he'd been another half-blood, I might've been the one with a mouthful of sand looking pretty damn lame.

"Jesus," Matt whispered, jumping back.

I looked up, expecting to see a shock and awe kind of look from him. Maybe even a thumbs up. Nothing, I got nothing from him. At the Covenant, I would've been applauded. But I kept forgetting I wasn't at the Covenant anymore.

Stimpy's dumbstruck gaze swung from his pal to me and quickly turned to fury. "You act like a man? You better be able to take it like a man, you bitch."

"Oh." I smiled as I faced him fully. "It's on like Donkey Kong."

Having the obvious body mass thing going for him, Stimpy rushed me. But he hadn't been trained to fight from the age of seven and he didn't have my literally god-given strength and speed. He swung a meaty fist toward my face and I spun around, kicking out and planting my bare foot in his stomach. Stimpy doubled over, throwing out his hands as he tried to capture my arms. I stepped into him, grabbing his upper arms and yanking him down as I brought my leg up. His jaw bounced off my knee and I let go, watching him fall into the sand with a grunt.

Ren stumbled to his feet, spitting out sand. He swayed and then took a swing at me. It was way off, and I could have easily dodged it. Hell, I could've stood still and he wouldn't have made contact, but I was on a roll now.

I caught his fist, sliding my hand down his arm. "Hitting girls isn't nice." I turned around, using his body weight to knock him off balance. He went over my shoulder, face first into the sand once more.

Stimpy climbed to his feet and staggered to his fallen friend. "Come on, man. Get up."

"Need help?" I offered with a sweet smile.

Both guys scrambled down the beach, looking over their shoulders like they expected me to jump on their backs. I watched them until they disappeared around the cove, smiling to myself.

I turned back to Matt, the wind blowing my hair around me. I felt alive for the first time in . . . well, years. I can still kick ass. After all this time, I can still do it. My excitement and confidence dried up and shriveled away the moment I got a good look at Matt's face.

He looked horrified. "How . . ?" He cleared his throat. "Why did you do that?"

"Why?" I repeated, confused. "It seems pretty clear to me. Those guys are dicks."

"Yes, they're dicks. Everyone knows that, but you didn't have to lay the smackdown on them." Matt stared at me, eyes wide. "I just . . . I just can't believe you did that."

"They were bothering you!" I planted my hands on my hips, past caring about the wind smacking my hair in my face. "Why are you acting like I'm some kind of freak?"

"All they did is touch me, Alex."

That was enough reason for me, but apparently, not enough for Matt. "Ren grabbed at me. I'm sorry. I'm not down with that."

Matt just stared at me.

I bit back the string of curse words that were forming in my mind. "Okay. Maybe I shouldn't have done all that. Can we just forget about it?"

"No." He rubbed the back of his neck. "That was too weird for me. Sorry Alex, but that was just . . . freaky."

My ever tenuous hold on my anger started to thin. "Oh, so next time you want me to stand here and let them kick your ass and molest me?"

"You overreacted! They weren't going to kick my ass or molest you! And there won't be a next time. I'm not down with violence." Matt shook his head and turned away from me, plowing his feet through the mounds of sand, leaving me standing all alone.

"What the hell?" I muttered and then louder, "Whatever! Go save a dolphin or something!"

He whirled around. "It's a whale, Alex, a whale! That's what I'm interested in saving."

I threw up my arms. "What's wrong with saving dolphins?"

Matt ignored me at that point, and about two minutes later, I truly regretted yelling that. I stormed past him to retrieve my sandals and bag, but I did so with grace and dignity. Not one single disparaging remark or cuss word escaped my tightly sealed lips.

A couple of kids glanced up, but none of them said anything. The few friends I had at school had been Matt's friends, and they liked saving whales too. Not that anything was wrong with saving whales, but some of them threw their beer bottles and plastic wrappers in the ocean. Hypocritical much?

Matt just didn't understand. Violence was a part of who I was as a half-blood, ingrained in my blood since birth and trained into every muscle in my body. It didn't mean I was going to snap and body slam someone for no good reason, but I would fight back. Always.

The walk home sucked butt.

I had sand between my toes, in my hair and up my dress. My skin chafed in all the wrong places and everything freaking sucked. Looking back, I could admit that I might've overreacted a tad. Ren and Stimpy hadn't been particularly threatening. I could've just let it slide. Or acted like a normal girl in the situation and let Matt handle it.

But I hadn't.

I never did. Now everything was going to be screwed up. Matt would go to school on Monday and tell everyone how I'd gone Xena Warrior Princess on the douchebags. I'd have to tell my mom, and she would freak. Maybe she'd insist we move again. I'd actually be happy about that; there was no way I could go back to school and face those kids after Matt told them what'd happened. I didn't care that school would be ending in a few weeks, anyway. I also wasn't looking forward to the major bitch-fest coming my way.

One I knew I deserved.

Clenching the little purse in my fist, I picked up my pace. Normally the neon lights from the clubs and the sounds of the nearby carnival put me in a happy mood, but not tonight. I wanted to punch myself in the face.

We lived three blocks off the beach, in a two story bungalow Mom rented from some ancient guy who smelled like sardines. It was kind of old, but it had two tiny bathrooms. Bonus points there—we didn't have to share. It wasn't exactly in the safest neighborhood known to man, but an iffy side of town wasn't anything that would scare my mom or me.

Bad mortals we could handle.

I sighed as I navigated the still crowded boardwalk. The night-life was a big thing here. So were fake ID's and super-tan, super-skinny bodies. Everyone looked alike to me in Miami, which wasn't very different from my home—my real home—where I'd once had a purpose in life, a duty I'd be obligated to fulfill.

And now I was pretty much a loser.

I'd lived in four different cities and attended four high schools in three years. We always picked large cities to disappear in and always lived near water. So far we'd only attracted a little attention, and when we had, we'd run. Never once did my mom tell me why, not even a single explanation. After the first year, I'd stopped getting mad when she wouldn't tell me why she'd come to my dorm room that night and told me we had to leave. I'd honestly given up asking and trying to figure it out. Sometimes I hated her for all of this, but she was my mom and where she went, I went.

Dampness settled in the air, the sky overhead quickly darkening until no stars shone down. I crossed the narrow street and kicked open the gate of the waist-high, wrought iron fence surrounding our little patch of grass. I winced at the screech as it swung open, scraping along the sandstone pavers.

I stopped in front of the door, looking up as I searched my purse for the key. "Crap," I muttered as my eyes roamed over the little garden balcony. Flowers and herbs grew like crazy, overflowing their ceramic pots and climbing the rusty railings. Empty urns I'd stacked in a pile weeks ago had toppled over. I was supposed to have cleaned up the balcony this afternoon.

Mom was going to be pissed for a lot of reasons in the morning.

Sighing, I pulled out the key and shoved it in the lock. I had the door halfway open, thankful it hadn't creaked and groaned like everything else in the house did, when I felt the most unfamiliar sensation.

Icy fingers ran up my spine, and then down. All the tiny hairs on my body stood up as the unerring sense of being watched came over me.

4

I quickly turned, my gaze darting over the little yard and beyond. The streets were empty, but the feeling only increased. Unease gnawed at my stomach as I stepped back and reached behind me, wrapping my fingers around the edge of the door. Nobody was there, but . . .

"I'm losing my mind," I muttered. "I'm getting as paranoid as Mom. Nice."

I went inside, locking the door behind me. The uncanny feeling slowly eased off as I tiptoed through the silent house. I inhaled and nearly gagged on the spicy aroma filling the living room.

Groaning, I turned on the lamp beside the secondhand, shabby couch and squinted into the corner of the room. Sitting beside our TV and the magazine rack full of *US Weekly* was Apollo. A fresh wreath of bay laurel wrapped around the marble cast of his head. Of all the things my mom had forgotten to pack the many times we moved, she'd never forgotten him.

I loathed the statue of Apollo and his stinky bay laurel wreath my mom replaced every godsforsaken day of my life. Not because I had anything against Apollo. I guessed he was a pretty cool god since he was all about harmony, order and reason. It was just the gaudiest damn thing I'd ever seen in my life.

It was only the bust of his chest and head, but engraved across his chest were a lyre, a dolphin, and—if that wasn't enough symbolic overload for the masses—there were a dozen tiny cicadas perched on his shoulder. What the hell did the annoying, buzzing insects that got stuck in people's hair even stand for? Symbolizing music and song my rosy left butt cheek.

I'd never understood my mom's fascination with Apollo or with any of the gods for that matter. They'd been on the absentee list since mortals had decided sacrificing their virgin daughters was a totally uncool practice. I didn't know a soul who'd ever seen a god. They'd run around and bred a hundred or so demigods and then let them have babies—the pure-bloods—but they never showed up on anyone's birthday bearing gifts.

Holding my hand over my nose, I walked over to the candle surrounded by more laurel and blew it out. Being a god of prophecy, I wondered if Apollo had foreseen that. Gaudiness aside, what was shown of his marble chest was pretty nice.

Nicer than Matt's chest.

Which was something I'd never be seeing or touching again. With that in mind, I grabbed the carton of double chocolate fudge ice cream out of the freezer and a large spoon. Not even bothering with a bowl, I climbed the uneven steps.

Soft light spilled out from the gap between my mom's bedroom door and the floor. Stopping in front of her door, I glanced at my room and then down at the ice cream. I bit my lower lip and debated bursting into her room. She probably already knew I'd snuck out earlier and if she didn't, the sand covering half my body would give it away. But I hated the fact that my mom was home alone on a Friday night. Again.

"Lexie?" The soft and sweet voice called from behind the door. "What are you doing?"

I nudged open the door and peeked inside. She sat at the head of the bed, reading one of those smutty romance novels with half-naked guys on the cover. I totally stole them when she wasn't looking. Beside her on the small bedside table was a pot of hibiscus flowers. They were her favorite. The purple petals were beautiful, but the only scent came from the vanilla oil she loved to sprinkle over the petals.

She looked up, a slight smile on her face. "Hi, honey. Welcome home."

I held up my carton of ice cream, cringing. "At least I'm home before midnight."

"Is that supposed to make it okay?" She pinned me with a look, her emerald eyes glittering in the dim light.

"No?"

My mom sighed, setting her novel down. "I know you want to go out and be with your friends, especially since you started seeing that boy. What's his name? Mike?"

"Matt." My shoulders slumped and I eyed the ice cream eagerly. "His name is Matt."

"Matt. That's right." She gave me a brief smile. "He's a really nice boy, and I understand you want to be with him, but I don't want you running around Miami at night, Lexie. It's not safe."

"I know."

"I've never had to . . . what do they call it? When privileges are suspended?"

"Grounding." I tried not to smile. "They call it grounding."

"Ah, yes. I've never had to 'ground' you, Lexie. I really don't want to start now." She brushed back the thick, wavy brown hair from her face as her gaze drifted over me. "Why in the name of the gods are you covered in sand?"

I inched inside her room. "It's a long story."

If she suspected I'd rolled around in the sand with the boy whose name she kept forgetting and then kung foo'd my way through two other guys, she didn't let on. "Want to talk about it?"

I shrugged.

She patted the bed. "Come on, baby."

Feeling a bit dejected, I sat and tucked my legs under me. "I'm sorry about sneaking out."

Her bright gaze dropped to the ice cream. "I believe you may be wishing you'd stayed home?"

"Yeah." I sighed, cracking open the lid and digging in. Around a mouthful of ice cream, I said, "Matt and I are no more."

"I thought his name was Mitch?"

I rolled my eyes. "No, Mom, his name is Matt."

"What happened?"

Looking at her was like staring in the mirror, except I was more like a mundane version of her. Her cheekbones were sharper, her nose a little smaller, and her lips more lush than mine. And she had those amazing green eyes. It was the mortal blood in me that watered down my appearance. I'm sure my dad must've been hotness to have caught my mom's married eye, but he had been very human. Hooking up with humans wasn't prohibited by any means, mainly because the children—half-bloods like me—were extremely valuable assets to the pures. Well, I couldn't be included as an asset any longer.

Now I was just . . . I didn't know what I was anymore.

"Lexie?" She leaned forward, snatching the spoon and carton from my hands. "I'll eat and you tell me what the idiot boy did."

I smiled. "It's all my fault."

She swallowed a mammoth chunk of ice cream. "As your mother I am obligated to disagree."

"Oh, no." I flopped on my back and stared up at the ceiling fan. "You're going to change your mind on that one."

"Let me be the judge of that."

I scrubbed my hands over my face. "Well, I kind of . . . got into a fight with two guys on the beach."

"What?" I felt the bed shift as she straightened. "What did they do? Did they try to hurt you? Did they . . . touch you inappropriately?"

"Oh! Gods no, Mom, come on." I dropped my hands, frowning at her. "It wasn't like that. Not really."

Thick strands of hair blew back from her face. Simultaneously all the curtains in the room lifted, reaching toward the bed. The book beside her flew off the bed and landed somewhere on the floor. "What happened, Alexandria?"

I sighed. "Nothing like that, Mom. Okay? Calm down before you blow us out of our own home."

She stared at me a few moments, and then the winds died down.

"Show-off," I muttered. Pure-bloods like my mom could command one of the elements, a gift the gods had bestowed upon the Hematoi. Mom had a thing for the element of air, but she wasn't very good at controlling it. Once she blew over a neighbor's car—try explaining that to the insurance company. "These guys started messing with Matt and one of them grabbed at me."

"Then what happened?" Her voice sounded calm.

I prepared myself. "Well, they kind of needed to help each other off the ground."

My mom didn't immediately respond to that. I dared a quick look at her and found her expression relatively blank. "How bad?"

"They're fine." I smoothed my hands down the front of my dress. "I didn't even hit them. Well, I kicked one of them. But he called me a bitch, so I think he deserved it. Anyway, Matt said I overreacted and he wasn't into violence. He looked at me like I was a freak."

"Lexie . . ."

"I know." I sat up and rubbed the back of my neck. "I did overreact. I could've just walked away or whatever. Now Matt doesn't want to see me anymore and all the kids are going to think I'm some kind of . . . I don't know, weirdo."

"You're not a weirdo, baby."

I gave her a droll look. "There's a statue of Apollo in our living room. And come on, I'm not even the same species as them."

"You're not a different species." She dropped the spoon in the carton. "You're more like the mortals than you realize."

"I don't know about that." I crossed my arms, scowling. After a few seconds, I glanced at her. "Aren't you going to yell at me or something?"

She arched a brow and seemed to consider it. "I think you've learned that action is not always the best response, and the boy called you such an ugly name . . ."

A slow grin pulled at my lips. "They were total douchebags. I swear."

"Lexie!"

"What?" I giggled at her expression. "They are. And douche-bag isn't a cuss word."

She shook her head. "I don't even want to know what it is, but it sounds revolting."

I giggled again, but sobered up when Matt's horrified face flashed before me. "You should have seen the way Matt looked at me afterward. It was like he was afraid of me. So stupid. You know? Kids like me would have applauded that, but no, Matt had to look at me like I was the antichrist on crack."

My mom's brows puckered. "I'm sure it wasn't that bad."

The painting of a goddess on her wall became a sole focus to me. Artemis crouched beside a doe, a quiver of silver arrows in one hand and a bow in the other. The eyes were unnerving, painted completely white—no irises or pupils. "No. It was. He thinks I'm a freak."

She scooted closer, placing a gentle hand on my knee. "I know it's hard for you to be away from . . . the Covenant, but you'll be okay. You'll see. You have your whole life ahead of you, full of choice and freedom."

Ignoring that comment and wherever it came from, I took back my ice cream and shook the empty carton. "Boo, Mom, you ate it all."

"Lexie." Cupping my cheek, she turned my head so I faced her. "I know it bothers you being away from there. I know you want to go back and I pray to the gods that you can find happiness in this new life. But we can never go back there. You know that, right?"

"I know," I whispered, even though I really didn't know why.

"Good." She pressed her lips to my cheek. "With or without a purpose, you're a very special girl. Don't ever forget that."

Something burned in the back of my throat. "You're like totally obligated to say that. You're my mom."

She laughed. "That is true."

"Mom!" I exclaimed. "Wow. Now I'm going to have self-esteem problems."

"That is one area you are not lacking in." She sent me a saucy grin as I smacked at her hand. "Now get off my bed and go to sleep. I expect you up bright and early. Your little butt better be out on that balcony, cleaning up that mess. I'm serious."

I hopped from the bed and shook my butt. "It's not that little."

Her eyes rolled. "Good night, Lexie."

I skipped to the door, glancing over my shoulder at her. She was patting the bed, frowning.

"Your windstorm knocked it on the floor." I went over and picked the book up, handing it to her. "G'night!"

"Lexie?"

"Yeah?" I turned back around.

My mom smiled and it was such a beautiful smile, warm and loving. It lit up her entire face, turning her eyes into jewels. "I love you."

I smiled. "Love you, too, Mom."

After dumping the empty carton and washing off the spoon, I scrubbed my face and changed into a pair of old jammies. Restless, I tinkered around with the idea of cleaning my room, an impulse that lasted long enough for me to pick up a few socks.

I sat on the edge of the bed, staring at the shuttered balcony doors. The white paint was cracked, showing a deeper layer in a pale shade of gray—like a cross between blue and silver, an unusual shade that struck an old yearning inside me.

Really, after all this time, to still even think about a guy I'll never see again was freaking ridiculous. Worse yet, he hadn't even known I'd existed. Not because I'd been some kind of wall-flower, wilting away in the shadows at the Covenant, but because he hadn't been allowed to notice me. Here I was, three years later, and chipping paint reminded me of his eyes.

That was so lame it was embarrassing.

Annoyed with my own thoughts, I pushed off the bed and went to the little desk in the corner of my room. Papers and notebooks I rarely used in class covered the top. If there was anything I loved about the mortal world, it was their school system. Classes out here were a piece of cake compared to what went on at the Covenant. Knocking the clutter to the side, I found my out of date MP3 player and earbuds.

Most people had cool music on their players: Indie bands or the current hits. I decided I must've been high on something—Apollo's bay laurel fumes?—when I'd downloaded these songs.

I clicked through—that's how out of date this thing was—until I found Van Morrison's Brown Eyed Girl.

There was something about the song that turned me into a walking cheese ball from the very first guitar riff. Humming along, I danced around my room, picking up discarded clothing and stopping every few seconds to flail about. I threw the pile in the basket, bobbing my head like a deranged Muppet Baby.

Starting to feel a little better about things, I grinned as I shimmied around my bed, clutching a pile of socks to my chest. "Sha la la, la la, la la, la la, la-la tee da. La-la tee da!"

I winced at the sound of my own voice. Singing was not a personal strength, but that didn't stop me from mutilating every song on my MP3 player. By the time my room was fairly decent, it was past three in the morning. Exhausted but happy, I tugged out the earbuds and dropped them on the desk. Crawling into bed, I flipped off the lamp and dropped down. Usually it took me a while to drift off, but sleep came easily that night.

And because my brain liked to torture me even while I slept, I dreamt of Matt. But the dream-Matt had dark, wavy hair and eyes the color of storm clouds. And in the dream, when his hands roamed under my dress, I didn't stop him.

A strange, satisfied smile pulled at my lips when I awoke. I kicked back the covers, stretching lazily as my gaze fell on the balcony doors. Thin sheets of light broke through the creases under the shutters and slid over the old bamboo throw rug. Specks of dust floated and danced in the rays.

My smile froze when I spotted the clock. "Crap!"

Throwing the bedspread to the side, I swung my legs off the bed and stood. "Bright and early" did not translate to waking up at noon. My mom had gone easy on me last night, but I doubted she'd feel the same if I added not doing my chores for the second day in the row. A quick glimpse at my reflection in the tiny bathroom mirror while I stripped confirmed I looked like Chewbacca.

I took a quick shower, but the hot water still went cold before I could finish.

Shivering from the wrath of the evil water heater, I changed into a pair of worn jeans and a loose shirt. Towel drying my hair, I started toward my door. I stopped, smothering a yawn. Mom was probably already outside in the tiny garden in the front. It was right below the balcony, facing the apartment buildings and row homes across the street. I tossed the towel on the bed and threw open the balcony doors like some kind of southern belle greeting the day, all ladylike and delicate.

Except it all went wrong.

Wincing from the glare of the bright Florida sun, I shielded my eyes and stepped forward. My foot snagged in an empty flowerpot. Trying to shake it off, I lost my balance and careened across the balcony, catching myself on the railing before I could topple over it headfirst.

Death by flowerpot would be a hell of a way to go.

Underneath my arms, the rickety-ass wooden plant stand swayed to the left and then the far, far right. Several pots of green and yellow tulips shifted all at once.

"Crap!" I hissed. Pushing off the railing and dropping to my knees, I hugged the plant stand to my chest. Kneeling there, for once I was grateful that none of my old friends had been around to see that.

Half-bloods were known for their agility and grace, not for tripping over things.

Once I got everything back to where it was supposed to be without killing myself in the process, I stood and leaned carefully over the railing. I scanned the flowerbeds, expecting to find Mom laughing her butt off, but the yard was empty. I even checked by the fence, where she had planted a row of flowers a few weekends ago. I started to turn back when I saw the gate was open, hanging to the side.

"Huh." I was almost positive I'd closed it last night. Maybe

Mom had gone to the Krispy Kreme to get doughnuts? Mmm. My stomach grumbled. I grabbed the garden spade out of the mess of tools piled atop the small folding chair, bemoaning another morning eating shredded wheat if there weren't doughnuts. Who did I have to kill to get some Count Chocula up in this house?

I flipped the spade over in the air, catching it by the handle while I gazed past the yard. The row houses across the street all had bars on the windows and paint peeling off the sides. The old women who inhabited them didn't speak much English. Once I'd tried helping one of them pull her garbage bags out to the curb, but she'd yelled at me in another language and shooed me away like I'd been trying to steal it.

They were all out on their stoops right now, cutting coupons or doing whatever it was that old ladies did. Traffic packed the street. It was always like this on a Saturday afternoon, especially when it was turning out to be a nice day for a beach trip.

My gaze crawled over the townies and the tourists as I continued to toss the spade in the air. It was always easy to pick out the out-of-towners. They wore fanny packs or abnormally large sun hats and their skin was either fish pale or sunburned.

A strange shiver coursed over me, spreading tiny bumps over my flesh. I sucked in a sharp breath, my eyes scanning the passing crowds with a will of their own.

Then I saw it.

Everything stopped around me in an instant. The air went right out of my lungs.

No. No. No.

He stood at the mouth of the alley, directly across from the bungalow and right beside the front porch where the old ladies sat. They glanced over at him as he stepped out onto the sidewalk, but they dismissed the stranger and returned to their conversation.

They couldn't see what I saw.

No mortal could. Not even a pure-blood could. Only half-bloods could see through the elemental magic and witness the true horror—skin so pale and so thin that every vein popped through the flesh like a baby black snake. His eyes were dark, empty sockets and his mouth, his teeth . . .

This was one of the things I'd been trained to fight at the Covenant. This was a thing that thrived and fed on aether—the essence of the gods, the very life force running through us—a pure-blood who had turned his back on the gods. This was one of the things I was obligated to kill on sight.

A daimon—there was a daimon here.

6

I wheeled away from the railing. Whatever training I'd managed to retain vanished in an instant. Part of me had known—had always known—deep down that this day would come. We'd been outside the protection of the Covenant and their communities for far too long. The need for aether would eventually draw a daimon to our doorstep. Daimons couldn't resist the pure-blood mojo. I just hadn't wanted to give voice to the fear, to believe that it could happen on a day like this, when the sun was so bright and the sky such a beautiful azure blue.

Panic clawed at the inside of my throat, trapping my voice. I tried to yell, "Mom!" but it came out a hoarse whisper.

I rushed through the bedroom, terror seizing me as I pushed and then pulled open the door. A crash sounded from somewhere in the house. The space between my bedroom and my mom's seemed longer than I remembered and I was still trying to call out her name as I reached her room.

The door opened smoothly, but at the same time, everything slowed down.

Her name was still just a whimper on my lips. My gaze landed on her bed first, and then on a section of floor beside the bed. I blinked. The pot of hibiscus had toppled over and broken into large pieces. Purple petals and soil were strewn across the floor. Red—something red—mingled among the blossoms, turning them a deep violet. My gasp drew in a metallic smell that reminded me of the nose bleeds I used to get when a sparring partner would get in a lucky shot.

I shuddered.

Time stilled. A buzzing filled my ears until I couldn't hear anything else. I saw her hand first. Abnormally pale and open, her fingers clawed at the air, reaching for something. Her arm twisted at an awkward angle. My head shook back and forth; my brain refused to accept the images in front of my eyes, to name the dark stain spreading down her shirt.

No, no—absolutely no. This was wrong.

Something—someone—braced half her body up. A pale hand clenched her upper arm and her head lolled to the side. Her eyes were wide open, the green somewhat faded and unfocused.

Oh, gods . . . oh, gods.

Seconds, it had only been seconds since I'd opened the door, but it felt like forever.

A daimon was latched onto my mother, draining her to get at the aether in the blood. I must've made a sound, because the daimon's head lifted. Her neck—oh gods—her neck had been torn into. So much blood had been spilled.

My eyes met those of the daimon—or at least, they met the dark holes where its eyes should have been. His mouth snapped away from her neck, gaping open to reveal a row of razor-like teeth covered in blood. Then the elemental magic took over, piecing together the face he'd had as a pure, before he'd tasted that first drop of aether. With that glamour in place, he was beautiful by any standard—so much so that, for a moment, I thought I was seeing things. Nothing that angelic-looking could be responsible for the red stain on my mother's neck, her clothes . . .

His head tipped to the side as he sniffed the air. He let out a high-pitched keening sound. I stumbled backward. The sound—nothing real could sound like that.

He let go of my mom, letting her body slip to the floor. She fell in a messy heap and didn't move. I knew she had to be scared and hurt, because there couldn't be any other reason why she hadn't moved. Rising up, the daimon's bloody hands fell to his sides, fingers twisting inward.

His lips curved into a smile. "Half-blood," he whispered.

Then he jumped.

I didn't even realize I still held the garden spade. I raised my arm just as the daimon grabbed me. My scream came out as nothing more than a hoarse squeak as I fell back against the wall. The painting of Artemis crashed to the floor beside me.

The daimon's eyes widened with surprise. His irises were a vibrant, deep blue for a moment, and then, like a switch being thrown, the elemental magic that hid his true nature vanished. Black sockets replaced those eyes; veins popped through his whitish skin.

And then he exploded in a burst of shimmery blue powder.

I looked down dumbly at my trembling hand. The garden spade—I still held the freaking garden spade. Titanium-plated, I realized slowly. The spade had been coated in the metal deadly to those addicted to aether. Had my mom bought the ridiculously expensive garden tools because she loved to garden, or had there been an ulterior motive behind the purchase? It wasn't like we had any Covenant daggers or knives lying around.

Either way, the daimon had impaled itself on the spade. Stupid, evil, aether-sucking son of a bitch.

A laugh—short and rough—bubbled up my throat as a tremor ran through my body. There was nothing but silence and the world snapped back into place.

The spade slipped from my limp fingers, clattering on the floor. Another spasm sent me to my knees and I lowered my eyes to the unmoving form beside the bed.

"Mom . . ?" I winced at the sound of my voice and the shot of fear that went through me.

She didn't move.

I placed my hand on her shoulder and rolled her onto her

back. Her head fell to the side, her eyes blank and unseeing. My gaze fell to her neck. Blood covered the front of her blue blouse and matted the strands of her dark hair. I couldn't tell how much damage had been done. I reached out again, but I couldn't bring myself to brush back the hair covering her neck. In her right hand, she'd clenched a crushed petal.

"Mom . . ?" I leaned over her, my heart stuttering and missing a beat. "Mom!"

She didn't even blink. During all of this, my brain was trying to tell me there was no life in those eyes, no spirit and no hope in her vacant stare. Tears ran down my face, but I couldn't recall when I'd started crying. My throat convulsed to the point I struggled to breathe.

I cried her name then, grabbing her arms and shaking her. "Wake up! You have to wake up! Please, Mom, please! Don't do this! Please!"

For a second I thought I saw her lips move. I bent down, placing my ear over her mouth, straining to hear one tiny breath, one word.

There was nothing.

Searching for some sign of life, I touched the undamaged side of her neck and then jerked back, falling on my butt. Her skin—her skin was so cold. I stared at my hands. They were covered with blood. Her skin was too cold. "No. No."

A door shut downstairs, and the sound broke through to me. I froze for a second, my heart racing so fast I was sure it would explode. A shudder passed through my frame as the image of the daimon outside flashed through my head. What color had his hair been? The one in here had been blond. What color?

"Hell." I scrambled to my feet and slammed the door shut. Fingers shaking, I turned the lock and whirled around.

There were two. There were two.

Heavy footsteps pounded on the stairs.

I rushed over to the dresser. Squeezing myself behind it, I

shoved the heavy furniture with every ounce of strength I had in me. Books and papers toppled over as I blocked the door.

Something slammed into the other side, shaking the dresser. Jumping back, I ran my hands over my head. A keening howl erupted from the other side of the door, and then it struck the door again . . . and again.

I whirled around, stomach twisting in painful knots. Plans—we had a stupid plan in place just in case a daimon found us. We modified it every time we moved to a different city, but each one boiled down to one thing: Get the money and run. I heard her voice as clear as if she had spoken it. Take the money and run. Don't look back. Just run.

The daimon hit the door again, splintering the wood. An arm snaked through, grasping at the air.

I went to the closet, pulling down boxes from the top shelf until a small wooden one fell to the floor. Grabbing it, I yanked it so fiercely that the lid ripped from the hinges. I threw another box at the door, hitting the daimon's arm. I think it laughed at me. I grabbed what my mom called the 'emergency fund' and what I referred to as the 'we are so screwed' fund and pocketed the wad of hundred dollar bills.

Every step back to where she had fallen ripped through me, taking a piece of my soul. I ignored the daimon as I dropped beside her and pressed my lips to her cool forehead. "I'm so sorry, Mom. I'm so sorry. I love you."

"I'm going to kill you," the daimon hissed.

Looking over my shoulder, I saw the daimon's head had made it through the door. He was reaching for the edge of the dresser. I picked up the garden spade, wiping the back of my arm over my face.

"I'm going to rip you apart. Do you hear me?" he continued, squeezing another arm through the hole he'd made. "Rip you open and drain you of whatever pathetic amount of aether you have, half-blood."

I glanced at the window and grabbed the lamp off the table. Tearing the shade off, I tossed it aside. I stopped in front of the dresser.

The daimon stilled as the glamour settled around him. He sniffed the air, eyes flaring wide. "You smell dif—"

Swinging with all my might, I slammed the bottom of the lamp into the daimon's head. The sickening thud it made pleased me in a way that would've concerned guidance counselors across the nation. It wouldn't kill him, but it sure as hell made me feel better.

I threw the busted lamp down and raced to the window. I pushed it open just as the daimon let out a string of creative cusses and threats. I wiggled into the window, perching there as I stared at the ground below, assessing my chances of landing on the awning over the small porch off the back of the house.

The part of me that had been in the mortal world too long balked at the idea of jumping from a second story window. The other part—the part that had the blood of the gods running through it—jumped.

The metal roof made a terrible sound when my feet slapped into it. I didn't think as I went to the edge and leapt once more. I hit the grass, falling to my knees. Pushing up, I ignored the stunned looks from the neighbors who must've come outside to see what was going on. I did the one thing I'd been trained never to do during my time at the Covenant, the thing I didn't want to do, but knew I had to.

I ran.

With my cheeks still damp with tears and my hands stained with my mother's blood, I ran.

After

7

A deep numbness settled over me as I stood in a gas station bathroom. I turned my hands over and rubbed them together under the rush of icy water, watching the basin turn red, and then pink, and then clear. I kept washing my hands until they, too, felt numb.

Every so often a spasm shot through my legs and my arms would twitch, no doubt a by-product of running and running until an ache had settled so far into my body that every step had jarred my bones. My eyes kept flicking to the garden spade as if I needed to assure myself that it was still within reach. I'd placed it on the edge of the sink, but it didn't feel like it was close enough.

Turning off the faucet, I picked it up and slid it under the waistband of my jeans. The sharp edges bit into the flesh of my hip, but I tugged my shirt down over it, welcoming the little stab of pain.

I left the dingy bathroom, walking in no particular direction. The back of my shirt was soaked with sweat and my legs protested the whole walking thing. I'd take a few steps, touch the handle of the spade through my shirt, walk some more and repeat.

Take the money and run . . .

But run where? Where was I supposed to go? We didn't have any close friends that we'd trusted with the truth. The mortal part urged me to go to the police, but what could I say to them? By now, someone would have called 911 and her body would've been found. Then what? If I went to the authorities, I'd be placed in the state system even though I was seventeen. We'd exhausted all of our money in the last three years and there were no funds left over except the few hundred dollars in my pocket. Lately, my mom had taken to using compulsions to get cheaper rates whenever we'd had bills to pay.

I kept walking as my brain tried to answer the question of what happens now? The sun was beginning to set. I could only hope the humidity would ease off some. My throat felt like I'd swallowed a dry sponge and my stomach grumbled unhappily. I ignored them both, continuing to put as much distance between my house and me as I could.

Where to go?

Like a sucker punch in the stomach, I saw my mom. Not how she'd looked last night, when she'd told me she loved me, that image of her escaped me. Now I kept seeing her dulled, green eyes.

A sharp stab of pain caused my step to falter. The ache in my chest, in my soul, threatened to consume me. I can't do this. Not without her.

I had to do this.

In spite of the humidity and heat, I shivered. Wrapping my arms around my chest, I barreled down the street, scanning the crowds for the horrific face of a daimon. Several seconds would pass before the elemental magic they wielded would have an effect on me. It might give me enough time to make a run for it, but they obviously could sense the little aether I had in me. It didn't seem likely that they'd follow me; daimons didn't actively hunt half-bloods. They'd tag and drain us if they happened across us, but they wouldn't seek us out. The diluted aether in us wasn't as appealing as that of the pures.

I wandered the streets aimlessly until I spied a motel that looked somewhat decent. I needed to get off the streets before nightfall. Miami after dark wasn't a place a lone, teenage girl skipped around happily.

After grabbing some burgers from a nearby fast food joint, I checked in at the motel. The guy behind the counter didn't look twice at the sweaty girl standing in front of him—with no luggage and only a bag of food—asking for a room. As long as I paid in cash, he didn't even care that I didn't show any ID.

My room was on the first floor at the end of a narrow, musty hallway. There were questionable sounds coming from some of the rooms, but I was more disturbed by the dirty carpet than the low moans.

The bottoms of my worn sneakers looked cleaner.

I shuffled the burgers and drink to my other arm as I opened the door to room 13. The irony of the number didn't pass me by; I was just too tired and out of it to care.

Surprisingly, the room smelled good, courtesy of the peach air freshener plugged into the wall outlet. I set my stuff down on the small table and pulled out the garden spade. Lifting my shirt, I inched down the band of my pants and ran my fingers over the indentations the blade had left in my skin.

It could be worse. I could be like my mo—

"Stop it!" I hissed at myself. "Just stop it."

But the aching pain welled up anyway. It was like feeling nothing and everything all at once. I drew in a shallow breath, but it hurt. Seeing my mom lying beside the bed still didn't seem real. None of this did. I kept expecting to wake up and find that everything had been a nightmare.

I just hadn't woken up yet.

I rubbed my hands on my face. There was a burning in the back of my throat, a tightness that made it hard to swallow. She's gone. She's gone. My mom's gone. I grabbed the bag of burgers and ripped into them. I ate them angrily, stopping every couple of mouthfuls to take a huge gulp from my cup. After the second one, my stomach cramped. I dropped the wrapper and rushed toward the bathroom. Falling to my knees in front of the toilet, everything came back up.

My sides ached by the time I fell back against the wall, pushing the heels of my palms against my burning eyes. Every couple of seconds my mom's blank stare flashed up, alternating with the look on the daimon's face before he'd burst into blue powder. I opened my eyes, but I still saw her, saw the blood that'd run over the purple petals, saw the blood everywhere. My arms started to tremble.

I can't do this.

I pulled my knees to my chest and rested my head on them. I slowly rocked, replaying not just the last twenty-four hours over and over again, but the last three years. All those times I'd had a chance to figure out a way to contact the Covenant and hadn't. Missed opportunities. Chances I'd never get back. I could've tried to figure out how to reach the Covenant. One call would've prevented this from happening.

I wanted a do-over—just one more day to confront my mom and demand we go back to the Covenant and face whatever had sent us fleeing in the middle of the night.

Together—we could've done it together.

My fingers dug into my hair and I pulled. A tiny cry worked its way past my clenched jaw. I yanked on my hair, but the hot flash of pain zinging across my scalp did nothing to relieve the pressure in my chest or the yawning emptiness that filled me.

As a half-blood it was my duty to kill daimons, to protect the pure-bloods from them. I'd failed in the worst way possible. I'd failed my mother. There was no way around that.

I had failed.

And I had run.

My muscles locked up and I felt a sudden rush of fury rise inside me. Balling my hands over my eyes, I kicked out. The heel of my sneaker slammed through the cabinet door below the sink. I pulled my foot free, almost pleased when the cheap particle board scraped my ankle. And I did it again and again.

When I finally did stand and leave the bathroom, the motel room was pitched in darkness. I tugged the chain on the lamp and grabbed the spade. Each step back into the shabby room hurt after forcing my sore muscles into such a cramped position in the bathroom. I sat down on the bed, not meaning to collapse there and not get back up. I'd wanted to check the door again— maybe block it with something—but exhaustion claimed me and I drifted off into a place where I hoped no nightmares could follow me.

8

Night turned to day, and I didn't move until the motel manager knocked on the door, asking for more money or for me to get out. Through a tiny crack in the door, I handed him the cash and went back to the bed.

I went on repeat for days. There was a general sense of time changing when I would get up and wobble into the bathroom. I didn't have the energy to shower, and this wasn't the kind of place that put out little bottles of shampoo, anyway. There wasn't even a mirror in here, just a couple of little plastic brackets framing an empty rectangle above the sink. Either moonlight or sunshine would break through the window, and I kept count of each time the manager visited. Three times he'd come to ask for money.

During those days I thought of my mom and I cried until I gagged into my hand. The storm inside me thrashed, threatening to pull me under, and under I went. I curled up in a small ball, not wanting to talk, not wanting to eat. Part of me just wanted to lie there and fade away. The tears had long since come to an unsatisfying end and I just lay there, searching for a way out. There seemed to be an empty void looming up ahead. I welcomed it, rushed in, and sank into its meaningless depths until the manager came the fourth day.

This time he spoke to me after I handed him the cash. "You need something, kid?"

I stared at him through the gap. He was an older guy, maybe in his late forties. He seemed to wear the same pinstriped shirt every day, but it looked clean.

He glanced down the hall, running a hand through thinning brown hair. "Is there anyone I can call for you?"

I didn't have anyone.

"Well, if you need something, just call the front desk." He backed away, taking my silence as the answer. "Ask for Fred. That's me."

"Fred," I repeated slowly, sounding like an idiot.

Fred stalled, shaking his head. When he looked back at me, his eyes met mine. "I don't know what kind of trouble you got yourself in, kid, but you're too young to be out here and in a place like this. Go home. Go back to where you belong."

I watched Fred leave and I shut the door behind him, locking it. I turned around slowly and stared at the bed—at the garden spade. My fingers tingled.

Go back to where you belong.

I didn't belong anywhere. Mom was gone now and—

I pushed away from the door, approaching the bed. I picked up the spade and ran my fingers along the sharp edges. Go back to where you belong. There was only one place I did belong and it wasn't curled up in ball on a bed in a craptastic motel on the wrong side of Miami.

Go to the Covenant.

A tingle ran along the back of my neck. The Covenant? Could I seriously go back there after three years, not even knowing why we'd left? Mom had acted like it wasn't safe there for us, but I always chalked that up to her paranoia. Would they allow me back without my mother? Would I be punished for running away with her and not turning her in? Was I fated to become what I'd avoided all those years ago when I'd gone before the Council and punt-kicked an old lady?

They could force me into servitude.

All those risks were better than being chomped on by a daimon, better than tucking my tail between my legs and giving up. I'd never given up on anything in my entire life. I couldn't start now, not when my life seriously depended on me not losing it.

And by the way the bed looked and how I smelled, I was officially losing it.

What would my mom say if she could see me now? I doubted she'd suggest the Covenant, but she wouldn't have wanted me to give up. Doing so was a disgrace to everything she'd stood for, and to her love.

I couldn't give up.

The storm inside me stilled and the plan began to form. The closest Covenant was in Nashville, Tennessee. I didn't know exactly where, but the whole city would be swarming with Sentinels and Guards. We'd be able to sense each other— the aether always called out to us, stronger from the pures, more subtly from the halfs. I'd have to find a ride, because my butt wasn't walking all the way to Tennessee. I still had enough money to get a ticket on one of those buses I usually wouldn't consider riding in. The terminal downtown had been closed ages ago and the nearest bus stop going out of state was at the airport.

That was one hell of a hike from here.

I glanced at the bathroom. No light shone through the window. It was night again. Tomorrow morning I could take a cab to the airport and get on one of the buses. I sat down, almost smiling.

I had a plan, a crazy one that may end up backfiring on me, but it was better than giving up and doing nothing. A plan was something and it gave me hope.

After waiting until dawn, I caught a cab to the airport and lingered in the near-vacant bus terminal. The only company I had was an elderly black man cleaning the hard plastic seats and the rats that scurried along the darker corridors.

Neither were very talkative.

I pulled my legs up on the seat, cradling the spade in my lap while I forced myself to stay alert. After existing in the void of nothingness for days, I still wanted to climb into my favorite jammies and curl up in my mom's bed. If it wasn't for every little noise causing me to jump out of my seat, I would've fallen out of my chair in a dead sleep.

A handful of people were waiting for the bus when the sun rose outside the windows.

Everyone avoided me, probably because I looked like a hot mess. The motel shower hadn't even been working when I'd finally tried it, and my quick rinsing in the sink hadn't included soap or shampoo. Standing slowly, I waited until everyone got in line and looked down at the clothes I'd been wearing for days. The knees of my jeans had been torn open and the frayed edges were stained red. A sharp pang hit me in my stomach.

Pulling myself together, I climbed the steps to the bus and briefly made eye contact with the bus driver. Right away, I wished I hadn't. With a head full of bushy white hair and bifocals perched on his ruddy nose, the driver looked older than the guy who'd been cleaning the chairs. He even had an AARP sticker on the sun visor and wore suspenders. Suspenders?

Gods, there was a good chance Santa Claus was going to fall asleep at the wheel and we all were going to die.

Dragging my feet, I picked a spot in the middle and sat down beside a window. Luckily, the bus wasn't even half full and so the body odor usually associated with these buses was below the norm.

I think I was the only one who smelled.

And I did smell. A lady a few seats ahead of me turned around, wrinkling her nose. When her gaze landed on me, I looked away quickly.

Understanding my questionable hygiene was the least of my problems, it still made my cheeks burn with humiliation. How at a time like this could I even care about how I looked or smelled?

I shouldn't, but I did. I didn't want to be the stinky girl on the bus. My embarrassment flashed me back to another horrendously mortifying moment in my life.

I'd been thirteen and just started an offensive training class at the Covenant. I remembered being thrilled to do something other than running and practicing blocking techniques. Caleb Nicolo—my best friend and an all around awesome guy—and I had spent the beginning of the first class pushing each other around and acting like monkeys on crack.

We'd been quite . . . uncontrollable when together.

Instructor Banks, an older half-blood who'd been injured while doing his Sentinel duties, had been teaching the class. He'd informed us that we'd be practicing takedowns and paired me up with a boy named Nick. Instructor Banks had shown us several times how to do it correctly, warning us that, "It has to be done this way. If not, you could break someone's neck, and that's not something I'm teaching today."

It had looked so easy, and being the cocky little brat that I'd been, I hadn't really paid attention. I'd told Caleb, "I so have this." We'd high fived like two idiots and gone back to our partners.

Nick had executed the takedown perfectly, sweeping out the leg while maintaining control of my arms. Instructor Banks had praised him. When it came to my turn, Nick had smiled and waited. Halfway through the maneuver, my grip had slipped on Nick's arm and I'd dropped him on his neck.

Not good.

When he didn't get up right away and had started moaning and twitching, I'd known I'd made a terrible miscalculation concerning my skill level. I'd put Nick's butt in the infirmary for a week and had been called the "Pile Driver" for several months after that.

Up until now, I'd never been so embarrassed in my life. I wasn't sure which humiliation was worse, though—failing in front of my peers or smelling like gym socks left forgotten in the hamper.

Sighing, I glanced down at my travel itinerary. There were two transfers: one in Orlando and the other in Atlanta. Hopefully one of those stops had some place I could clean up a little better and grab some food. Maybe they'd also have drivers who weren't nearing their expiration dates.

I looked around the bus, smothering my yawn with my hand. There were definitely no daimons on the bus; I imagined they'd loathe public transportation. And—from what I could tell—I didn't see any possible serial killers who looked like they'd prey on dirty chicks. I pulled the spade out and shoved it between me and the seat. I dozed off pretty quickly and woke up a few hours in, my neck cramping something fierce.

A couple of the people on the bus had these neat little pillows I'd have given my left arm for. Wiggling in my seat until I found a position that didn't feel like I was cramped in a cage, I didn't notice I had company until I lifted my eyes.

The woman who'd sniffed the air earlier stood in the aisle beside my seat. My gaze fell over her neatly coiffed brown hair and pressed khaki pants, not sure what to make of her. Had I stunk up the bus?

Smiling tightly, she pulled her hand out from behind her back and held a package of crackers out toward me. They were the kind with peanut butter in the middle, six to a pack. My stomach roared to life.

I blinked slowly, confused.

She shook her head, and I noticed the cross dangling from a gold chain around her neck. "I thought . . . you might be hungry?"

Pride sparked in my chest. The lady thought I was some homeless kid. Wait. I AM a homeless kid. I swallowed the sudden lump in my throat.

The lady's hand shook a bit as she pulled back. "You don't have to. If you change—"

"Wait," I said hoarsely, wincing at the sound of my own voice. I cleared my throat while my cheeks heated. "I'll take it. Thank . . . thank you."

My fingers looked especially grubby next to hers even though I'd scrubbed them in the motel bathroom. I started to thank her again, but she'd already moved back to her seat. I stared down at the package of crackers, feeling a tightening in my chest and jaw. Somewhere I'd read once that was a symptom of a heart attack, but I doubted that was what was wrong with me.

Squeezing my eyes shut, I tore into the package, eating so fast I really couldn't taste anything. Then again, it was hard to savor the first food I'd eaten in days when tears clogged my throat.

9

At the transfer in Orlando, I had several hours to try to clean up and grab some food. When the bathroom was free and it didn't look like anyone would be coming in, I locked the door and approached the sink. It was hard to look at myself in the mirror, so I avoided doing so. I stripped off my shirt, holding in a whimper as several sore muscles pulled. Choosing to ignore the fact I was kind of taking a bath in a public restroom, I grabbed a handful of rough, brown towels that were sure to make my skin break out. Dampening them and using the generic soap, I cleaned up as quickly as possible. Ghosts of deep purple bruises still marred the skin from my bra to my hip. The scratches on my back—inflicted when I'd wiggled through my mother's bedroom window—weren't as bad as I thought they'd be.

All in all, I wasn't that bad off.

I was able to score a bottle of water and some chips from a vending machine before boarding the next bus. Seeing the remarkably younger driver made me feel so much more relieved, since it was starting to get dark out. The bus was fuller than the one from Miami had been, and I was unable to fall back asleep. I just sat and stared out the window, running my fingers along the edge of the spade. My brain kind of clicked off after I finished the bag of chips and I ended up staring at the college-aged boy several rows ahead. He had an iPod, and I was jealous. I really didn't think about anything during the next five or so hours.

It was around two in the morning when we unloaded at

Atlanta, arriving ahead of schedule. Georgia's air was just as thick with humidity as Florida's had been, but there was a smell of rain. The station was in some kind of industrial park surrounded by fields and long forgotten warehouses. We seemed to be on the outskirts of Atlanta, because the dazzling glow of city lights appeared a couple of miles away.

Rubbing my aching neck, I shuffled into the station. A few people had cars there waiting for them. I watched college boy rush over to a sedan and a tired-looking but happy middle-aged man climbed out and hugged him. Before my chest could tighten again, I turned away to seek out another vending machine to raid.

It took me several minutes to find the vending machines. Unlike the ones in Orlando, these were all the way back near the bathrooms, which I found gross. I pulled out the wad of cash and separated a few singles from the hundreds.

A shuffling sound, like pants dragging along the floor, caught my attention. I looked over my shoulder, scanning the dimly lit corridor. Up ahead, I could see the glass windows of the waiting room. After freezing to listen for several moments before I dismissed the sound, I turned back to the machine, grabbed another bottle of water and another bag of chips.

The idea of sitting for the next few hours made me want to break something, so I took my meager goodies and headed back outside. I kind of liked the wet smell in the air and the idea of getting rained on wasn't too bad. It would be like a natural shower of sorts. Munching on my chips, I headed around the terminal and past a rest stop full of truckers. None of them whistled or propositioned me when they saw me.

This, in a way, totally ruined my whole image of them.

Across from the rest stop turnoff were more factories. They looked like something straight out of a haunted house reality TV show—broken or boarded up windows, weeds overflowing the cracked pavement, and vines trailing up along the walls. Before

Matt had decided I was a giant freak, we'd gone to one of those carnival haunted houses. Come to think of it, I should have known he'd be a wuss. He'd screamed like a girl when the guy had come out at the end and chased us with a chainsaw.

Smiling to myself, I followed a narrow path around the rest stop and tossed my empty bottle and bag into a trash bin. The sky was full of heavy clouds and the loud purr of the tractor's engines was comforting in an odd way. In four hours I'd be in Nashville. Four more hours and I'd find—

The sound of breaking glass startled me. My heart leapt in my throat. I whirled around, expecting to be faced with a horde of daimons. Instead I found two young guys. One had thrown a rock through the window of a maintenance building.

What rebels, I thought.

I moved my hand away from where I had the spade shoved into the back of my pants, studying them. They weren't much older—or cleaner—than me. One was wearing a red beanie . . . in May. I wondered if there was some kind of weather situation I was unaware of. My gaze drifted to his partner, whose eyes kept bouncing from his friend to me.

And that made me nervous.

Beanie boy smiled. The off-white shirt he wore clung to his scrawny frame. He didn't look like he was getting three square meals a day. Neither did his friend. "How ya doin'?"

I bit my lip. "Good. You?"

His friend gave a sharp, high-pitched laugh. "We're doing okay."

Knots began to form in my stomach. Taking a deep breath, I started to edge around them. "Well . . . I've got a bus to catch."

Giggles shot a quick look at Beanie Boy, and damn, Beanie Boy could book it. Within a second, he was standing in front of me and had a knife pointed right at my throat.

"We saw ya with the money back at those machines," said Beanie Boy, "and we want it."

I almost couldn't believe it. On top of everything, I was being robbed.

It was official. The gods hated me.

And I hated them.

10

In stunned disbelief, I lifted my hands above my head and exhaled slowly.

The one without the knife gaped at his partner. "Man, what are you doing? Why'd you pull a knife? She's just a girl. She's not going to fight us."

"Shut up. I'm running this show." Beanie Boy grabbed my arm as he leered in my face, pressing the tip of the knife under my chin.

"This wasn't part of the plan!" argued the guy who didn't seem to want to stab me. I eyed him hopefully, but he was staring at his partner, his hands opening and closing at his sides.

Great, I thought, I'm being robbed by unorganized criminals. Someone's definitely getting stabbed and it's probably going to be me. Instead of fear, I felt a hot stab of annoyance. I so did not have the time for this crap. I had a bus to catch, and hopefully, a life to reclaim.

"We saw ya getting the food." He inched the tip of the knife down my throat. "We know ya have money. A whole wad of cash, right, John? Must be a lot of hooking to get that kinda money."

I wanted to kick myself in the face. I should've been more careful. I couldn't pull out a wad of cash and expect not to be robbed. Surviving a daimon attack only to have my throat slashed for a few hundred dollars? Dammit, people sucked.

"Did ya hear me?"

I narrowed my eyes, figuring I was about five seconds from going ballistic. "Yeah, I heard you."

His fingers dug in my skin. "Then give us the damn money!"

"You're going to have to get it yourself." My gaze went to his friend. "And I dare you to try it."

Beanie Boy motioned toward John. "Get the money out of her pocket."

His partner's eyes darted between his friend and me. I hoped he'd refuse, because he was so going to regret it if he didn't. That wad of cash was all that I had. In it was my ticket for the next bus. No one was getting that.

"Which pocket?" the one holding me asked. When I didn't answer, he shook me, and that was it.

My bitch switch was flipped and, well, my sense of self-preservation went right out the window. Everything—everything that'd happened boiled up inside me and burst. Did these wannabe gangstas actually think I was afraid of them? After everything I'd seen? My universe went red. I was going to stomp the ever-loving crap out of them.

I laughed in Beanie Boy's face.

Bewildered by my response, he lowered the knife a fraction of an inch.

"Are you freaking serious?" I wrenched my arm free and grabbed the knife from his fingers. "You're going to rob me?" I pointed the knife at him, half tempted to prick him with it. "Me?"

"Whoa, now." John backed up.

"Exactly," I waved the knife around. "If you want your bal—"

A shiver went down my spine, icy and foreboding. An innate sense kicked in and every fiber of my being screamed out a warning. It was the same thing I'd felt before I'd spotted the daimon from the balcony. Panic punched a hole in my chest.

No. They can't be here. They can't.

But I knew they were. The daimons had found me. What I couldn't wrap my head around was why they had. I was just a freaking half-blood. I wasn't even a snack pack to them. Worse yet, I was like Chinese food to them—they were going to be craving aether again in a few hours. Their time would be better spent hunting down pures. Not me. Not a half-blood.

Clearly distracted, Beanie Boy took advantage. He shot forward, grabbing and twisting my arm until I dropped the knife in his waiting hand. "You stupid bitch," he hissed in my face.

I pushed him with my free hand as I scanned the area. "You have to go! You need to go now!"

Beanie Boy pushed back and I stumbled to the side. "I'm done messing with you. Give us the money or else!"

I gained my balance, realizing these two were too stupid to live. So was I for hanging around and trying to convince them. "You don't understand. You have to go now. They're here!"

"What's she talking about?" John turned around and scanned the darkness. "Who's coming? Red, I think we should—"

"Shut up," Red said. Light from the moon broke free from the heavy clouds, glinting off the blade he jabbed at his friend. "She's just trying to freak us out."

Part of me wanted to bolt and let them deal with what I knew was coming, but I couldn't. They were mortals—obscenely stupid mortals who'd pulled a knife on me—but there was no way they deserved the kind of death coming their way. Robbery attempt or not, I couldn't let this happen. "The things that are coming are going to kill you. I'm not try—"

"Shut up!" yelled Red, swinging on me. Once again the knife was at my throat. "Just shut up!"

I looked at John, the saner of the two. "Please. You've got to listen to me! You need to go and you need to make your friend go. Now."

"Don't even think it, John," warned Red. "Now get over here and get this money!"

Desperate to get them out of here, I dug in my pocket and pulled out the wad of cash. Without thinking, I shoved it at Red's chest. "Here—take it! Just take it and go while you still can! Go!"

Red looked down, his mouth dropping open. "What the—"

A cold, arrogant laugh froze the blood in my veins. Red whirled around, squinting into the darkness. It was almost like the daimon materialized out of the shadows, because the spot had been empty a second ago. He stood a few feet from the building, his head cocked to the side and his horrific face twisted into a gruesome smile. To the boys, he looked like a yuppie in Gap jeans and a polo shirt—an easy target.

I recognized him as the daimon I'd hit over the head with a lamp.

"This is it?" John looked at Red, visibly relieved. "Man, we hit the lotto tonight."

"Run," I urged quietly, reaching behind me and wrapping my fingers around the handle of the garden spade. "Run as fast as you can."

Red glanced over his shoulder at me, snickering. "Is this your pimp?"

I couldn't even respond to that. I zeroed in on the daimon, my heart doubling over as he took a slow, lazy step forward. Something wasn't right about the daimon. It was . . . too calm. When the elemental magic took over, amusement flickered over his arresting features.

Then, when I was pretty sure I couldn't be having a crappier week, a second daimon stepped out of the shadows . . . and behind her stood another daimon.

I was so screwed.

II

My hand was still up in the air, clenching the four hundred and twenty-five dollars along with my bus ticket. Perhaps it was shock that held me in that position. My brain quickly flipped through my lessons at the Covenant, the ones teaching us about pure-bloods who'd tasted aether and turned to the proverbial dark side.

Lesson number one: they didn't work well together.

Wrong.

Lesson number two: they didn't travel in packs.

Wrong again.

Lesson number three: they didn't share their food.

Wrong again.

And lesson number four: they didn't hunt half-bloods.

I was so going to kick a Covenant Instructor in the face if I ever made it back there alive.

John took a step back. "Too many people at this—"

The first daimon held up his hand and a gust of wind came rushing from the field behind the trio. It shot down the dirt path, slamming into John's chest, sending him flying through the air. John hit the back of the rest stop, his surprised shriek cut off by the snapping of his bones. He fell into the shrubs, a dark, lifeless lump.

Red tried to move, but the wind was still coming. It pushed him back and knocked my arm down. It was like being caught in an invisible tornado. Hundred dollar bills, a bunch of singles, and my bus ticket flew up in the air, caught and tossed by the wind. A hole opened in my chest as the rushing wind took them up and up. It was almost as if the daimons knew that, without those things, I was trapped. Completely, freaking trapped.

Lesson number five: They could still control the elements.

At least the Covenant Instructors had gotten that part right.

"What's going on?" Red backed up, stumbling over his own feet. "What the hell is going on?"

"You're going to die," said the daimon in Gap jeans. "That's what's going on."

I reached out, grabbing Red's flailing arm. "Come on! You've got to run!"

Fear rooted Red to the spot. I pulled on his arm until he twisted around. Then we were running, me and the guy who'd held a knife to my throat moments before. Flat laughter followed us as our feet left the dirt path and crashed through field grass.

"Run!" I yelled, pumping my legs until they burned. "Run! RUN!"

Red was so much slower than I was and he fell—a lot. I briefly considered leaving him there to fend for himself, but my mother hadn't raised me that way. Neither had the Covenant. I yanked him back to his feet, half tugging him across the field. Incoherent babbling came from him as I dragged him on. He was praying and crying—sobbing really. Lightning zipped overhead and a crash of thunder jolted both of us. Another bolt of light split the dark sky.

Through the fog rolling over the field, I could make out the shapes of more warehouses beyond a cluster of ancient maples. We had to make it there. We could lose them, or at least we could try. Anywhere was better than being out in the open. I pushed harder—pulled on Red harder. Our shoes tripped in the tangled weeds and my chest was hurting, the muscles in my arm straining to keep Red on his feet.

"Move," I gasped as we dashed under the canopy of trees,

darting to the right. It seemed better than running in a straight line. "Keep moving."

Red finally fell in step beside me. The beanie was gone, revealing a head full of thick dreads. We dipped around a tree, both of us stumbling over thick roots and underbrush. Low hanging branches slapped at us, tearing at our clothing. But we kept running.

"What . . . are they?" Red asked breathlessly.

"Death," I said, knowing no better way to describe them to a mortal.

Red whimpered. I think he knew I wasn't kidding.

It came out of nowhere then, slamming into us with the ferocity of a freight train. I hit the ground face first, inhaling spit and dirt. Somehow I kept ahold of the spade and rolled onto my back, praying we'd just gotten tackled by a chupacabra or a minotaur. Right now either would be far better than the alternative.

And I was not that lucky.

I stared up at the daimon as he picked Red up and held him several feet off the ground with one hand. Thrashing wildly, Red screamed as the daimon smiled, although he didn't see the rows of razor teeth that I could. Full of panic and terror, I rolled to my feet and rushed the daimon.

Before I could reach them, the daimon drew back his free arm and a burst of flames encompassed his hand. The elemental fire burned unnaturally bright, but the gaping eyeholes remained dark. Seemingly indifferent to the horror playing out across Red's face and his terrified screams, the daimon placed his fiery hand on Red's cheek. The fire sparked from the daimon's hand, swallowing Red's face and body within seconds. Red shrieked until his voice cut off, his body nothing but flames.

I stumbled backward, choking on a silent scream. The taste of bile filled my mouth.

The daimon dropped Red's corpse to the ground. The

moment his hands left the body, the flames vanished. He turned to me and laughed as the elemental magic cloaked his true form.

My brain refused to accept reality. He wasn't the daimon from Miami or the one who had spoken behind the rest stop. A fourth. There were four of them—four daimons. Panic raked at me with fresh, sharp claws. My heart pounded fiercely as I backed up, feeling a cold desperation well up inside me. I whirled around and found him now standing in front of me. Nothing moved as fast as a daimon, I realized. Not even me.

He winked.

I darted to the side, but he mimicked my movements. He shadowed each step I took and laughed at my pathetic attempts to get around him.

Then he stilled, letting his hands fall harmlessly to his sides. "Poor, little half-blood, there is nothing you can do. You can't escape us."

I clenched the handle of the spade, unable to speak as he stepped to the side.

"Run, half-blood." The daimon tilted his head toward me. "I'll enjoy the chase. And once I catch you, even the gods won't be able to stop what I will do to you. Run!"

I took off. No matter how much air I dragged into my lungs as I ran, it didn't seem like I could breathe. All I could think as branches snagged strands of my hair was that I didn't want to die like that. Not like that. Oh, gods—not like that.

The ground became uneven; each step sent a spike of pain up my leg and through my hips. I broke free from the trees as another rumble of thunder drowned out every sound except that of the blood pounding in my temples. Seeing the outline of the warehouses, I pushed my sore muscles harder. My sneakers left the weed-covered earth and pounded across a thin layer of gravel. I darted between the buildings, knowing wherever I went I might have only a few stolen moments of safety.

One of the buildings, the furthest from the woods, was

several stories tall while the rest looked squat in comparison. The windows on the ground floor were either broken or boarded up. I slowed down, peering over my shoulder before I tried the door. I kicked at the rust-frozen handle and the surrounding wood cracked and gave way. I ducked inside and shut the door behind me.

My eyes roamed the dark interior, searching for something to secure the door with. It took several seconds for my eyes to adjust, and when they did, I could make out the shapes of abandoned work benches, presses, and a set of stairs. I struggled to get my fingers to stop shaking as I shoved the spade back into my pants. Grabbing a work bench, I yanked it toward the door. The screeching sound it made reminded me too much of a daimon's howl, and it also seemed to send things scurrying in the shadows. Once I'd barricaded the door, I rushed the stairs. They creaked and shifted under my weight as I took the steps two at a time, keeping a death grip on the metal railing. On the third floor, I went straight to a room with a large set of windows, dodging discarded benches and flattened boxes. A startling realization hit me as I peered out the window frantically, scouring the ground for daimons.

If I didn't make it to Nashville—if I ended up dead tonight— no one would even know. No one would even miss me or care. My face wouldn't even end up on the back of a milk carton.

I flipped out.

Leaving the room, I hit the rickety stairs and kept climbing until I reached the top floor. I raced through the dark hallway, ignoring the startled squeaks. I threw open the door and tumbled onto the roof. The storm continued violently overhead as if it had become a part of me. Lightning streaked across the sky, and a crack of thunder vibrated through my core, mocking the cyclone of emotions building inside.

Going to the edge of the roof, I peered through the fog. My eyes scanned every inch of the nearby woods and grounds where I'd just been. When I saw nothing I rushed to each of the other sides and did the same.

The daimons hadn't followed me.

Maybe they were playing with me instead, wanting me to believe I'd somehow outsmarted them. I knew they could still be out there, toying with me like a cat does with a mouse before it pounces and it rips the poor thing apart.

I went back to the center of the roof, the wind whipping my hair around my face. Lightning flashed overhead, casting my long shadow across the rooftop. Waves of sorrow crashed over me, coupled with anger and frustration. Each swell cut me from the inside, lancing open wounds that would never really heal. Bending over, I covered my mouth with both hands and screamed just as the thunder rolled through the dark clouds.

"This isn't it." My voice was a hoarse whisper. "This can't be it."

I straightened, swallowing down the burning lump in my throat. "Screw you. Screw all of you! I'm not dying like this. Not in this state, not in this stupid city and sure as hell not in this pile of crap!"

Fierce determination—so hot and full of rage—burned through my veins as I climbed back down the stairs and to the room with the windows. I dropped down on a pile of flattened boxes. Pulling my legs up to my chest, I leaned my head back against the wall. Dust coated my damp skin and clothing, sucking most of the moisture out.

I did the only thing I could do, because this couldn't be the end for me. With no money and no bus ticket, I might be trapped here for a while, but this wasn't how I was going to go out. I refused to even entertain the possibility. Closing my eyes, I knew I couldn't hide here forever.

I ran my fingers over the edge of the blade, preparing myself for what I would have to do when the daimons came. I couldn't run anymore. This was it. The sounds of the storm melted away, leaving a cloying humidity, and off in the distance, I could hear the roar of the trucks passing in the night. Life went on outside these walls. It couldn't be any different inside them.

I will survive this.

ACKNOWLEDGEMENTS

I would like to thank my Mom and Dad for allowing me to write random stuff with permanent markers all over the walls of my bedroom when I was a teenager and not killing me. To Jesse, thank you for playing Barbies and Nintendo with me. Thank you to Jerry and all my family, extended and close, for being the awesome sauce. A special shout out to whoever created zombies. Whenever I feel like I'm having a bad day, I take a peek at the living dead and totally feel better about myself. Thank you to my sister Dawn, who is probably the only person in this world who wants to see my face on a shirt and not on the back of a milk carton. Ricky Bobby—I don't know what I would've done without the endless distraction you and your sidekick have provided me whenever I've reached an impasse in my writing (Thank you, baby Jesus).

So very thankful for my friends—Dawn, Lesa, Amber, Amber number 2, Shelly, Kelley, Lisa, Tracy, Ashlee, Jen and everyone else—for not disowning me because I choose to spend time with imaginary friends. My betas and awesome writing friends—Brenda St. John Brown, Kimberlee Turley, Claire Merle, Lisa Rogers, Stephanie Sauvinet, Catherine Peace—all helped me not make a complete idiot out of myself when it came to revisions and all that good stuff. Remember those names, because they will be your favorite authors real soon. Thanks to Carissa Thomas for helping me brainstorm while I played the waiting game. And love and hugs to all the wonderful members of Query Tracker Forum for always being supportive, kind, and ingenious.

Oh, *Chewie*—my *Chewsters, Chewtoy*, also known as Chu-won Martin, you were my first friend to actually read anything I wrote and not laugh. You will always hold a special place in my heart.

None of this would have happened without my editor and the wonderfully supportive and enthusiastic team at Spencer Hill Press: Kate, Debbie, Osman, and Kendra. Kate—wow, I don't even know what to say. Without you, *Half-Blood* would still be an annoying and useless file on my computer. You are remarkable and I'm indebted to you.

Michael—thank you for putting up with me when I spend more time with inanimate objects than you. Love you.

Did you think I was going to forget Loki? Ha. Loki, I love you. You're the best damn dog in the world. I also would like to thank those who looked at me like I was insane when I said I wanted to be a published author. Because of you, I'm achieving that dream.

And finally, huge thanks to Julie Fedderson—you rock my world with your insanely right-on critiques and hilarious comments. Julie, we need to share that bottle of wine sometime soon. I have such a writer crush on you.

In the *Covenant* series:

Half-Blood

Pure

Deity

Apollyon

Sentinel

Daimon: the prequel
to *Half-Blood*

Elixir: a *Covenant*
novella

Enjoyed this book?
Want more?

Head over to

CHAPteR 5

for extra author content,
exclusives, competitions – and lots
and lots of book talk!

Our motto is
'Proud to be bookish',

because, well, we are ☺

See you there ...

f Chapter5Books 🐦 @Chapter5Books